*To Maddie Field, for feeding and clothing me
and my family at a truly awful time*

Sharps

K. J. PARKER

www.orbitbooks.net

ORBIT

First published in Great Britain in 2012 by Orbit

Copyright © 2012 by K. J. Parker

Excerpt from *The Hammer* by K. J. Parker
Copyright © 2011 by K. J. Parker

The moral right of the author has been asserted.

A CIP catalogue record for this book
is available from the British Library.

ISBN 978-1-84149-926-0

Typeset in Horley OS by M Rules

Printed and bound in Great Britain by
Clays Ltd, St Ives plc

Papers used by Orbit are from well-managed forests
and other responsible sources.

MIX
FSC C104740

Orbit
An imprint of
Little, Brown Book Group
100 Victoria Embankment
London EC4Y 0DY

An Hachette UK Company
www.hachette.co.uk

www.orbitbooks.net

Ever since she was a little girl, she'd had a recurring dream. She was on top of the stupid pillar, looking down into a deep, still green pool, where the blurred outlines of huge fish drifted lazily just under the surface. Then, quite suddenly, she was in the dried-up pool, looking up, as water poured out of a broad pipe twenty feet above. In no time at all the pool was full – with water, with fish, with dead bodies drifting like the fish; a dead man floated past on his back, and she knew he was her husband. But she neither sank nor drowned; the water lifted her up, right to the top of the pillar, where she'd come from.

She knew about the pillar, of course; it was her father's one good story, and he told it on every possible occasion. The rest of the dream's imagery bothered her, so much so that when she was fourteen, she sneaked out of the house and went to Temple, and asked the priest if he had any idea what it all meant. The priest listened gravely and carefully, and when she'd finished he wore a puzzled look, as though some of it made sense and some of it didn't.

"Well?" she asked.

"I'm not a fortune-teller," the priest replied, fabricating a smile. "If I didn't know better, I'd say you'd been reading Saloninus' *Phocas and Leontia*, and it's given you nightmares. But that's not exactly a suitable text for a well-brought-up young lady."

"Never heard of it," Iseutz replied.

"Quite." The priest rubbed his nose with thumb and forefinger. "Well, there's a scene in *Phocas* where the heroine's in a shipwreck, and her husband's corpse floats past her on the water. I suppose you might've overheard someone talking about it, and it stuck in the back of your mind. That's all I can think of, sorry."

She sighed. "Is there any way of stopping it? It's getting so I'm afraid to go to sleep."

"Prayer," the priest replied; and although she didn't actually believe in the divinity of the Invincible Sun, she gave it a try, and the dream stopped, and for ten years she thought no more about it.

General Carnufex became known as the Irrigator following the destruction of Flos Verjan, the second city of Permia, in the thirty-seventh year of the War. By the time Carnufex took command, the siege had already lasted two years. Three outbreaks of plague had taken a severe toll of the besieging army, and the near impossibility of securing regular supplies, given the city's position in the valley formed by three mountain ranges, had prompted the chiefs of staff to order that what remained of the army should be recalled, with the loss of all the territorial gains made during the previous five years' campaigns.

Carnufex spent a month rounding up as many of the local civilian population as he could catch, accumulating a workforce of some twenty thousand men, women and children. He set them to work diverting the courses of the four major rivers that flowed from the mountains into Lake Prescile. By employing innovative engineering techniques learned from the captive silver-miners, he contrived to cut deep channels through solid rock to lead the river water down into the Verjan valley. When the work was complete and the dams were finally breached, the ensuing torrent flooded the city so completely that it remains underwater to this day.

There are few more depressing sights than your own blood. The whole of his left trouser leg was drenched, the degree of saturation you get from one of those sudden, furious summer rainstorms that only last a minute or so but soak you to the skin. But it wasn't rain, though; it was blood. There comes a point – he remembered being told about it by a medical student, but he hadn't paid attention – when the loss is too great and there's no way back. Shortly before, or was it shortly after you reach that point, you start to feel a bit drunk. You lose your focus, and you'd really quite like to close your eyes and take a nap, even though you're well aware you probably won't be waking up again. It's not exactly a happy feeling, the medical student had said, but it's not mortal terror and fear either. It doesn't hurt much, and mostly you can't be bothered.

Shortly before or shortly after. He relaxed, letting his head rest against the bell-chamber wall. If I die, he thought, at least I won't have to face up to the consequences of my actions. I really wouldn't want to have to go through all that; all the fuss, unpleasantness and embarrassment. The thought made him smile. They'll come bustling up the bell-tower stairs, he thought, following the mile-wide blood trail; they'll kick down the door and they'll find me gone – almost as good as escaping. There'll be no arrest, no miserable, humiliating night in the cells along with the drunks and the uncouth street people, no heartbreaking glimpse of his parents' faces in the public gallery of the court while the prosecutor spells out in graphic detail the exact true account of all the incredibly stupid things he'd done; no unbearable waiting in the condemned cell, no bowel-loosening terror as the first rays of light came through the window on the appointed morning. Escaping from all that was very nearly the same as getting away with it completely. He grinned and looked down at his red, shiny-wet leg. Come on, he said, bleed faster.

It'd be nice, at the very least, if he could die before he had to explain to his father exactly what he thought he'd been playing at, what had possessed him. Well, Dad, it was like this. I went to the lecture hall, not to listen to the lecture I was supposed to be attending, but because it's *the* best place for meeting girls. I meet a lot of girls. Not through random serendipity. I go looking for them. I meet girls the way cousin Huon and his aristocratic chums and their highly trained dogs meet wild boar in the woods. A good place – please don't construe this as advice, Dad, I'd hate it if you ended up in a bell tower somewhere – is the lobby of the lecture halls. The girls you meet there are just about perfect: upper-class, smart, eager to defy convention. They're allowed out on their own, and all you have to do is watch which lecture they come out of. If it's literature, you can start up a conversation about the use of imagery in late Mannerist poetry. If it's natural philosophy, go for a detailed critique of Saloninus' theory of insubstantiality. Provided you've done your basic background reading, piece of cake.

Dad, I met this girl. Actually, she was quite interesting. She had a lot to say about social factors in Segimerus' agrarian reforms, and I rather liked her take on the ten per cent land tax. But there's a time for chat and a time for getting the job done, so I curtailed the academic discussion and we went back to her house, her father being guaranteed absent until the House rose. Thanks to you constantly badgering me about it, I take an interest in politics, so I knew they were debating the Law of Property Reform Bill, a topic guaranteed to generate more heat than a volcano. He'd be at it all night, and wouldn't be home before dawn. Ideal.

I guess I'll never know the outcome, Dad – maybe you could write it on a piece of paper for me and burn it, like prayers to the dead in Temple – but my guess is that the Optimates did a deal on Clause 16. Ironic, yes? As a hot-headed young radical, that's exactly what I wanted to happen. But if my theory is correct, it led directly to my death. Does that make me a martyr to the cause of fair redistribution of public land? It'd be nice, but I don't think so. Pity. In my more hopelessly romantic moments, I'd have said that it was a cause worth dying for. I guess it depends on how you construe the word cause. Cause meaning primary factor, yes. But that won't get me a place in the pantheon of heroes of the revolution. Of course I've only ever been a hot-headed young radical because it goes down well with the sort of girls you meet at the lecture halls.

The point being, Dad, her father came home earlier than expected, while we were still hard at it. The sad part of it is, she was nothing special. She moaned and groaned a lot, but I could tell her mind was somewhere else entirely, and I thought, the hell with this, let's get it over with and I can go home. So I turned her over and upped the tempo a bit; at which point the door opened.

I can see how it must've looked to her father. The yowling must've been audible all through the house. He hears the cries of someone apparently in great fear and pain. He sprints up the stairs. The noise is coming from his daughter's room. He kicks open the door. I'm on top of her, holding her wrists and working like a stoker, she's yelling like she's being murdered. I ask you, Dad. What was the poor man to think?

Here's what I saw. The door bursts open, and there's this huge, tall, fat man. He's staring at me as though I was some kind of unimaginable monster, horns, tail, fangs. There's this split second when we're looking straight at each other. Then I hear the silvery whisper of a rapier blade sliding against the chape of a scabbard.

You remember learning fencing in the schools, Dad? The first thing they teach you is the salute. You make a courteous bow to your opponent. You lift your hat, you do this flourish with your left hand – I'm hopeless at it, apparently – and then you straighten up and bring your sword slowly and decorously into the guard position. It wasn't like that. As soon as I heard that hiss, I jumped off her – squatting jump, like a frog. He lunged while I was actually in the air, caught me about six inches above the left knee. I felt no pain as the blade went in; they tell you that, and you don't believe it, but it's true. I could feel the thing inside me; I felt it being pulled out as I hit the floor. I remember thinking, that's it, I'm dead, like I'd given up. But my hands were grabbing in empty space, and my right hand found my trousers, where I'd dumped them on the floor.

You remember how you taught me Davianus' parry with the cloak held in the left hand, where you gain a little time by tangling the other man's blade. It works with trousers. He made a sort of roaring noise and withdrew, and my right hand found the hilt of my rapier. I'd hung it on its belt over a chair. I pulled it out of the scabbard, which tipped the chair over. It got in his way as he lunged the third time, and I was able to double-bunny-hop backwards, making myself a little room. He lunged a fourth time, and halfway through the lunge, he died. It was only when I saw the truly amazed look on his face, just as the light went out in his eyes, that I realised I'd performed a textbook demi-volte – you know, where you sidestep out of line while counter-thrusting – and the thrust had gone straight through the side of his head. In one ear and out the other, like Grandma used to say.

Picture the scene. There's me, stark naked, blood pumping down my leg, holding a sword that disappears into the side of a man's head – perfect stranger, never seen him before in my life – and sticks out the other side. About thirty seconds earlier, I'd been making a disinterested sort of love to a girl whose main interest in the proceedings was seeing how hard she could yell. It happened so quickly, most of it was sheer comedy, and there's my life changed for ever and, viewed with hindsight, nearly over.

And let's not forget the other guy. I've always been a bit cynical about protestations of remorse, and the bastard had been trying to kill me. Even so, I promise you, a lot of what I felt was sheer dumb horror at what I'd just done. Partly because I knew without having to stop and reflect that there'd be consequences, but mostly at the rank obscenity of violent death. To stab a man through his ears, for crying out loud, how disgusting is that? There's this technical term in law, an act of gross indecency. If what I'd just done didn't fit that description, I have no idea what would.

Then he collapsed sideways, almost dislocated my wrist as he pulled off the sword; and I didn't think, I ran. I think I trod on his face scrambling over him. I just wanted to get out of there, away from that appalling sight. I bolted through the door, found myself on a sort of landing. I could see the top of the stairs. There was some old man coming up them. I bumped into him and knocked him down, felt absurdly bad about that. Down the stairs; the front door was open. Out into the street.

What would you do if you saw a naked, bleeding man, trousers in one hand, unsheathed rapier in the other, sprinting up the sidewalk at you? No disrespect, Dad, but you can keep your answers, because they'll be wrong. I'll tell you. You'd stand perfectly still, staring, with your mouth open, while the naked man rushes past you. That's what they did, my honest, decent fellow citizens, too stunned to move, not having had time to figure out whether what they were watching was comedy or tragedy. As for me, I'd never run in my bare feet before, or at least not since I was too young to remember. Actually, it's surprising how much traction you get. I remember noticing how warm the pavement was. Anyhow, long story short, I caught sight of the Tower of Revisionary Martyrs, and next thing I knew, I was struggling up the stairs to the bell chamber. I'll be safe there, I thought. Yes, quite. Really stupid thing to do. Good idea at the time.

Anyhow, Dad, that's where I died. And I'm glad about that. Mainly because, when they tell you all about it, when they tell you your son committed rape and murder but died before he could be arrested, you'll be able to not-believe. You won't have to face me confessing, yes, I did those incredibly stupid things; and all right, it wasn't actually rape and it wasn't technically murder; but I think you could forgive those two misdemeanours rather more easily than the total, utter stupidity of which I'm really and truly guilty. You'll be able to go to your grave convinced that there was more to it than met the eye, there was some perfectly plausible explanation proving my complete innocence, which nobody will ever know. So really, I don't mind, Dad. Really, believe me, it's better this way.

He lifted his head. He could hear boots on the stairs.

*

"You know the fantasy," Phrantzes said cautiously, "where instead of going home down Cornmarket you take the short cut through the slave market, and you see this beautiful young girl for sale, and you immediately fall in love."

Corbulo smiled. "That one."

"Yes. And you buy her and set her free, and she says, I don't want to be free, I think I'm in love with you, so you get married and spend the rest of your life introducing her to fine art, literature and classical music, for which she has an instinctive appreciation."

Corbulo looked at him. "You marry yours, do you?"

"It's just a fantasy."

"Even so."

"Actually." Phrantzes opened the rosewood box and took out a handful of brass counters. "It's not exactly like that," he went on, sorting the counters into columns of five. "But there are similarities."

Chess games aside, it was the first time he'd managed to reduce Corbulo to silence. Worth it, just for that. He laid out three lines of counters on the board; and then Corbulo said, "Go on."

"Well, for one thing she's not a slave."

"Ah."

"*Was* a slave, once, but that was a long time ago. And I guess she's not exactly a girl any more. She's thirty-seven."

Corbulo frowned. "That's two things she isn't. What *is* she?"

Phrantzes placed three more counters; two on the thousand line, one on the hundred. "She used to be a prostitute," he said.

"Used to be."

"Retired. Has been, for some time."

"I see."

"These days, she works in the office."

Corbulo laid down his pen. "In a brothel."

"Yes, but in the office. She keeps the books and looks after the housekeeping side of things. You know, wine, candles, sending out the laundry."

"In a brothel."

Phrantzes sighed. "I met her," he said irritably, "at a concert." Corbulo barked out a short, projectile laugh, but Phrantzes ignored him. "At the New Temple, in aid of the refugees. Lord Bringas' house orchestra. They were playing the Orchomenus flute sonata."

"The hell with that," Corbulo said. "What was she doing at a concert?"

"Listening," Phrantzes replied. "She's very fond of music."

"Really."

"Yes, really." Phrantzes rolled up his right sleeve, so as not to disturb the counters, and began to make his calculation. "I was late arriving. I trod on her foot getting to my seat."

Corbulo sighed; a long sigh, the last third of it for effect. "I'm reminded," he said, "of Paradaisus' epigram concerning horticulture."

"Remind me."

"You can lead a horticulture, but you can't make her think."

Phrantzes clicked his tongue. "Anyway," he said, "in the interval I apologised properly for standing on her foot, and she was terribly nice about it, and we got talking."

"And?"

"And that was all," Phrantzes said. "But then I ran into her again at the post-Mannerist exhibition at the Cyziceum."

"Also an art lover."

"Yes. We looked round the exhibition together. I must say, she had a very interesting perspective on Zeuxis' use of light and shade."

"Of course she did," Corbulo said. "And then you went to bed together."

"Certainly not."

"Later, then."

"Several weeks later, if you must know."

"For free?"

Phrantzes sighed, and Corbulo pulled a face. "Sorry," he said.

"But you'll forgive me if I reserve the right to be just a little bit sceptical. How old are you exactly?"

"Fifty-one," Phrantzes snapped. "Two years younger than you."

"Quite."

"But in considerably better shape. I exercise three times a week at the baths, and I fence most days at the school in Coppergate. The instructor reckons I'm very well preserved."

"That's what they said about Tiberias the Third when they unwrapped the bandages."

"She doesn't think I'm too old."

"She's no spring chicken herself."

"Age," Phrantzes said, "is irrelevant where two people have deep, sincere feelings for each other."

"Absolutely."

"I didn't expect you to understand," Phrantzes said, jotting down the result of his calculation and sweeping the counters back into their box. "I think that at my age, after a long and frankly pretty tedious life, I deserve a little happiness."

"Of course you do." Corbulo looked away. "Maybe this isn't the best way of achieving it."

"How the hell would you know? You've always been miserable, for as long as I've known you."

Corbulo shrugged, a big, wide manoeuvre that in no way rejected the assertion. "I'm your oldest friend," he said, "not to mention your business partner. In circumstances like this, it's my duty to be miserable.

Phrantzes turned his head and scowled at him. "You're worried she might get hold of my share of the business."

"Yes," Corbulo replied. "Among other things."

A frozen moment; then Phrantzes grinned. "It'll be all right, I promise you," he said. "She's a lovely girl. You'll like her."

"I'll do my best. But no promises."

"Your best is all I can ask for." Phrantzes opened the big blue ledger, and wrote in the date at the top of the page. "She's making dinner for us tomorrow night. Bring Xanthe if you like."

"At the brothel?"

"No, you idiot, at my house." He took a pinch of sand from the pot and sprinkled it on the wet ink. "Will Xanthe come, do you think?"

"When I tell her about it?" Corbulo beamed like a sunrise. "No power on earth could conceivably stop her."

"Well?"

Corbulo took off his coat and hung it on the hook behind the door. "If you must know," he said, "I think you've made a wise choice."

Phrantzes looked at him. "Wise," he repeated.

"Wise. Sensible, even."

"*Sensible* . . ."

Corbulo nodded, and settled down on his stool. "I think she represents a sound medium-to-long-term investment, offering worthwhile returns with an acceptably low risk factor."

Phrantzes rolled his eyes, while Corbulo took off his gloves, stacked them on the edge of the desk and unstoppered the ink bottle. "Really," he said. "I was sceptical at first, but—"

"*Sensible*, for crying out loud."

Corbulo shrugged. "You're a middle-aged bachelor, set in your ways, no experience of women. Quite suddenly you decide to fall in love. While I wouldn't recommend such a course of action, if you feel you must do such a thing, you've chosen the right woman to fall in love with. I think," he added.

"You think."

Corbulo examined the nib of his pen, then reached in his pocket and found his penknife. "Yes," he said. "And Xanthe agrees with me. In fact, she thinks you're a very lucky man. She suggested," he went on, reaching into his other pocket, "that you might find this useful."

He produced a book; old, its binding cracked and starting to crumble at the edges, the middle of the spine carefully repaired with scrap parchment. Phrantzes picked it up, squinted at the title and raised his eyebrows.

"It belonged," Corbulo said, "to my father."

"Ah."

"Quite. Even so," Corbulo went on, "I gather it's still pretty much the standard work on the subject. I haven't read it myself, of course."

"Of course."

"Just dipped into it, here and there. It's got pictures."

Phrantzes was blushing. "I'm not a complete novice, you know. There have been—"

"I'm sure," Corbulo said. "Didn't mean to imply otherwise. But Xanthe said, and I agree with her – well, the disparity of experience could be a problem, if you see what I mean. It's the same as any new venture. A little background reading is always helpful."

Phrantzes looked at the book as though he expected it to bite him. Then he grabbed it and thrust it into a drawer. "Thanks," he said.

"Don't mention it."

"I won't," Phrantzes replied earnestly. "Ever again. And neither will you."

It was, everyone agreed, a charming wedding, in the circumstances. The bride disappointed nearly everybody by wearing a plain demure blue dress and a dark veil. She didn't invite any guests. The four chairmen who carried her in the traditional covered litter from her lodgings to the Temple wore the livery of the Silversmiths & Clockmakers, but nobody could bring themselves to ask why.

Corbulo and Xanthe opened the dancing in an estampie, a small man and a large woman moving with practised, almost telepathic grace. For a while, nobody moved, they were too busy watching. Eventually Astyages from the assay office and his wife joined in, and not long after that there was shuffling room only on the floor. Phrantzes and his bride opened the second dance, a slow and formal quadrille; his part in it was mostly standing perfectly still, which made sense to all who knew him. She proved to be an exquisite dancer, which surprised nobody.

After the dancing there was music, from the Carchedonia Ensemble, and a calligraphy demonstration provided by Master Histamenus from the Lesser Studium. The main event, however, was an exhibition bout of single rapier between the two finalists in that year's Golden Lily; Gace Erchomai-Bringas and Suidas Deutzel. It came as a complete surprise to the groom, who'd known nothing about it. Corbulo had arranged it all, and the Association had been pleased to declare it an official match, in honour of a former triple gold medallist. They fenced with sharps (a superb case of antique Mezentine cup-hilt rapiers, the bride's gift to the groom). After six three-minute rounds in which both combatants performed magnificently, Deutzel eventually won in the seventh with a half-inch scratch to the back of Erchomai-Bringas' right hand. The prize, a silk handkerchief embroidered with the Association crest, and fifty nomismata, was awarded by the outgoing chairman of the Association, who made a short but witty speech saying that if Phrantzes had been twenty years younger, nobody would ever have heard of either of these two pretenders, et cetera. There was polite applause, and the two fencers were given something to eat.

"Complete nonsense, of course," Phrantzes said later, as he poured the chairman a drink. "Even at my best, either of those young thugs would've made mincemeat of me. It's one of the few good things about getting old. I'll never have to face one of the younger generation in a serious match."

The chairman nodded sagely. "The game's changed a lot since our day," he said. "People moan about it, of course, but I believe it's no bad thing. When you think how much footwork has improved since we did away with amateur status ..."

"I agree," Phrantzes said (and he noticed that his wife was looking sweetly patient, and realised he'd been talking to the chairman for far too long). "There's no two ways about it, the standard of fencing is ten times better than it was twenty years ago. The only danger is, nowadays everybody's watching, rather than fencing themselves. We're turning into a nation of—"

"Darling," his wife interrupted, "I think the Senator is about to leave."

So Phrantzes had to go and say good night to the Senator, and once he'd gone the party cooled down quite quickly and people began to drift away. As they waited outside for their chair to be brought round, Corbulo said to Xanthe, "It's a terrible admission to make, but I still don't know the wretched woman's name. I tried to catch it during the ceremony, but of course he mumbled, and obviously I can't ask him now and I can't spend the rest of my life referring to her as 'your good lady'. Did you happen to . . .?"

"Sphagia," Xanthe said.

"What?"

"Sphagia," she repeated slowly. " S-P—"

"Good grief."

"It's a Thelite name," she said, "meaning 'rose'. Or, if you pronounce it Sphagia, with the long *a*, 'blood sausage'. I expect he's got a nickname for her by now. You'd have to, wouldn't you?"

Their chair appeared beside the mounting block. As they climbed in, Corbulo asked, "Was that one of the Carnufex boys I saw?"

"Yes. Addo, the youngest."

"Good heavens. I never realised Phran knew those sorts of people."

"From fencing," Xanthe explained. "It's a pity you never fenced. We might have got to meet some decent people, instead of all your dreary business contacts. Shit," she added, as her foot slipped off the running board and landed in a puddle of icy water. "Now look what you've made me do."

Suidas Deutzel left the wedding early and went straight home, passing the Sun in Splendour, the Beautiful Revelation of St Arcadius and the Charity and Chastity without even stopping to sniff at the door. He hadn't drunk anything at the wedding either.

"Well," she said, as he let himself in, "did you win?"

He nodded. "Fifty nomismata."

"Thank God."

He dropped into the one functional chair and closed his eyes. "Sharps," he said. "They made us fight with bloody sharps. I really don't see the need for that sort of thing. It's barbaric."

"The money," she reminded him.

"What? Oh, right." He reached in his pocket and produced first the handkerchief, which he frowned at and threw on the floor, and then the purse of coins, which he held out to her. She snapped it up, teased it open and started to count.

"It's all there," he said.

"You counted it?"

"They're decent people."

"No such thing." The coins clicked together in the hollow of her hand. "Fifty."

"See?"

"Now then." She sat upright on the floor, forming short columns of coins with the practised touch of a banker. "Ten for the rent. Ten for Taducian – we owe fifteen, but he can go to hell. Three for the poll tax. Twelve to pay back last month's house-keeping. Fourteen for your cousin Hammo – it'll be worth it just to keep him off my back, I'm sick of him pouncing on me every time I put my head round the door." She held up one coin. "And that's for us to live on, till you can earn some more."

He stared at her. "You're kidding me."

"One nomisma," she confirmed grimly. "And if you so much as look at a bottle, I'll kill you. Understood?"

He sighed. "I thought we'd be all right," he said.

"Oh, we are," she replied. "At least, by our standards. We're bloody rich, with one nomisma. Of course we still owe for the coal, the water and the window tax, but I can stave them off for another week."

"I'm sorry," he said bitterly. She didn't reply. Instead, she crawled across the floor and retrieved the handkerchief.

"You can have it if you like," he said.

She was examining it. "I can get nine trachy on that," she said.

"It's worth—"

"Nine trachy," she said, "to us, at Blemmyo's." She turned it over and picked at the hem with her fingernail. "Was the chairman there?"

He nodded.

"Did you ask him?"

"I sort of hinted," he replied defensively.

"Did you ask him?"

"Not in so many words." Her face hardened. "Look, it was a social occasion, all right? People lolling around drinking and enjoying themselves. It wasn't exactly the time and the place for touting for work."

"You didn't ask him."

"I'll go round to the office tomorrow," he said angrily. "All right?"

"Do what you like."

He sighed melodramatically and lay back in the chair, surveying the room. There wasn't a lot to see. Except for the chair and the mattress (the bailiff's men had taken the bed frame) there was nothing there apart from the range, which was built into the wall, and an empty fig crate, on which rested the three-foot-tall solid-gold triple-handed cup that you got lent for a year for being the fencing champion of the Republic of Scheria. She used it to store their arsewipe cabbage leaves in.

"You could go back to work," he said.

She gave him a furious look. "Believe me, I'm tempted," she said. "At least I'd be warm, instead of freezing to death in this icebox. But unfortunately they're not hiring right now. Maybe in the spring."

His eyes widened. "You asked."

"Grow up, Suidas."

"I didn't mean *that*," he said awkwardly. "I thought maybe a few days a week in a shop, something like that. Just till we're all right again."

"Suidas." When she was really angry, she always spoke softly. "I was principal soubrette at the Palace Theatre. I'm damned if I'm going to work myself to death in a shop just because you're completely useless with money." She paused, to let him know she meant what was coming next. "If I go back to work, I'll leave you. Up to you. Your choice."

He looked at her. "For crying out loud, Sontha," he said wearily. "Do you think we live like this because I want to? It's just . . ."

He didn't bother with the rest of it. No point. He had his ultimatum, and it was perfectly reasonable. He'd never been able to argue with her, because she had the infuriating knack of being in the right all the time; and Suidas had been a fencer so long that he'd become incapable of not acknowledging a clean hit.

"Well?"

"Fair enough," he said (and her face changed to unreadable). "I'll go and see the chairman tomorrow, I promise. And anything that's going, I'll take."

It hadn't been the right thing to say, and she slept with her back to him that night, while he lay awake and tried to think of something else he could possibly do, besides fencing. But he couldn't; so just before dawn, he got up and shaved, using the cup as a mirror. His other shirt was being pressed under the mattress and he couldn't very well retrieve it without waking her up; not a good idea at such an intemperately early hour. Luckily, the cold weather meant he hadn't sweated too much the previous

evening, so yesterday's shirt was just about wearable. He buckled
on his sword belt, thought for a moment and took it off again, in
case he ran into the bailiff's men in the street.

In his sleep he heard someone repeating his name over and over
again: Giraut, Giraut, Giraut Bryennius. He opened his eyes
and saw light, which wasn't what he'd been expecting.

"I'm alive," he said.

"Indeed." A woman's voice, possibly the one he'd just heard,
but he wasn't sure. "There's no justice."

A moment of confusion; then the joy of discovering that he
hadn't bled to death in the bell tower after all; then the horrible
recollection of what he'd done, and what was going to happen to
him.

"Look at me," the voice said.

He turned his head. His neck hurt.

She was middle-aged, with streaks of grey at the sides of her
head; a stern, plain woman who immediately made him feel
stupid. She was wearing black, and smelt very faintly of roses.

"You're in the infirmary of the Lesser Studium," she said.
"You lost a great deal of blood and you're still very weak, but the
brothers tell me you'll live." She smiled at him, cold as an archaic
statue. "Perhaps that's not what you wanted to hear. If I was in
your shoes, I'd rather have died before they found me."

"I'm sorry," he said. "I don't think I know you."

Her face went through the motions of laughter, though she
made no sound. "Of course you don't," she said. "You've never
seen me before. You killed my husband."

Oh, he thought. "I'm sorry."

"You're sorry," she repeated. "Well then." She picked up a jug
and a cup from the table beside the bed, poured some water and
handed it to him. "It's all right," she said, "I haven't put poison
in it. Go on."

Now she mentioned it, he was painfully thirsty. He drank,
spilling water down his chin.

"I really am sorry," he said. "About your—"

"No you're not." She said it calmly, as if correcting a trivial error. "You're sorry for yourself, and deeply embarrassed. You have no idea what the proper form of words is for apologising to the widow of your victim." She put the jug down and settled herself in her straight-backed chair, her hands folded in her lap. "My husband," she went on, "was a pig. He was a boor and a bully, forever making a fool of himself with the female servants, shamefully neglectful of his family and absolutely hopeless with money. I was married to him for twenty-seven years. The reason you're here, rather than in a cell in the Watch house, is that I went to the Prefect and asked him for clemency. Theoretically, you've been remanded into my custody while the court decides what's to be done with you. In practice, they've more or less left it up to me to decide."

He stared at her. She was looking straight at him, frowning slightly, as if he was some rather unsatisfactory object she'd bought on a whim and paid too much for. He remembered something else, and said, "I'm really sorry about your daughter."

"Oh, her." She shrugged. "I got the truth out of her. She's never been able to lie to me, though not for want of trying. I knew it was a mistake allowing her to go to college, but her father insisted." She paused for a moment, as though taking time to ratify her own decision. "I'm in the interesting position," she said, "of being able to decide what happened. Once I've chosen a version of events, it'll be accepted as true and nobody will question it. I can decide it was rape and murder or a stupid misunderstanding and involuntary manslaughter. Usually only the Invincible Sun can retrospectively alter the course of history, but apparently on this occasion He's delegated that power to me. As you can imagine, I've given it a certain amount of thought."

She stopped again and looked at him; creating suspense, just for wickedness, because she could. Eventually she leaned forward just a little – there was something rather motherly about the way she sat, almost as if she was about to read him a story. "I was strongly tempted to allow my dislike for my late husband to influence me into letting you get away with it," she went on. "He'd have been absolutely furious at the thought that his killer might walk free, and he was always so very pompous when he was angry. On the other hand, our family enjoys a certain position in this city. It really wouldn't do if people got the idea that someone could kill the head of the Chrysostomas and not be punished for it. Also," she went on, reaching down to a velvet bag on the floor and taking out a small embroidery frame, "there's you to consider."

She stopped talking long enough to thread a needle with red embroidery silk. His mother was the same. She'd been doing needlework so long she couldn't think properly unless she was stitching at something.

"I spoke to your parents," she went on. "Your mother was inclined to be hysterical, and your father ... That reminds me." From her bag she took a folded sheet of paper. "He asked me to give you this. Go on, read it."

He took the paper and unfolded it. Not his father's atrocious handwriting; he'd had it written out formally by a professional clerk.

> WHEREAS my son Giraut Bryennius has by his wicked and unforgivable conduct disgraced himself and his family for ever and WHEREAS my said son Giraut stands by the will of my father Jilaum Bryennius and sundry other family trusts hereinafter specified to inherit certain properties more specifically described in the schedule hereto NOW THIS DEED WITNESSES that I Tancre Bryennius entirely disinherit and dispossess my said son Giraut of all properties real and personal in being or hereafter acquired that would otherwise—

"If you like," she said gently, "I can talk to him for you when he's had a chance to calm down. The fact remains," she went on, "that even your own parents agree that you're basically worthless. I think your father blames himself and your mother blames him, but really, that's none of my business. The point is," and she paused to pick exactly the right place to insert her needle into the cloth, "you may be entirely without value to society; my husband, for all his many faults, was not. I don't suppose you follow current affairs, but he was a leading light of the Redemptionist faction; very much a radical, and remarkably, something of an idealist. It's rather a pity he didn't bring his enlightened thinking home with him in the evenings, but the fact remains, politically he was a good man, possibly even a great one, which is probably why I put up with him for so long. And you killed him."

The silence that followed was so oppressive that he felt he had to say something, even though anything he said would undoubtedly make him feel worse. "I'm sorry," he said. "I didn't know."

"Of course you didn't. And even if you had, it wouldn't have made the slightest difference, when my husband was lashing around with his sword trying to kill you. That's men for you," she added, "always looking for the easiest response instead of the best." She lifted the embroidery frame to her mouth and bit through the last inch of thread; neat and efficient, like a hawk. "Because of you, the land reform bill, the slavery bill and quite probably the poor relief bill won't go through this session, and maybe not at all. I don't suppose you care very much, but I do. Which is why," she went on, licking the end of a new length of thread, "you're going to Permia."

His eyes opened very wide. "Excuse me," he said, "but you don't mean—"

"Yes." Her expression hadn't changed, but suddenly he felt very cold. "Congratulations," she went on. "You've been chosen to represent the Republic."

He didn't understand. "As a diplomat?"

She actually smiled. It didn't help. Quite the reverse. "Good God, no."

"It'll be the first officially sanctioned tour of Permia since before the War," the chairman said. "As you can imagine, it's been an absolute nightmare setting it up, but now it really does look like it's going ahead. According to Senator Glycerius, it's the biggest diplomatic coup of our generation." He unstoppered the wine jug. "Really, it's the only thing we and the Permians have in common, apart from the War itself."

"I never knew they even liked fencing."

The chairman laughed. "They're crazy about it, absolutely crazy. More so than we are, even. It's all they ever talk about. Glycerius says that if you go into any bar in Luzir Beal, you can be sure they'll be talking about the latest results in the Nationals. All sections of society, from the mine workers to the great nobles in the hill country. They're obsessed with it. Every kid in Permia wants to be a fencer when he grows up."

Suidas was watching the wine jug. He hadn't been offered a drink yet, so he'd had no opportunity to refuse. "I didn't realise," he said. "I suppose we never thought about them as people, back then."

"You were in the War? I'd have thought—"

"Boy soldier," Suidas said, without expression. "I was with the Fifteenth."

Without asking, the chairman poured two glasses. It looked very red, like the other red stuff; clear and rich and smooth. I'll take the glass, he told himself, but I won't drink it.

"Anyway," the chairman went on, "you don't need me to tell you what's riding on this. If it's a success – well, who knows? We could be in the history books, you and me. If it goes wrong, we might very well start another war. It matters that much."

"Oh come on," Suidas said. "It's just fencing."

The chairman turned round slowly, like a man carrying a log on his shoulder. "You're wrong," he said. "It's really important you understand what's at stake here. Half of the Senate wants another war. They still think we can win, God help us. They think Permia's on its knees, and one final shove will have them down."

"Maybe they're right."

The chairman winced. "My son was a captain in the Seventh," he said. "He'd have been thirty-two, the first of last month. For pity's sake, Deutzel, you were there. You know what it was like."

Suidas shrugged. "I'm in no hurry to be back in uniform," he said.

"It's not just our side," the chairman went on, placing one glass on the table next to Suidas' chair. "The Permians are pretty desperate. The whole country's in a mess, they really don't know what to do next . . ."

Suidas frowned. He didn't follow the news if he could avoid it. "This is that business with the new mines in Choris Androu."

"Exactly." The chairman nodded fiercely. "Of course, the real effects won't start to bite for a while yet, not until the contracts expire. After that . . . " He shrugged. "What happens if you deprive an entire nation of its livelihood? We have no idea, it's never happened before. You've got some people saying it's the best possible thing, our oldest and most bitter enemy on their knees, starving in the streets. Or they'll tell you it's a disaster just waiting to happen, tens of thousands of angry Permians with absolutely nothing left to lose. The Bank wants peace, naturally. The nobility's saying that now's the best possible time to finish them off, like we should've done seven years ago." He shivered a little, and spread his hands in a hopeless gesture. "It's not like we're exactly a model of political and social stability right now. I really don't know what to make of it, and neither does anyone else. It's a mess. But if there's anything we can do to help, any-thing at all – well, it's obvious, isn't it?"

Suidas didn't think anything was obvious, but he held his tongue. "I'm not sure," he said. "If it's as bad over there as you say . . . "

"The job pays twenty-five thousand nomismata."

That shut him up like a slap across the face. The chairman looked at him and smiled. "Correct me if I'm wrong," he said, "but I get the impression you could use the money."

"Yes."

The chairman nodded slowly. "You'll do it, then."

Twenty-five thousand nomismata. "Yes."

"Splendid." The chairman frowned and looked away. "I'm so glad you agreed. If you'd refused, I was authorised to use blackmail and entrapment, or in the last resort we'd have framed you for a murder or something of the sort. I know," he added quickly, as Suidas opened his mouth and no words came out. "These people I'm dealing with, they're – well, you wouldn't think it was possible, not in a civilised society. God only knows what they'd be capable of, and I'm in absolutely no hurry to find out. But I guess, with so much at stake . . . " He shook his head. "I promise you'll get the money. It'll be paid into an account in your name at the Bank on the day you leave here for Permia. As soon as you get home, you'll be authorised to draw on it. Or, if – well, if things don't go so well, you can leave it as a bequest in your will. You have my personal guarantee it'll be honoured."

Suidas looked at him. "This is insane," he said. "I'm a professional fencer, not a—"

"I know," the chairman said.

The Bank's decision to repossess the Golden Spire temple and convert it into their headquarters led, needless to say, to a furious response from both the Studium and the public at large. The Bank's response was that the move was entirely reasonable and logical. They urgently needed larger premises; that wasn't in dispute. Twelve years ago the Studium had borrowed the sum of seven million nomismata, to pay its war tax and fit out three privateer regiments. The privateers, far from returning a substantial profit from battlefield spoils and the plunder of captured enemy towns, had been wiped out in their first serious engagement.

Furthermore, the war loan stock the Studium received from the Treasury in return for its tax payments had been downgraded to junk status following the Great Crash. There was, therefore, no realistic prospect of the Studium repaying its loan in the middle or long term. The Bank had tried to be realistic and had agreed to annual interest-only payments for twenty years. Five of these payments had not been made, which meant the compromise agreement was null and void. The only security available to the Bank was the Studium's realty, and they held mortgages on nine of the great City temples. They'd had all nine independently valued. The Golden Spire was worth five million, but the Bank was prepared to accept it in full and final settlement. Since they needed offices rather than a very large chapel, they had no option but to convert the building. However, they were only too happy to undertake to do so in as sympathetic a manner as reasonably possible. The internal fabric would remain substantially unchanged except for the addition of new partitions. None of the frescoes, reliefs and mosaics for which the Golden Spire was famous throughout the civilised world would be damaged or altered in any way, and the public would be given access to them on five designated open days every year, which was rather more than the Fathers had ever been prepared to allow. Finally, if at any time during the next fifty years the Studium found itself in a position to be able to pay off the original loan plus the interest accumulated to the date of foreclosure, the Bank would transfer the Temple back to their ownership, having first restored it to its original state and condition. They couldn't, they felt, say fairer than that.

The Studium didn't agree; the public did. The transfer was ratified by plebiscite 4/23, a majority of seventeen wards to five. Since the Patriarch refused to sign the transfer documents, the Bank obtained a court order and instructed the Land Registrar to amend the register. On the day the Bank took formal possession, three monks tried to chain themselves to the Antelope Gate and set themselves on fire. Two of them had either faulty tinderboxes or insufficient strength of purpose; the third was severely burned, but was put out in time by Bank guards, carrying water from the Fountain of Symmachus in their helmets.

The architect's plans designated the East Cloister as the site of the new boardroom, but it wouldn't be ready for at least eighteen months. The Board therefore met in the chapter house, with its magnificent mosaic ceilings by Theophano the Elder and its notoriously poor acoustics. On the day in question it happened to be raining heavily. Forty-six buckets were brought in to the chamber to catch the drips and prevent further damage to the tesselated floor (attributed to Chrysophanes, third century AUC); together they sounded like a huge musical instrument played by a hesitant beginner.

The first hour was taken up with routine business; formal repossession of the estates of the Leucas and the Blemmyas, and the sealing of several hundred conveyances and mortgages in favour of the existing tenants. Then Mihel Tzimisces, chairman and chief executive officer, announced that the Carnufex family had paid off the last instalment of capital and interest on its loans, and its debt was therefore extinguished. He personally fixed the Bank's seal to the deed of redemption, which was dispatched to General Carnufex by special messenger.

The courier entrusted with this mission rode directly to the Irrigator's country house at Bluewater, pausing only to change horses at the Bank's way station at Ridgeway Cross. He handed the deed, with Chairman Tzimisces' covering letter, to the house steward, who signed the receipt. The courier returned to the city by way of Monsacer, where he stopped for a drink at the Blessed Annunciation in the abbey foregate. There he happened to meet the abbot's cupbearer, who'd been in the same regiment as him during the War. The cupbearer reported back to the abbot, who immediately wrote to the Patriarch's chaplain, who reported to evening Chapter.

"The only thing that surprises me," one of the canons commented, "is that he left it so long to pay the damn thing off.

Everybody knows the Irrigator did pretty well out of the War. He can't have been short of money."

"Tax reasons," suggested one of his colleagues. "You get basic-rate relief on interest payments on war loans with private providers. I'd have thought you'd have known that."

The canon shrugged. "Not that it matters. I'd have liked to have seen them try putting the old man out on the street. They'd have been lynched before they got five yards."

The abbot, a third cousin of the General, frowned. "The Carnufex," he said, "and the Phocas, and the elder branch of the Bardanes; they're pretty much all that's left now. And the Phocas aren't what they were. I gather they had to sell a lot of land towards the end."

"And guess who bought it," said the prior.

"I hadn't heard that," the abbot said.

"Quite true. It was all perfectly proper and above board, but they might as well not have bothered. Who else was going to buy it anyway? Nobody's got any money."

Another canon, a huge man with a bald head and a long black beard, laughed. "The Bank hasn't got any money," he said. "Not of its own, at any rate. It's all borrowed from the Western Empire, at stupid interest. It's perfectly obvious what's happening, but nobody's prepared to recognise it for what it is. I guess they're afraid they'd have to do something about it if they did."

"Who would *they* be, in that context?" the abbot asked quietly. "For all practical purposes, the Bank is the government now. I don't really see them prosecuting themselves for procedural irregularities."

The big canon gestured helplessly. "If the people really understood what's going on . . . "

The abbot smiled at him. "My dear fellow," he said. "You've always had the gift of seeing complex issues in such delightfully simple terms. It's a tremendous asset in matters of doctrine, but you'd be wise to avoid politics or finance. The people are better off than they've been for a hundred years."

There was a brief, awkward silence. Then the prior said, "In the short term, maybe."

"Nonsense." The abbot closed his eyes for a moment, then opened them again. "We really mustn't allow ourselves the luxury of belittling our enemy's achievements. It's an undisputed fact that the Bank is guided by the best of motives, and has achieved more for the public good than we or our friends in the nobility have managed to do in living memory."

"The best of motives," someone repeated. "All things considered, I'm inclined to doubt that."

"Really?" The abbot gave him a puzzled look. "I believe their motives are simple and straightforward. Having lent tens of millions to the nobility so they could finance the War, the Bank realised that we were losing, and if we lost the War all those loans would default and they'd be ruined. What else could they possibly do except foreclose on the loans, bankrupt the nobility, take over effective political control and end the War as quickly as possible? Oh, it took a great deal of courage and a considerable leap of imagination; but looked at objectively, it was the only thing they could have done. Then, faced with the backlash from a dispossessed former ruling elite, they did the only sensible thing and bought the everlasting love of the common people. They sold them the freeholds of the land they'd hitherto been tenants of, and since there was never any question of the peasantry being able to pay for the land, they took two-hundred-year mortgages with capital repayment deferred for seventy years. In practical terms, the peasants pay their rent to the Bank, not the big house on the hilltop; everything stays the same, but everything's changed for ever. It's every politician's dream, and they contrived to find a way of doing it quietly and without bloodshed. I really do have the greatest respect for Tzimisces and his people, and I wish they were on our side and not our sworn enemies. But there it is. And if you're waiting for the Phocas and my cousin Herec to rise up and drive the Bankers out of the Golden Spire, I suspect you'll be waiting for a very long time, during which you could've been doing something useful."

In the exact centre of the iconostasis above his head, the single silver tear on the cheek of the Lady of the Moon reflected the glow of the twelve brass lamps on the pedestals surrounding the Low Stations. The lamps had been gold once, before the war tax was levied on monastic institutions. The abbot maintained that the brass ones gave a better light, because of the improved reflectors.

"The government's weak," the big canon broke in, "everybody knows that. They can't command a majority in the House, so they're doing everything by plebiscites. You can't run a country that way. All it'd take would be one bad thing happening, and then they'd lose the people, there'd be a vote of no confidence in the House and they'd be out. That's what happened to the Zonaras three hundred years ago, and it'll happen again. The question is, how much damage will they do in the meantime?"

"Define damage," the abbot said calmly. "Surely the point is, hamstrung politically as they are, they can't do anything much, beyond what they've done already. They've made the mistake of thinking that once you've got power, you'll live happily ever after, like princesses in fairy tales. But the essential nature of power is that it's an ongoing process. And, as I just said, they can't really do anything."

"Which is how they'll ruin everything," the big canon maintained. "What we need most of all right now is strong government." He paused, suddenly aware that he was almost shouting. "If they make a mistake and the City people turn against them . . . "

"There you go," the abbot said sadly, "hoping for a miracle. Much as I recommend prayer in the ordinary course of business, I'm not inclined to rely on it in something as important as this. There's also the small matter of who you intend to pray *to*. I can't help but think that your mat's pointed in the direction of my cousin Herec. And, as I think I made quite clear, that would be a vain hope. The army isn't going to clean up this mess for us. It's the only disaster in recent history that it's not directly responsible for, and I can assure you, it has no interest whatsoever in getting involved." He glanced down at his fingernails, which were dirty and ragged; he'd been working in the vineyard that morning, and hadn't had time to make himself presentable. "I suggest you reserve your prayers for the Invincible Sun. After all, that's what we're here for, supposedly."

An elderly canon, who hadn't said anything yet, leaned forward and folded his hands neatly in his lap. "I agree that the condition we're in is fairly dreadful," he said. "The question is, surely, are they any better off? I suggest that, since we've come so far and lost so much, it'd be a terrible waste not to go the last mile, especially if it's downhill."

The abbot smiled at him. "That's what so many people are saying, inside the House and outside. Even one or two in the Bank, so I'm told." That got him their undivided attention, but he raised his hand. "I'm reminded of the story of King Atoches and the oracle." Blank faces; he nodded. "King Atoches asked the prophetess whether he should risk everything on a final pitched battle with the Tant Fue. She replied that if he took the field, he'd overthrow a mighty kingdom. And so he did; his own. They say that his dying words were a homily on the ambivalence of prophecy, but since his body was never found, I imagine that was a later addition to the story. If we provoke a new war, I'm quite certain we'll destroy a mighty kingdom, possibly two. That certainty isn't enough to lead me to endorse a specific course of action."

The prior made a show of gathering up his papers. "Someone is going to have to do something," he said. "On balance, I think I'd rather it was us. I don't really trust the nobility, I have nothing but contempt for the Bank, and that only leaves the enemy, who are in no fit state to make rational decisions about anything. It's not an ideal state of affairs by any means, but it's the one we're stuck with. As Baventius says in the *Rope*, if you're sinking

in the sea and you can't swim, you might as well try and catch a
fish on your way down."

"Actually, it's the *Two Brothers*." The abbot lifted a finger to
signify the formal conclusion of the meeting. Nobody moved. "I
propose we adjourn and meet again in two days' time. I don't
suppose anything will have changed by then, but there's always
prayer."

Still nobody moved, so the abbot gathered up his papers and
walked out of the room. He crossed the yard, climbed the seventeen stairs to his cell, dropped into his chair and massaged his
knees. Every day, a little bit harder, just to do ordinary things,
like walk and climb stairs. In comparison, extraordinary things,
like gently guiding the destiny of the nation, were child's play.
He reached across his desk for his ink bottle, hesitated, and
instead picked up his copy of *The Greater Devotions*. It was the
copy he'd made himself, when he was fourteen years old, and
these days the letters were too small for him to read, but he knew
the words by heart, so it hardly mattered. He recited the five sec-
ondary collects, the singular confession and two of the prayers
for indecision. Then he flipped back the hinged lid of the ink
pot, picked up his pen and began to write:

Symbatus, Abbot of Monsacer, confident in salvation, to
Senator Brenart Trapezius, greetings.

He hesitated, lifted his head and craned his neck a little to see
out of his window. It was high on the wall (to discourage idleness
and distraction) and looked out over the roof of the stables; to
see the hills beyond, you had to stand on a chair, something the
abbot hadn't dared try for the last five years. On either side of the
window hung ancient icons, blackened by centuries of candle
smoke. It would be wrong to clean them. It was enough to know
that the holy images were there under the dust and grease; looking at them, a man might be misled by their beauty. The abbot
sighed. He'd nagged his parents into letting him join the Order

because he loved drawing and painting and looking at beautiful pictures. After nine years in the scriptorium, he'd produced what was still acknowledged to be the most perfect miniature illuminated missal in the world; whereupon he'd been transferred to the Chancery and taught accountancy, before his soul became irrevocably polluted with beauty. It was mere chance that he'd proved to be even better at accountancy than painting. Curiously, saving and making large sums of money for the Order hadn't been regarded as a mortal temptation to vanity.

Doubtless you can explain why

He stopped writing. Senator Trapezius was notoriously devout, but he was still a senator, not likely to take kindly to being lectured, even by his Father in the Invincible Sun. He put the sheet of paper to one side – it would do for lining a binding in the scriptorium – and started again.

Delighted as I was to hear that my cousin Herec Carnufex has been able to repay his debt to the Bank in full and is now clear of his mortgages, I must confess that I was slightly puzzled by the news that he is not to be pursued for arrears of interest on late instalments and penalty charges. You know as well as I do – better, of course, since you are a distinguished statesman and I am just a monk, wholly separated from the world – that if we are to have peace, the hawk faction must be kept in check; and the only means at your disposal is control over the warrior nobility through debt and encumbrance. My cousin Herec is a wealthy man. He made a great deal of money out of the War, and spent it on improving his estates (scientific agriculture and all that sort of thing); accordingly, he's rich in assets but poor in ready cash. He could, and should, be controlled through extended debt. You have now lost this hold over him.

Of course, I don't regard my dear cousin as an inherently dangerous man. I am, in fact, rather fond of him. When we

*were boys together, I regularly used to beat him at fencing,
single-stick, archery and wrestling, something which I have
never failed to remind him of on the all too rare occasions on
which we meet; he was better than me at boxing, but only
because of his slightly longer reach. These days, as a
conscientious servant of the Invincible Sun, I deplore in general
terms his bloody profession, while applauding the role he played
in the preservation of the state and true religion. I also beat him
regularly at chess, something a tactician of his standing would
not wish to be widely known.*

*What matters is the general principle. No doubt, when your
committee comes to consider similar applications for discharge
from other members of the nobility, you will bear what I have
just said firmly in mind.*

*Now to other, more important matters. The rose you so
kindly gave me last year has taken surprisingly well to our harsh
and bitter soil, and at his most earnest request I have sent a
cutting of it to the patriarch of En Chersin. He is a competent
gardener, and I therefore confidently expect that within our
lifetimes, the Trapezius rose will be propagated and appreciated
throughout the length and breadth of the Western Empire.*

He finished the letter, dusted it with sand, folded it and put
it on the pile for sealing. He had other letters to write (there
were always letters to write, reports to read, accounts to scruti-
nise, petitions to approve or dismiss) but he felt exhausted,
after such a small effort. He wondered, in a general sort of way,
if he was dying – slowly, in a discreet and dignified manner, of
some perfectly acceptable condition. The man to ask would be
Brother Physician, but of course he couldn't do that. He could
go to the library and consult medical texts, but he decided
against it; he'd have to ask the librarians to find the appropriate
books and bring them to him, and that would be as good as
announcing to General Chapter that there was something
wrong with him. The sensible thing, he decided, would be to

assume that his time was limited, in the earnest hope of being pleasantly surprised. On balance, in spite of the evidence, he doubted it. The Invincible Sun (that lifelong-familiar but still largely incomprehensible entity) clearly had more work for him to do, but felt it necessary to make that difficult work harder still by burdening him with physical weakness. Blessed be the name, et cetera.

Although he tried to concentrate on the service, he was preoccupied throughout evening responses, and the prior had to tap him on the shoulder to let him know proceedings had ended. Instead of taking the evening meal in the refectory with the Brothers, he asked for bread, cheese and black tea in his cell. To clarify his mind, he let the fire go out, took off his robe and sat in his shirt, until he was so cold he couldn't feel his feet. That didn't help; so he shook the problem off like a wet dog and glanced over some of the routine reports. One item (minutes of the House foreign affairs subcommittee) caught his attention. He ate the bread and cheese, which he'd forgotten about. The tea was cold, so he drank water instead.

On the second shelf of his bookcase was an old, sad-looking *Imitation of the Divine*; a home-made wooden board and pigskin binding, repaired several times over the years by men whose principal business hadn't been bookbinding; on the inside front cover, in peasant fashion, nine generations of his father's family had recorded births, marriages and deaths. The earliest entries, written in lamp soot and oak gall, were a soft brown colour and barely legible. The most recent additions, far out on the right-hand side of the page, were in his own superb formal-cursive, in black with red capitals. The names were the four sons of Herec Carnufex:

Sphacterius (b. 1577 AUC)
Cortemanduus (b. 1579 d. 1598 AUC)
Stellecho (b. 1581 AUC)
Adulescentulus (b. 1590 AUC)

He counted on his fingers. Young Addo would be – what, twenty-four, already? Just about right, he decided, for what he had in mind. It had been twelve years, half Addo's lifetime, since he'd last seen him. He remembered a thin, sad boy who felt the cold but refused to show it, a good chess player, would probably have been a reasonable musician if he'd been allowed to continue his education; just another aristocratic face, instantly forgettable, the epitome of the younger son.

Well, he thought; a pity, but it can't be helped. That would still leave Sphacterius (about whom he knew nothing) and Stellecho (famous in cockfighting and dog-racing circles) to carry on the family name, for what that was worth. If I had a son of my own, he told himself, I'd send him instead; but I don't, so young Addo will have to do. Besides, once Herec had made up his mind about something . . .

(He'd never mentioned it to anyone, naturally, but from time to time the abbot had nightmares about the drowning of Flos Verjan. The water had come down so fast, in such unspeakable volume, that there wouldn't have been time to evacuate the city, even if it hadn't been under siege and bottled up tight. Conservative estimates put the death toll at seventy thousand, but the method by which that figure had been calculated made no allowance for the very poor, the homeless, refugees from the surrounding country-side – everyone, basically, who wasn't on the electoral roll or a member of a guild. In his dream he was standing in the market square – he'd never been to Flos Verjan, but for some reason he could picture it very clearly – and looking up into the mountains, watching clouds that weren't clouds but great masses of water falling slowly towards him, like shapeless, distorted hands, both menacing and imploring. Whenever he had the dream, he would order a special mass for the dead, with candles and a full proces-sion, both choirs and a double distribution of alms. What if anything that was supposed to achieve he wasn't entirely sure. He could only hope that the Invincible Sun would find a way of trans-lating so much retrospective effort into some positive outcome)

High time our family did its bit, the abbot decided, and wrote another letter.

After three weeks of treatment, Giraut Bryennius was certified as fully healed of his wounds and discharged from the infirmary of the Studium. As ordered, he presented himself at the Fencers' Guild meeting house, where he was expected. A smartly dressed young man in Guild livery showed him to his room, a small space on the third storey with one long, narrow window, clean white walls and a mattress on the floor. Next to the mattress was a compact heap of clothes, which he recognised as his own. On top of the heap was a brand-new, expensive-looking rapier.

She meant it, he thought. Just for a moment, he contemplated using the rapier to force an exit, and running away. Wiser counsels prevailed. Only an idiot would consider fighting his way out of the Fencers' Guild, and besides, where would he go?

He resisted the temptation, which in spite of everything was quite strong, to draw the blade and examine it. Instead, he picked up his clothes and folded them neatly, then sat on the mattress and waited for something to happen. Nothing did, for a very long time. He really wished he had something to read, even if it was only the Hymnal.

Quite some time later, a different young man in the same livery turned up and led him back the way he'd come, down two flights of stairs on to a broad marble landing. The young man held a tall panelled door open for him, and he went in.

The room he found himself in was probably the most beautiful interior he'd ever seen. He guessed it had once been a chapel; the walls were covered from floor to ceiling with religious frescoes – the usual subjects: the Sun in glory, the apotheosis of Man, the Reckoning, the Second Partitionist Council; he could probably have named the artists if he'd been able to concentrate, but at the time it didn't seem to matter. The ceiling was mosaic on a gold background, the implacably perfect face of the Invincible Sun looking past him at something more interesting.

There were five tall, wide windows, curtained in purple brocade embroidered with heraldic motifs. On the polished oak floor lay Mezentine and Eastern Empire carpets, which he couldn't quite bring himself to step on; any one of them was worth a decent hill farm, including the stock and barn contents. There were also four chairs, with impossibly thin legs and rails, gilded and upholstered in red silk. One was empty. On the other three sat two men and a girl, none of whom he'd ever seen before.

There was a man of about thirty; a touch above average height, deep-chested, his fine fair hair touching his shoulders, just starting to thin on top, a square, good-looking face and a weak chin. A broad shiny scar stretched an inch inwards from the web between his thumb and forefinger. There was a tall, thin young man, about Giraut's age, who sat looking down at his hands. He was dark, with a narrow face, a very long, straight nose and big ears. He looked up as Giraut came in, smiled, then looked away. The girl was probably the tallest of the three, long in the body, broad-shouldered, with a sharp, plain face and short sandy hair pulled back behind her ears. She was wearing a man's riding jacket, a little too small for her; her thin wrists stuck out from the sleeves and her hands were big and long-fingered. She scowled at him as though a great many things were his fault, then folded her arms tightly and looked at a curtained window.

The older man stood up slowly, as though his legs were stiff from a long ride. "Presumably you're Giraut Bryennius," he said. He had a slight accent that came through on the long vowels, like copper shining through worn silver plating.

Giraut nodded. "Is this the fencing team?"

The older man grinned. "That's us. I'm Suidas Deutzel, the lady is Iseutz Bringas, and that over there is the honourable Adulescentulus Carnufex."

The tall young man mumbled, "Addo, please," then looked away again. He was beautifully dressed in grey velvet, with a mark on the left lapel where he'd recently spilled something.

"Sit down," Suidas said, and pointed to the empty chair;

maybe he thought he was training a dog, Giraut thought. He sat down and waited. Suidas frowned, then went on, "Do you know about all this stuff?"

Not the easiest question to answer. "We're a national fencing team, and we're going to tour Permia," he said. "That's about it."

Suidas nodded. "That's more or less all we know," he said. "Apart from, I don't know about you, but we aren't exactly volunteers. How about you?"

Giraut looked at him. He'd heard the name, of course, but had never seen him fence. Deutzel was a Western Empire name, but the accent was all City. He looked about as trustworthy as a rope bridge, though Giraut didn't feel inclined to hold it against him, under the circumstances.

"I was encouraged to join," he said.

"He killed a senator," the girl said. She had a low but perfectly clear voice. "Isn't that right?"

Giraut opened his mouth but couldn't seem to make a noise.

"So presumably," the girl went on, "it was this or the rope. Remains to be seen if you made the right choice."

Suidas looked blank, then carried on as though he hadn't heard her. "I'm team captain, for my sins. I don't actually know what you're fencing. Are you sword and buckler?"

Giraut shook his head. "Rapier."

"Oh. That's two rapiers, longsword and ladies' smallsword." He shrugged. "Any good?"

Giraut thought for a moment. "Yes," he said. "Better than I thought I was, anyhow."

"Else he wouldn't be here," the girl said.

She was getting on Suidas' nerves, he could tell. "I don't seem to remember seeing your name in competitions."

"I've never entered," Giraut replied. "My father wouldn't let me, said it'd distract me from my studies."

"So you haven't got any real experience at competition level?"

"No."

"Right." Suidas nodded. "It just gets better and better. Never mind." He noticed that he was standing up, seemed to realise there was no need for him to do so, and sat down. "Is what she said true?"

"Yes," the girl called out.

Giraut nodded. "It was sort of self-defence," he added.

"Sort of," Suidas repeated. "Well, that's none of my business. Our business," he amended firmly. "Apparently someone's going to come along at some point and tell us something. They can't be in any desperate hurry, because we've been here for a very long time." He looked up at the ceiling, frowned, and went on, "I guess, since we're going to be teammates, we really ought to make some sort of effort to talk to each other."

"Why?" the girl said loudly.

Suidas pulled a face. "I know she comes across as annoying to begin with," he said. "But once you've got to know her a bit better, you'll find it makes no difference whatsoever. I'll start, then. I'm Suidas Deutzel, I'm thirty years old—"

"We all know who you are," the girl snapped.

"Fine." Suidas turned round slowly. "You next, then."

"Go to hell," the girl said.

"Thank you, that was really helpful. You?" He looked at the thin young man, and Giraut noticed that he was making an effort not to scowl. "Well, come on, then."

The thin young man started to stand up, then thought better of it. "I'm Addo," he said. "My father—"

"We know about him," Suidas interrupted.

"Yes, of course. Well, I'm twenty-four, I've got two brothers, older than me, and there was another one who died in the War. Apparently I'm going to be fencing longsword, though I'm really not that good. My brother Stellecho—"

"Has it occurred to anybody to wonder," the girl said, talking through him like a needle through cloth, "why they're sending the Irrigator's son to Permia on a *goodwill* mission? Either it's some kind of a joke, or what they really want to do is start another war."

Addo went bright red and turned away. Suidas scowled, and said nothing. There was a long, painful silence, which gave every indication of lasting for ever and ever. Then the girl said, "Well, I think it's strange, anyhow. And the rest of you aren't exactly the brightest and the best. A murderer and a drunk—"

"And you," Suidas said. "Quite. I can tell we're all going to get along just fine. Maybe we should just sit here quietly till someone comes."

"You please yourself," the girl snapped, and took out a book. Giraut noticed she held it almost at arm's length. Suidas sighed, lay back in his chair and closed his eyes. Addo had his back to them all. Giraut placed his hands on his knees and tried hard to look at the artwork on the walls, but his mind slid off it like smooth-soled shoes on ice.

An infinite time later, the door opened. A bald, bearded man in some kind of robe or habit came in, looked at the four of them and (Giraut distinctly saw his face change) palpably wilted. But he was evidently a determined man. He cleared his throat, smiled and said, "Ladies and gentlemen, welcome to the Fencers' Guild."

Suidas clearly knew him. Addo probably knew him by sight. The Bringas girl ignored him completely. He took a couple of steps forward and realised there wasn't a chair for him. At once, Addo jumped up and went and stood against the wall. The newcomer hesitated, then took the chair and moved it a little so he was a few feet away and facing them. One of nature's lecturers, Giraut concluded.

"My name," the newcomer said, "is Jifrez Bardanes, I'm the chairman of the Guild. Some of you know me already, of course." He avoided Suidas' eye as neatly as a dancer. "First, I'd like to thank you on behalf of the Guild and, indeed, the Republic for your participation in this project." He kept a straight face as he said that; Giraut's respect for him increased dramatically. "The importance of the job you're about to do can't be overemphasised. It's really no exaggeration to say that the future of the peace rests in your hands. It matters that much."

It was, of course, precisely the wrong thing to say. Suidas frowned terribly at the ceiling, Addo went ghastly white, and the Bringas girl turned a page. Giraut was doing his best to stay perfectly still.

"I'd hoped to be able to introduce you to your coach and team manager," the chairman went on. "Unfortunately, that's not possible right now, so for the time being you'll have to make do with me. Now, I'm sure you have questions. I'll do my best to answer them for you."

He stopped and looked round. There could never have been such a silence since the beginning of the world.

Phrantzes came home from work to find a Watch captain sitting in his favourite chair, and two armed guardsmen standing behind it. The captain didn't get up. Sphagia was nowhere to be seen.

"Jilem Phrantzes?"

"That's me, yes."

"You're under arrest." The captain lifted a finger, and the two guardsmen moved forward, like chess pieces, and stood level with Phrantzes' shoulders.

"I beg your pardon?"

"As a citizen," the captain recited, looking over Phrantzes' shoulder, "you have the right to appeal to the Praetor. Should your appeal not be heard within thirty days, you have the right to apply to the City Prefect. You are obliged to answer any questions I may put to you truthfully, and failure to do so will lead to a prosecution for obstructing justice. Do you understand?"

Phrantzes stared at him. "What am I supposed to have done?"

The captain nodded, as if he'd just been given his cue. "Possession of obscene literature, contrary to the Sexual Offences and Blasphemy Act, AUC 1471." He reached behind him and produced a book. It was the one Corbulo had given him as a wedding present.

"That?" Phrantzes said.

"A proscribed text, according to the seventh schedule to the Act." The captain's face was completely blank. If he hadn't known better, Phrantzes would have sworn he was trying not to laugh.

"But everybody's got a—" Phrantzes stopped short. "It's not mine," he said. "I've never seen it before. It must belong to one of the servants."

The captain gave him a mildly disapproving look. "We have detained your domestic staff for questioning," he said, "and also your wife." He paused, to let that sink in, and went on, "I do hope you'll co-operate fully with our investigations."

It was a long time – not since the War, in fact – since Phrantzes had felt real fear. He recognised it straight away. He knew it would make his voice higher, and he'd probably start sweating; the symptoms were like a mild fever, only wildly accelerated. He'd have no chance of lying convincingly. "It's mine," he said.

The captain nodded again. "Of course it is," he said. "Your business partner gave it to you as a wedding gift. He inscribed the flyleaf. I must ask you to accompany me to the Watch house, where you will be formally charged."

They put him in a closed carriage, and nobody spoke. At the Watch house (he didn't actually know where it was; ridiculous, he'd lived all his life in the City) he was politely but ruthlessly searched. They confiscated his tiny ivory-handled penknife and led him down a flight of stone stairs to a long corridor of cells. He could hear someone, presumably a prisoner, banging on a door. Nobody else seemed to have noticed. They put him in a tiny white box with a stone ledge and no window, and left him there.

It was bitterly cold in the cell. No doubt that was what made him shiver, though it was hard to see how it could have accounted for the sweating.

He was sitting on the ledge when a different captain opened

the door and told him to follow. Back into the corridor, escorted by the captain and three guards; up four flights, along a low-ceilinged passageway, and through a door.

The room was as white as his cell, no window, a table and two chairs. In one chair sat an old man in a monk's habit. He was reading a book, using a powerful glass. He looked up, smiled, and thanked the captain politely, as though he was a waiter. The captain went out, closing the door behind him.

"Jilem Phrantzes," the old man said. "Do please sit down. Forgive me for not getting up, but these days my knees don't work terribly well. My name is Symbatus, I'm the Abbot of Monsacer."

Phrantzes hesitated for a moment. The man was old and feeble and they were alone; for a split second he considered grabbing the old fool in a stranglehold and using him as a human shield as he made his escape. Too ridiculous for words. He sat down.

"You've got me rather than a secular magistrate because technically, sexual offences and blasphemy is an ecclesiastical jurisdiction," the abbot said. "Of course, under ordinary circumstances we delegate our authority to the secular power. Did they keep you waiting long?"

"I don't know," Phrantzes said truthfully.

The abbot nodded. "My fault," he said. "They sent a carriage for me, but I move frightfully slowly these days. All those stairs." He pulled a face. "But I'm here now, and so are you. I expect you're wondering what on earth is going on."

"Yes."

The abbot smiled, and closed the book. It was Phrantzes' copy of *Mysteries of the Bedchamber*, the one Corbulo had given him. "It's been years since I saw a copy of that," the abbot said. "My late father had one. I remember walking in on him once when he was reading it. He went bright red in the face and yelled at me for entering a room without knocking first. It was ages before I figured out what that was all about." He pushed the book into the middle of the table with his forefinger. "Actually, I'd forgotten what mild stuff it is, compared with what passes for literature these days. Half of it's a closely reasoned debate about the indivisibility of the three aspects of the Invincible Sun – rather good, actually, I've got half a mind to quote it in a homily one of these days and not say where the text comes from. It'd be interesting to see how many of my learned brethren recognise it. Of course, they used to put great slabs of theology in everything in those days."

He stopped talking. Phrantzes guessed he was doing a fairly realistic impression of a dithering old man. He kept quiet, and eventually the abbot looked at him.

"Unfortunately," the abbot went on, "by some ridiculous oversight, it's still on the forbidden publications list. Which is quite ludicrous," he added with a smile, "because practically everybody in the City who can read has owned a copy at some point in their lives, though I imagine it comes as a bitter disappointment to most of them. We couldn't possibly prosecute you just for having one, we'd be laughed out of court. It'd be a complete waste of time and an embarrassment for the Prefect's office."

Another silence. Phrantzes was sure he was supposed to say something at this point. He kept his mouth shut and waited.

"So really," the abbot went on, "you'd have been all right if you hadn't lied to the Watch captain, in front of two witnesses. Now *that* is a genuine offence, for which I believe the penalty is an unlimited fine, up to three years in prison, or both. Also, the prosecution doesn't have to give details of the original investigation in open court. All they have to do is satisfy the judge, in camera. So you can be tried and found guilty of obstruction, and nobody need ever know that the original offence you were being questioned about was, well, a bit of a joke, really. If you ask me, it's a bad law and wide open to abuse, but there, I'm not a legislator, so it's not up to me. I'm dreadfully sorry," he said, "but you would appear to be in a bit of a fix."

Phrantzes looked at him. He felt a great surge of anger, which dissipated as quickly as it had come, followed by a deep, lingering terror. He couldn't have said a word if he'd wanted to.

"Before you ask," the abbot went on apologetically, "your wife, obviously, had nothing to do with it at all. I gather she's being held at the convent of the Sublime Revelation. It's a pretty dreary place but they're quite decent women there, for nuns. She'll be fine, though I imagine she'll be most dreadfully worried about you. The main thing," the abbot went on, as Phrantzes' hands clenched on the arms of his chair, "is to get you out of this as quickly as possible. Don't you agree?"

"What the hell," Phrantzes said slowly, "could anybody possibly want from me?"

The abbot sat up a little straighter in his chair. "During the War," he said, "I believe you served on the staff of General Carnufex. My cousin," he added, and there was something; not pride, but a sort of warmth. "He speaks very highly of you, as an administrator."

"I was a clerk."

"Oh, a bit more than that. You don't get to be a major if you're just a clerk."

"I organised supply convoys," Phrantzes protested. "Itineraries, estimated travel times, that sort of thing. Just paperwork, that's all."

"And you did it very well, according to cousin Herec. And he's not easily impressed, as I'm sure you know."

"He always gave me the impression he thought I was an idiot."

The abbot smiled. "That's just his way. He was an extraordinarily pompous boy, I remember. He used to lecture the gardeners until they chased him away, and then he hid in the rose bushes. Don't tell anyone that, by the way. He'd be furious, and he'd know it was me that told on him. Now then," the abbot went on, "after the war, you won four gold medals in the national championships."

"Three."

"Sorry, three. Still, a remarkable achievement. I believe the record stood until quite recently, though I have to confess, I don't follow fencing. We're not supposed to, in an enclosed order, though that doesn't seem to stop the younger men taking an interest. When I first took over as prior at Monsacer, there used to be a regular sweep on the winter League. I made myself very unpopular when I put a stop to it."

Phrantzes stared at him. "What's fencing got to do with anything?"

"Please bear with me," the abbot said kindly, "I'm coming to that. The business you run with your friend Corbulo. How's it doing?"

"Not too badly, I suppose."

The abbot scratched his head. "You export raw wool to the Western Empire, and you import finished goods. You'll have to excuse me," he went on, "I'm just a priest, I really don't know the first thing about international trade or any of that sort of thing. Am I right in thinking you inherited your share in the firm from your father?"

"Yes." Phrantzes suddenly felt an urge to talk, as if that might somehow help, though he was fairly sure it wouldn't. "He and Corbulo's father founded the business, back before the War. My father died and Corbulo's retired, and we took over. We'd worked in the business all our lives, of course, except when we were away at the War."

"So you've known Corbulo . . .?"

"Since we were kids."

"You've always got on with him?"

"He's like a brother, I guess. Things changed a bit when he married Xanthe, naturally, but not all that much."

"Ah yes." The abbot nodded, as though they'd reached some fascinating crux in the argument. "She's a Rhangabe, isn't she? Benart Rhangabe's youngest daughter."

"That's right."

"Rather a good marriage for a merchant."

Phrantzes shrugged. "They lost a lot of money in the War. I sort of got the impression that they were glad to get her off their hands. Of course, Corbulo and Xanthe are devoted to each other."

"You know Rhangabe's brother, the Senator, was killed recently."

Phrantzes nodded. "It was quite a shock," he said. "Not that Xanthe and her uncle were particularly close. But a man like that, getting stabbed to death in his own home ..."

"Defending his daughter's honour." The abbot frowned. "What do you think should happen to the young man responsible?"

Phrantzes shrugged. "I really couldn't say," he said. "Hanging him wouldn't bring the Senator back."

"You surprise me. I'd have thought you'd want to see justice done."

"Well, he's been caught." For some reason, Phrantzes felt he should choose his words carefully. "I'm sure he'll get a fair trial, and the court will do what's best."

"You have a touching faith in our justice system."

"Well, yes. Or I used to. Look, I'm sorry, but what's all this got to do with me? Please, tell me what you want and I'll do it. I just want to get out of here."

But the abbot didn't seem to be listening, or maybe he was a bit deaf. "Mihel Rhangabe was a radical," he said. "Do you agree with what he was trying to do?"

Phrantzes pulled a confused face. How could he be expected to remember details of points of current affairs that didn't really concern him very much, when he'd just been arrested on a spurious charge and interrogated by an elderly lunatic? "By and large, I suppose," he said. "I mean, banning slavery, that makes sense."

"Go on."

Phrantzes considered for a moment, collecting his thoughts

like a general rallying his surviving troops after a massacre. "You've got two dozen or so aristocrats owning huge factories producing high-volume, low-quality woollen cloth," he said. "They've got a thousand or so slaves working hand looms; practically no overheads, they produce the raw material themselves, so they can trim their profit margin and make their money by selling in bulk to the Western Empire. But in the Empire, they don't have slaves, instead they've got machines that'll do the work of a hundred men and only need one man to work them. What we should be doing is buying in those machines. But we can't, because there's no money in it, because the big landlords have their slave factories. Get rid of slavery, you can take the woollen cloth trade away from the aristocrats, which is the only way you'll be able to keep it in this country in the face of Imperial competition. Carry on the way things are now and we'll be reduced to selling raw wool instead of finished cloth, and that won't last long, believe me. We'll be in exactly the same mess as Permia, or maybe even worse."

"Interesting," the abbot murmured. "Go on."

Phrantzes wanted to stop and consider what the question really was, but by now he couldn't help himself, just as a drowning man can't help thrashing his arms. "Also," he said, "you've got thousands, tens of thousands of slaves, all getting fed barley bread, which we've got to import from the West, which just makes the balance of payments problem worse. Free those men, put them on farms of their own in the Demilitarised Zone, where they can feed themselves and produce a saleable surplus, and you're a big step closer to solving the foreign exchange deficit. Also, once we've got people living in the Demilitarised Zone, with a damn good reason for defending it, maybe the Permians won't be so keen to invade it again. At the moment, it's just empty, practically a desert. We can't send our own people there, we lost so many men in the War we can't farm our own country, let alone colonise the DMZ. Get rid of slavery, you solve two problems in one go, and it won't cost the Exchequer a bent trachy."

The abbot pursed his lips. "It's refreshing," he said, "the way you address the issue without any recourse to arguments based on morality. In my line of work, I hear so much about right and wrong, I sometimes lose sight of the real issues. Thank you." He stood up, staggered a little, put a hand on the table to steady himself. "Cramp," he said. "I find sitting still for too long very trying." He walked slowly and painfully to the door, and opened it. "I think that's everything," he said. "For now."

Phrantzes opened his mouth, closed it again, said, "I can go?"

"Not quite," the abbot replied. "But you can wait out here in the corridor instead of in a cell. Progress of a sort, I'm sure you'll agree."

A guard came in and stood over Phrantzes; he took the hint and stood up. His left foot had gone to sleep, and the pins and needles made him wince. He walked to the door, suffering agonies because he daren't hobble. Then he paused, because there was one question he had to ask, come what may.

"How did you know to search my house?" he asked.

The abbot beamed at him. "Now that," he said, "is a really good question. Goodbye."

They'd been given a different room to sit in. This one had at one stage been a salle d'armes. It still had the polished oak floor, scuffed and shining, the pale oak-panelled walls and the high windows, placed to catch the early light. But someone had filled it with chairs and put in a fireplace, a huge grey stone affair rather ineptly carved with the arms of the Guild. At the far end was a large board, inscribed with dozens of columns of names in small gold script. Giraut guessed they were the past winners of some prize or other, but he couldn't be bothered to look.

At least their shared misery had got them past the sulking stage, though they still weren't talking much. The girl had lent Addo her book (he recognised the title; a two-hundred-year-old verse epic of forbidden love and high-minded anguish among the ruling elite of the Eastern Empire, written by someone who'd never been there), and he was sitting in the far corner reading it. The girl had found a stack of blank writing paper, and was carefully folding each sheet into the shape of some stylised animal, before slowly tearing it to pieces. Suidas was doing his midday exercises, a revolting sight. Not for the first time, Giraut considered the probability of there being a guard outside the door; but even if there wasn't, where would he go, and what on earth would he do for money?

Suidas completed his course of fifty one-arm press-ups and started doing star jumps. This, apparently, was more than Iseutz could bear. "Do you have to do that?" she snapped, and he stopped, scowled at her and then suddenly grinned.

"Sorry," he said. "It's just, when I'm feeling like shit, I exercise."

"That would explain why you're so healthy," Iseutz said. "I vote we go out into the corridor, find someone and demand to know what's going on. Well?"

"You can if you like," Suidas said.

"Fine. How about you?" She hadn't aimed the question at anybody in particular. "You," she said, turning in Addo's direction. "Mister Born-in-the-Purple. Well?"

Addo looked up from the book. "We could do," he said. "If you think it'd help."

Iseutz clicked her tongue. "How about you? Sorry, I didn't catch your name."

"Giraut. And no, I don't think it'd serve any useful purpose."

"Fine. We'll all just sit here till we die of old age."

"Or starvation," Giraut said. "I don't know about you, but I'm hungry."

"Well, there you are, then." Iseutz stood up. "Let's go and find young Mister Giraut something to eat, before he fades away. There's got to be a kitchen or something in this place."

Addo said, "I'm not sure we ought to just help ourselves without asking."

"Who's going to stop us?" Iseutz laughed, rather high and

scratchy. "We're the finest swords in all the Republic. We'll cut our way through to the kitchen if we have to."

"It's not midday yet," Suidas said. "The angle of the sun through the window," he explained. "I've been watching it, and I make it about an hour before noon."

"Please yourself, then." Iseutz sat down, folded her arms and scowled at the floor. "At least they could've given us a chessboard or something like that."

Addo looked up. "Excuse me," he said. "Do you play chess?"

"Yes. Why?"

"I've got a chess set in my pocket. You know, the little travelling ones."

Giraut was impressed. They were made in a far province of the Eastern Empire; ivory and some kind of incredibly hard black wood. You could rest them on the palm of your hand. Each piece had a tiny peg in the base, which fitted into holes in the middle of the squares. You could buy one second-hand for less than the price of a town-centre house, but they didn't come up very often.

Iseutz glared at him with barely controlled fury. "Why the hell didn't you mention it earlier? We could've been playing chess, instead of sitting here like idiots."

"I didn't think anybody would want to give me a game. I'm not a very good player."

"Excellent. I don't like losing."

"I'll play the winner," Suidas said.

"If you want. But we've got to make it interesting. Say, five nomismata?"

Suidas frowned. "I haven't got five nomismata. Sorry."

"That's all right, you can owe me. What about you, Giraut? Do you want a game, after I've slaughtered these two?"

Giraut thought about it for a moment. "For five nomismata."

"Yes."

"All right."

Iseutz disposed of Addo in a dozen moves, though Giraut

had the feeling he wasn't really trying. He counted the coins out of a heavy green silk purse. Suidas refused to play, which made Iseutz extremely angry. Giraut stepped in to keep the peace, and found himself sitting across the tiny board, facing a standard opening.

He tried to spin it out, but he was never much good at deception. As soon as he'd taken her queen (in self-defence; what she lacked in skill she made up in aggression), it was obvious she was going to lose, but she fought on until he couldn't stand it any more, and executed a simple checkmate. She looked at him, her face milk-white and her lips an impossibly thin line, and pushed Addo's five coins across the table at him. Then she got up and stood beside the window.

There was a long silence. Then Suidas said, "I'll give you a game, if you like. Not for money."

What the hell. He enjoyed chess, and he was good at it. He found that Suidas was a high-class player, maddeningly slow at times, extremely cautious, with a defence he couldn't break down, in spite of some quite inspired gambits he hadn't thought himself capable of. In the end he lost deliberately. Suidas thanked him for the game, in such a way as to suggest he didn't want another. They left the chess set on the table. Addo made no move to reclaim it.

Giraut must have fallen asleep. He woke up in a spasm of terror, and for a moment he was sure the man standing in the doorway must be the hangman, or at best the chaplain waiting to hear his last confession. But the newcomer walked past him, an old man levering himself along with a stick; so much effort and determination required to accomplish something Giraut did without thinking. If that was me, he thought, would I go to all that trouble just to move myself five yards?

"Ladies and gentlemen." His voice was high, dry and brittle, and he spoke quietly, to make them all shut up so they'd be able to hear him. "You don't know me. My name is Symbatus, and I'm the Abbot of Monsacer." He saw Addo lift his head. "For my sins, I'm one of the organisers of the tour you're about to take part in. Don't worry," he went on, "I'm not going to preach a homily. I'd like to introduce you to Jilem Phrantzes, who's kindly agreed to be your coach and team manager."

Understandably enough, given its history, Permia is not a religious country. There are a few Eastern Didactic monasteries in the mountains, where a few grim old men still recite the Seven Offices, and the capital has a fire altar and a temple of the Invincible Sun, mostly for the convenience of foreigners. By and large, however, the Permians have no great interest in the divine. Occasionally, one or other of the mildly hysterical mystery cults that periodically sweep through the Eastern Empire breaks out in some of the smaller fields and is allowed to burn itself out. Nothing of the kind is allowed to take hold in the major fields, with their necessarily large and volatile populations, for fear of disruption and lost production.

Director Kalojan was, therefore, something of a curiosity. A highly placed Board member, responsible for seven major mines in the Home fields, he'd been a sincere and open devotee of the Divine Flame for most of his adult life. It was generally accepted that he'd picked up the habit as a student in Chosroene, at that time the third best university in the Eastern Empire, where he'd been sent to study mathematics and natural philosophy. Although he made no secret of his faith, he never seemed to allow it to interfere with his duties as a company officer; nor did he ever try to convert any of his colleagues, although he was delighted to discuss moral and spiritual issues. He gave a quarter of his income to the poor each year, endowed a chaplaincy at the fire altar, and wore a small silver signet ring engraved with the insignia of the faith. That was all.

Kalojan did, however, attend services at the altar, which made the assassin's job relatively simple. At the conclusion of the morning office, celebrants are required to file past the altar steps, dropping a handful of incense into the brazier as they pass it.

They then leave the building through the narrow door, which symbolises the true way of the believer. Part of the symbolism lies in the fact that only one person can go through it at a time (just as no teacher or priest can achieve another man's salvation; each believer must find truth on his own). Thus, when Kalojan walked out of the altar house into the fresh air on the morning of his sixty-third birthday, he was alone; his usual bodyguards were only a pace or two behind him, but that was enough of an opportunity for the killer to step forward and stab him through the right ear with a Mezentine left-hand dagger. Two of the bodyguards gave chase, but the killer eluded them easily in the crowded streets of the Fruit Market. Kalojan died instantly.

The first reaction to his death was astonishment. Company directors used bodyguards because, by the very nature of their office, they could expect to be attacked at any time. Of all the Board members, however, Kalojan had been considered the least offensive to the greatest number. He belonged to no permanent faction, had no ambition to seek higher office, had made no serious enemies and was, unusually for a Board member, liked and respected by the mine workers.

The obvious suspects, therefore, were the Beautiful and Good, the only people who might conceivably have wished him harm, simply because he was a fair and honourable man with the interests of both the Company and the workforce at heart. Too obvious. It was soon being argued in the camps and taverns that if someone wanted to make it look like the Beautiful and Good were out to cause trouble, Kalojan was the perfect target; after all, nobody else could have wanted him dead, so it had to be them. Suspicion soon centred on the Board, who were widely suspected of preparing a last all-out campaign against the remnants of the military aristocracy. There were several riots in the western fields, and three miners were killed at the Blue Bird mine after the prefect sent in the Blueskins. The Empire, choosing to interpret the murder as motivated by anti-religious feeling, registered an official protest and demanded a full investigation, to be observed by three archdeacons of the Fire Church. Meanwhile the Rasen family made a statement, basically saying that the rumours were true and they had proof (which they didn't offer to share), and calling on war veterans to rally to the family's castle at Sirven and prepare to defend it against further Company aggression. All the Board could do at first was to draw attention to the fact that the murder weapon was of Mezentine origin, suggesting the involvement of the Republic, the Western Empire, or both, a hypothesis that met with no public interest whatsoever.

With so much noise being made about the affair in every part of the country and stratum of society, the report of the investigating officer passed largely unnoticed, in Permia at least. The investigator admitted that he had no substantial clues as to the killer's identity, allegiance or motive. The bodyguards had been unable to give him a helpful description – the man was medium height, medium build, inconspicuously dressed and masked, and all they could say about him for sure was that he could run very fast. Nobody had noticed any suspicious-looking strangers waiting outside the altar house at any time before the attack. The usual sources had nothing to offer on the subject of recent negotiations for the hire of an assassin, the provision of a safe house or the laundering of any substantial sums of money. The only concrete evidence was the weapon, which the killer had left behind presumably so as not to attract attention once he was clear of the scene. The weapon was easy enough to identify, though such objects were rare in Permia: a duellist's dagger, designed to be held in the left hand, primarily to deflect the opponent's sword; of exceptional quality and finely engraved with a characteristic leaf-and-scroll pattern, it bore Mezentine guild approval marks and the monogram of a famous sword-making firm. The guild marks revealed that it was over a hundred years old. It was, therefore, a valuable item in its own right, though worth considerably less on its own; weapons of this kind were almost invariably sold as part of a case (two exactly matching rapiers and daggers, for use in duelling), the value of a complete set greatly exceeding the sum of its parts. The investigator could only conclude that it had been acquired by theft, probably by a thief who had no idea of the true value of what he had stolen, and that the murderer had chosen it because it would be harder to trace back to him than, say, a newly made knife bought from a cutler's stall in the market. However, no theft of such an item had been reported in the City in the last eighteen months, nor had any of the principal handlers of stolen goods heard of such a thing being offered for sale.

Eurid Aten was able to make a certain amount of play with the report in his speech to the Conclave of Lodges a week after the murder. The dagger, he said, was, if honourable members would excuse the pun, a two-edged clue. It was all very well the investigating officer looking up his records for thefts of fancy knives in the City, where people couldn't afford such things and wouldn't want them if they could. A Mezentine-made duelling set was, however, exactly the sort of status symbol you'd expect to find in a Beautiful and Good castle or manor house; had the investigator bothered to write to the heads of families to ask if any of them had an empty space in a trophy of arms they couldn't account for? In reply, Tepan Masav pointed out that a great many Beautiful and Good heirlooms had been sold off during and shortly after the War by impoverished households. Furthermore, at least two dozen castles and many more lesser houses had been stormed and plundered by the enemy – loot from these sources could easily have changed hands many times since the armistice. Equally, the Beautiful and Good had no monopoly on fine Western antiques, very few of which had ever been exported outside the frontiers of the Empire, so it was just as likely, if not more so, that the dagger had been acquired abroad (which, in Masav's view, was where the assassin undoubtedly came from, and his paymasters as well). In any case, surely it was impossible to believe that a member of a great family would use or cause to be used a family heirloom for such a purpose, precisely because of the implications to which the honourable member had been good enough to draw Conclave's attention.

The report of the day's proceedings in Conclave was one of the documents included in the weekly diplomatic bag sent by the Republic's accredited representatives in Permia to the House. Before he left the City, the messenger stopped, as usual, at the Praetor's office, where the dispatches were carefully unsealed, read and sealed up again. He then took the Old West Road through the mountains, crossed the border at the Triangle Pass, and followed the road across the Demilitarised Zone to the Republic's way station C15, where he handed the bag on to the second-link courier, who rode through the night, bypassing C14 and reaching C13 just before dawn. The third-link courier carried straight on to C10 (C11 and C12 hadn't been rebuilt yet), and the fourth-link rode without stopping, reaching the House just before the start of the morning session.

All that effort; somehow, the opposition had got hold of the investigator's report two full days before the official courier arrived, and were able to ambush the foreign secretary with the Mezentine dagger story before he'd had a chance to read his brief.

"Which means," the Abbot of Monsacer explained to a select committee of the Bank directors, "they must have a direct line of communication that's at least two days faster than ours, presumably crossing the mountains somewhere south of the Blackwater and not going through the Demilitarised Zone at all."

"That's not possible," one of the directors objected. "All the mountain passes are guarded. You can't just slip across the border, not unless you happen to be a bird."

"Maybe they've found a new way over," someone suggested.

"I doubt it," the director replied. "Every place you can possibly get through was found during the War. Mostly," he added with feeling, "by the enemy."

"Then they must have an understanding with the guards somewhere," said someone else. "Like General Promachus used to say, no fortification built by men is strong enough to keep out a donkey loaded down with gold coins."

"The likeliest explanation would be that money is changing hands at some point," the abbot said gently. "In which case, our chances of finding out how they're doing it are fairly remote. I think we must just accept it as a fact of life and move on."

"But it's maddening," someone said, "having to learn the news from the enemy, when we're spending a fortune on couriers and way stations. Also, I don't like not being in control of the news supply. If people find out things we don't want them to, any form of coherent government becomes impossible."

The abbot smiled sadly. "All we can do is try and cope, and discredit wherever possible," he said. "A few patently untrue stories, planted in such a way as to suggest they originated with the opposition's news service, might redress the balance a little, but that's your field of expertise, not mine. I'm more concerned with the message, rather than the manner of its delivery." He paused, and looked slowly at the men sitting around him. "I don't suppose any of you gentlemen had anything to do with the assassination."

There was a moment of perfect silence. The abbot nodded. "I was fairly sure you hadn't, but it's as well to be open about this sort of thing, among ourselves."

"As far as I can see," an elderly director said, "it's little short of a disaster for us. Anything that destabilises the Permian government—"

"Kalojan wasn't that important," a younger man interrupted.

"No, but he was a moderate, and you can bet your life he'll be replaced by someone more extreme," someone replied. "Could be a hawk or a dove, it depends who can capitalise best on the fuss they're making over it. Looking at this report, chances are it'll be the military. Everyone seems to think it was a crude attempt to discredit them."

"That's what concerns me," the abbot said. "Personally, I'm inclined to believe that the Beautiful and Good were behind it.

Their response has been so swift and well-orchestrated, it seems to me that it must have been prepared in advance; and they could only have known the Director would be killed if they themselves arranged it. In cases like this, I'm simple-minded enough to suspect the party that benefits most. The question is, what can we do about it?"

That led to another silence. Then someone said, "There isn't anything. Is there?"

"Oh, there's always something," the abbot replied mildly. "For example, we could arrest someone, tell the Permians that we've caught the murderer and he's confessed, and then arrange for him to die escaping or hang himself in his cell. We would then apologise fulsomely to the Permian government, confessing that the murderer was a rogue intelligence officer who exceeded his orders, and that we're taking all possible measures to make sure nothing of the sort ever happens again. There'd be an almighty row, for a week or two, but in due course the Permians will be left with the impression that we're serious about peace and honest enough to own up to our mistakes. People respect you when you admit you've done something wrong, even if you haven't."

Another dead silence. Then someone said, "Could we do that?"

The abbot laughed. "Of course," he said. "But I don't think the situation quite warrants it. Better to keep that trick up our sleeves for when we actually need it."

"It's a thought, though," someone said. "What if we could frame someone like General Andrapodiza? Or the Irrigator, even. Two birds with one stone."

The abbot frowned slightly, and the speaker remembered, a little too late, that the Irrigator was family. "I'd counsel against trying to be too clever," the abbot said quietly. "The repercussions at home might be unfortunate. Also, there's a difference between bearing false witness against a nonentity and a man of power and influence. One should always bear in mind the consequences should one be found out. Personally," he went on, "I would be inclined to let this affair blow over. It may well be that the Permians will catch the guilty party, in which case matters will doubtless sort themselves out. What we should do is increase our efforts in other, safer directions."

"Ah," someone said. "You mean the fencing tour."

"More than ever before, it's vital that the tour is a success," the abbot said. "What we have here is a chance to get in touch directly with the Permian people, rather than their divided and absurdly conflicted representatives. We have the tremendous advantage, from our perspective, that even after seventy years of war, there's remarkably little hostility towards us at grass-roots level."

They stared at him. "Are you sure about that?" someone said.

"Moderately sure," the abbot said quietly. "And I've taken the trouble to research the point. I've made discreet enquiries of village brothers and City chaplains, men who are so much more in touch with popular feeling than we could ever hope to be. I'm particularly interested in the views of war veterans; they're the real formers of opinion on this issue, and we're extremely fortunate, in that regard, that the Permians chose to fight with mercenaries rather than their own people. If you ask an old soldier, he'll tell you that he hates the Aram Chantat, and if he had his way the Blueskins would be rounded up and wiped off the face of the earth. Most likely, though, the Permians he'll have encountered would have been refugees, women, old men, children. You'd be surprised how many of the veterans we've heard from talk about how they shared their food with starving villagers – I don't suppose they actually did, but it shows that they'd have liked to, which is what's important. Of the rest, a fair proportion feel guilty about raping and robbing defenceless women. The consensus would seem to be that the War was the fault of the mine owners and the Beautiful and Good, and the ordinary people were as much victims as we were."

"I don't suppose they feel the same way in Permia," someone said.

"To a certain extent, I think they might," the abbot said. "At least, as far as attributing the blame for the War is concerned. In a class-ridden society like Permia, the common people tend to hate their social superiors rather more than the foreign enemy; which, I firmly believe, is how we come to have peace. On that level, we share a primary objective: destroying the power of the military aristocracy in our respective countries and ensuring that power stays in the hands of the leading commercial interests. I'm convinced that an East Country shepherd and a Permian miner have quite a lot in common; they blame the bosses, not the foreigners. Also," he went on, "they're both obsessive about organised sports. It's more or less the only bright note in their otherwise fairly miserable lives."

The silence that followed was submissive, if not entirely convinced. The abbot waited for a moment, then said, "Talking of which, I'm pleased to be able to tell you that Jilem Phrantzes, my choice for coach, has kindly agreed to join the team, which means the touring party is now complete. All that remains—"

"Phrantzes," someone interrupted. "That name rings a bell."

"My congratulations on the excellence of your memory," the abbot said. "I envy you. These days I find it's all I can do to remember where I left the book I was reading last evening. As I was saying, all that remains is to finalise the details of the tour dates, which I'm happy to leave to Phrantzes and his staff. As soon as that's done, we can begin."

Leaving the Republic and heading into the Demilitarised Zone, the Great West Road is, of course, the Great East Road. Once clear of the wide, messy skirt of willow shacks and semi-permanent tents on the east side of the City, where most of the refugees still live, the road climbs slowly but steadily through orchards and grass-keep meadows on to the eastern plateau, once moorland but now painstakingly improved into thin, wet pasture. The only trees are wiry thorns, bent into ridiculous shapes by the wind, and the lines of copper beeches, planted into the enclosure-dividing earth and stone banks a century ago by a generation of optimistic improving landlords hoping to form windbreaks. Halfway through the War, the roots began to break through the sides of the banks, gradually ripping them apart; there was nobody to do anything about it, since everybody was away. The rain got into the splits and fissures, washing out the earth, and the wind slowly prised out the trees, like bad teeth, and pushed them over. Most of them are lying on their sides now, still with a taproot in the soil to keep them alive, but growing sideways, like old men who have fallen and can't get up.

Beyond the plateau the hills rise and fall, and it's easy to see where the improvers' optimism ran out. The bald tops grow only a little woody-stemmed heather, while the steep-sided valleys and combes are too wet to graze safely except at the height of a dry summer. Sensibly, the road follows the central ridge, which runs fairly straight through the middle of the moors. A hundred years ago there were cottages, wrapped round on all four sides with tall beech hedges. But the low eaves of their turf roofs have long since reached the ground and melted away into it, leaving long, strangely regular grass mounds that eventually collapse as the roof timbers rot away, briefly revealing a blackened table or two legs of an overturned stool. These days, the shepherds cart up wheeled huts for the summer grazing, stopping where it's easiest to cut into the peat seam, to keep the stove going. The only continuously inhabited structure on the moorland stretch of the road is way station C9, where they keep three changes of horses for the couriers, and the stationmaster sells stale bread and flat beer to travellers as a sideline. During the war, C9 was a fortified inn, the Hope & Endurance, headquarters of the 17th Dragoons, a defence-in-depth cavalry unit whose job was to shadow Aram Chantat and Blueskin raiding parties and, if possible, ambush them on their way home, when they would be careless with success and encumbered with loot. But the Blueskins never got that far – too cold, they said, and nothing worth taking – and the Aram Chantat were never that careless;

mostly, the hundred or so dragoons stayed in the Hope and tried to keep warm. These days, apart from the shepherds, the only visitors tend to be romantic poets and well-bred young ladies of the mercantile class, who come in splendidly equipped coaches to record in charcoal and watercolour the savage beauty of the wilderness.

"I managed to get us warrants to put up at the way station," Phrantzes said, raising his voice so as to be heard over the rumble of the wheels, "so with any luck we won't have to camp out overnight."

Nobody said anything. Phrantzes, apparently satisfied that he'd done his duty, ostentatiously closed his eyes and leaned as far back into his seat as he could get – not particularly far, since the headrest was too low and narrow for a man of his size. Hardly surprising; the carriage had been designed for four young ladies and their paints, easels and hampers. Somehow they'd managed to cram five men and a tall girl into it, with all their gear strapped to the roof. It had been the only wheeled vehicle available, apart from farm and carriers' carts, and according to Phrantzes they'd been lucky to get it.

The sixth passenger was reading a book. Giraut was filled with awe and admiration; he'd tried to read at the start of the journey, but the movement of the carriage, lurching and wallowing on four catapult-steel springs over the rocks and potholes, had made him feel disastrously sick, so he'd spent the last nine hours looking out of the window instead. But the sixth man – Phrantzes had described him as a political officer, with no further explanation offered – was snuggled in his seat, a warm scarf round his neck, apparently engrossed in his book (Iseutz had made several barely disguised attempts to read the title off the spine, but the lettering was too small), a picture of deep content. It helped that he was short and slight, with little short-fingered hands, and so the seat and the headrest were just the right height for him. At one point, three hours out and in the middle of a ferocious hailstorm, he'd offered round a small enamelled tin of pale brown honey cakes, and hadn't seemed in the least offended when nobody except Phrantzes took one. He'd taken one himself and stowed the tin under his seat, and the offer hadn't been repeated; a pity, Giraut thought, since by the looks of it, the tin contained the only food on the coach.

It was raining again, and Giraut couldn't help thinking about all their spare clothes, fencing gear, footwear and other possessions, up on the roof in six large canvas sacks. He told himself that there'd be a nice roaring fire at the way station, where they'd be able to dry out their stuff and buy or borrow a tarpaulin. It was, he suspected, one of those promises he made himself from time to time that somehow didn't get kept, but he put it out of his mind. Phrantzes was pretending to sleep, the political officer was reading, Suidas was staring down at his fingertips as if trying to read something written very small indeed on his nails, Addo was sitting up straight with his hands folded in his lap – he seemed capable of holding this pose almost indefinitely, and it made him practically invisible, like one of the magic cloaks in fairy tales – and Iseutz was picking at a scab on the back of her left hand. According to Phrantzes, the tour was going to last for three months. Although Giraut felt properly grateful to the Invincible Sun for the amazing second chance he'd been given, after apparently screwing up his life beyond all hope of redemption, he couldn't help wondering if a short stay in a condemned cell and a brisk walk to the gallows might not have suited him better after all.

A sudden lurch, a dull thumping noise, and Giraut found himself kneeling on the carriage floor, with his head in Phrantzes' lap. The carriage had stopped moving. "What the hell . . .?" Iseutz demanded. The political officer, who was next to the door, leaned his head out of the window and sighed. "It looks like we've just lost a wheel," he said.

Phrantzes made a soft moaning noise. Suidas, who'd somehow managed not to get thrown across the carriage when they stopped so suddenly, was already on his feet, climbing daintily behind Giraut's back on his way to the door. It wouldn't open when he tried the handle, so he scrambled and swung himself through the window, a performance so swift and graceful as to defy analysis.

"He's right," Giraut heard him call out. "Nearside front wheel's off, and it looks like the axle's busted. We're screwed."

The political officer frowned, put down his book (having first marked his place with a handkerchief), and placed his hand on the door handle. For him, it opened easily. He stepped down and closed the door behind him.

"Now what?" Iseutz said.

Giraut hadn't taken to Phrantzes, but he couldn't help feeling sorry for him. He looked like a hunter who's discovered that the rabbit he's just shot was actually his best friend kneeling behind a bush. "I have no idea," he said. "The nearest place is the way station, but I don't suppose they've got anyone there who can mend axles."

"You'd need a blacksmith," Addo said – Giraut was startled for a moment; the voice seemed to have come out of thin air. "You've got to dismount the axle, forge-weld it back together, straighten it and then put it back. Or if it's broken off too short, you may need to make up a new one. It happened to us once when we were driving out to our country place one summer," he explained. "We were stuck in a little village somewhere for three days."

"Three days." Iseutz looked as though she'd just been condemned to death. "I can't possibly—"

"The nearest blacksmith is probably back in the City," Phrantzes said quietly. "Which means someone would have to walk back there, carrying the axle."

"And what the hell are we supposed to do?" Iseutz snapped at him. "Just sit here and starve?"

"Walk to the way station, I suppose," Phrantzes said. "At least you'll be warm and dry there. I'll have to send a message back to the City and tell them to tell the Permians we'll be a week late.

This is going to ruin everything. We won't possibly be able to make the schedule."

"Excuse me," Giraut said, and stood up. He couldn't get the door handle to open, so he climbed out through the window. It wasn't nearly as easy as Suidas had made it look.

He found Suidas lying on his back, half under the carriage, looking up at a snapped-off length of steel bar. The political officer and the coachman had apparently vanished into thin air. "How bad is it?" Giraut asked.

"I've seen worse," Suidas replied. "I did a bit of time on caravan duty in the War, we were always getting held up with shit like this."

"Addo says we need a blacksmith."

Suidas grinned at him. "For a proper job, yes," he said. "But it's, what, two hours to the way station; something like that, anyway. Not too far."

"How do you know that?" Giraut had to ask.

Suidas seemed surprised at the question. "I looked at a map before we left," he said. "And I've been keeping tabs on landmarks as we've passed them, which gave me our average speed. If I'm right, we're about twenty miles from C9 – which figures; if we hadn't had this, we'd have got there just before nightfall, which makes sense. So, what I'm saying is, if we could fix it just enough, as opposed to properly, we could probably get to the station all right."

Giraut frowned. "How on earth can you fix something like that without the right tools?"

"You'd be amazed what you can do if you absolutely have to," Suidas replied, hauling himself out from under the carriage and sort of bouncing to his feet. He seemed almost absurdly cheerful, as if something good had happened. "Right, let's see what we've got."

"Such as?"

Suidas was looking round. "I once saw an old supply carter replace a busted axle with a chunk of oak gatepost and an axe," he said. "Of course, we haven't got either of those, but I expect the principle's the same." He put his foot on the hub of the back wheel and sprang up on to the carriage roof. "Of course it'll be dark soon, which really doesn't help. Any idea where the creep's got to? Not to mention the coachman."

The creep was presumably the political officer. "Sorry, no idea," Giraut said. He could hear voices inside the coach – well, Iseutz's voice, raised and unhappy, interspersed with short silences, which presumably represented Phrantzes' attempts to reply. It was colder outside, and it was just starting to spit with rain, but he felt no great desire to get back in.

"Screw them, then. Are you going to help?"

Giraut nodded, and for some reason he felt pleased too. Maybe it was just good to be doing something, after a long period of things being done to him. "What can I . . .?"

"These bars." Suidas was pointing to the luggage rack, the basis of which consisted of six steel rods, about as thick as a thumb. "Of course, the axle's considerably thicker, so we'd have to shim the wheel with belt leather or something of the sort. The real problems are, one, getting one of those rods out, two, fixing it to the underside of the carriage. It'd be a piece of cake if we had a cold chisel, a big hammer and a dozen long nails."

Giraut looked at him. "What have we got?"

Inside the coach, Iseutz chose that moment to say something trenchant about her view of the situation. "Motivation," Suidas said. "Now then, there must be some sort of carrier's box some-where on this thing. Long wooden trunk, with a lid. It's where the carter stores all his junk."

Giraut looked up. "You're sitting on it," he pointed out.

"Well done, that man." Suidas jumped up. "Right, let's see." He stood up, raised his foot and stamped on the lid of the box, smashing it. For some reason, Giraut found this mildly dis-turbing. "Oh come on," Suidas said mournfully, pulling out an armful of spare reins, some rope and a coil of thick iron wire. "If I have to walk to the way station with that bloody woman whining all the time, there'll be bloodshed, I can promise you that. On army wagons there was always a big hammer, an axe, six-inch nails, useful stuff. This is just ... "

Giraut crawled under the coach and had a look for himself. The steel axle, what was left of it, passed through two loops welded to the high point of the arched springs. Suddenly, as if in a moment of divine revelation, he saw what Suidas had in mind: one of the iron bars from the luggage rack, clamped to the floorboards of the coach with about two dozen long, bent nails. He could see how it would've worked with an ordinary cart, built from massive timbers you could drive a nail deep into. But the coach was light and flimsy; nails would pull out of those delicate boards, or pull through and shatter the wood. He was about to point this out, but realised that Suidas wasn't in the mood to hear something like that. Then another thought struck him. He measured the diameter of the broken axle against his forefinger.

"Those rods," he said.

"Well?"

"Roughly an inch thick?"

"More or less. But like I said, we could pack out the axis hole in the wheel with something."

Giraut grinned. The luggage rack stretched the full width of the coach; slightly more, in fact. The broken axle was two and a bit inches across. And if he pulled it off, he'd suddenly be a hero and everybody would like him. As it happened, the Invincible Sun was sulking behind a cloud at that precise moment, but Giraut nodded gratefully in His direction nonetheless.

"Come down here a minute, will you?"

"Why?"

"Because we don't need one bar," Giraut said. "We need four."

They called Addo out to give them a hand. The look of gratitude he gave them suggested he'd be their friend for life.

Fortunately, Addo was a good deal stronger than he looked.

Together, he and Suidas were able to lift the coach while Giraut pulled the broken axle out from the other side. Then he hauled a couple of similar-sized rocks under it to prop it up, while they lashed into a bundle the four luggage-rack bars they'd eventually managed to prise loose, wrapping the spare reins round them as tight as they possibly could. This bundle they inserted into the steel loops welded to the springs.

"One axle," Suidas said delightedly. "Of course we won't be able to go more than walking pace, and it'll be bumpy as hell, but never mind."

In order to get the wheels back on, they had to lift the coach up higher. Iseutz and Phrantzes were pressed into service as auxiliary lifting power, while Giraut crammed in flat slabs of stone from a nearby derelict wall. By now it was nearly dark, so they snapped off the pretty gilt brass coach lamps and lit them; it was just enough light to work by. It wasn't straightforward. The other wheel didn't want to come off the old axle, and neither wheel wanted to go on the new one. The drizzle turned to rain, which made hands slippery and dissolved the ground under their feet into greasy, thin mud. Iseutz insisted on offering advice, most of it perfectly reasonable, which Suidas seemed to regard it as a point of honour to ignore. Eventually, however . . .

"Knock the stones away," Suidas shouted, "and let's see what happens."

To keep the wheels from sliding off the axles, they'd bound the ends tightly with spare rein, knotted and intertwined into balls the size of a closed fist. That had been Addo's suggestion, and Suidas didn't think much of it. But it held. Addo led the horses on; the wheels rolled, creaked, wobbled in two planes, but stayed on. It was, Giraut couldn't help thinking, something of a miracle.

"What about the luggage?" Addo asked.

They'd had to take it off the rack and dump it on the ground, of course, to break out the improvised axle rods. There wasn't enough left of the rack to tie it to, and there most definitely wasn't room for all of it inside.

"We'll take the fencing gear," Suidas said, after a long silence. "They'll have to send someone from the way station to pick up the rest of the stuff. Probably they can catch us up on the road later."

The wooden crate took up the space they'd been using to put their feet. Faced with the prospect of spending the rest of the ride with his knees tucked under his chin, Giraut volunteered to ride up top with Suidas, even though the rain showed no sign of letting up. He was so wet already, it couldn't possibly matter. But that's all right, he told himself. The huge log fire at C9 will have us all dry in minutes. In spite of everything, the wet, the pain in his back and shoulders and where he'd skinned his knuckles against the hub, he felt serenely happy, in a way he couldn't remember having felt before.

"I really would like to know where that so-called political officer's got to," Suidas said, wiping rain out of his eyes with the back of his hand. "I mean, we're in the middle of nowhere, and he just disappears. It doesn't make sense."

But just as the coach was about to move off, he appeared, trotting towards them out of the darkness, with the coachman following on behind him. They were wet through, which was some consolation.

"Where the hell were you?" Suidas yelled at him, but he was through the door and into the coach before either of them could stop him. The coachman climbed up on to the box, only to find there wasn't room for him.

"You can damn well lead the horses," Suidas snapped. "First, though, you can tell me where you and that arsehole went off to."

But the coachman shook his head and climbed down. Suidas yelled at him some more, but it was too dark to see if he was taking any notice. The coach lurched forward; it was actually limping, as if it had feet rather than wheels, and each quarter-turn

of the ludicrously improbable axle made the boards under
Giraut's feet shake.

It would, of course, have been quicker to walk. There was no
way of telling how long it took, because there was nothing to
gauge the passage of time by. Suidas claimed to be making some
kind of scientific observation based on his extrapolation of the
circumference of the wheels; but when they blundered into a
deep pothole and he was nearly thrown off the box, he admitted
he'd lost count, so his findings were necessarily flawed. After a
very long time, however, he started making worried noises.

"We should be able to see the lights by now," he said. "I
mean, the damn place is right next to the road, and there's only
one road, so we can't have taken a wrong turning, so it's got to be
there, and we've got to reach it soon. But we ought to be able to
see the lights. They keep a big storm lantern burning all night,
for the government couriers."

"You've been here before." Giraut found it hard to get the
words out. He was wet and cold, so his teeth were chattering, and
every bump of the four-lobed axle jarred his jaw.

"During the War. Of course, they didn't show a light then, so
you had to find it by dead reckoning."

"That's what you were doing."

"Trying to," Suidas said. "But it wasn't my job back then, so
I've never done it for real. I just know the general principle. It's
like how they did the military survey of the DMZ: a dozen men
in raggedy old clothes, counting their paces under their breath.
Amazingly accurate, as it turned out."

More time passed, and Suidas said they'd better light the one
remaining coach lamp (the other had got smashed while they
were playing with the axle). "If we miss it and have to go back,
she'll go on about it for the rest of the trip, you can bet your life."

Entirely believable; so they lit the lamp. It meant they could
see the rain, each slanting line golden in the yellow light, like
strands of hair, but not much else. It didn't help them find C9.

"What the hell's that?" Giraut heard Suidas call out; he was hauling on the reins with one hand and the brake with the other. The coach stopped. Giraut couldn't see anything.

"There's something blocking the road," Suidas said. "If we'd run over it, it'd have snapped the springs, sure as eggs. What the hell does that clown of a carter think he's playing at?"

He jumped down, and after a moment's thought Giraut followed him. The obstacle proved to be a thick, square-section wooden beam, lying across the road. Suidas swore and lifted the lamp over his head, then started yelling, "Everybody out! Now!" It took Giraut rather longer than he'd have liked to admit to figure out that if you wanted to wreck a coach or a cart in the dark, presumably with a view to robbing it, you could do worse than lay a beam across the road.

The coach door opened. The political officer came scurrying out. He had a lantern of his own, a tiny little thing that gave out an extraordinary amount of light for its size. Behind him came Iseutz, then Addo, then Phrantzes last of all, stumbling like someone who's just woken up out of a deep sleep. The political officer noticed the beam and lifted his lantern. "I think we should all move away from the coach," he said, in a quiet voice that everybody heard quite clearly. "There's a building over there," he added, and they could just make it out against the slightly paler darkness of the sky. "I'll go ahead and take a look. Wait here till I call."

He disappeared, taking the light with him; they couldn't see him, only a glowing yellow cocoon moving away. "What the *hell* is going on?" Iseutz demanded.

"Someone put a big chunk of wood across the road," Suidas replied. "It's what we used to do in the War, to block a convoy. It's really lucky we were only crawling along. If we'd been going at anything like normal pace, the lead horses would've broken their legs. But they just stepped over it, and I saw it in time."

"Who would want to do that?" Addo asked.

That was clearly a very good question, which was probably

why nobody tried to answer it. "That political bastard is always disappearing," Suidas said, to no one in particular. "Someone had better tell me what he's supposed to be doing on this trip, or I'm going to get very unhappy."

"It was a condition of the tour," Phrantzes said, and everybody else turned and looked at him. "Any official delegation going into Permia has to be accompanied by a political officer. That's what they told me," he added defensively. "I wasn't told anything about him, just that he'd be joining us."

"He makes my skin crawl," Iseutz said. "He just sits there reading his stupid book and smiling, and he doesn't feel the cold. Can't we leave him behind somewhere, or something?"

The light went out, and Giraut felt a surge of panic. *Why* had the light gone out? Its absence made the world a much darker place than it had been when they'd been moving. "Now where's he got to?" Iseutz said. "I vote we put him on a lead, like a dog."

There was a long silence. Giraut had to wipe rainwater out of his eyes so he could see, though it was too dark for him to make out anything except very subtle gradations of black and dark blue.

"If you'd all care to follow me." It was the political officer's voice, though Giraut couldn't place where it was coming from. "This way."

"Where are you?" Suidas said.

"Head directly away from the coach. That's right, keep going. Follow that line, and you'll come to a stone wall. I suggest we camp there for the rest of the night, it'll provide a degree of shelter from the weather."

"And he can see in the dark," Iseutz said bitterly. "That's not natural."

They found the wall by bumping into it. The political officer was there before them. "I'd prefer not to light the lamp again," he said. "I'd recommend keeping the noise down, if you wouldn't mind. Nothing to worry about," he added, cheerful and in no way convincing. "I think we might all try and get some sleep."

"Look, what the *hell*—"

"Shh," the political officer said gently; and it worked, because Iseutz didn't speak again.

Giraut wedged his back against the wall, pulled his completely sodden lapels round his running-wet face, and sat staring into the impenetrable darkness. He didn't know who was on either side of him. He'd have given two hundred nomismata for a weapon, if he'd had two hundred nomismata.

But, somehow or other, he must've fallen asleep at some point, because the next thing he did was open his eyes. He saw pale red light, the first stain of dawn. He could hear Iseutz talking.

"... complete bloody shambles, and we haven't even reached the border yet. What's going to happen when we're in Permia, assuming we manage to get that far, I dread to think. That man Phrantzes is obviously completely useless, the political man is most definitely not on our side, Deutzel's decided he's in charge but he's an idiot. I was under the impression this jaunt was supposed to be *important*, but ..."

From context, therefore, she was talking to Addo, and the rest of them weren't there. He looked round and saw the two of them, tucked under the wall like a handkerchief in a woman's sleeve. He stood up, winced as the cramp announced itself, and looked round.

He could see the coach, about thirty yards away. Beyond it there was a large grey square building, which had to be C9. So that was all right; except, if that was the way station, why were Iseutz and Addo still out in the open, still in their wet clothes, sitting on the ground?

"Excuse me," he said.

Iseutz broke off in mid sentence. "Oh look, he's back from the dead. Sleep well?"

"What's happened?"

"There's nobody here," Iseutz said crisply. "The place is deserted, doors locked, shutters down. Deutzel reckons the way-station people put the plank of wood there before they left, though why he thinks he's such an expert I really couldn't say. Phrantzes was absolutely useless. I said to him, perhaps you'd care to explain why a bunch of government servants suddenly take it into their heads to abandon their post, without a word to anybody, and take off into the night . . . "

Giraut could think of a reason. How stupid would it be, how grossly in keeping with his life so far, if between their departure from the City and their arrival here, war had been declared and the way stations closed, leaving them to wander cheerfully in their dainty little coach into the first tidal wave of Blueskins and Aram Chantat? Clearly the same thought had occurred to the political officer, which was why the lantern had gone out so abruptly, and why they'd spent the night hiding behind a wall.

"Excuse me," he said, "I think I'll go over and see what's happening."

"Suit yourself," Iseutz said angrily (he had no idea what he'd done). "Don't expect to get any sense out of those morons, though."

He passed the coach, and saw that the horses had been taken out of the shafts; he couldn't see them, and wondered if anybody else had noticed they weren't there. As he got closer to it, the building depressed him. It was grey stone, giving an impression of monstrously thick walls and tiny, grudging windows behind sheet-iron shutters. Iron? The door was sheet iron too, closed with two broad, flat bars secured by padlocks as big as his hand.

Phrantzes was sitting on an upturned box beside the door. He lifted his head as Giraut approached, and nodded politely.

"What's going on?" Giraut asked.

"I'm sorry to say I have no idea," Phrantzes replied. "According to what I was told, this station is open and functioning. Unless this isn't C9, of course. But Suidas Deutzel says it is, and he was here in the War."

"Where is Suidas?"

"Seeing to the horses," Phrantzes replied. "There's a stable out back. It was locked up, but he was able to break the lock off.

Luckily there was some hay in the loft, because there's no grazing around here to speak of." Phrantzes smiled bleakly at him. "I'm afraid I'm not making a very good job of being your team manager," he said. "It's fortunate Suidas Deutzel seems to know what to do. I asked him if there was any way I could help, but he didn't seem to think there was."

Giraut looked away. He wasn't really in the mood for granting absolutions. "So what do we do now?"

"I really don't know," Phrantzes said. "Suidas doesn't think the improvised axle will get us back to the City, and we can't stay here, we've got no food, we can't get into the building. I suppose we could sleep in the stable, but what would that solve? We don't even know if the authorities are aware this station's been abandoned, so we can't rely on them sending anybody to find us. The next station is thirty miles further down the road, on the border of the DMZ. But if this one's been closed, we can't rely on the next one being open. And it's twenty-seven miles back to the City."

None of which, Giraut reflected, answered the original question. "Where's the political officer?"

Phrantzes frowned. "He went off with the coachman, didn't say where they were going. I asked him if he knew any reason why the station would be closed, but ..." He shrugged. "The thing is," he said, "they've got my wife in a convent. I don't suppose they'd actually do anything to her, but you really don't know with these people, they're capable of anything."

Giraut pretended he hadn't heard any of that. "So you think we should walk back to the City?"

"I don't know," Phrantzes snapped, as though the question was totally unreasonable. "I have no idea why we're here or what we're supposed to be doing, or why everything is suddenly my fault. I'm a wool merchant. What do they expect me to do, grow wings and fly them all to Permia?"

Giraut decided that none of this was helping. "I think I'll go and look at the coach," he said, and walked away.

The stable was just the main blockhouse in miniature, except with no windows and a wooden door. It was open, and Giraut saw a closed padlock dangling from the mangled wreck of a hasp still bolted to the frame. Suidas Deutzel, he guessed, had found something to take his feelings out on. He went inside, and found Suidas forking hay out of the loft.

"Which suggests they left in a hurry," Suidas said. "Standard procedure on evacuating a military facility, you remove all materials likely to be of use to an enemy. Which specifically includes animal fodder. Also, there's a tin plate with a chunk of bread and a bit of cheese on the ledge over there, by the door. Someone didn't stop to finish his dinner."

"Suidas," Giraut said. "Do you think war has started?"

Suidas considered his reply. "The thought crossed my mind," he said. "Especially when I saw the bar in the road. But no, I don't think so. If they'd declared war, they'd reinforce a strong-point like this, not just abandon it. I mean, two padlocks aren't going to keep out the Aram Chantat. On the other hand, why the hell lock up a way station and just leave? I've thought about it and I can't imagine why they'd do that."

"You don't think so."

That made Suidas angry, though he made an effort to keep his temper. "I'm guessing, I could be wrong. Maybe some lunatic's started a new war, I don't know. I'm this close to getting on one of these horses and riding like hell for the City." That seemed to have exhausted his anger; now he just looked worn out. "What do you think? Do you reckon that's what's happened?"

Giraut shrugged. "I don't know the first thing about it." It occurred to him to confess, although he had no idea why. But it seemed important. "I should've been in the War," he said. "I turned fifteen two months before the peace. But my dad knew someone who knew someone, and I got deferred. And then it was all over."

Suidas grinned at him. "You weren't the only one, believe me. You know what? Nobody wanted kids that age. I should know, I was drafted at fifteen. At that age, you're far more trouble than you're worth. It screws up the whole platoon. You can't keep up, you haven't got a clue, you get on the guys' nerves. Then someone starts yelling at you, someone else sticks up for you, leave the kid alone, and next thing you've got bad feeling, fighting, everything goes to hell. Everyone's scared stiff that if there's a scrap you'll get yourself in trouble and they'll feel obligated to look out for you, which means someone'll get killed on your account. It's bad enough in a fight, God knows, without having to look after some useless kid. The sergeants and the officers knew it, so did the brass. The politicians hated it, because for some reason the voters objected to having their fifteen-year-old children sent to the front. But the nobility insisted, talked about manpower shortages and having to make up their quotas somehow. Then again, all conscripts are basically useless in a war. That was a great advantage the Permians had, using mercenaries. We only got peace because they ran out of money. So," Suidas said, turning aside to stick his pitchfork into the hay, "don't beat yourself up about it, all right? It's no big deal, really. I just wish my dad had known somebody."

Giraut nodded; he wished he hadn't said anything. But he didn't seem to be in control of what came out of his mouth. "But if there's a war now, I'll have to go."

Suidas lifted a load of hay on the fork. "In my day, cutting off your little toe was the favourite," he said. "Of course, they put you on a compulsory labour detail, and you spend the war in a supply depot hauling sacks around. Another good one was criminal blasphemy. You piss on the steps of the altar, that's five years. They tell me you get a better class of person in prison during a war, because all the hard cases take enlistment parole, so it's only draft-dodgers and a few old men. And for criminal blasphemy they won't even consider you for enlistment, because it might bring down the wrath of the Invincible Sun on your unit. I knew a kid who chopped his balls off with a pair of shears. They wouldn't even take him for compulsory labour, reckoned he was too weird. So no, you don't have to go. It's up to you what you think it's worth. Me, I didn't argue. Got me out of the house and away from my mother. We didn't get on." He leant the fork against the wall and sat down on the edge of the loft floor. "There's worse things than war," he said. "If you're lucky, you'll be all right."

An hour or so after sunrise, the political officer reappeared, though without the coachman; he'd sent him back to the City, he explained, to get another coach. In the meantime, they'd have to stay where they were.

"But there's no food," Iseutz said slowly, as though to an imbecile. "We haven't had anything to eat since we left home."

The political officer pulled a sad face. "Rest assured," he said, "there'll be plenty of food when we reach C11."

"We're going on, then." Addo had spoken. "I thought—"

"Of course," the political officer said. "There's absolutely no reason why we should alter our plans because of this. It's unfortunate, of course, but I expect we can make up time once the new coach gets here."

"Excuse me." Iseutz took a step forward. She was a head taller than him. "I'd like to know precisely who you are and what you're doing on this stupid trip. Well?"

"Certainly," the political officer said. "My name is Yvo Tzimisces, I'm a facilitator working for the diplomatic service, and I'm here to smooth over any difficulties we may encounter once we get to Permia. That's all," he added, with a smile. "Really."

"Excuse me." Addo looked as if talking was hurting him worse than a broken arm. "Are you any relation of Mihel Tzimisces, the Bank director?"

"My second cousin," the political officer said. "It's a large family. Well, I think that's more or less everything. I suggest we all make ourselves as comfortable as possible until the coach gets here."

*

Giraut went back to the hay loft. It was dry there. He took off his coat – with difficulty; the sodden wool was starting to turn into felt, and it was as stiff as leather – and hung it over a rafter. There was no realistic possibility of it drying out, but he felt obliged to try. He buried himself in the hay, which was dusty and made his eyes itch. He was colder now than when he'd been sitting out in the rain, and he wondered if that was the first sign of a fever.

After a while, Iseutz came in and sat down on a feed bin. She hadn't seen him and he didn't announce his presence. She took a book from her pocket and opened it, found that the pages were soaked through and dropped it on the floor. A little later, Giraut heard a strange noise, which he couldn't immediately identify. At first he thought it was mice, but realised it was Iseutz, crying.

That made him all the more determined to avoid detection, so he made himself stay perfectly still. The noise went on for what seemed like a very long time, then gradually died away.

"I've been looking for you." Suidas' voice, though Giraut couldn't see him from where he was lying. He closed his eyes. It made it easier to concentrate on listening, and if they saw him, he could pretend to be asleep.

"Well?"

"Our political officer," Suidas said. "You reckoned there was something odd about him, right?"

"Yes."

"I hate to say this, but I think you may be right." A short pause; presumably Suidas was finding something to sit down on. "Our political friend's very well connected, isn't he?"

"Is he?"

"Don't you know anything about current affairs? Mihel Tzimisces is the chairman of the Bank."

Silence. He wished he could see her face.

"And that's not all," Suidas went on. "I don't suppose you noticed, but he's got these marks on his neck . . ."

"Like little red scars. Three on the left and two on the right."

"That's right." Suidas' voice had changed; he was clearly impressed. "I've seen marks like that before."

His pause was presumably for effect. "Well?" she said impatiently.

"During the War," Suidas said. "High-ranking field officers wore these fancy breastplates. All-in-one jobs, not the scale stuff. It was a particularly stupid design. It was so young aristocrats could look like heroes of antiquity; you know, in statues and paintings."

"So?"

"So," Suidas went on, "the neck opening on this particular pattern was a bit too small, and they tended to chafe. People dealt with it by wearing scarves. That was fine for the staff, who spent most of their lives sitting around in meetings. But in the field, you got unbearably hot, so you dumped the scarf and put up with the chafing. And it left little scars. Yvo Tzimisces was a senior officer on active service; a senior captain, possibly even a major. A fighting officer, not a desk ornament."

Another pause; then Iseutz said, "I don't quite see . . ."

"Think about it. The chairman's cousin, and in the War he was a senior officer. What's he doing playing nursemaid to a sports team?"

"He can see in the dark," Iseutz said. "That's creepy."

"What you mean is," Suidas replied, "he's used to night operations. Also his knack of making himself scarce. He's not political, he's military, must be. And a pretty unusual sort of military, come to that. The Tzimisces aren't one of the old army families, they're not noblemen. You didn't get to be a major unless you were the right sort of person; not unless you were very good indeed at doing something that needed doing properly. I think we're in very distinguished company. It'd be nice to know why, though."

A longer silence this time. Then Iseutz said, "I think, when the coach gets here, we should insist they take us straight back to the City. If we all say we want to go home, they'll have to let us go."

"I'm not so sure about that."

"The hell with you." Her voice rose a little; brittle, and it had sharp edges. "You're enjoying yourself, aren't you? You're having *fun*. Ever since the stupid wheel came off the stupid cart. What's *wrong* with you? You're treating all this shit like it's some sort of *adventure*. Of course they'll have to let us go. We're not prisoners."

"Actually." Suidas' voice was as cold as ice. "Two of us are — that's Giraut and Phrantzes. The Carnufex boy's here because Daddy told him he had to, which is much the same thing. I don't know what they did to you."

"Fine. You?"

"They're paying me a very large sum of money. Which I need," he added. "Desperately. All right?"

Another silence; then Giraut heard a shout, from outside the stable. It was repeated, this time closer: "Suidas Deutzel? Are you in there?" Phrantzes' voice.

"Yes. What?"

"Could you please come out here? Quickly."

Giraut gave them a moment, then jumped down from the loft and followed them outside. He found Phrantzes, Addo and Tzimisces.

"There are twelve men approaching from the north-west," Tzimisces said. "They aren't soldiers, but they do have weapons. I would imagine they're robbers, highwaymen, whatever you like to call them. They'll know we're here, because they'll have seen the coach."

Iseutz broke the silence. "So what? We haven't got anything worth stealing."

"I don't suppose they'll see it like that," Tzimisces replied quietly. "Clothes, boots, anything at all. Times are hard in these parts, I'm afraid."

"Let them have them," Phrantzes said. "So long as we co-operate, they have no reason to harm us."

"Ah." Tzimisces shook his head, just a small movement.

"That's not how they do things, I'm afraid. We're going to have to defend ourselves. Which shouldn't be a problem," he added briskly, before anyone could speak. "After all, you're all trained swordsmen, aren't you?"

"We haven't got any weapons," Suidas yelled at him.

"On the contrary. The crate is in the coach."

"They're *foils*," Iseutz snapped. "Bits of wire with a knob on the end. They're not *real*."

"Better than nothing," Tzimisces said, and his tone of voice told them the discussion was closed. "I'll open up the crate. If it's all right with you, I'll borrow one for myself."

"Go ahead," Suidas shouted at him. "It won't do you any good."

Tzimisces scuttled to the coach. "It must've been them," Suidas said. "They put the bar there, to block the road."

"What's going to happen?" Giraut asked.

"Guess."

Tzimisces came back with a bundle of sheathed swords under his arm: three rapiers, a longsword and a smallsword. In his hand he carried another, short and wide, with a bare hilt, a pattern Giraut had never seen before. "Here you go," he said. "I suggest we fall back to the blockhouse. If we fight with our backs to it, they won't be able to take us in rear."

Giraut could see them now, a dozen shapes on the skyline. They appeared to be walking at normal speed, like ordinary people on their way somewhere; it was impossible, surely, that they were coming to do anybody any harm; that that was what death looked like. He watched them grow ever so slightly bigger. Ludicrous, he thought. Perfect strangers don't just stroll up to you and start killing you. The world simply doesn't work like that. He felt a nudge on his arm; Tzimisces was holding out a sheathed rapier, and he realised he was supposed to take it. He reached for it, but his fingers wouldn't close properly, and he dropped it on the ground.

"What the hell makes you think—" Iseutz said.

"Go to the blockhouse, please." Tzimisces' voice was perfectly calm, and Giraut thought: Suidas is right, he's a soldier. What the hell is going on here?

"At least let's try talking to them," Phrantzes said.

"I'm sorry." Tzimisces put a hand gently on Phrantzes' sleeve and towed him away, like a kindly child guiding a blind man. "Actually, it's them I feel sorry for. For pity's sake, gentlemen," he added, with just a feather of an edge to his voice, "you're *fencers*. There's absolutely nothing for you to be worried about."

Oddly enough, Giraut found that helped. Perfectly true, he thought; I spent years in the fencing school, learning to fight. The whole point of it is, once you've learned the orthodox way, you need never be scared of anybody ever again. That's why it's such an important part of a gentleman's education. He realised he hadn't drawn in a breath for quite some time. When he tried, it was like swallowing mud. "Mr Bryennius," Tzimisces called out; he and the others were halfway to the blockhouse. Giraut took a step. His knees weren't working properly. Suidas had to go back and grab him by the arm.

"I think you've got this all wrong," Iseutz was saying, louder than usual, her eyes fixed on the skyline. "I think they're just a harmless bunch of shepherds or something, and you're completely overreacting."

"Too many of them to be shepherds," Tzimisces said. "And shepherds don't tend to go around heavily armed. Also, we haven't seen any sheep. Believe me, there's nobody in this area with a legitimate reason for being here. Now, I'd like you all to draw your swords and make ready. Now, please."

Giraut did nothing of the sort; his hands were shaking, and his mind was somewhere else entirely – in a bedroom, back in the City, where he'd killed someone. He heard someone say, "What the hell is this?" but he chose not to enquire further. The approaching men were now close enough that he could make out their faces. They looked frightened. But they kept walking.

I can't do this, he thought. Really, I can't.

(He tried thinking through the stages of a formal set: ward, measure, single or double time, retreat, ward, measure. He could do all that. But his mind insisted on superimposing on the known formalities of the set the image of a big man, a fat man, taken completely by surprise by death, sliding off the point of his rapier on to the floor, from human to garbage in one split second. He told himself: if you won't fight them, they'll kill you. He was unable to make it a compelling argument.)

He could see them quite clearly. The one nearest to him was a short man, thin-faced, big eyes, quite a delicate face, sharp chin. He had a strip of grain sack wrapped round his neck for a scarf, and an old, worn-out coat, what Giraut's mother would have described as only fit for charity. The sleeves were too short, and Giraut could see the bones of the wrist of the hand that gripped a staff hook so tight that the knuckles showed white. He thought; how in God's name do you defend against everyday farm tools with a rapier? Not in any of the books. A hell of a time for making it up as you go along. The man looked at him, and Giraut understood him. He's doing what I'm doing, he thought; converting me in his mind from a human being into a target. He's done that before. Well, we both have.

And, under other circumstances, we could sit together over a few beers and compare our experiences, human mind to human mind: what did you feel, the first time you killed someone? Was it so quick and instinctive that you didn't have time to think about it? Did the other guy strike first? Or did you have to make the first move, an act of will, like plunging your hand into icy water on a cold morning? How did you bring yourself to do that, exactly?

Suidas was yelling something: orders, suggestions, a warning; like it mattered. Giraut thought: a wise man once described violence as just another form of communication, and another wise man called fencing a conversation in steel. He wasn't convinced, not unless you could wake up a dead man and ask him, how was it for you? So he looked at his enemy-to-be and tried to see him as a target, like the dummy in the fencing school, stuffed with straw, hanging from a sort of gibbet by a rope coming out of the top of its head, all the principal vulnerable areas hatched in red. They talked about sizing up your opponent. That made him think of looking at girls, the way he used to do. Turn people into objects and you can do any damn thing to them.

The measure was closing. There are three measures in classical single rapier: long, in which neither man can reach the other; middle, where each can make contact by taking one step forward; close, where each can strike a mortal blow without moving their feet. Just before long measure, he pulled the rapier out of its sheath –

(Odd; because you can't sheathe a foil; the button on the end would jam as you tried to draw it.)

– and tried to do the right thing, look at the enemy over the point of the sword. But he couldn't see the point, only the man behind it; whom he couldn't kill, because he'd already killed a man, and kill one, kill them all . . .

Middle measure, and the man swung his hook, a big, two-armed, hedge-cutter's movement, exposing heart, throat, half a dozen prime targets, but Giraut found he couldn't move. Instead, his lungs seemed to clamp up tight, and he felt suddenly, desperately cold. Oh well, he thought, and the long-handled hook described a broad, slow arc, like the Invincible Sun's curved journey from east to west, to sunset, and all he could do was close his eyes so as not to see it actually happen.

He heard a scream, and assumed it was his own. But, curiously enough, it wasn't. Something barged into him from the front. He hadn't anticipated that, and it sent him sprawling; he tripped over his own heels and fell backwards, bashing his head against the blockhouse wall.

"What the hell," someone was shouting, "happened to you?"

Giraut opened his eyes, and found he was looking straight at the sun, an ambiguous situation, in context. When you die, as everyone knows, you stand before the Invincible Sun and are weighed in the balance, and a great voice comes out of the heart of the fire, and asks you—

"Well?"

It was Suidas, bending over him, absolutely furious. "You froze," he shouted. "You just stood there. *Iseutz* had to rescue you, for crying out loud."

Just behind Suidas he could see a pair of boots. They were very old and heavily patched, lying on their sides, and there were legs still in them. "What happened?"

"That's a bloody good question," Suidas roared at him. "You're a fucking liability. You could've got someone killed."

"Leave him alone," said somebody Giraut couldn't see. It was a high voice, and very, very tense.

"For God's sake . . ."

"Leave him *alone*." She clearly wasn't in a mood to be argued with. Giraut thought: according to Suidas, she just saved my life. Now why would anybody want to do a thing like that?

The legs inside the boots weren't moving. Also, they were lying all wrong. It occurred to him that they were the legs of the thin-faced man, and that the long conversation he'd just had with him must have been a dream, or some mechanically induced aberration resulting from the blow to the back of his head. He couldn't remember what they'd finally agreed, which was frustrating.

"You," Iseutz said, bending over him so that her hair fell down over her eyes, "are pathetic."

All he could say was, "What happened?"

"That one was going to chop you with a long-handled hook. Fortunately, I got there in time. And you," she went on, "are a complete waste of good luck. Get up, for pity's sake. You look ridiculous."

She was holding out her hand. He grabbed it, and was hauled to his feet. "Thanks," he said.

"Go to hell," she said, letting go of his hand. He staggered, and found his balance.

"Even so," he said. "I'm sorry. I just froze. I couldn't—"

"I'd sort of gathered that," she said. "Hell of a time to get religion. You can kill a duly elected member of the Senior House, but show you some peasant with a hedging tool and suddenly you're a pacifist. Next time you're on your own, understood?"

Next time, he thought. "Are you all right?"

"Like you care." She walked away, and Giraut could see past her. There were bodies lying on the ground, a number greater than ten. It occurred to him to wonder if any of the others hadn't been as lucky as him. He looked round, and saw Addo, standing quite still, looking at the longsword he was holding; and beyond him Phrantzes sitting on the ground while Tzimisces did something with a bandage. They'd got away with it, apparently; no thanks to Giraut Bryennius.

Well, he thought, they'll have to let us go home now.

He felt a sudden great need to apologise to somebody. The logical person would be Phrantzes, he decided, so he walked over to where he was sitting. Phrantzes looked up and nodded awkwardly (so he knew what'd happened, evidently).

"That ought to do it," Tzimisces was saying. "It'll be all right, it's really just a scratch. Ah, Giraut, I was just coming to talk to you. How are you feeling?"

"Fine," Giraut said. "Look, I'm really sorry."

"That's all right," Tzimisces replied, his tone of voice cancelling out his words. "Happens to us all at some point. Extremely impressive intervention from the Bringas girl. Tongue like a razor, but she kept her head splendidly, I thought. I do believe she'll prove to be a real asset to the project."

Unlike someone else who didn't need to be specified by name. "She saved my life."

"Yes." Tzimisces looked at him; he felt like he was being squeezed dry. "And to think I was worried she'd go all to pieces. Women can be tigers sometimes. Well, it looks like nobody's too badly hurt. I'll write a full report as soon as we get to Permia."

"We're still going to . . . "

"Of course." He'd said the wrong thing. "As soon as the coach arrives. Now, unless anyone needs me for anything . . . "

"Excuse me." Addo had materialised behind Tzimisces' shoulder. Tzimisces turned round and smiled at him. "Excuse me," Addo repeated, "but I was just wondering. Why were all the swords in the fencing box sharp?"

It was as though he had just punched Tzimisces in the face, but not hard enough to put him down. "Just as well for us they were, don't you think?"

"Oh, absolutely." Addo looked like somebody's pet dog, but he was standing his ground. "I just thought, it's rather strange. We should've been issued with foils, surely."

"Ah well." Tzimisces smiled again. He had perfect teeth, apart from one missing right at the front. "If I was as much of a true believer as I suppose I ought to be, I'd say it was a miracle. Being something of a sceptic, I prefer to think that there was a mistake at the office. Phrantzes," he said, turning and looking straight at him, "you put in the requisition. You did specify foils, didn't you?"

Phrantzes nodded.

"There you are, then. My guess is, they didn't have any foils in stock in the armouries, so they sent us sharps instead. It doesn't matter. We can get them bated when we reach Permia."

He started to walk, pausing to nudge something out of the way with his foot. It was a head, with no body attached. Giraut just managed to make it to the corner of the blockhouse before he threw up.

"Are you all right?" Addo's voice.

He nodded. "I'm fine," he said. "I just never saw . . . "

"Of course. My fault, I'm afraid." Addo made it sound like he'd broken a cup. "Only, there were two of them coming at me at once, and I had to hit out a bit. And I hadn't realised the sword was sharp."

"That's perfectly all right," Giraut heard himself say, and

then add: "At least you didn't freeze up, like I did. I think I owe you an apology."

"My dear fellow, certainly not." Addo moved an inch closer. "This isn't the army, none of us signed up to fight to the death, so to speak. Actually, in a way it does you credit."

Giraut looked at him. "Cowardice?"

"Being reluctant to take someone's life. That's hardly something to be ashamed of." Addo stopped, and turned red. "I'm sorry," he said, "I don't suppose you want to hear my opinion about anything. I imagine you'd prefer to forget all about it."

Yes, Giraut thought, in roughly the same way I'd quite like to have wings. But yes, let's forget all about it, and talk about the weather. "Did you hear what he said? We're still going to Permia."

Addo nodded. "I thought we would be. Tremendously important diplomatically speaking, and so forth. Look," he went on, lowering his voice and leaning a bit closer, as though he was just about to suggest they sell their souls to the Devil. "Would you like a drink? Brandy," he added. "I've got a small flask. It might, well, cheer you up a bit."

"Yes," Giraut said quickly. "Please," he added. Addo handed him a small, exquisite silver flask, in the shape of a sitting dog. It had tiny blue sapphires for eyes. He fumbled out the stopper and swallowed four times. "Go ahead," he heard Addo say, "finish it off. I don't actually drink myself, so you're more than welcome to it."

There were two swallows left; then he handed back the flask. "Thanks," he said. "I feel better now."

"You've had a shock," Addo said. "My father. He doesn't drink either, but he always carried brandy with him, during the War. He said it did more good than most of the medical corps."

The brandy was burning his throat where vomiting had made it raw. He nodded weakly. "I can believe it," he said. Then, for no immediately clear reason apart from curiosity, he asked, "Were you in the War?"

Addo shook his head. "My father kept me off the draft," he said. "My papers came shortly after my brother was killed."

"Did you want to go?"

"No." Addo's face twisted into a painful grin. "For what it's worth, I'm a pacifist. I don't think war's justifiable, ever. If there's another one, I'll go to jail rather than join up."

With that, he walked away. Giraut propped himself up against the blockhouse wall. The brandy was making his head swim, and he wished he hadn't drunk it. His clothes were still wet, clinging to him like the wife of a departing soldier, and the damp wool smell was disgusting. On the positive side, he told himself, I'm still alive. On the other page of the ledger, I've marked myself out indelibly as a coward, I've almost certainly mortally offended Addo, and my life's been saved by a *girl*.

Later the sun came out, almost but not quite enough to dry his clothes. Nobody was talking; they stood or sat against the blockhouse wall, facing the direction a coach from the City would come from. There was, of course, nothing to eat. Suidas found some water, a dull brown trickle on the slope just below the blockhouse, but the rusty pan from the stable he filled with it sat undisturbed in the sun; nobody was quite that desperate, at least not yet. Tzimisces was writing something in a small brown book, with ink from an exquisite traveller's inkstand that he'd called into being from the apparently limitless pockets of his coat, and an ivory-handled gold-nibbed pen. Two buzzards circled overhead for quite some time, but went away eventually. Addo and Iseutz started a game of chess. After half a dozen moves she lost a castle, immediately resigned and stalked away. Suidas went into the stable, and Giraut heard a lot of banging noises, the reason for which he couldn't be bothered to speculate about. Phrantzes just sat, a short measure away from one of the dead bodies, staring at the road.

It was beginning to get dark when Giraut heard what he was sure was hooves on the metalled road. He sat up. It was notoriously difficult to judge these things, but he felt sure the sound was coming from behind them; the east, the other direction, the wrong way. He went over to Phrantzes, and said, "Did you hear something just now?"

Phrantzes shook his head. "But I'm slightly deaf on my left side," he said. "My wife gets very impatient sometimes. What did you hear?"

"Sounded like horses," Giraut said. "Of course, I could be wrong."

Phrantzes broke his fixed eye contact with the road and turned his head a little. "I wasn't expecting the coach to get here before morning, at the earliest," he said. "Of course, our messenger may have run into a routine patrol, or maybe the relief garrison for this post. You'd have thought—"

"There it is again," Giraut interrupted.

"You're sure it's horses?"

"That's what it sounded like."

Phrantzes nodded sharply, as if accepting a good offer. "It's about time something went right," he said. "I'll tell Tzimisces."

He stood up and walked away. Giraut stayed where he was. The sound he'd heard was definitely behind them; in which case, it was coming from the general direction of Permia. That made him shiver, although of course that was ridiculous. They were still well inside the territory of the Republic, with the whole of the Demilitarised Zone between them and their neighbour, with whom there was no cogent reason not to believe they were still at peace. Phrantzes was talking to Tzimisces, who carefully marked the place in his book and stoppered his inkwell before standing up. Suidas came out of the stables, with a bundle of smashed planks under his arm. "Did anybody just hear horses?" he called out.

This time, it was plain and unmistakable, the clatter of shod hooves on stone. "It's from behind us," Iseutz said. "That's not right."

"That's just the wind playing tricks," Phrantzes said. "Or it could be the garrison from here, coming back, if they went east."

Giraut could think of other explanations, the most comfortable of which was that it was the bandits' friends arriving with a wagon, to load up and carry away their expected takings.

"I think I'll just take a walk over that way," Tzimisces said quietly, and pocketed his book, pen case and inkwell. They watched him until he was out of sight on the eastern skyline. The sound was continuous now.

"We should get away from the buildings," Suidas said. "They'll see the coach, of course, but that can't be helped. Best place would be the bank we slept under last night. It'll be dark soon, so it should be all right."

"What the hell are you talking about?" Iseutz said; and then, Giraut guessed, the answer to her question dawned on her, and she went very pale. "You think . . . "

"Let's just be sensible and get out of sight," Suidas said. His voice was quiet and harsh, like a fine saw cutting slowly. "No, leave the weapons," he added sharply, as Addo moved towards the packing case. "If it's who I think it is, it's quite important that we're just civilians. Come on."

They followed him to the bank and lay down, as they'd done the previous night. Giraut couldn't see the road from where he was. The light was still good, although the sun was just about to set. There can't be another war, he thought.

He heard someone close to him catch his breath, and a moment later a horseman appeared, roughly level with where Giraut lay. When the horseman was no more than five yards away, he stopped and shifted a little in his saddle, turning his head and shoulders to face the bank.

He rode a black mare with a single white star on its forehead, bigger than any horse Giraut had ever seen before. He was fully armoured – not the chainmail shirt and breeches that the Republic issued as standard, but the laced-together small steel plates of the Eastern Empire, flexible as linen, reckoned to turn arrows at point-blank range. On his thighs and knees he wore steel splints, with articulated steel shoes. At his cuffs and neck,

Giraut could see the pale yellow fur lining of his coat, teased out to keep the steel from chafing; he also had a red wool scarf up to his chin. His tall conical helmet was made from a single piece of steel – too difficult for the smiths of the Republic, who riveted four smaller plates to a frame – and the edges were rolled and roped; the rivet heads that secured the lining were gilded, and he wore a foot-high plume of white horsehair that nodded gently even when he was still. He shivered slightly, and with his free hand pulled his scarf a little tighter round his neck. The small part of his face that was still visible between scarf and helmet was dark brown, the colour of polished and waxed mahogany; he had a thin line of moustache on his upper lip, and a small, neat black tuft on his chin. He was a Blueskin.

Well, Giraut thought, so we're at war after all. At least it wasn't the Aram Chantat, who never took prisoners. He felt like a child who's inadvertently wandered into a room where the grown-ups are sitting, and they break off their serious, mysterious conversation and look at him. The saddlecloth was green velvet, he noticed, worn and dirty but fifteen nomismata a yard in the Cloth Market, if you could find any. In his left hand he held a long spear, with a blue-painted shaft.

The Blueskin was looking straight at him.

Giraut realised he was paralysed. It wasn't fear of death; he knew what that felt like now, and the symptoms were subtly different. Besides, he'd faced death in the bell tower, and it hadn't affected him nearly as strongly as the Blueskin's stare. It was more the way he imagined he'd feel if he'd woken up and found an angel standing over him: awe and wonder and a kind of terror that wasn't anything to do with possible harm to his body. He couldn't move, because to move in the presence of such an entity would be an abomination, unless he was ordered to, in which case refusal would be an equally appalling sin. He felt as though he was waiting for a verdict.

"Excuse me," the Blueskin said.

Nobody moved, though Giraut could feel a massive build-up

of furious energy, like the air just before a thunderstorm, - somewhere to his right. The Blueskin frowned slightly.

"Excuse me," he repeated, a little louder and slower, "but would you gentlemen happen to be Jilem Phrantzes' party?"

He spoke in the most beautifully clear, pitch-perfect upper-class accent, the sort you only hear on the stage, or in a country castle. Well, of course he did. That was the accent of the Empire, which the nobility preserved as jealously as a saint's shinbone in a gold casket. The voice itself was remarkable enough. The words simply didn't make sense.

"Get *down*," he heard Suidas hiss; but Phrantzes was getting to his feet, looking mortally embarrassed. "I'm Phrantzes," he said.

"Thank goodness for that," the Blueskin said, a puzzled frown on the small patch of his face still vulnerable to the cold. "We're here to find you. I'm Lieutenant Totila, Diplomatic Escort Corps. Look, why don't you fellows get up off the ground? It must be terribly uncomfortable."

There were nine of them in all, lancers, seconded to the civilian authorities to escort the honoured guests from halfway into the Demilitarised Zone to the Permian border. Lieutenant Totila produced his diplomatic credentials, which Tzimisces, suddenly reappearing, confirmed were entirely in order.

"You were late showing up," Totila explained, "and we were a bit concerned, because we'd heard rumours of bandit activity on your side of the line from your chaps at the frontier station. They were going to come out and see what'd happened to you, but I sort of volunteered, because, well, no offence, but we're a damn sight faster than your people. I get the impression we were right," he added, looking pointedly at a decapitated corpse lying a few yards away. "Though you seem to have coped perfectly well without us. Well, of course you would. It must've come as a bit of a shock to them, when they found out who they were up against."

The lancers had a beautiful foldaway grill, on which they were cooking a complicated-looking mixture of dried fish, sausage and rice in a copper pan. They didn't seem inclined to hurry, and the smell was driving Giraut out of his mind. "Oh, just field rations," Totila had said, when asked, as the lance corporal measured wine out of a flask with a little pewter cup, to add to the sauce. "But I imagine anything'll taste all right if you've been stuck out here for a day without any grub."

There was also fine soft wheat bread, which was all Iseutz would accept; she sat on the edge of the circle, trying very hard not to enjoy it. Tzimisces sat next to Lieutenant Totila, balancing a tin plate on his cupped left hand, exactly like the lancers were doing. The wine from the flask made the best stuff they sold in the Republic taste like brine.

"Everyone's terribly excited, of course," Totila said. "Actually, I don't follow the fencing as closely as the Permians do; I did a bit at the Academy, and you've got to study form if you're posted in Permia or you'd be left out of all the conversations. But it's been all they've been talking about for months, this tour of yours. There's pictures of you up all over the place."

"Pictures," Giraut said. "That's crazy. How do they know what we look like?"

"They don't," Totila said, with a faint smile. "They're not what you'd call wonderful likenesses, but that's the Permian artistic tradition for you. What you ought to look like, not what you actually do, if you see what I mean. You wait till you see them. But do try not to laugh, they're a sensitive lot."

"It's a Permian tradition," Tzimisces said with his mouth full. "A sort of sideshoot of religious icons. Always full-face, and wearing clothes five hundred years out of date."

Totila laughed. "You've got it," he said. "Really rather beautiful in their way, once you get over the not looking a bit like what they're supposed to be. They reckon they paint the soul, not the body."

There was a thoughtful silence; then Addo said, "Are there any of me?"

"Of course," Totila said. "In full armour, naturally, since you're a longswordsman. Actually, yours are pretty much like you."

"I take after my father," Addo said.

"Quite," Suidas said. "I don't suppose they've forgotten what the Irrigator looks like in Permia."

Totila looked down at his hands. Iseutz said, "Please don't tell me there's any of me."

"You're very popular," Totila said cheerfully. "Although," he went on, as Iseutz drew breath for a reply, "they paint you as a man, of course."

Everyone except Suidas managed not to laugh. Iseutz opened her mouth, and for once nothing came out.

"Artistic conventions, you see," Totila went on, carefully not looking at her. "All swordsmen in Permian art are, well, men. Women are angels or abstract personifications, usually," he added blithely, "with no clothes on. But the aspect of you they want to portray is you as a fencer, so they have to make you into a man. You've got a wonderful big red beard, practically down to your waist."

Even Suidas had more sense than to make a sound. Totila went on: "The paintings are only the start of it, actually. There's specially written lives of all of you – entirely made up," he added, as Giraut winced violently, "since they don't actually know anything about you. There are ever so many ballads celebrating your glorious deeds; you pay a street singer a couple of coppers and he sings them to you, right there in the road. I gather there's a blank-verse drama in the works. Someone told me rehearsals were just starting when I left Joiauz about ten days ago. You'll be expected to go to that. It's a great honour."

"I never realised they were such a creative people," Phrantzes muttered.

"Oh, they aren't," Totila said. "At least, the painters are home-grown, but the poets and musicians are generally from the Empire. Anything Eastern is the height of chic, so they tell me. There's a certain amount of local talent as well, of course. They black up their faces with walnut juice to perform, but nobody's fooled by that."

"Anybody dressing up and pretending to be me is going to wish she'd never been born," Iseutz said icily. "That I can promise you."

"Actually, it'd be a man," Totila said. "No women on the stage in Permia. And please, I must ask you most sincerely not to make any sort of fuss about it. That would be taken as a most serious insult. You'd be rejecting a special honour, you see. They wouldn't like that at all."

"She's only joking," Tzimisces said firmly. "She knows perfectly well how important this project is. Don't you?" he added, and his voice was quite quiet and very intense, like a lover's. Iseutz hesitated, then nodded briskly. "There you are, then. And thank you for forewarning us. It's just as well you told us, or we'd have been taken by surprise."

"Anyway," Totila said – gratitude seemed to make him uncomfortable – "it'll be the best of everything for all of you once you get there, which I hope will make up for the frightful time you've had so far. Talking of which," he added, sitting up a little, "I don't know what you had in mind for continuing your journey, but if you haven't got any hard-and-fast plans" (Suidas made a sort of grunting noise, which Totila didn't seem to hear), "then might I suggest that you ride on with us? I've already taken the liberty of sending back to our post for a fast chaise, which ought to be here by morning—"

"That's not possible," Suidas interrupted. "Here to the DMZ, it's thirty miles."

Totila smiled. "We can move quite quickly when we want to, you know. It'd be quicker if I'd sent for saddle horses rather than a vehicle, but I honestly couldn't recommend riding them, not if you aren't used to them. I don't think you'd be in any fit state by the time you got to Joiauz."

Phrantzes said, "We've already sent back for a carriage." Nobody heard him, because at the exact same moment Tzimisces said, "Thank you, that'd be perfect, if it's no trouble."

"That's settled, then," Totila said. "With any luck, if you don't object to forcing the pace a bit, we can make up some of the lost time. Naturally I'll send ahead to let them know you've been held up. Might have to bring the first bout forward a little, though. It really wouldn't do to disappoint all those people. I gather a lot of the miners are coming into town specially for the match."

The troopers gave them their blankets – thick, soft wool, dark blue – and broke up the stalls in the stable for firewood, which they hadn't dared do, since it was government property. They slept in the stables, with the Blueskins standing guard outside in case the robbers' friends came back. Giraut was just falling asleep when Suidas came across and sat down beside him.

"Nice enough people, don't you think?" he said.

Giraut nodded. "They've gone out of their way to be nice to us, anyhow," he said.

"Oh, they would do," Suidas said quietly. "They don't do anything by halves, the Blueskins. You've seen what their kit's like, and they've got the most amazing medical support for their men in the field. There's a doctor with each company, and you should see their field hospitals. You wouldn't believe what they can do. Our so-called doctors killed more of our boys than the enemy ever did, but the Blueskins'll sew you back together and have you back on your feet in a few weeks. I knew a man who'd been picked up off the battlefield three parts dead. The Blueskins found him and took him to one of their hospitals, and he was good as new."

Giraut frowned. "One of ours?"

"Sure," Suidas said. "And they look after their prisoners really well; better food and clothes and shelter than they'd have got from their own units, that's for sure. They're remarkable people, the Blueskins, in many respects they make us look like kids, or savages."

"I thought you hated them."

"Ah well." Suidas yawned, and lay on his back. "The thing is, they obey orders, immediately and without question. That's what makes them such good soldiers, of course. So, if they're told to look after you and treat you right, that's what they do. But if orders come down to kill all the prisoners, they don't stop and think, they do it. Burn the town, rape the women, kill the children; it'd never cross their minds to disobey an order. And you can see how it'd be no problem to them. After all, they're so much better than us. To them, it's just like pouring boiling water on an ants' nest."

Giraut propped himself up on his elbow. "I couldn't imagine Lieutenant Totila killing civilians," he said.

"Totila wouldn't have been in the War," Suidas replied, "he's too young. They don't enlist under eighteen in the Empire. But if he was told to cut our throats, we'd all be dead inside three minutes, you can count on it. On balance, I think I prefer the Aram Chantat. You know where you are with savages. Couple of times in the War, the Aram Chantat were told to massacre a village. They looted everything they could take with them, but they didn't kill anyone. Too much like hard work, they said, and what's in it for us? No kudos in killing kids, their knucklebones aren't worth stringing."

"What?"

Suidas laughed. "That's how they keep score," he said. "They cut off the left index fingers and thread the knuckles into a necklace. They wouldn't want any that're too small, they'd get laughed at. Of course, nine times out of ten they were told to wipe out a village and they did it. But just occasionally people got lucky, if the Aram Chantat felt they were being asked to do more than they'd been paid for. They have a horror of being exploited, I guess."

"Would you two please keep the noise down," Iseutz called

out from the other end of the stable. "Some of us are trying to get to sleep."

The chaise arrived while Giraut was still asleep. When he woke up, the stable was empty. He went outside and saw it standing in front of the blockhouse. He'd never seen anything like it before.

It was smaller than the coach they'd come in, but the passenger compartment was much bigger. It sat up on its springs like an eager dog, and its wheels looked impossibly thin and spindly. There were six horses in the shafts, matched pairs of greys, chestnuts and piebalds. The chaise was painted bright red.

"We'll go back and pick up the luggage you had to dump," he heard Totila saying. "We should be able to get it back to you before you reach Joiauz. In the meantime, you're welcome to hold on to the blankets and whatever. I'm just sorry you've had to rough it like this."

"Please don't apologise," Phrantzes replied. "After all, we're still inside the Republic, so if anyone's to blame, it's us. Me," he added, with a sad smile.

"I think you've done remarkably well," Totila said. "Your makeshift axle's very impressive. I'm sure I wouldn't have thought of that, in your shoes."

"Can we go now, please?" Iseutz interrupted. "The sooner we start, the sooner we'll get there, and presumably there'll be somewhere I can wash. I feel like I've been buried in a dunghill for twenty years."

The seats were amazing: soft, padded, upholstered with some sort of cloth like velvet. Even Addo had enough room for his legs. "It's just an ordinary post chaise," Totila said apologetically. "I commandeered it from the courier service. Still, it ought to get you to Joiauz. They're tough little things, built for bad roads. Once we're in Permia, of course, we can transfer you over to something a bit more comfortable."

"Oh," Iseutz said. "Don't they have bad roads in Permia, then?"

"Built by Imperial engineers," Suidas said. "Isn't that right?"

"Well, quite a lot of them," Totila replied. "Three-hundred-odd years ago, of course, before Independence. And we patched them up to a certain extent during the War. Enlightened self-interest, you see, so the carts can get to and from the mines."

Giraut found it almost impossible to stay awake the next day. The chaise was more comfortable than any bed he'd ever slept in. He could barely feel its motion, and the cushions seemed to mould themselves to the shape of his back, easing away his weight so that he felt like a creature of pure intellect, purged of the gross necessities of the flesh. He felt as though he could write a theological tract, if only he could keep his eyes open.

"Nobody said anything about *pictures*," Iseutz was saying bitterly. "I don't like these people. Did you notice how he never once looked at me, even when I was talking to him? Like I wasn't really there."

"The Imperials have a rather different attitude to women in their society," Tzimisces said smoothly. "Tremendous respect, of course; they practically invented the notion of chivalry. But men and women don't mix much, in everyday life. I expect he was a little bit frightened of you."

Iseutz made a sceptical noise, rather like Suidas' snores (he was fast asleep, wedged into the corner) but a trifle higher and sharper. "They're certainly different from us in a lot of ways," Phrantzes said. "I remember when we had a trade delegation from the Eastern Empire, just after the War—"

"I don't suppose we'll be having very much to do with them," Tzimisces went on. "The actual number of Imperial troops in Permia these days is quite low, about five regiments, and two of them are engineers. Truth is, they just can't afford them. Same with the Aram Chantat. They paid most of them off seven years ago, just to get rid of them. The majority of them left, but I gather there's still a few units in the south, making trouble. Well away from where we're going, I'm delighted to say."

"What about the Permians themselves?" Addo had become a

great deal more talkative since they'd met Lieutenant Totila. Nice for both of them to have someone of his own class to talk to, Giraut supposed, even if one had a different colour skin and the other was the son of the Irrigator. He vaguely remembered that Flos Verjan had been an Imperial city, built before the Permians broke away from the Empire.

"Oh, they're all right, once you get to know them," Tzimisces said. "Basically they're the same as us, only they were an Imperial province for seven hundred years and we were never conquered. Let's say we've got more in common than we've got differences."

"Even after seventy years of war?" Iseutz said. "I find that hard to believe."

"The War is something we have very much in common," Tzimisces replied. "They didn't want it, neither did we. It was the great families on either side who insisted on fighting. I think you'll find it's their own upper class they hold grudges against, not us." He adjusted the blanket he'd spread across his knees; he looked disconcertingly like an old lady taking carriage exercise. "What's made all the difference is the Regia process. That changed everything. It's what led to the peace."

"The what?" Giraut asked.

Tzimisces smiled. "The Regia process," he repeated. "A discovery by natural philosophers in the Eastern Empire, whereby you can use some sort of chemical to get silver out of low-grade ore that couldn't be refined using the traditional method. It means that it's now cheaper for the Eastern Empire to produce silver domestically, instead of importing it from Permia. In response, the Permians have had to cut their silver prices dramatically. Their economy's in ruins, which is why they can't afford to fight another war. Also, the Empire no longer has a vested interest in propping up the old aristocratic regime, since they're no longer dependent on Permia for their silver supply. As a result, the military aristocracy's out of power and the mine owners have taken over the country. Our kind of people,"

Tzimisces added, "people we can hold a reasonable conversation with. That's why we need hearts-and-minds exercises like this one, to win over the working classes. Once they realise we're just ordinary people, like them, there'll be no appetite for another war."

Suidas woke up sweating, and opened his eyes. He was in the chaise. Everyone else was dead.

No, that was another occasion. Everyone else was asleep, a subtle but important difference. Tzimisces' head was lolling forward, his nose buried in his muffler. Iseutz had her head on Addo's shoulder (worth seeing their reactions when they woke up). Giraut's head was leaning against the panelling, his mouth open. Phrantzes was sitting upright, taking every precaution possible to avoid touching anybody, even in his sleep. Suidas breathed in deeply and blew the breath out again through pursed lips, as though he'd just had a lucky escape.

He'd been dreaming; a new one this time, though thematically linked to the usual repertoire. He'd dreamt through yesterday's fight, watching it from a distance, as though analysing the performance of a promising student. He saw the enemy, a one-eyed man in a scarecrow coat that had once been military issue, so a veteran, like himself. He was quite tall, and thin, and he'd got a messer.

(Here they fight with messers. God help them.)

Suidas hadn't ever killed a man with a rapier before. It was child's play. The opponent came at him in a crude, instinctive low back guard, presumably looking for an opening for an ascending cut in sixth. Suidas had obligingly opened his own low guard, provoking a closing of the measure. Then all he'd had to do was go in off the opponent's right arm, in single time, punching a neat hole in the upper stomach. Then he'd stepped back, because dying men sometimes lash out. But this one wasn't going to, so he closed the measure right up, carefully positioned the point on the hollow between his collarbones, and gently but firmly pushed the point in until it met bone. Piece of cake.

As it should've been, of course, because the rapier, against soft-skinned game, is the best killing tool ever invented. He remembered looking over the dead man's shoulder just before he toppled backwards; no additional targets. There had been a slight tug on the hilt as the body fell off the blade. At which point Suidas had taken a breath to scream with, and opened his eyes.

Twenty-five thousand nomismata, he told himself.

He breathed out again, slowly, consistently, to stop himself from hyperventilating. Twenty-five thousand nomismata was a good enough reason. It was a future, something he hadn't had for a very long time. It was enough to set up a high-class fencing school in a fashionable district of the City, with a long panelled salle, practice rooms, a dining room and kitchen, and a comfortable apartment on the upper floor where she'd be happy to stay. It was a pleasant, honest retirement, no more sharps, not ever; just foils.

He remembered how his stomach had lurched when they opened the crate, and all the swords inside it had been sharp. Weapons, not sports equipment. He'd toyed with the idea of simply disarming his opponent – easily done, if he'd got a rapier or a spear or a single-hand sword or even a longsword. But no, the bastard had to have a messer. Here they fight with messers. God help them.

He'd picked it up, later, when it was all over. It was a typical blacksmith job: blade two feet long, inch and a half wide, curved, single very sharp edge. The blade was slightly twisted, the forging blemishes and the firescale marks hadn't all been drawfiled out, and the single deep fuller hadn't been ground smooth inside. You wouldn't bother, for a tool that would mostly be used for cutting coppice, hedging and butchering the occasional pig. There was one in every barn, in Permia.

He'd wrapped it in a scarf he'd taken from one of the dead bodies and shoved it in the packing case. Just looking at it made him feel sick, but you never knew when something like that might not come in handy. They always did, didn't they?

He tried to picture the salle, with its high windows curtained in figured brocade – everybody goes to Deutzel's, it's the only place to learn. He used to be rapier champion, you know. They'd say it with a slight hint of wonder, because who'd have thought the cheerful, bald fat man with the big welcoming smile and delightful manners had once been a professional fencer?

He was in the War, you know. No, they wouldn't say that. They'd have no reason to.

What he wouldn't give for a stiff drink right now. But he'd promised, and he knew that if he so much as looked at a bottle she'd know, and when he got back home there'd be an empty room and a short, well-phrased letter. He realised he was flexing his right hand over and over again, the way the doctor had taught him, to build up the strength in the tendons.

So, he asked himself, by way of distracting his own attention, what was a Scherian highway robber doing with a Permian messer? Not a very taxing question, particularly since he'd also been wearing the ghost of an army greatcoat. He'd picked it up in the War, of course. Loads of men brought them back as souvenirs, trophies of war; that'll come in useful round the farm, they'd thought, not like the swords and pikes and other dedicated military junk you found on battlefields. They'd even started doing home-made copies, because they were such useful things.

Quite. He looked at the scar. It had been a Blueskin doctor who'd sewn it up. Marvellous people, the Blueskins, if you caught them on a good day.

And now we're going back to Permia, he thought. Of all the stupid things to do. For twenty-five thousand nomismata, which was quite ridiculous in itself. There had to be more to this than met the eye. After all, nobody in their right mind . . .

He wanted the others to wake up, to stop the thoughts churning round inside his head. It was no way to live, constantly besieged inside your own mind, like Flos Verjan before the

Irrigator opened the sluices. He accidentally-on-purpose nudged Giraut's foot, but he only grunted and carried on sleeping.

But, he told himself, the past changes, like everything else. The further away you got, the vaguer it became, until you reached the point where your memories, unless corroborated by witnesses, were unreliable evidence. If there were no witnesses – well, a memory was property, after all. When there were no other witnesses to claim title to it, the memory belonged to you. It was no crime to bend it a little, to dull the edges, put a button on the point so it was no longer sharp. Only a fool would carry an unsheathed knife in his pocket.

Which would be fine if you could live without sleeping; or if, like some incredibly lucky people he'd met over the years, you never remembered your dreams when you woke up. And only a fool would go back to Permia, even for twenty-five thousand nomismata, if he didn't absolutely have to.

He looked out of the window and saw the nodding white plume of a Blueskin helmet.

Well, it could've been the Aram Chantat. From time to time, the people who lived in the tenement below cooked fish with saffron and garlic, and the last time they'd done that – he had no memory of it at all, but apparently Sontha managed to get past him and ran to the Guild house; it took four trained fencers to get the sword away from him, and one of them was cut up quite badly. All because of the smell of fish and saffron, mixed with the sweet air you get just after it's rained. The Aram Chantat ate a lot of fish; odd, for an inland nomadic people, but apparently they traded furs for dried stockfish somewhere down on the coast; knowing they had a taste for it, the Permians had supplied it as standard rations. Of course, he'd been drinking back then, though not (as far as he could remember) on the night in question. The sword he'd used (this was one thing he could remember) had been a messer; a souvenir he'd brought back from the War, in case it came in useful for something. Needless to say, it wasn't the only one, but he hadn't told her about the others.

The dead veteran's messer was up on the roof, in the packing case, with the other weapons. He could almost feel it up there, watching him. Of course, a messer was basically just an over-grown knife. Nobody would think of *fencing* with one of the damn things. Except that there was a page of drawings, in Lecapenus' *True Art of Defence*: two men, in ordinary street clothes, face off against each other with big, curved knives. Instead of the usual rubric, technical stuff about transitions between wards, footwork, possible defences and ripostes, there was just one line: *Here they fight with messers. God help them.*

(In fact, now he came to think of it, there was a war souvenir in his carriage trunk right now, carefully wrapped in heavy blue cloth, under his clean shirt and the selection of rare and sought-after fencing manuals he'd brought with him to sell in Permia, which with any luck the Guild library would never miss. But his trunk had been dumped off the coach when the axle broke, and with all these bandits about, there was little chance he'd ever see it again. Probably just as well. Only a fool would take a messer *into* Permia, after all.)

The chaise must have gone over a pothole or a rock in the road; there was a very slight lurch, barely noticeable, but it was enough to wake up Phrantzes. He opened his eyes and stared at the opposite side of the compartment, and a look of shock and great sorrow passed over his face, quick as a cloud across the sun on a windy day. Suidas reckoned he knew exactly how he felt.

"Still here," he said sympathetically.

"Excuse me?"

"It's all right," Suidas said. "You haven't missed anything, by the way." He glanced out of the window. "If I'm right, we're about an hour from the border. This thing goes like the wind."

"Was I asleep for long?"

Suidas nodded. "The best way to travel, in your sleep," he said. "You miss out all the tedious sitting still. The worst way is walking, of course. I've always hated walking. It's *primitive*."

"I enjoy a pleasant walk myself," Phrantzes said mildly. "My wife and I like to walk beside the river in the evening. We have a dog, you know."

"Suit yourself," Suidas replied. "Now, presumably there'll be some of our people at the border. Then we can find out what's really going on."

Phrantzes looked worried. "How do you mean?"

"Well." Suidas wasn't quite sure where to start. But he'd been chewing at the various issues in the back of his mind for a long time; it was unreasonable to expect someone else to be as far along as he was. "Don't you think it's strange," he said, "that we turn up at a way station in our own country – an important station, mark you, not just some branch auxiliary – and find it all shut up and deserted, with the road booby-trapped? Well?"

"Inconvenient, certainly . . . "

"First," Suidas said firmly, "abandoning a military installation without express orders is gross dereliction, they can hang you for it. Second, they knew we were coming, right? You sent ahead. We should've been expected."

"That was what I was told."

"Quite. And everybody's been going on about how important this mission is, haven't they? But we get there – a bit behind schedule, but everybody who uses the road knows how you can get held up – and guess what, the place is all closed down, nobody there. Doesn't that make you wonder, just a little bit?"

"Well, yes," Phrantzes said. "But you seem to be suggesting there's something sinister about it. I'd be more inclined to put it down to a breakdown in communications."

"You think that's a plausible explanation?"

"Oh, definitely," Phrantzes said. "During the War I was on General Carnufex's staff. I was responsible for materiel shipments over several sectors. Nothing would surprise me after that. We used to have a rule, formulated by some wise man whose name temporarily escapes me; ninety-nine times out of a hundred, things that look like treason or malice turn out to be simple incompetence."

Suidas nodded calmly. "And a bunch of robbers turning up out of nowhere, at the precise moment we're there," he said. "That's just coincidence."

Phrantzes considered his reply for a moment. "Not really coincidence," he said. "I assume that they were – well, that was what they did for a living, and they'd been doing it for a while. They probably have lookouts on the road—"

"They choose to mount their ambush," Suidas said over him, "in the back yard of a government way station. Now, unless they knew it was all shut up, that's about the most stupid thing they could possibly do; there should've been a garrison in that station, soldiers specifically to hunt down and destroy bands of high-waymen. There's miles and miles of empty country where they could've attacked us. It makes no sense."

Phrantzes frowned. "Therefore," he said, "they must've known the station was closed."

"Fine. But when you were making the final arrangements for our departure, you had someone send ahead to let them know we'd be coming. Nobody got back to you and said, actually, that station's been closed."

"No," Phrantzes admitted, "no, they didn't."

"Fine. So, when you sent ahead, a couple of days before we set out—"

"The day before."

"The day before. And at that time, the station was open, and nobody knew anything about any plans to close it. We get there twelve or so hours behind schedule, not that much later than we should've been, and the place is empty and the road's blocked. And," he added, "there's a bunch of bandits hovering round the station; so they must've known it was closed, but the government didn't. Well?" he added. "That's not just some clerk screwing up in the transit office, is it?"

"It could be," Phrantzes said slowly, "a routine evacuation, due to rotation of personnel. A junior officer in the relevant department failed to notify the central office."

"And your people, checking ahead? Even if the garrison was about to go off shift, wouldn't they mention that? Oh, by the way, if your people show up here in two days' time, the place'll be all closed up?"

"They may have assumed we already knew."

"And the bandits?"

"They saw the garrison leave," Phrantzes said, "and saw an opportunity. Coaches would stop at the station; much easier to attack a stationary coach than trying to stop one while it's moving. Especially," he added happily, "since they were on foot."

Suidas thought for a moment, then shook his head. "I don't think so."

"It would then have been the bandits," Phrantzes added, "who put the bar in the road."

"Ah yes," Suidas said, "the bar. That punches a hole in your easier-to-attack-a-stopped-coach theory. All they've got to do is bar the road, like you're saying they did, and the coach stops dead. No need for any running about."

Phrantzes shrugged. "Then perhaps the garrison put the bar there when they left the station," he said. "For all I know, it's standard operating procedure."

"In peacetime? Hardly."

"Then it must have been the bandits."

Suidas sighed irritably. "And then," he went on, "who should show up but the Blueskins? On our side of the line. And they're not even supposed to be in the DMZ, let alone on our side of the line."

"Oh, Lieutenant Totila's explained all that," Phrantzes said firmly. "And his papers are entirely in order. And lucky for us he did turn up," he added. "Otherwise—"

"And there's him," Suidas said quietly, nodding his head at Tzimisces. "Even you must've noticed how he always seems to melt away just before something bad happens."

"He's an accredited political officer seconded from the foreign office."

"Right. One last thing." Suidas was starting to fidget with his hands, rubbing the scar on his right hand with his thumb. "How many way stations are there between C9 and the DMZ?"

Phrantzes' eyes opened a little wider. "Seven."

"And we're nearly at the border. And we haven't stopped."

A moment's silence. Then Phrantzes said: "Totila said he wanted to make up the lost time."

"Stopping at way stations isn't optional. Not if you're Permian soldiers on Scherian soil, anyhow. You'd have to stop and show your papers. And we haven't left the road, so we haven't just bypassed them all. Even if Totila's decided to break the rules and just ride on by without stopping to show his pass, there should've been some *reaction*. The station garrisons should've scrambled their horsemen and come after us, or ridden ahead across country so the next station down the line could bar the road. No, the only conclusion I can draw is, *all* the stations between C9 and the DMZ have been closed down." He stopped, giving Phrantzes an opportunity to speak. No reply. "Now," he said, "why would anybody do that?"

A look of panic crossed Phrantzes' face, but it soon passed. "It's entirely possible," he said, "that from time to time, all the stations are closed down simultaneously, for some reason. Don't ask me what it could be," he added quickly, "I'm not an expert."

"You used to be."

"That was seven years ago, and there was a war on. Things are almost certainly different now. It's equally possible that nobody thought to tell me that just such a closedown would be taking place at the same time as we set out for Permia. Furthermore," he went on, as Suidas opened his mouth, "the local bandits would quite likely know the closedown timetable, and make use of it in their business. In fact, if there is a regular network closedown, that's precisely what they'd do. It might also be the case that the Permians know about it, and my office doesn't; which would explain why Permian units are standing by. To cover for our people," he added forcefully, "in a spirit of mutual co-operation and trust. Well," he added, "it's possible. Isn't it?"

"You seem to think so."

"Rather more possible," Phrantzes said, "than some enormous conspiracy against us, involving multiple arms of government, requiring enormous effort, employing highly unreliable agents such as common highwaymen, not to mention wildly, bizarrely oversophisticated for the purpose. If someone wanted to kill us," he added quietly, "there are much easier ways in much more convenient places. Also," he went on mildly, "we're still alive. I put it to you: anybody with the resources to concoct a conspiracy on the scale you're imagining would surely have got the job done. They wouldn't have gone to all that trouble, and then relied on a small group of bandits with farm tools to overcome the four finest swordsmen in Scheria."

Suidas scowled at him; then he changed the scowl to a smile. "That reminds me," he said. "The swords, in the crate. How did they suddenly, magically turn from foils to sharps?"

Phrantzes slowly shook his head. "I don't think that's going to help your case," he said. "If I was plotting to murder us, I wouldn't surreptitiously replace our fake weapons with real ones. Counterproductive, don't you think?"

Suidas glared furiously at him for a moment, then burst out laughing. "I'm sorry," he said. "When I'm bored, I start thinking about things. You're probably right," he added. "I remember a time in the War, we were taking food to the siege of Flos Verjan, and we were promised they'd have finished building a bridge over the Renec, like we'd been asking them to do for I don't know how long. So we got there, no bridge; and then a bunch of engineers showed up, told us they'd just got their orders to start building it. And then, of course, that was cancelled, because the Irrigator moved the Renec seven miles to the east and we didn't need to cross it any more. I guess it's just something like that, and I've built up this wonderful theory—"

"I remember that bridge," Phrantzes interrupted. "I was the one who tried to get it built."

"You're joking."

"No, certainly not. I was in charge of supplies to Flos Verjan, and it seemed ridiculous that our convoys had to go the long way round, adding two days to the journey, when a simple bridge would take a few men a week to build. Of course, the general wouldn't allow a bridge there because he was planning to divert the river, but I was far too low down the hierarchy to be told about the grand design. So I spent a great deal of time and energy lobbying for what I saw as an entirely reasonable project, and of course I was wasting my time and making a fool of myself." He smiled. "I remember how angry I felt, and how inappropriate that seemed, because of course the flooding of Flos Verjan was the biggest victory in the War, and I was upset because it got in the way of my personal bridge. Later, of course, I could see how ridiculous I'd been about it, but at the time . . . "

The chaise was slowing down. Suidas pulled the window down and stuck his head out. "Looks like the border," he said. "There's a blockhouse, and a gate across the road, and a couple of soldiers."

"There you are then," Phrantzes said cheerfully. "Everything normal."

Suidas couldn't be bothered to argue. He was watching the soldiers. He tried to imagine how he'd react if he was a border guard and he was suddenly faced with a squad of Blueskin cavalry he hadn't been told about, coming *out* of Scheria. At such short notice he couldn't properly reconstruct such a complex train of emotions, but he was fairly sure he wouldn't just stand there looking bored, which was what the two soldiers were doing.

He reached across and prodded the side of Tzimisces' nose with his forefinger. "Wake up," he said, as Tzimisces grunted and opened his eyes. "We're at the border."

"What? Oh, splendid. I'd better have a word with the station officer."

Sliding out from under his travelling rug, Tzimisces opened
the door and melted out of the carriage. Suidas listened hard, but
he couldn't hear voices. "You were on Carnufex's staff in the
War?" he said.

"That's right," Phrantzes said.

"How long?"

"About eight years. Before that I was at GHQ."

Suidas nodded. "Not a field officer, then."

"Not really. I did spend a certain amount of time up around
the lines, but . . ."

"They're opening the gates, anyway," Suidas said. "I think
I'll just get out and see if I can . . ."

"Better not."

There was something in Phrantzes' voice that made Suidas
hesitate; and then Tzimisces came back, climbing into the chaise
and under his rug so fluently that it was hard to believe he hadn't
been there all the time. The chaise started to move.

"Thanks for waking me up," Tzimisces said. "Well, I had a
quick word with the captain, and everything's fine. Totila's troop
is going to escort us right though to Joiauz, and they've arranged
for a cart to meet us in the Zone with food and tents and blankets
and so forth, so we shouldn't have to rough it too much."

"Why are all the way stations shut down?" Suidas demanded.

Tzimisces didn't even blink. "Some ridiculous misunderstanding," he replied. "The captain explained it to me. Once
every three months or so, the way stations do an invasion drill.
Part of it involves closing down the network and shadowing an
imaginary invasion force, like we did in the War when the Aram
Chantat launched their raids. Apparently, some fool scheduled a
drill and nobody thought to mention it."

Suidas looked at him. He was sure Tzimisces had been asleep,
right up to the moment he'd woken him. "Well," he said, "that
explains it."

"Indeed. I shall have to mention it in my report. Of course,
the Permians will hear about all this and we'll look rather silly,

I'm afraid. The fact that they had to rescue us, on our own soil, will play very well in some quarters, I fancy. Still, it could've been worse." He smiled. "I suppose you know this road quite well."

"It's been a while," Suidas replied.

"Oh, I don't suppose it's changed all that much since your day. More potholes, I imagine. There simply isn't the money for road maintenance."

Suidas smiled bleakly and said nothing; after a moment, Tzimisces picked up his book and started to read. This time, the title on the spine was just visible: scrawly brown handwriting, *Pescennius and Berenice*. Suidas smothered a grin. He remembered Sontha buying a copy of it in the bookseller's market, as a present for her mother, one of whose many faults was a penchant for poisonously soppy verse romances. Tzimisces' copy had a distinctly home-made look, though Suidas couldn't really imagine the political officer sitting on a high stool in the writing room of the City Library, slowly and painfully copying out the text as the light from the tall east-facing windows slowly dwindled. Rather more likely, he decided (though on no evidence, he admitted to himself, as he drifted off to sleep), the book was the forfeited property of some political prisoner put to death on a trumped-up charge, and Tzimisces was reading it as part of a twisted attempt to get into its deceased owner's mind. Well, it was a theory, anyway.

Tzimisces wasn't the only one reading. Iseutz opened *Principles of Political Theory* at random and made a valiant attempt at the first paragraph on the left-hand page. It was written in ordinary modern Imperial Standard and she knew what all the words meant, but those words in that particular order seemed to deflect her mind, like a good parry in Third.

> *The institution we commonly refer to as democracy would,*
> *properly speaking, be more aptly termed an elective, or even in*
> *many cases a sortative, oligarchy, where the democratic element*

consists merely of the selection, often by random, perverse or
otherwise unsound procedures, of the membership of the
personnel of the ruling elite. Further vitiating factors include
the process whereby candidates are chosen and promoted – the
self-limiting caucus, the various forms of patronage, actual and
indirect corruption; issues regarding voting procedure, electoral
colleges, oversight and the proportion of votes received required
to constitute a genuine mandate; the discretion of a purportedly
representative body to dissolve or prolong its term of office, to
co-opt, to form coalitions. When we compare the patterns of
legislative activity of such representative democracies with
oligarchies based on qualification by birth, property or faction
membership, we find a significant correlation in terms of—

She frowned, and read it again. It still didn't make much
sense. But the creep Tzimisces had read it, apparently for pleasure, and if he could manage it, so could she. Even so, when she'd
agreed to swap books with him, she hadn't realised she was getting such a raw deal. Lifting her head slightly, she saw that the
creep was several pages into *Pescennius* and giving every indication of enjoying it. At the very least, she decided, she had to give
him credit for being able to read her handwriting.

She closed the book and opened it again, the way fortune-tellers
in the Flower Market did when purporting to tell you who you
were going to marry. The idea was, the first letter of the first word
on the left-hand page was the initial of your future husband.

Although.

But of course you had to be trained, or an old peasant woman
with hill-country blood, or it didn't work. She scowled at the
book and fought back the urge to throw it out of the window.
There was, of course, a certain amount of leeway, since the tradition didn't specify whether the initial was your one true love's
first name or surname. She tried again.

Generally.

She smiled; another myth exploded. She read:

*Generally speaking, military dictatorships contain from the
outset the seeds of their own undoing. One has only to
contemplate the vicissitudes of the Western Empire in the sixth
and seventh centuries AUC to form the inescapable view that—*

The hell with that. She realised that she was gripping the
book so tightly that her nails were cutting half-moon grooves in
the pages. I will *not* be defeated by a book, she told herself, and
read the whole chapter. Then she closed the book and put it
away in her pocket.

Her great-great-grandfather, according to family tradition,
had been a hermit. At that time, there had been a fashion for rich
noblemen to decorate the grounds of their estates with follies –
ruined castles, abandoned monasteries, hermitages. The propri-
etor of the estate where her family had worked as farm labourers
for generations came back from the customary grand tour of the
Eastern Empire determined to go one better. He had a column
built, forty feet high, on the top of the hill overlooking his ornamental lake. In the Mesoge, far to the east of the capital, he had
ridden across part of the great desert, where the most extreme
ascetics retired to live lives of perfect solitude and contemplation;
to which end they climbed to the top of pillars and columns and
sat, perfectly still, sunk in meditation for years at a time. That, he
decided, was real class; so as soon as the column had been raised,
he let it be known that he was looking to hire an ascetic to go and
sit on it. No qualifications or previous experience were required,
since the ascetic would be purely for show. The duties would
consist simply of sitting quite still whenever anybody might be
watching. Supplies of food and water would lugged up a long
ladder twice a week (there was a cunningly hidden recess in the
top of the column, so the pots and baskets wouldn't be visible
from the ground) and the applicant would be permitted to wear
thick woollen hose under his ascetic rags during the winter
months. Iseutz's great-great-grandfather, who by all accounts
was precious little use for anything else, was the only man on the

estate to apply for the job, and he did it, well and conscientiously, for two years, until the novelty wore off and he was allowed to come down. Two years' arrears of quite generous pay were waiting for him, and although he managed to drink a significant proportion of it, enough was left to enable him to set up a little dry-goods business, which his wife and daughter ran so successfully that his grandson was able to go to school and become a great success in the banking sector.

It was a pity, Iseutz had often felt, that she hadn't inherited her ancestor's ability to sit still. She thought of him from time to time, imagined him surveying the grand, gorgeous vista – the lake, the great house, the parkland and the mountains beyond – like some divine audience, almost like the Invincible Sun himself, possessed of the leisure of his betters, enjoying the spectacle they'd spent so much time, effort and money on creating, the complete effect of which only he could see. The right sort of man could be quite happy up there, provided it wasn't raining, simply observing, collecting data, slowly and scientifically collating and refining the results of his observations into a coherent unified theory that would explain— There, the daydream broke down. But the patience, the ability to watch rather than take part; that would be nice, she often thought. Of course, they'd never have got her up there because she was scared to death of heights, and if they had managed it, she'd have jumped off the column after five minutes from sheer intolerable boredom. But in any case, such an opportunity was unlikely to present itself in her lifetime. Nobody had that kind of money any more.

Outside the window, the landscape was changing. They'd been climbing steadily for several hours, and now they appeared to have reached a plateau of sorts. The road ran along the top of a broad ridge, slowly dropping away into what she guessed was a deep river valley. On the other side, she saw hillsides purple with heather, with occasional patches of yellow gorse. Green gullies marked the courses of small streams. There were no trees anywhere. A long way away, she saw the white tops of mountains.

She tried to imagine what all this enormous empty space would look like reduced to lines on a map, and concluded that they'd crossed into the Demilitarised Zone, previously known as the Debatable Land, the cause and principal arena of the War. She'd learned all about it from her tutor, a thin, harassed man with a bald head and a stringy white beard, who'd come both highly recommended and cheap. The problem, he'd told her, was that when the Eastern and Western Empires had fought each other to a standstill, two hundred years ago, they hadn't been able to agree a boundary in this sector. Rather than allow the negotiations to founder over a trivial scrap of moorland, they'd agreed to defer a decision and set up a boundary commission. Both sides then issued their unilateral declarations of victory, and pending the commission's report, they'd reached an informal agreement whereby both sides used the land for summer grazing – it was, after all, useless for anything else. The commission took its time; before it could announce its findings, the Aram Chantat burst into the Eastern Empire, the Suessones attacked the West, and the frontier provinces of Scheria and Permia took advantage of the resulting chaos to break away from their Imperial masters. Fighting off the barbarian invasions left both empires too weak to reclaim their lost provinces (no great loss, in any case). Scheria and Permia declared and secured their independence and found that they'd inherited a little piece of the Great War. Scheria, having considerably greater manpower at its disposal, immediately occupied the Debatable Land and parcelled it out among the leading families, who sent in their shepherds. Not long afterwards, the first major silver strike was made in Permia, whose military aristocracy suddenly realised that they could now afford to pay for a war of their own.

He told a good story, she'd say that much for him. When she came to read round the subject for herself, she realised it wasn't quite as straightforward as that. Scherian historians advanced a fairly convincing case for the land having originally belonged to the semi-nomadic tribes from whom the Scherians claimed descent. Permian authors drew attention to the ruins of a once significant city, now almost totally obliterated, whose monuments bore inscriptions in the long since extinct Middle Zeuxite language, which the Permians were believed to have spoken before they were conquered by the Eastern Empire, a thousand years ago. Another thing her tutor hadn't told her – quite possibly he hadn't known it himself – was that before the Great War, Western Imperial surveyors had reported substantial deposits of iron, copper and lead in the Debatable Land. Nothing had been done about it, of course, because the deposits were a long way down inside the hills, and the West lacked the technical skill necessary for deep-cast mining, so the minerals would have been too expensive to exploit. But deep-cast mining was what the Permians did best, and it was logical to assume that that was why they'd been prepared to fight so long and so hard for what was otherwise a modest expanse of second-rate sheep pasture.

Bearing all that in mind, she took another look at the landscape. It still struck her as vacant space to be got through as quickly as possible, devoid of any possible interest or value. There were no houses, none at all, and she found that sort of emptiness disturbing. Even her distinguished ancestor would've gone mad out here, she decided, with nothing to look at but heather. There was nothing to suggest that people had ever been here, or that they existed anywhere in the world. She shivered, opened her book again, and soon fell asleep.

She dreamt, as she often did, of the drowning of Flos Verjan. There was no reason for this, except perhaps that her father had told her about it once when she was quite young, and her imagination had seized on it and made it real. She imagined herself standing in the market square, which was really the Bakers' Market in the City, and looking up at the surrounding mountains, and seeing a great white and blue sheet of water falling towards her – an extraordinary thing, based on nothing in her own experience, but unmistakably vivid, and she'd never doubted for a moment what it was; rather like an abstract concept suddenly transformed into matter. It wasn't ice, because it moved as it fell, and it wasn't a waterfall, because every waterfall has sides to it, after a fashion, and this was entirely unconfined. Besides, she'd never seen a waterfall, although there was a picture of one in one of her school books (so badly drawn it could be anything). She stood with her neck craned back, watching from underneath as it fell, and fell, and fell; it was impossible to judge its speed because it was so huge and so shapeless, so there was no immediate impression of it getting bigger as it came closer. She felt no urge to run, because she knew it'd be pointless. The water was so big, there'd be no chance of getting clear. She could see a rainbow through it; quite pretty, in a way. She knew instinctively that when it reached her, she'd drown, and wake up. She knew that drowning here was waking up on the other side, which raised a number of quite intriguing issues about the nature of life, death and resurrection that she'd have liked to follow up on once she was awake (but when she tried to think them through afterwards, her mind seemed foggy and sluggish; she could feel the connections and insights and sparks of intuition evading her, and it made her angry). She was vaguely aware that all the people she'd ever known were standing next to her, and if she turned her head she'd be able to see them, even the dead ones, but instead she kept her eyes fixed on the falling water. Also, very much at the back of her mind, she felt a furious rage against the Irrigator, who had somehow brought himself to do this utterly inhuman thing, just to win a war and cause a map to be slightly redrawn.

This time, as the water fell, and fell, and fell, she knew that the man standing beside her, also looking up, was the Irrigator's son – not Addo, but the one who, she vaguely knew, had died in the War. It was a silent dream this time, but she was sure he was muttering something about sending his only begotten son to die for all the people – which was absurd, because General Carnufex had four sons, everybody knew that, though of course one of them had been killed in action. As the water surged down to touch her, and she opened her eyes and saw Addo, head against the bulkhead, eyes closed, dribbling slightly, she realised that it had been a sort of play on words, the Irrigator's son and the Invincible Sun, the son of the invincible Irrigator, the son of the Sun sent to die for the people every night and be resurrected every morning, to the greater glory of his Father in heaven. For some reason she found that intensely annoying, as though she'd been playing silly word games with herself, and had somehow contrived to lose.

Addo had woken up and was looking at her, and she realised she must've made a noise. She did that, apparently; spoke or even screamed in her sleep, though not necessarily when she was having nightmares.

"Are you all right?" he asked.

"Fine."

"You made a sort of—"

"Yes," she snapped. "But I'm fine now."

He winced, and she suddenly felt rather stupid. Maybe, she thought, I'm blaming him for my dream, which would be silly. She remembered that he had a chess set, and that she'd finished her book and traded it for one she really didn't want to read, although she could never admit that. They had a long journey ahead of them. It would, therefore, be in her best interests to be nice to the son of the Irrigator.

She glanced at him and wanted to smile. He was having the most terrible trouble deciding where to aim his eyes. He couldn't look at her, because she'd just snapped at him. But they were sitting opposite each other, and it was a small, enclosed space. His only real option was to look out of the window. "Do you mind if I have the blind down?" she asked, standing up and yanking it shut. "The sun's in my eyes."

It wasn't, of course. He mumbled a sort of consent. Now he couldn't look out of the window. She gave him her best friendly smile.

"How about a game of chess?" she said.

*

He tried to lose, but he wasn't that good. He managed to spin it out, at any rate. She fought to the very last. He tried to engineer a stalemate, but made a careless move that proved to be checkmate. She glowered at him, but said, "Another?"

"If you like."

Winning at chess was one of those things he couldn't help, like being his father's son. Winning came naturally; losing was something he'd had to work at, and he didn't quite have the tactical flair necessary to lose convincingly at will. Against a poor or mediocre player he was generally all right, but someone with just enough ability to be awkward, like Iseutz, presented him with real difficulties. For the second game he tried to think long-term, building a complex and far-reaching strategy based on what he'd learned about her play in the first game. She liked to attack strong pieces, so he devised a beautiful trap for his own queen. She took the bait eventually, only to sacrifice her own queen in the process. That left him with a significant advantage in capital pieces (the idea was that once his queen was dead, she'd be able to mop them up at her leisure) and he won again, this time quite quickly.

"That was smart," she said, her voice sheer ice. "Sacrificing your queen like that. I really fell for it, didn't I?"

"Actually, it was just carelessness." He knew straight away that he'd said the wrong thing. Outwitting her with a magnificent ploy was bad enough; making a stupid mistake and then going on to win an overwhelming victory was ten times worse. He had no idea how to recover from that. But she offered him another game, and he made up his mind that this time she was going to win, no matter what.

Unfortunately, it didn't work out. He'd set her up a knight fork that should've been mate in three, but ten moves later she gave him a look that felt as though it had flayed half the skin off his face, and resigned. "Another?" he said.

"All right."

Maybe, he thought wildly, as the inevitable slaughter

proceeded, she's letting *me* win, just to make me suffer. Maybe she's an absolute genius at the game – not so implausible as it might seem; you'd have to be damned good to lose against the chances he'd been offering – and what she enjoys is the embarrassment and guilt of her opponent. The first imperative of war, his father always insisted, was to define victory; to work out exactly what you wanted to achieve. Depending on what her agenda was, she stood to gain considerably more from losing than winning. His father was, of course, notoriously bad at chess. He always lost when playing against promising junior officers or enemy generals. But of course, in losing, he gained valuable information about their strengths, whereas if he won, all he'd have demonstrated was that he was more clever than them, which he knew already.

After she'd lost, she pulled up the blind and looked out of the window. The sun, he confirmed, was on the other side of the chaise, as he'd suspected.

But Dad, he heard himself saying, *I'm really not interested in tactics and strategy and the art of war. Don't be stupid, Addo.* The voice, gentle, contemptuous and kind. *Strategy and tactics are everything. They're the whole of life. War is just a tiny part of it.* And then, by more or less direct association, his own voice, almost a year ago now, telling her, *I never argue with my father, it's like arguing with the sea. You remember the story about the man who argued with the sea, Lyssa? You remember what happened to him?* And she'd frowned and said no, and he'd smiled and said, *He got very, very wet.* The last but one time he'd seen her, and she'd called him spineless, and yelled at him because he didn't disagree.

Everything. Well, he was his father's son, in that respect at least. He worked out an exit strategy before standing up and closing a door, or offering round a plate of biscuits.

(And always, always in the back of his mind his mother's voice: *Nobody ever suggested you're stupid, Addo. It's just . . .* And then, for once, her exceptional command of language failed her, and she waved her hands vaguely instead. *We should've put you into the priesthood, but your grandfather wouldn't hear of it.* He reflected on that, not for the first time that day or any day. His father was his father's son, and so it went on. And back to Lyssa's voice, saying, *Poor Addo. You inherit so much more than land in the landed bloody aristocracy.*)

At least there was no longer anything stopping him from looking out of the window. He saw moorland, empty, bleak and bizarrely purple (the colour of emperors; in the Eastern Empire, it was treason if a commoner wore purple. A distant ancestor on his mother's side had died for a faint purple stripe in the weave of an imported scarf. The family was very proud of her, for some reason). Somewhere around here, if he remembered his ancient history, was the tomb of Ataulf the Great. Of course there was no point at all in looking out for it, because it was lost for ever, like so much else, but someone with a proper feel for history ought to feel a slight frisson, passing through the country where the mightiest of all conquerors lay buried. He inspected his soul: no frisson. Oh well.

His mind kept trying to get back to the question he'd asked after the fight with the bandits, which nobody had answered and nobody except him appeared to find interesting: why had the swords in the packing case been sharps instead of foils? Various answers came to mind, and he knew he could make any of them plausible enough to be credible, if he wanted to. He'd been taught how to do that sort of thing, at great expense, by the finest logicians and rhetoricians money could buy in Scheria. They would argue that if something was so believable that you sincerely believed it, and enough people sincerely believed it too, then it must be true. He'd never been able to win that argument (only partly because he was too well brought up to contradict his betters), but he'd never really accepted it. Someone had put sharp weapons in that crate instead of foils, either through negligence or by design, and until he knew the answer to the question, it would be a crime against scientific method to assume, believe or accept anything at all about his current situation. But the others didn't seem particularly bothered. They seemed happy to jump over it, like the knight on the chessboard.

(If I was a chess piece, he wondered, which piece would I be? Not a king or a queen, naturally. Not a knight, because however hard I try, I can't jump over anything, or come at problems from right angles. Not fierce and strong enough to be a castle, and no son of the Carnufex could ever be a pawn, so presumably I'm a bishop. Should've been, only my grandfather wouldn't hear of it.)

He realised he was looking straight at Iseutz. Luckily she didn't seem to have noticed; she was staring out of the window, rapt in contemplation of the heather. *A plain girl*, his mother would say. *Probably prettier than she looks*, would be Stellecho's verdict, immediately followed by, *Don't even think about it, little brother. There wouldn't be enough left of you to bury*. Not that he'd even considered thinking about it. Suidas didn't like her, or at least they were always bickering, and Suidas said things about her behind her back. Lyssa would've noticed him looking at her and smiled, in that way she had that made him wish he'd never been born. Father probably wouldn't be able to see her, because her father was something in the Bank. The Irrigator had severe difficulty noticing people who weren't of good family, unless they were soldiers.

She really doesn't want to be here, he thought. Suidas is here because he needs the money, for Giraut it was this or the rope, and I'm here because I got a direct order from a superior officer. But as far as he knew, she wasn't governed by that sort of imperative; he assumed she'd been bullied or nagged into it, or maybe she'd actually wanted to go at the time, to get away from home and her family. That was actually quite plausible. Addo wasn't entirely sure what women actually *did*; in the Carnufex household, it seemed to be mostly needlework, while the Phocas daughters sketched and played suitable musical instruments (not woodwind, because a lady doesn't puff out her cheeks like a bullfrog). He couldn't imagine Iseutz doing anything like that.

She'd noticed him. It was too late to break eye contact. She scowled at him, and said, "What?"

"I'm sorry?"

"You were looking at me. What is it?"

Oh well, he thought, why not? "I was just wondering," he said, "what made you come on this trip."

She gave him a look of horrified fascination, as though he'd just kissed her or pulled her hair. "What?"

"I'm sorry," he said immediately. "None of my business, of course. I was just curious."

The gamble paid off. There was a short struggle inside her, and then she relaxed very slightly. "If you must know, I was given a choice, by my father. Well, it wasn't a choice exactly, more like a threat. Well, a bluff. You see, they wanted to marry me off to some idiot in my father's department at the Bank. Something political, I'm sure you know the sort of thing. I wasn't having it. I was so angry. And then my mother chipped in with *Well, dear, you do realise you're not getting any younger, and most girls your age* and all that, and I just lost my temper with both of them. And my father said, *So what do you intend doing with your life, if you're not going to get married?* And all I could think of was fencing, because I was ladies' junior champion when I was sixteen; and Mother just laughed, but Father got this look on his face and said about how they were sending a team to Permia, and some important people had been to see him to ask if I could go, but he'd said no, because I was just about to get married. So I said, *Fine, then, I'll go to stupid Permia.* And after that, well, I couldn't really back down. It'd have meant marrying this clown of Father's, and that'd have been my life down the sink. And I thought, well, how bad can it be? Compared to marrying a moron, I mean. So here I am."

Addo nodded slowly. "Do you like fencing?"

"Yes, actually. At least, I like it when I win. How about you?"

He frowned. It wasn't a question he'd ever been asked, or

expected ever to have to answer. It was a bit like *Do you enjoy breathing?* "Yes," he replied, surprising himself slightly. "I enjoy it the same way I like chess."

"You like winning."

He shook his head very slightly. "When you're fencing, you've got to concentrate, you can't let yourself think about anything else. You've got to be alone in your mind. I think that's what I like about it."

She frowned, as though she hadn't entirely understood him but was nevertheless intrigued by what he'd said. He felt strangely pleased by that. "Me too," she said. "Also, I like being able to jab at people as hard as possible and not get into trouble for it later."

He nodded sagely. "You should try longsword," he said. "You'd like that."

"Not allowed. Not ladylike."

"That's a shame. You'd be good at it."

The moment that followed was of a sort he recognised: the disengage, after a well-fought point of attack, riposte, counter, bind, simultaneous withdrawal to long measure. It was a moment when, generally speaking, you felt respect and a kind of warmth for your opponent, a special luxury of fighting with foils. Usually it was followed by a long pause, as each participant tried to tempt the other into making the next attack, because it was when attacking that you were most vulnerable. His father said that people communicated most when they fought.

(*You know what*, she'd said to him once. *Your father doesn't actually know everything about everything.*

True, he'd replied. *He knows very little about embroidery.*)

"Your father's General Carnufex."

Yes, I know that. "Yes."

She gave him a solemn look. "My brother Hamo was in your father's regiment in the War," she said. "He joined at fifteen, worked his way up to first lieutenant in the light cavalry. Then your father sent his squadron to capture a bridge. But he didn't really want the bridge, it was just a diversion. Like you sacrificing your queen, in the chess game."

Addo knew what was coming. Another dead brother, for whose death he was responsible by birth and inheritance. The only decision left to him was whether to play his own dead brother, or to retreat behind his guard.

"He was lucky," she went on, and Addo caught his breath. "They took the stupid bridge and chased away the enemy, and then they just sat there waiting for the rest of the army to catch them up. But nobody came. He said he felt such a fool, like he'd been stood up by a girl, and his men were looking at him. He started thinking that maybe he'd captured the wrong bridge. Well, they waited till it was starting to get dark, and Hamo really didn't want to be out there at night, away from the rest of the army, where the Aram Chantat could creep up on them, or anything. So he led his squadron back to camp, and everybody was really surprised to see them. They assumed they'd be dead. But it turned out your dad had screwed up, and the enemy didn't take the bait. They didn't send their mobile reserve or whatever it's called to try and protect the bridge, so when your dad launched his main attack, he got a really nasty shock."

Addo nodded. "Did they win?"

"I suppose so. Or if they didn't win that day, they won later on."

"And your brother was all right? He survived the war."

"Oh yes. He's always been lucky, Hamo. He's married to a very distant poor relation of a junior branch of the Phocas, so you can see, he's really made something of himself."

Addo grinned. "Unlike you," he said.

"Quite. What about you? Shouldn't you have been married off by now?"

"I'm my father's mobile reserve," Addo replied. "That's not strictly true, I'm more his defence in depth. He's keeping me for an emergency, where he needs to make a marriage alliance quickly. Always keep a reserve, he says."

"So." She looked at him thoughtfully. "No emergency yet, then."

"None he hasn't been able to cover without committing his heavy cavalry." He took a breath, and said, "I thought you were going to say my father got your brother killed. I hear that quite often."

"Yes," she said. "I suppose you do." She shrugged. "Hamo was sure he was going to get court-martialled and hanged for abandoning his position, but nobody ever mentioned it again. He couldn't stay there, though. He said he owed it to his men to get them back safe."

"He was a good officer," Addo replied. "He did the right thing."

"But it was all pointless. The trick didn't work."

"That wasn't his fault. And he used his head, and probably saved a squadron of cavalry. I'm sure my father approved of what he did. In fact, I know for certain. Your brother would've heard about it if my father wasn't pleased."

She clicked her tongue. "It'd be far better for everyone if people stuck to chess," she said.

"My father's a rotten chess player."

She grinned at that. "Worse than me?"

"You'd slaughter him."

She laughed – not an attractive sound in itself, but it gave Addo more pleasure than a clean and acknowledged hit – and Giraut woke up. He blinked and said, "What's the matter?"

"Nothing," Iseutz said. "Why?"

"I thought I heard a scream."

Addo managed not to laugh. Iseutz shot Giraut a poisonous look and stuck her head back into *Principles of Political Theory*, where it stayed until the chaise stopped for the night.

"Explain to me," Abbot Symbatus said icily, "why C9 was abandoned and the road blocked. I'll be fascinated to hear what you have to say."

Fulco Phocas opened his mouth and closed it again. He wasn't quite sure why he was there, or on what authority this ferocious old priest was cross-examining him, but he knew from his experiences in the war that you recognise the enemy by the look in his eye, not where you find him or what he happens to be wearing. Besides, a priest wouldn't dare to treat a member of the joint chiefs of staff with such obvious disdain if he wasn't sure he had the backing of overwhelming strength. Just because Phocas didn't know what that strength consisted of didn't mean it didn't exist.

"What can I say?" He tried charm, in the form of a smile. Didn't work. "One of those ridiculous misunderstandings. They happen. It's just unfortunate that it had to happen at such a particularly inconvenient time."

He waited for a reply, but the abbot didn't speak, or move. To break the silence before it crushed him flat, Phocas went on, "The standard operating procedure is for way-station garrisons to serve a three-month tour, after which they're relieved and assigned to other duties for six months, and then sent back again. Basically, we've got three shifts of experienced way-station guards, and we rotate them. It was time for the duty shift to be relieved, but for some reason we're still looking into, the relief shift wasn't mobilised. The duty shift waited for the relief shift to show up, but they didn't, so they closed up their post and marched back to their home camp. They shouldn't have done that, of course," Phocas added quickly, "they should've stayed put till they were relieved, but they didn't. Naturally, there's going to be a regimental enquiry."

The abbot was looking at him, keenly, motionless, as if concerned that the slightest movement would cause his rare and timid quarry to take flight. After a long pause he said, "I'm rather surprised to learn that something like that can happen. I thought the entire ethos of the military was founded on rigid discipline and orders passed along the chain of command."

"Ah, well." Phocas tried a vague hand gesture, and immediately regretted it. "In wartime, yes. But a peacetime army's a rather different animal. Not quite the same sense of urgency, if you follow me. And, to be absolutely frank with you, not quite the same calibre of men as we had in the War."

No reaction. Phocas discovered he'd started speaking again. In fact, he was gabbling.

"Back then, you see," he was apparently saying, "we had the best and brightest at our disposal, whether they liked it or not. These days, we have to make do with volunteers. And there's no money, so we can't afford the sort of people we'd like to have, they can make five times as much working for the Bank. And the old families, with their sense of duty and public service, were pretty well wiped out in the War. What's left of them is needed back home, to manage their estates." It wasn't what he'd wanted to say; indeed, it was something of an overstatement of the case for the prosecution. But he had an idea it was what the terrifying old gentleman wanted to hear, so he felt himself constrained to say it. "Anyhow," he added lamely, "they're all right now and safely on the way to Permia, so no harm done."

Shortly after that, Abbot Symbatus allowed General Phocas to escape, and poured himself a drink of water, to ease his sore throat. He was fairly sure that Phocas had told him what he believed to be the truth. That, if anything, was rather more disturbing than a pack of lies.

The next day was the Feast of the Redemption. He got through it with gritted teeth, managing to complete the procession to the high altar without stumbling or having to hold on to anyone, though each step was agony. Between the ceremony and his customary address to the novitiates (a chair was provided, which he grimly refused to sit in), he sat on the floor of his cell with his back to the wall and prayed for the pain to stop. It didn't, which suggested his prayers weren't finding favour for the time being. He couldn't sleep that night, so he crawled out of bed, called for his fire to be built up until it was hot enough to peel skin at two paces, and sat in his chair in front of it. Heat didn't seem to work any more, so he resolved to accept the pain as a form of divine communication, and put it out of his mind. It wasn't, after all, as bad as the kidney stone had been, and he'd lived with that for a month before his prayers were answered and it stopped, quite suddenly, in the middle of Chapter.

Since he was awake, and in his chair with his desk in front of him, and since there was absolutely no chance that he'd be able to get to sleep that night, he decided that he might as well make himself useful. There was a small stack of letters (thin, crisp parchment; they reminded him of the flatbread his mother used to order for his birthday), and he picked up the one on the top. It was from the Prior of Conessus, asking permission for one of his monks to take stylitic vows for five years, with a gentle hint that should the request be granted, Monsacer might find itself moved to contribute towards the not inconsiderable expense of raising the necessary pillar.

In spite of the pain, Symbatus grinned. He'd always found the stylites faintly ridiculous, but that was probably because of his own family history: his great-great-grandfather had fallen victim to the ornamental-hermit craze of the late Regency, and had spent a huge sum of money the family couldn't really afford on a folly pillar, complete with a lavishly paid pretend stylite to sit on top of it. The ruins of the pillar were still there, on the hill overlooking what was now the Irrigator's country seat. He'd been to look at it when he was twelve years old. It was a wonderful thing. It had been built hollow, like a chimney. Mostly this was on grounds of hygiene; under the base of the column was a seven-foot-deep sump and soakaway (the hill was chalk); but it also meant that the stylite's food, water and other supplies could be sent up via a basket and winch without the operation being visible from the footpath (which was as close as anyone ever got). The remains of an iron ladder still clung to the inside of the chimney, so it was perfectly possible for the stylite to sneak down at night, or when nobody was looking, to stretch his legs. His cousin's eldest boy, Sphacterius, had told him once that he'd actually climbed the column, and discovered a little alcove cunningly built into the top of it, large enough for a man to sit comfortably; presumably the stylite ducked in there out of the rain. All in all, it sounded like a fairly pleasant existence, and he couldn't help wondering whether the terrifying saints of the past had had similar creature comforts built into their own pillars; if, in fact, they'd cheated. He hoped they hadn't.

He read the petition again and scribbled on the back of it: petition granted, but gentle hint firmly ignored. He put it on the other side of his desk, then reached across and picked it up again. Under his previous annotation he added: *Height of pillar not to exceed twenty-five feet.* The closer you were to the ground, the easier it was for people to see, the harder it was to cheat. It would be a beautiful irony of the Faith, he told himself, for someone to achieve salvation by doing honestly what those he sought to emulate had achieved by fraud.

The next letter was a furious rebuttal by a subcommittee on doctrinal orthodoxy of a trivial, tiny heresy that had broken out somewhere he'd never heard of in the far west of the Western Empire. It was probably the answer to his prayers, because in spite of the pain, it sent him straight to sleep.

Giraut woke up and looked out of the window.

"My God," he said. "What happened here?"

"Nothing," Suidas said. "We're in Permia."

It looked a bit like a quarry, except that it was huge; in fact, it was everything, as far as the eye could see. The road ran down the middle of a valley, with bare-stone mountains rising sharply out of a wilderness of shale. There was a little yellow grass, a few grey ferns, no trees of any sort anywhere. Here and there boulders as big as houses stuck up out of the ground. Otherwise, it was featureless and utterly bleak.

"It's supposed to look like this?" Giraut asked.

"Please don't say anything like that in front of our hosts," Tzimisces murmured. "They're fiercely proud of their country."

Giraut looked at him. "Why?"

Tzimisces smiled and didn't answer.

They stopped around mid morning, beside the first thing vaguely resembling a watercourse Giraut had so far seen in Permia. It was a little brown trickle running in an absurdly deep gully. Dead weeds about five feet high lined the banks. One of Totila's men ran a bucket down on a rope, for water for the horses.

"Is it all like this?" Addo asked.

"No." Phrantzes opened the chaise door. "The east of the country is rather more like what we're used to at home, only it's quite high, and flat. In summer the grass comes up to your waist." He climbed out, and they followed him, realising for the first time how stiff and cramped they were. "This region has never quite recovered from its time under the Eastern Empire," Phrantzes went on. "It was parcelled out among absentee landlords, who thought it'd be a good idea to graze large herds of goats here. For the wool, so I gather. It was particularly fine, suitable for luxury-grade cloth. After they'd eaten off all the grass, the wind blew the topsoil away. Before that, apparently, this was first-class arable land, but it got depopulated during the Fifty Years War."

Giraut frowned. "The what?"

"Five hundred years ago," Addo said. "Though it wasn't really a war. More a series of border skirmishes."

"It's horrible," Iseutz said solemnly. "Let's get back in the coach."

They sat in silence for a long time. Then Iseutz looked at Phrantzes and said, "You know a lot about Permian history."

"I read a book," Phrantzes said mildly.

"So what's this town like that we're going to first?"

"Joiauz," Tzimisces interrupted smoothly. "It's the third largest city in Permia. It's a mining town, of course. Most of it's still being rebuilt." He smiled. "We were rather rough with it during the War, weren't we, Deutzel?"

Suidas frowned at him. After a moment Addo said, "It was a major base for Aram Chantat raids into Scheria. My father decided—" He stopped.

"Indeed," Tzimisces said. "We took Joiauz by storm. It was General Carnufex's first substantial command and one of the first real successes of the war. However, I can assure you that the place where you'll be staying has four walls and a roof."

The chaise stopped sharply, the inertia lifting Giraut several inches out of his seat. "Now what?" Iseutz snapped, then saw the look on Suidas' face. He was staring out of the window, and the look on his face was somewhere between terror and a kind of hunger. Giraut craned his neck to see past his shoulder.

He saw a man on a horse, possibly one of a group. The horse was small, barely larger than a child's pony. Its rider was small too, and he looked very young, no more than sixteen, with a few wisps of golden hair on his upper lip and chin. He was wearing a fur cap that covered his ears and neck, and a long blue woollen gown down to his ankles. His feet were bare. He was riding bareback, but he had a quiver slung over his horse's neck, with a short, unstrung bow sticking out of it. His fingers were long and delicate, like a girl's. He was smiling, listening to something someone was saying; then he laughed, and his face lit up. His nose was long and straight, and he had pale blue eyes. He reminded Giraut of the icons of the firstborn of the Invincible Sun.

"That's them, isn't it?" he whispered to Suidas, who nodded.

"What is it?" Iseutz said. "I can't see from where I'm sitting."

"Aram Chantat," Tzimisces said quietly. "Would you please all sit still and stay quiet. There's absolutely no cause for alarm."

Giraut carried on staring. The last thing he'd expected was that the Aram Chantat would be beautiful. It made no sense: beautiful as an angel, but next to him Suidas was as taut as a bowstring, and he could see Tzimisces' left hand shaking very slightly, until he closed his right firmly around it. He could hear Totila's voice, higher than before, with a distinctly nervous edge to it. *Even the Blueskins are terrified of them, and they're on the same side*. But he was sure Totila could snap the young horseman's delicate neck like the stem of a flower.

He heard several men laughing; then Totila said something else, and the horseman abruptly moved out of sight. The chaise rolled forward and rapidly picked up speed.

"What's the *matter* with you two?" Iseutz was demanding. "You look like you've seen a ghost or something."

Suidas gave her such a ferocious scowl that she shrank back an inch or so. "Just a routine patrol, I should imagine," Tzimisces said softly. "Nothing to worry about." He turned his head a little and looked at Suidas. "Chauzida?"

Suidas nodded. "I think so," he said. "Either that or Rosinholet. Northerners, at any rate."

"You're sure?" The point seemed to matter.

"Oh yes." Suidas breathed out slowly. "Trust me, I know my Aram Chantat sects. Some of the easterners wear blue, but they don't go barefoot. And the bone structure's northern."

"Ah well," Tzimisces said. "Small mercies."

Iseutz's eyes opened wide. "Did he just say Aram Chantat?"

"That's right," Phrantzes said, and his voice was tense but quiet. "You couldn't see them from where you're sitting, Iseutz, but we were just stopped by half a dozen Aram Chantat horsemen. However, Lieutenant Totila showed them some papers, and they let us pass."

"Papers?" Suidas objected. "They can't read."

"They can recognise a seal," Tzimisces said. "Besides, we're being escorted by a squadron of Permian cavalry."

"Then why'd they stop us?" Iseutz said.

"Because they can," Suidas said. "They like scaring people. Especially the Blueskins." He smiled. "They've been fighting the Empire for centuries, on and off. Very occasionally, the Blueskins win."

"Please don't use that expression now we're on this side of the border," Tzimisces said pleasantly.

Suidas pulled a sad, angry face. "I don't know what else to call them."

Tzimisces laughed. "Imperials will do just fine. Best of all, don't call them anything. That way, nobody can take offence, and we might actually achieve something."

"The first thing I'm going to do when we get to this Joiauz place," Iseutz told nobody in particular, "is have a bath. I haven't washed properly for days. I *smell*."

Suidas lifted his head. "Yes," he said.

She scowled at him. "So do you."

Suidas shrugged. "I was in the army."

"What's that got to do with it?"

"It's my fault," Phrantzes muttered. "I'm supposed to have organised this trip, and it's all been a complete disaster."

He was expecting to be contradicted, but nobody said anything. After a while Tzimisces said, "Don't beat yourself up over it. There's obviously some problem with the way-station garrison rotations. It can't be helped."

"I should've made sure everything was in place," Phrantzes insisted. "Checked and double-checked. I'm sorry."

"Well now," Tzimisces said, "if you feel that strongly about it, when we get to Joiauz I can write home and ask them to send out someone else. That's if you feel you've failed in some way."

Phrantzes looked at him. "No, that won't be necessary," he said quietly. "I'll just have to try harder from now on."

"That's the spirit," Tzimisces said.

There was a long silence. Then Addo said, "Is it my imagination, or are we going uphill?"

Giraut glanced out of the window, and nearly choked. On his side of the chaise, there was nothing at all. Thin air.

"Quite right," Tzimisces said. "Joiauz is built on a hill. Well, more than a hill. We had a devil of a job here, in the War. They collapsed the road, and we had to rebuild it, with the Permians rolling rocks on to our heads. It's fully restored now, of course," he added, as Iseutz shot him a horrified stare. "Superb engineers, the Permians. It's amazing what they've achieved in such a short time."

"Would you mind very much if we had the blinds down?" Addo said, after he'd looked out. "I'm afraid I'm rather stupid about heights."

Nobody minded in the least, and they all sat perfectly still until the chaise eventually stopped, quite some time later. The door opened, and Totila was standing there, looking decidedly cheerful.

"Joiauz," he said. "Come in and have something to eat."

The sun was just beginning to set, and the light was gently red. It suited the soft yellow stone of the tall buildings on three sides of the square they found themselves in. The fourth side was open; the head of a grand stairway, leading down to the lower town. It was an extraordinary view, a wild jumble of red-tiled roofs, green domes, bell towers, fire pillars and soaring brick chimneys. But there were pieces missing, like empty squares on a chessboard; closer examination showed these to be ruins not yet rebuilt. In the middle of the square was a fire pillar at least a hundred feet tall.

"There's a reception," Totila was saying, "in the Guildhall. But I expect you'll want to freshen up first."

A small procession was heading towards them across the square. At the head were two short, bald men in long red robes, followed by a giant in grey velvet. Behind them was a column of old men in black gowns. Giraut wanted to run away, but he couldn't think where to run to. The procession halted, close enough that he could see the gilt buttons on the bald men's cuffs. The giant stepped between them and cleared his throat.

"On behalf of the Fencers' Guild and the freemen of Joiauz," he said, in a rather high-pitched voice with a curiously nasal accent, "we welcome you to our city."

Nobody moved. We're supposed to say something or do

something, Giraut thought, and nobody knows what it is. Nothing can happen till we've said or done it. We could be here for the rest of our lives.

Tzimisces nudged Phrantzes, who opened his mouth, closed it again and said, "Thank you."

Clearly that wasn't right, but the two bald men, after a moment of stunned silence, nodded abruptly and advanced on Tzimisces and Phrantzes. Tzimisces skipped back out of the way, and Phrantzes was left to accept the cold, harsh embrace. Then a small boy hopped out of nowhere holding a big silver key. He gave it to one of the bald men, who gave it to Phrantzes, who looked at it for quite some time and then stuck it in his pocket. Giraut heard Tzimisces moan softly. Then the column about-faced and marched back into the building they'd come out of, leaving the fencers alone with Totila's men in the otherwise deserted square.

"Did I do something wrong?" Phrantzes said.

"Yes, but never mind," Tzimisces said briskly. "I'm sorry, I thought you'd been briefed on protocol. Not to worry. Let's get inside and have some food."

It was the biggest room Giraut had ever been in. You could've held a small steeplechase in there without moving more than a couple of tables. They had it all to themselves.

"I'll be leaving you now," Totila said, and his voice soared up to the great domed roof, bounced off the stunning gold mosaic of the Fire God in Splendour, and chased itself between the pillars for a while. "I expect there'll be someone along soon to tell you what's happening."

Far away in the distance, across a vast black-and-white tiled floor, was a table on a dais. There were cups and plates on it; the rest of the tables were bare. "I guess we're supposed to help ourselves," Addo said. He didn't seem particularly overawed by his surroundings, which made Giraut wonder what his house looked like inside. He looked round for Tzimisces, who wasn't there. He heard footsteps, impossibly loud, which he assumed were Totila's, leaving.

They crept up on to the dais as quietly as they could. There was bread and cheese, long red sausages and a big silver vat of what Giraut guessed was that celebrated Permian delicacy, fermented white cabbage. It was a sort of puddlewater brown, and Giraut could've sworn he saw it move.

"God help us," Iseutz said under her breath, and put a couple of slices of bread on a plate.

Giraut stared at the food, decided that the cheese was probably all right, and looked round for something to cut into it with. There wasn't anything. "Excuse me," he said, "but has anybody got a knife?"

No reply. On Tzimisces' instructions, they'd left anything that could possibly be construed as a weapon in the chaise. Giraut leaned forward and tapped the cheese with his fingernail. It was rock solid, sealed in a plaster rind. He turned his attention to the sausages, but they were too big to get in any mouth that would conceivably qualify as human. That left the bread and the pickled cabbage. He took three slices of bread. It was like eating wood. He washed them down with a cup of water, which tasted funny. Welcome to Permia.

"He's disappeared again." Iseutz had materialised next to him. He saw that she'd nibbled the crust of one of her slices of bread. "Hadn't you noticed?"

"Presumably he's meeting with the Permian officials."

"Rubbish. He's slipped out to an inn. He's probably eating roast lamb right now. My God."

"What?"

"Look."

He followed her pointing finger, and saw Addo, munching a handful of the pickled cabbage. He noticed her staring at him and smiled feebly. "It's actually not that bad," he said, with his mouth full.

"You can't eat that stuff. It's not fit for human consumption."

"The Permians eat it," Phrantzes said.

"Proving nothing."

Phrantzes shrugged. He'd piled a small heap of the stuff on his plate, along with a slice of the wooden bread, but he wasn't eating. "There'll probably be food at the reception," he said hopefully.

"What makes you think that?"

He didn't reply. Iseutz shook her head, slammed her plate down on the table and folded her arms. "This isn't good enough," she said. "We're supposed to be important, aren't we? So why have they dumped us here in this cowshed with nothing but stale bread and nowhere to wash? We'd be better off in prison."

"Not really," Giraut said mildly. It had the effect of shutting her up, which was what he'd aimed at. Of course, he hadn't been in prison, or at least if he had, he'd been unconscious all the time. But she wasn't to know that.

"What is this place exactly?" Addo asked suddenly.

That was a question Giraut had asked himself and then forgotten to answer. "I don't know," he said. "I assumed it was some sort of Guild house."

"Fencers' Guild, maybe," Suidas put in. "Well, it's big enough, God knows. If you moved all these tables out of the way, you'd have a really first-class salle. And it figures, doesn't it? Presumably we're the guests of their Fencers' Guild."

Iseutz dragged her foot across the floor. "You could fence here, granted," she said.

"Look." Phrantzes was pointing at the far wall. It was covered with dark wood panels, on which were long columns of dates and names. "Previous champions, I assume."

"Well, that explains that, then," Iseutz said briskly. "You know, this makes the guild house back home look like a chicken coop. It's more like a temple."

"But with a better floor," Suidas said. "And the lighting's good." He looked round, counting under his breath. "You could get a thousand spectators in here, no trouble at all."

"More," Giraut said. "There's a gallery, look."

"And this isn't even the capital city," Iseutz said. "Someone's spent a great deal of money on this place."

"They had a great deal of money to spend, at one time," Phrantzes said. "Before the War, of course."

Iseutz walked out into the middle of the floor. "If we had our stuff," she said, "we could get some practice. All that sitting in coaches, I'm amazed I can move at all. I practise forms three hours every day back home. This is the longest I've gone without practising since I was seven."

Suidas grinned. "If you want to do some forms, go ahead," he said.

She scowled at him. "Not with you watching."

"There's going to be twelve hundred people in here when we do the match."

"That's different."

Addo was looking up at the high windows. "We ought to be able to borrow some foils," he said. "They're bound to have some, if this is the Fencers' Guild. I don't know about you, but I like to get the feel of the kit before a match."

"I want to know where my foils have got to," Iseutz said. "For one thing, they're quite expensive. I know they were collected from our house. Presumably they're sitting in some transit office."

"I can fence with more or less anything," Giraut said. "But she's right, we need to practise before the match."

Phrantzes realised that they were all looking at him. "I'll go and see if I can find someone," he said unhappily.

Suidas sat down on the edge of the table. "A decent meal, a good night's sleep in a bed and a proper workout with the gear we'll be using in the match," he said. "Otherwise I'm not fencing. It'd help," he added sternly, "if we all agreed. I mean, if we all refuse, there's not much they can do."

Giraut looked away. "We don't want to make trouble," Addo said. "Still, it's not exactly unreasonable, what you're saying.

And I'm sure that's what we'll get; it's just they're not terribly good at communicating. I expect Tzimisces is organising it all right now."

"It shouldn't be him, though," Suidas said. "He's the political officer, not the team manager. It should be Phrantzes dealing with that kind of thing."

"Oh, him," Iseutz said. "He's useless."

"Keep your voice down," Suidas said quietly. "He's coming back."

Phrantzes stood in the doorway and tried to think what he was going to say. They'd noticed him, and were looking at him. Oh well, he thought. He walked forward. He felt like he'd been running.

"There's been a change of plan," he said.

They waited for him to say more. Then Suidas said, "Well?"

"The reception," he said, speaking very clearly, "has been postponed."

"Yes?"

Phrantzes nodded. "It'll be held after the match. Here, in the Guildhall."

The Bryennius boy looked relieved. Suidas Deutzel shrugged. "Fine," he said. "So when's the match?"

"In about an hour."

The reaction was more or less what he'd expected. Iseutz screamed, "*What?*" Suidas and Giraut stared without speaking. Addo Carnufex let his head droop forward, as though he'd been expecting something of the sort. It could have been worse, Phrantzes told himself. Generally speaking, the worst happening was always marginally better than the worst anticipated.

"That's completely—" Iseutz started to say, but Suidas cut her off with a slight gesture of his hand; a born sergeant, that man.

"That's unacceptable," he said, furiously calm. "We've been travelling for days, we haven't slept properly, we haven't trained, we've had no food, we haven't got our kit . . ."

Phrantzes felt his stomach lurch. He expected the words to come out in a squeak or a whisper, but he managed to say them perfectly clearly. "Actually, you've got everything you'll need."

He hadn't expected then to understand. But Addo Carnufex lifted his head and looked straight at him, and he got the impression that somehow, he knew.

"I'm really sorry," Phrantzes went on. "The thing is, the arrangements were made in advance, and well, we weren't expecting to be held up so long on the road. A lot of people have travelled for days to see the match. If we tried to postpone it, there'd almost certainly be a riot. I know it's dreadfully short notice, but there's really nothing we can do. I'm sorry, but there it is."

"Phrantzes," Addo said, still looking straight at him, "where are our foils? And the masks, and the jackets and stuff?"

This time, his voice nearly broke. He managed to cover it with a fake cough. "You won't be using foils," he said.

As Iseutz shrieked and Suidas roared and Giraut stared open-mouthed, Phrantzes realised he felt much calmer, now he'd actually said it. The terrible thing he'd brought with him all the way from the City was out now, loose, beyond his control. It was a shamefully blissful release.

"The Permians don't use foils," he said, raising his voice over theirs. "At least, only in practice, and for children's matches. Certainly not at the professional level. That's why we were sent out with sharps. That's what we'll be using."

There was a long, long silence. Then Iseutz said, "They want us to fight with *real swords*?"

"I'm afraid so."

Suidas had recovered from the initial shock. "That's barbaric," he said. "I'm not doing it."

"I'm sorry, but we can't back out now," Phrantzes said gently. "There's over a thousand people waiting in the square behind this one. Most of them have been there all day. If we try and back out now, there will almost certainly be bloodshed."

"The hell with that," Suidas thundered at him. "If we go out and fight with sharps, there'll quite definitely be bloodshed, and I'm having no part of it. And you can tell that bastard Tzimisces—"

"Phrantzes," Addo said, talking quietly over him and silencing him straight away, "did you just find out? Or did you know all along?"

Some questions really matter. This was one of them. In such cases, Phrantzes told himself, it's not always expedient to tell the truth. "No," he said. "They sprang it on me just now. They assumed we knew. I asked for foils, like you wanted me to, and they looked at me and said, *What do you want foils for?* I'm sorry," he added. "There's obviously been the most appalling breakdown of communications. But there's nothing we can do about it now. You're going to have to fight with sharps, that's all there is to it."

Two Permians – short, black-bearded, in white tunics and grey trousers – brought in the crate and set it down in the middle of the floor. They stared at the Scherians briefly, as if in the presence of gods and monsters, then withdrew quickly.

"We can refuse," Iseutz repeated, yet again. "We just stand up and say sorry, there's been a really stupid mistake, we aren't fighting tonight. What can they do?"

Nobody answered her. Suidas lifted the lid off the crate and let it clatter on the floor. He reached inside and took out a rapier. Then a strange look passed across his face.

"Phrantzes," he said. "Where's the other rapier? There's only one in here."

"That's for Giraut." Phrantzes leaned across, took the rapier out of his hand and passed it to Giraut, who took it, fumbled and nearly dropped it.

"What am I supposed to use, then?"

"You won't be fencing rapier," Phrantzes said.

"But that's insane," Suidas protested. "I'm the Scherian rapier champion."

"Yes, but rapier's not all that popular here." Phrantzes listened to himself saying the words, but it sounded like someone else's voice. "What they really like is the Permian long knife, and nobody else in Scheria . . .'

(*Here they fight with messers. God help them.*)

"That's totally ridiculous." Iseutz's voice, high and ragged. "You can't expect him to fight a style he doesn't know, especially with sharps. That's just utterly unreasonable."

Suidas had gone milk-white. He took a step back, tripped over his own heel and fell, landing on his backside. Addo stepped forward, and Iseutz shouted, "Leave him alone."

Phrantzes felt like he was about to throw up. "I'm sorry," he heard that voice say, "but you've got to. I'm really sorry."

"This is stupid," Addo said. "I'll do it."

There was a moment of perfect silence. Then Phrantzes said, "What did you say?"

"I'll do it instead of him. Can't you see, the poor man's having a fit or something."

It was as though a fist was slowly unclenching in his chest, the fingers forcing his ribs apart. "You can't," he said. "You don't know . . . "

"I know broadsword and sword-and-buckler. How different can it be?"

"You're fighting longsword," Phrantzes said desperately. "You can't do both."

"Fine. Suidas can do longsword, I'll do this Permian knife thing. I don't mind. I'm quite good at sword-and-buckler."

"There's no buckler. It's just the knife."

"Not to worry," Addo said, and with only the tiniest modulation of pitch his voice was cold and savage, admitting no contradiction. "I'll just have to pick it up as I go along."

Phrantzes gawped at him, then looked down at Suidas, who was still on the floor. "You can't let him," he said. "He'll be killed. For pity's sake, he's the general's son."

Dead silence. Then Addo said quietly, "I think we all know

that, thanks. And really, I don't mind. Suidas can fight longsword, and I'll do the Permian knife. Giraut can do rapier, and Iseutz can do smallsword. What are the conventions?"

Phrantzes looked at him as though he was talking a different language. "What?"

"The scoring conventions. With sharps, I mean. Do we fight till someone gets cut, or what?"

"It's rather more complicated than that." Phrantzes realised, after he'd said it, that if he hadn't known they'd be fighting with sharps, he oughtn't to know the sharps rules. "It varies from weapon to weapon. The fact is," he said (his teeth were starting to chatter), "I'm not absolutely sure myself. They sent us a rule book . . ."

"They sent you a rule book," Iseutz repeated.

"But it's full of technical terms, and nobody really understands what they mean. Really, I need to meet with the Permian officials and get them to explain them to me."

He found that Addo was looking straight at him; no anger, hatred or contempt, nothing as human as that. He was a source of information, and an imperfect one at that. "All right," Addo said quietly. "You go and find someone to ask, and then come back and tell us. We won't run away, I promise."

After Phrantzes had gone, nobody said anything. Suidas slowly got up and walked away. Iseutz turned and hissed, "*Addo* . . ."

"It's all right," he replied, firm and perfectly calm. "My father and I fight with sharps at home."

Her eyes went wide. "You *what*?"

"He says it's the only way to learn. We've been doing it since I was seventeen, and we've never hurt each other. Just concentrate on your measure, that's the main thing. If you aren't there, you can't be hit."

She turned sharply away from him. Giraut happened to be in the way. "You talk to him," she snapped. "He won't listen to me. Tell him he's being ridiculous."

"Don't look at me," Giraut said. "I don't want to fight anybody with real swords."

The fury faded slowly from her face. "You'll be all right," she said.

"After the last time? After I froze, and you had to . . ."

"It'll be all right," she said, and it was more of an order than a reassurance. "It's just a fencing match, right? You know how to fence."

"Not with sharps. I could get killed. I could—"

"They don't fence to the death," Iseutz said firmly. "They can't do, it simply wouldn't work, they'd run out of fencers. It's an *organised sport*. There's got to be proper conventions."

"Yes, but we don't know what they are. It's *dangerous.*"

For some reason, that made Suidas laugh. "And you can pull yourself together," Iseutz said savagely. "You're not going to let Addo fence for you, he's never even seen one of these Permian knife things." She hesitated. "You have, though, haven't you? Phrantzes said—"

"It's all right." Addo shouldered past her without actually making contact – a wonderfully delicate piece of footwork, Giraut couldn't help noticing – reached down, grabbed Suidas' wrist and hauled him to his feet. "Suidas, listen to me. You'll be all right fencing longsword?"

Suidas frowned, as though the question involved complicated mental arithmetic, then nodded.

"Splendid. That's settled. It's settled," he repeated, as Iseutz opened her mouth. She closed it again. "We all know what we're doing, and Phrantzes will be back in a minute or so with the scoring conventions, so we can think about how we're going to do this. It's just fencing," he said. "We're *good* at fencing. Nobody's going to get hurt, I promise you."

There was a moment of stillness and quiet; then Iseutz said, "Do you really train with your father with real swords?"

Addo nodded. "He's very good," he said. "He was army champion five years in a row when he was a young man.

He says the only thing foils teach you is how to be a good loser."

The first bout was single rapier. The crowd were still settling in as Phrantzes went through the local rules. It took him quite some time. When he'd finished, he said, "Have you got that?"

Giraut shook his head. "Not really."

"Any of it?"

"No."

Phrantzes took a deep breath. "Go for a disarm," he said. "You can do that?"

Giraut nodded.

"A disarm will win you the match," he said. "If you get stabbed, just stop. Don't move, drop your sword; that ends the bout. Keep your distance." He straightened up. The crowd were cheering the entrance of the other man. "And for crying out loud, don't kill him. Do you understand?"

Giraut gave him a hopeless look. "I'll try."

"Don't just try," he said. "If one of us kills a Permian champion, basically we're all dead. Do your best to win, but for God's sake be careful. All right?"

The other man was standing in the middle of the floor. Giraut stood up. His knees didn't seem up to supporting his weight, so he had to go forward or else fall over. He took a deep breath, but it caught in his throat. "They fence in a straight line," Phrantzes called after him. He had no idea what that was supposed to mean.

He was a tall man, about twenty-seven years old, with a narrow face, a small nose and clear brown eyes. He wore a green shirt, with dark horn buttons. Giraut relaxed very slightly. He was happier against opponents who were taller than him, and he could see the man was nervous; there were traces of sweat on his forehead, and he was holding his scabbarded rapier tightly enough to make his knuckles stand out. He wore old scuffed shoes, which was a bad sign; presumably they were comfortable, or lucky. There were no scars on his face or the backs of his hands, which ruined Giraut's favourite theory about how points were scored in this miserable country. As Giraut advanced to just short of long measure, he smiled: nervous, polite, well-mannered. Giraut smiled back, then pulled his face straight. The salute, he was pleased to discover, was roughly the same as at home. He made a bit of a mess of it, bringing his left hand across his body rather than level with his knee. He'd have been yelled at for that back home.

They fence in a straight line. What the hell? Didn't everybody?

The other man had drawn his sword and was waiting for him, but he didn't know what to do. Somewhere in the crowd someone laughed; private joke, maybe. He guessed, and assumed a basic business guard: high first, with his feet a little too close together, leaving his chest very slightly open. Well, there was a chance the bastard would fall for it, though it wasn't very likely.

But he did. He lunged, foot and hand together, long legs and a long arm instantly closing the measure. Giraut felt his back foot move to the right, and he twisted his body with it, watching only the point of the other man's rapier. He saw the point go past him, and felt his wrist turn and his own sword stop, but he didn't dare take his eyes off the end of the other man's blade. He saw it drop and fall to the ground with a clatter like a blacksmith's forge. He glanced down the length of his own rapier, and realised he'd stuck his opponent's sword arm, the point passing two inches above the elbow, between the muscle and the bone, and out the other side. He dragged it clear quickly, as if hoping to get it out before anybody noticed what he'd done, and took two quick steps back.

There was dead silence. The other man looked at him: shock, fear and anger. *They don't know about the demi-volte.* It hit Giraut like a hammer. They fence in a straight line; which means they don't know about stepping sideways.

Somewhere a very long way away, somebody started to clap. It was a dull, thumping noise, like the sound of someone driving in fenceposts a mile away across a valley. He counted five claps, and then others joined in, a pattering, like rain on a slate roof, then a surge and a thunder, loud enough to be uncomfortable. The other man was staring at his arm – there was blood everywhere; he clamped his hand over it, and blood oozed between the fingers and dripped on the floor, splashing in fat drops. Giraut dragged in a breath. He desperately wanted to apologise, but his mouth was dry. I didn't mean to do that, he wanted to say, I was really just getting out of the way, and I forgot the sword was sharp. At which point it occurred to him that he'd missed. The demi-volte, which he'd practised so many times he could do it with his eyes shut and still come up half-inch perfect against a target, involved a short thrust to the windpipe. He'd missed by eighteen inches. If he hadn't, his opponent would've been dead before he hit the floor.

Two men in fancy robes bustled up and pulled the other man away, leaving Giraut alone in the middle of the floor, staring at where he'd been, the dropped rapier and the wet, messy puddle of blood, shameful, like a child weeing down its leg. *It was an accident*, he tried to tell them; like the other time, accident, misunderstanding, instinct. This time, though, they were clapping and shouting and whistling and waving; on the edge of his vision he could see they were brandishing flat wooden panels about eight inches square. It nearly stopped his heart when he realised they were *pictures of him*, or supposed to be, at any rate. Someone grabbed his left wrist and towed him off the floor; he walked away backwards, the tip of his rapier scraping across the black and white tiles.

"Nicely done," said Phrantzes' voice in his ear. "Next time, though, try and spin it out a bit, can't you? We don't want to look like we're showing off."

Iseutz was fighting a slim, dark girl a head shorter than her; irrelevantly, she was serenely beautiful, like an angel in an icon. She was also visibly terrified. Understandable, after Giraut had concluded his bout with a single pass, so quick and subtle that hardly anyone had seen it. Her arm shook as she made her salute, and as soon as Iseutz levelled into a low third guard, she skipped back three paces. Iseutz stayed exactly where she was, and for a long ten seconds nothing at all happened. Then the Permian girl started to close the measure, edging in a half-pace at a time, stopping just outside full measure as if she'd come up against an invisible wall. The strange noise that followed was actually Iseutz, clicking her tongue.

In the audience, people were blowing their noses, peeling boiled eggs, opening bottles. Someone shouted something; it wasn't friendly encouragement, and there was a short blast of laughter. The Permian girl went bright red in the face, closed the measure with a single long skip and lunged. Iseutz parried on the back step, the Permian disengaged neatly, feinted high, swept low and was parried and riposted in coaching-manual style. It was proper fencing. The crowd fell silent.

Addo could see Iseutz was doing everything she could to keep from hitting the Permian girl. She was good; better, she was convincing. She timed and placed her attacks to force her opponent to defend in depth, keeping her own right shoulder up and forward, perfectly side on, the absolute minimum target. It was a beautiful performance but not a strategy; she was tiring the Permian girl out, because (not knowing the scoring rules) it was all she could think of to do. The Permian was clearly in two minds: she wanted to stay as far away as possible from the devil woman trying to kill her, but she'd lost confidence in her defence, so she was trying to control the bout by relentlessly attacking. He could see Iseutz itching to disengage and counterattack, practically every time the Permian came at her. It was an astonishing display of self-control, which she was having to disguise from the crowd and her opponent.

Eventually Iseutz's tactics worked. The Permian was getting tired, dragging her feet, overstriking. Iseutz let two chances pass, presumably because she wasn't absolutely sure. Then she closed

in for a beginner's-level disarm, flicking the sword out of the
wretched girl's hand and gently pressing her swordpoint on the
side of her throat until she yelped her surrender. She's found out,
Addo realised, just how good she is. There'll be no living with
her after this.

"What was all that about?" she panted to him as she plodded
off the floor, carefully not looking back at the frantically cheering
crowd. "I was better than that when I was twelve."

Addo grinned. "I can only assume they're lulling us into a true
sense of security."

"They're rubbish."

"I do hope so," Addo said. "I really do hope so."

Iseutz tried to kick off her shoes, but they stuck to her feet.
She put a hand on his shoulder, lifted one foot and slowly
dragged the shoe off it. "I thought they were mad keen on fencing in this country," she said. Then the other shoe. Then she let
go of him and spread her toes on the tiles. "Who's next?"

"Suidas," Addo said. "Then me."

It came to him in a flash of inspiration, in the middle of the
salute. Pretend he's a student, and you're teaching him to fence.

That made it simple. The teacher makes the student do what
he wants him to; he's always better, always in control, but striv-
ing to draw the student out, encourage him to have confidence in
himself, right up to the point where the teacher bats the sword
out of his hands, trips up his feet and grins at him, flat on his
back and looking up the fuller of a blade resting lightly on his
neck. Confident, yes, but not overconfident. Barring some ridiculous accident, there's never any danger of either party getting
hurt, because the instructor knows exactly what he's doing.

It made for a good show, too. Suidas made his pupil work
with the edge, never giving him room to threaten a thrust, while
always keeping him covered with the point, just in case something went wrong. He taught him why you shouldn't allow
yourself to be cramped up, the virtues of the close, binding style,

the pre-eminence of leverage and economy of movement. He let him slash ferociously, until the edge of his beautiful Type Eighteen longsword looked like an old farm saw, then taught him a few basic lessons in mechanical advantage. When he was clearly too tired to be able to take anything else in, he drew him into a wild lunge, sidestepped and knocked him silly with the pommel as he tumbled past, on the grounds that humiliation is the best teacher of them all.

"They're useless," Suidas said cheerfully, slamming the longsword back in the case and collapsing on to a bench. "And the crowd love us. Listen to that, will you?"

Addo was listening, but he was inclined to put a slightly different interpretation on the vast noise behind him. It had changed just a little since Suidas made his fancy bow and stalked off the floor, while stewards dragged his unconscious opponent away. They don't care about rapier or smallsword or longsword, he decided. That's not what they came to see.

Phrantzes was standing next to him. He had something wrapped in a cloth. "It's quite a good one, apparently," he was saying. "I borrowed it from the Master of the Guild, it's his own personal messer."

There was something wrong with Addo's throat; it felt tight and sore, and he wondered if it was the early stages of glandular fever. He thought about it and realised it was probably fear; the real thing, as opposed to the mild anxiety he'd lived with most of his life. And what a truly wonderful time to make its acquaintance.

Phrantzes put the cloth bundle down on the table with a bump. Addo stared at it, then pulled away the cloth; it tangled in something, and he realised his hand was shaking. The crowd was chanting something. It sounded like a name. He made a special effort, steadied his hand and removed the cloth.

It looked like a farm tool. The hilt was two slabs of unpolished wood (ash, he guessed, though he didn't really know about that sort of thing) riveted to the tang, which was just an extension of the blade, which was about two feet long, roughly a thumb-length wide, single-edged and slightly curved. It had a clipped point, not much use for thrusting, and a false edge, half-sharp. The true edge was thin and sharp as a razor. A fine tool for hedging or sharpening fence posts, so long as you were careful how you used it. One careless slip and you could do yourself a serious injury. It made him feel slightly sick just looking at it.

"That's a messer, is it?" he heard himself say.

"Apparently," Phrantzes replied.

You'd have to be mad to fight with something like that; or desperate, or too poor to buy a real weapon. There wasn't even a proper crossguard, to keep the other man's blade from riding up in a bind and slicing into your knuckles. He could see no defences, no wards, maybe one or two extremely dangerous parries; and it was short, presumably front-heavy, so almost certainly horribly quick. And it was what twelve hundred Permians had come to see.

"I think they're ready for you," Phrantzes said.

He picked up the messer, but somehow it slid through his hand and clattered on the table. Instinctively he shrank back, terribly aware of the sharp edge, temporarily out of control, which would slit his flesh on the slightest contact. *Pull yourself together, for pity's sake*; the voice in his head sounded just enough like his father to make him obey. *If you're this scared of your own sword, then God help you when you face the other man.* He reached out and closed his fingers tight around the hilt; firm, like a good handshake, like shaking hands with the only friend and ally he had in the room.

Longsword was easy; it was *safe*. You had three feet of steel to hide behind, and both hands to guide it with. That and a good guard, and you could hold off a small army. This thing was grotesque. He looked up at Phrantzes and saw he was terrified too. He smiled. "Wish me luck," he said.

"Of course."

"Oh well," he said, and walked out on to the floor.

The other man was over six feet tall, slim, broad-shouldered, with a shaven head and a badly healed scar running from his left eyebrow down to his chin. He wore a sleeveless white shirt and knee breeches, and his feet were bare. There were smaller scars on his forearms, white lines under the thick black hair, like animals hiding in undergrowth. Watching from the wings, Suidas couldn't make out his name, even though everybody in the crowd was yelling it; something like Langros, but it wasn't that. Standing next to him, Addo looked like a girl.

Here they fight with messers.

He tried to look, but he couldn't. His eyes closed, and the volume of sheer crude noise crashed over him like a wave; and he was in Permia, and he was nineteen years old, and it was raining.

Later, much later, he'd found out what had happened. The Irrigator, the greatest strategic genius of the age, had sent a squadron of cavalry to fail to capture a bridge, by way of a diversion, to draw away the Permian infantry. But something went wrong. The cavalry succeeded; they captured the bridge, and the Permians withdrew their infantry back down the road, along which the Irrigator, expecting it to be empty, had sent a supply convoy.

It hadn't mattered, because as soon as he realised what had happened, the Irrigator sent three hundred dragoons to deal with the Permian infantry, who were wiped out and ceased to be a nuisance. But before that ...

They'd driven straight into them. It was a comedy. The Permians took them for their own wagons, they took the Permians for their own auxiliaries; it was only when they were close enough to see the rank emblems on the officer's tunic facings that the convoy realised something was wrong, and if they'd kept their heads and just kept on going, they'd probably have got away with it. But some idiot with a bow shot an arrow. The

Permians looked stunned, then figured it out. The Scherian carters were armed, after a fashion. There was a very short fight.

He'd done the right thing, to begin with. He jumped off the box of his cart and ran, which was what the old-timers had told him to do, and everything would've been fine if it hadn't been for the rain, which had turned the bottoms of the ruts in the road to greasy mud. He slipped and landed on his hands and knees, and when he'd tried to scramble up, the end of his scabbard was lodged between his ankles and he fell over again; and then there was a Permian coming straight at him.

He didn't look like a problem. He wasn't a soldier. At that stage in the war, they were hauling men out of the mines and sending them straight to the front. He had no uniform, no armour or helmet, no spear or shield; just a short sword or a long knife. He had one boot and one bare foot – lost the other boot in the mud, most likely.

Suidas Deutzel fancied himself as a swordsman. The government had bought him a brand new Type Fifteen, which he hadn't had a chance to use on anybody yet. The Type Fifteen was the finest single-handed sword ever issued; everybody said so. And the Permian was in the way, blocking the road. He had to go. Suidas jumped to his feet, drew his sword and composed himself magnificently into a high front guard.

The Permian kicked his left kneecap with his booted foot. He fell over.

He landed in deep mud, sitting in a wagon-wheel rut that came up almost to his waist. The sides of the rut gripped him, and the mud was too soft to give him a footing. He couldn't move. He lifted his sword. The Permian kicked it out of his hand and it sailed away, end over end, an asymmetric curling flight into the edge of his field of vision. The Permian raised his right hand and swung. Instinctively, Suidas put his own right hand up in front of his face. The front inch of the messer sliced through the web between his thumb and forefinger. It didn't hurt. As the Permian lifted his arm for another stroke, Suidas understood why there was no pain; he was going to die, he was dead already, there's no feeling in dead flesh. His bladder and sphincter relaxed. He opened his mouth. The horror of the moment of death swelled up inside him, worse than any pain.

The finishing cut never came; obviously, because here was Suidas Deutzel, ten years later, still alive. The next thing he remembered was waking up on a bed in a big tent, looking into the brown, weary face of a Blueskin doctor, who'd just spent half an hour sewing his right hand back together. He remembered the hospital tent, the prisoner-of-war stockade and the prisoner exchange perfectly, every detail. After the exchange, he re-enlisted, forced his way into a good line infantry regiment and spent the last two and a half years of the war at the front. He kept score: seventeen Blueskins, twenty-three Aram Chantat and forty-six Permians. He returned home with seven bravery medals, a field commission (no pension) and a long pearwood box the size of a coffin, which took two men to lift it. At first he kept the box next to his bed; but when his drinking led to money problems and there was a real danger of the bailiffs confiscating his possessions, he left it at his uncle's house, sealed in five places to keep the old man from temptation. Not that the contents of the box were worth anything, at least not in Scheria. In Permia, maybe: seventy-three messers, some of them barely used. He kept the rest of them in another safe place, which nobody at all knew about.

It wasn't going well. After the first disastrous exchange, Addo concentrated on keeping out of the way. But the Permian was as agile as a cat and showed no signs of getting tired, which was more than he could say for himself. He didn't dare wipe the blood out of his eyes, in case the Permian chopped his exposed hand off; that meant he had to squint, just when he needed to be able to see perfectly. He tried not to pay any attention to the jeering from the crowd, but it was starting to get to him, because they were quite right. He *was* a coward, he *was* scared shitless, and he was one small mistake away from the end of his life.

The Permian grinned at him, feinted left, dodged right, fooled him; at the last moment he somehow contrived to cringe out of the path of the cut. He did a backwards standing jump, nearly toppled, caught his balance just in time. The messer swished past the tip of his nose.

Pointless, he thought, and foolishly stubborn; like a chess player grimly, selfishly playing out the very end of a game when he's down to his king and the other man's still got his queen and both castles. But his body kept moving, the thickness of a sheet of paper away from the fast, sharp edge. He could feel his concentration slipping. It'd be so easy to give up, allow the Permian to demonstrate the self-evident truth, that he was the better man. Keeping going was dishonest, like pleading not guilty when everybody knew you'd done it.

The Permian fooled him again; he wasn't sure how, but he saw the messer coming and knew he couldn't quite get out of the way this time. He felt it brush against him, he didn't know where. Instantly he relaxed, and heard the clatter of his own messer on the tiles. There was a great roar, and he slid to the ground, landing in a puddle of something. To his shame, he smelt that it wasn't blood. Hell of a way to go.

More noise, deafening, the joy of perfect strangers at his miserable undoing. Then someone was dragging him along by his feet, and he was still alive.

"Don't beat yourself up about it," Phrantzes was saying. "Everybody loses sooner or later."

An Imperial surgeon was sewing up his face. The pain was appalling, but he kept still and quiet because he was too ashamed to wince. Iseutz was watching, but his eyes were blurred and he couldn't see her expression. Probably just as well. His left trouser leg was warm and soaking wet. He ought to be wishing he'd died, but he couldn't. Too weak to die, too humiliated to live. The surgeon leaned forward – for a moment he thought he was going to kiss him, but instead he bit neatly through the suture and turned away. "He'll be fine," he heard the surgeon say. No he won't. Not ever.

"You were lucky," Phrantzes said. "Four inches down and he'd have cut your jugular vein. As it is, you'll just have to grow a beard."

Giraut was peering over Phrantzes' shoulder. He'd seen people look like that at funerals, paying their respects to the white, cold dead. Behind him, Tzimisces was talking loudly to three men in dark red gowns. He laughed, and one of the men nodded vigorously.

"Anyway, it's over and we're all more or less in one piece," Phrantzes went on. "Which is a hell of a lot more than I could've hoped for not so long ago. Well, you'll have to excuse me, I've got to go and talk to the Permians about this reception. Well done."

Well done. Was he trying to be funny?

Perhaps the worst thing about the world at that moment was that it was so horribly full of people. No sooner had Phrantzes gone away than Iseutz and Giraut came and hovered over him. "Are you all right?" Iseutz asked. Giraut stood a pace behind her – long measure – wearing an embarrassed-in-the-presence-of-suffering look.

He nodded. He had a good excuse for not talking, though it was in fact a lie. The wound was only just starting to stiffen up.

"You did pretty well not to get killed," Iseutz said.

He managed to shut her up with a grunt, followed by an exaggerated wince. "Sorry," she said, "you can't talk, I understand. I'm going to speak to the creep about this. That wasn't fencing, it was ... " She opened her mouth, but maybe the word she'd chosen was too big to get out from between her teeth. "I'll talk to him," she said. "I'll make sure he listens."

She patted him lightly on the shoulder, and his flesh crawled. She turned away quickly. Giraut nodded gravely and bolted after her. Addo screwed his eyes shut, but that pulled on the cut on his forehead, which was just starting to scab over. He could feel his heartbeat through both wounds, as though being damaged was his only evidence that he was still alive.

"We can be pleased with ourselves," Tzimisces said. "It all went off extremely well."

He looked perfectly at home: a wine glass in his hand, a freshly pressed shirt under his gown, the reception politely raucous behind him. He was smiling. He reminded Phrantzes of a lizard.

"In fact," he went on, "it's hard to see how it could've gone better, in the circumstances. We won three out of four events, they won the only match they care about, nobody got killed, so we're all still friends. No harm done, and I think we can say we've made a pretty solid start."

Phrantzes could think of nothing to say. Fortunately, he wasn't called on for a contribution.

"I had a word with the representatives of their Board of Control," Tzimisces went on, "and off the record, they don't mind in the least if we wipe the floor with them in rapier and longsword. Quite the reverse. Apparently they're quite concerned about the recent trend towards what they regard as effete Western disciplines. If we can put their fencers off fighting rapier, so much the better; they'll stick to messers, which is the traditional form, and that'll please the Board. Longsword's always been a minority form here, and we didn't completely humiliate them, so they're not bothered about that. As for the girls, they're ambivalent about women in the sport, to say the least. There's a long tradition of it, granted, but ..."

Phrantzes nodded and made an I'm-listening noise. He'd looked all round the room, but he couldn't see Suidas anywhere. He became aware that the lizard had stopped talking, and tried to remember where the conversation had got to.

"I don't see young Deutzel anywhere," Tzimisces said. "He really ought to be making the rounds. After all, he's our national champion."

Phrantzes got away with a nod.

"What was all that about, by the way?" Tzimisces went on. "Deutzel was supposed to be fencing messer, wasn't he? Only I made rather a thing of it: our champion, their national form. Perhaps next time you change the game plan, you might have a word with me first."

"It was a last-minute thing," Phrantzes managed to say.

"Fair enough." Tzimisces was looking thoughtfully at him, as if trying to decide if he was safe to eat. "And we've got to hold something in reserve for the big match in the capital, so it's worked out quite well. Maybe we should have Bryennius fence messer at the next place."

"I don't——" Phrantzes cut himself short and took a breath. "I don't think he's up to it," he said. "It wouldn't be safe."

That, apparently, was a good enough reason. "Well, we don't want anything like that," Tzimisces said. "So, we'll stick with Carnufex for Beaute, and save Deutzel for the grand finale. Yes, I'm quite happy with that." He gave Phrantzes what was presumably meant to be a warm smile. "Congratulations," he said. "You've handled it all very well indeed."

I haven't done anything, Phrantzes wanted to yell. Just as well he didn't; it'd have sounded like he was a prisoner being dragged away. "Thank you," he muttered.

"But you'd better just cut along and find Deutzel," Tzimisces added. "I know he's been dry for quite a while now, but this would be a very bad time for him to have a relapse."

Phrantzes hadn't thought of that. "I'll find him," he said, and fled.

Addo chose a Permian at random, cleared his throat, smiled and said, "Excuse me, but where's the . . .?"

The Permian looked at him; not unfriendly, but puzzled. "Excuse me?"

"The . . . um."

"The what, sorry?"

"I wish to urinate. Where should I go?"

The Permian frowned and pointed to a door. "Thank you," Addo said, and headed for it.

Outside, the air smelt of rain. Addo looked round. It was too dark to see beyond the dim leakage of light showing through the half-open door. He unbuckled his belt and lowered his trousers.

"Addo? Is that you?"

He froze. He hadn't seen Suidas, crouched on the ground in the shadows. He mumbled an apology and hauled his trousers up, as Suidas slowly dragged himself to his feet.

"How are you feeling?" Suidas said.

"Oh, could be worse."

Suidas shook his head. His face was in shadow. "There'll be a scar," he said.

"Not to worry. It's not like I was ever a thing of beauty."

Suidas moved away a little. "The important thing," he said, "is finding a way of dealing with it. In my case, I killed every Permian I could find. Then, after the war, I drank myself stupid. I wouldn't recommend either of those. On balance, they caused more problems than they solved. I'm sorry," he added.

"What for?"

"Fine." Suidas shook his head. "It doesn't alter what happened, though. But I really am sorry." Suddenly he laughed. "Ludicrous, isn't it? Here we are again, in Permia, only this time the orders are *don't* kill Permians. A man could get seriously confused."

Addo looked at him carefully. "My father says you were a war hero."

"Does he? Then it must be true, mustn't it?"

"When I agreed to come here, I asked him who I'd be going with. He made some enquiries. He let me read the dispatches, about the time when you—"

"You don't want to go believing everything you read," Suidas said. "And don't ever talk about that stuff again. Please," he added. "All right?"

"Of course."

"Wonderful. And now I'll leave you to pee in peace. You must be bursting."

The lodgings provided for them had once been a temple, built before the Empire came, before it split into East and West. The names of its gods were still discernible, engraved on pedestals of missing statues, written under painted figures faded into blank silhouettes; but the language and alphabet had been mislaid at some point, and nobody knew what they meant. Each of the party was given a chapel to sleep in: a plain, narrow bed in the centre of a huge square room with an impossibly high vaulted ceiling; no other furniture. No fireplace, either. Instead, they were each provided with a small iron charcoal brazier, military issue.

"Don't use the bloody things, whatever you do," Suidas warned them. "No chimney. You'll be dead by morning from the fumes."

Iseutz stared up into the belly of the dome above her head, shivered and decided she'd risk it; better to suffocate painlessly in her sleep than freeze to death. Eventually she got the thing lit, using the last of the tinder she'd brought from home. The brazier gave out a faint orange glow, not nearly enough to read by, and no perceptible heat. She pulled the sheets and the one thin blanket off the bed, wrapped them around her like bandages, and looked round for a corner to huddle in. It was, of course, a circular room.

Giraut's room was on two levels. There was a raised section, like a stage, where a high altar had once stood. The floor was veined green marble. He lay down on top of the bed and immediately fell asleep.

Addo's chapel was being used as overflow storage for the Fencers' Guild library. There were books stacked everywhere on the floor; you could've built a fortress out of them and held off an army. There was also a lamp. He lit it, picked up a book at random and lay down on the bed, propped up against the head-board so his face wouldn't touch the pillows. The book was an early edition of *The Fencer's Mirror*, a text he was well acquainted with. But this version was about a hundred years earlier than his father's copy, with strange, stick-like figures instead of the mag-nificently muscled, superbly bearded demigods he'd grown up with, and the guards and moves they illustrated were ever so slightly different. He leafed slowly through until he came to a picture of two men facing each other with long, curved knives. *Here they fight with messers. God help them.* He retrieved the bread and cheese he'd liberated from the reception and settled down to read.

In spite of the cold, Suidas eventually fell asleep, and dreamt, as he did occasionally, of the destruction of Flos Verjan. In his dream, he was standing on a bridge, looking down into the tur-bulent waters of a river. Suddenly the river rose, as if waking up, and lifted the bridge, with him still on it, and swept it away. He turned his head and saw the city; the river was taking him there, he was riding on its back like a cavalryman. He was so high, he was looking down on the city, as though he was approaching the edge of a waterfall. Through a curtain of fine spray he could see streets, buildings, crowds of people staring up at him. *I can't help that*, he thought, and the wave started to fall, the streets and the people grew larger. It was all right, though; all he had to do was cross the bridge and he'd be safe. He took a step, but there was someone in the way, a Permian with a messer in his left hand. He turned, but the same man was blocking the other side – which shouldn't be happening, because the general had sent men to secure this bridge, no matter what the cost. He reached for his own messer but it wasn't there.

Phrantzes couldn't get to sleep, so he lay awake and worried about his wife, stuck in a convent with sixty elderly, hostile nuns. It'd be cold there (Sphagia despised the cold) and there'd be bells every hour to call the nuns to prayer, and she snarled like a tiger if anything disturbed her sleep, and they ate bare bread and salted porridge, so the poor girl must be starving. After three or four hours of that, he got up and lit the lamp, sat on the edge of the bed and tried to think what to do about Addo.

Tzimisces was given a room, but he didn't sleep there.

Giraut was woken by Lieutenant Totila, looking singularly beautiful in gilded parade armour and a floor-length purple cloak with a white fur collar. "Breakfast," he said. "In the chancel."

"The what?"

"Through the door," Totila said, "left down the corridor till you come to a pair of bronze and silver gates. Straight through, you can't miss it."

Nor did he. It was vast, and the walls were decorated with frescoes of the torments of the damned in Hell. There was a table in the middle of the floor, like an island in an ocean. Iseutz was there, and Phrantzes. They were eating honey cakes.

"Morning," Phrantzes said brightly. "Lieutenant Totila, won't you join us?"

Totila smiled. "On duty, alas. I just thought I'd let you know I've been assigned to escort you as far as Beaute. I hope that's all right."

"Excellent," Phrantzes said, and Iseutz gave him a sour look. "You've taken such good care of us so far."

Totila smiled, turned crisply and marched out, his heels clattering on the black slate floor. Giraut sat down. There was one honey cake left; also a big loaf that looked like a millstone and a tall brown stone jar.

"What's in the jar?" he asked.

"Pickled cabbage."

"Ah." He reached for the loaf. There was nothing to cut it with. He took the last honey cake.

"Political Officer Tzimisces," Iseutz said, "is nowhere to be found. I looked in his room and his bed hasn't been slept in. Of course, that's presupposing he sleeps in a bed, instead of hanging upside down from a hook in the ceiling."

Giraut frowned. "Is there a hook?"

Iseutz nodded. "As it happens, yes, there is. Probably for hanging a thurible from."

"A what?"

"Incense burner. My cousin's a priest," she explained. She turned to Phrantzes. "Well, where is he?"

"I'm sorry, I haven't the faintest idea. I was hoping to talk to him myself."

They heard footsteps and saw Addo coming towards them. He looked tired, and had a book under his arm. "You're too late," Iseutz called out. "We've eaten it all."

Addo sat down, took a folding knife from his pocket and cut a slice of bread. "What's in the—"

"Guess."

"Pickled—"

"Yes."

"Right." He bit into the bread, and the noise it made was just like what Giraut imagined breaking teeth would sound like. "We're going to have to do something about food," he said.

"I imagine Lieutenant Totila would be the man to talk to," Phrantzes said. "The Imperial stuff was really rather good. And that was just field rations. He's going to be our escort, by the way, at least as far as Beaute."

Addo swallowed hard to clear his mouth. "Does anyone know when we're leaving?"

"I'm afraid not," Phrantzes said. "That's one of the things I need to talk to Tzimisces about."

"Where's Suidas?" Iseutz asked.

"I haven't seen anybody," Giraut said.

"Escaped, probably. Deserted. Or wandered off in search of sausages. Not that I give a damn, provided he brings us some." She turned, grabbed the book Addo had leaned up against the pickle jar, and squinted at the spine. "What's that you're reading?"

"*Principles of Elementary Swordsmanship*," Addo replied. "I found it in my room. There's a lot of books in there." He smiled at her. "No poetry, though. Unless you count fifteen thousand lines of blank verse about poleaxe fighting."

"Read it," she replied. "Birthday present from my uncle," she explained. "Not a complete dead loss, because it was good-quality parchment, nice and thick. I pumiced it down and used it as a commonplace book."

"That's all right, then," Addo said, gently retrieving the book and closing it. On the wall opposite, an army of the dead, skeletons in full armour, were slaughtering people in a marketplace; they wielded short, wide swords, a bit like messers. "Actually, there's some quite interesting stuff in there. Early texts from the late Separatist period, things I've heard about but never thought I'd ever see a copy."

"Fill your pockets," Iseutz said with her mouth full. "I don't suppose they'll be missed, and we've got a long ride ahead."

Addo looked vaguely shocked. Phrantzes took a sip of milk (which was all there was to drink) and said, "I need to have a word with Suidas. I'll go and see if he's in his room."

After he'd gone, Iseutz said, "I wonder what that's all about."

"Excuse me?"

"Well," Iseutz said, "I imagine our glorious national champion is in big trouble. If he isn't, he should be."

"But he won," Addo said.

"He shouldn't have been fighting longsword at all," Iseutz snapped back. "He was meant to be doing that short sword thing, but he chickened out. Went all to pieces. If you hadn't rescued him, God knows what'd have happened."

Addo looked away. Iseutz sighed impatiently. "Well, it's not good enough," she said. "The rest of us are here because we have no choice, but as far as I can gather, he's being paid a very large sum of money. And he's supposed to be competent with those billhook things."

"Messers," Addo said quietly.

"Whatever. As it is, the moment he sees one, he goes all boneless, and you nearly get killed."

Giraut looked at Addo. "I think he realises that," he said gently.

"It wasn't his fault," Iseutz said. "I think you did remarkably well," she went on, looking past rather than at him, "considering you'd never seen one before, and it was sharps. The point is, you shouldn't have had to. I mean, Deutzel's a *professional*."

"None of us expected to be fighting with real swords," Giraut said. "And you just don't know when you're going to go all to pieces. Believe me."

"It's all right, really," Addo said. "I mean, if this was a war, if we were soldiers, we'd be—"

"But it isn't and we aren't." Iseutz glowered at him and he looked away. "I think the whole idea is, we're here so there *won't* be a war and we *won't* be soldiers. To which end, we ought to have someone who knows what he's doing fencing big-knife."

Addo grinned. "That lets me out, then."

"And me," Giraut said quickly.

"But it's fine, honestly," Addo said, before Iseutz could get going again. "I've been doing single sword and sword-and-buckler for years, the moves aren't all that different, and Suidas is better than me at longsword."

"Is he?"

"He's very good," Addo said. "And clearly, for reasons we don't know and probably wouldn't understand if we did, he has got some sort of problem with messers, which means he can't do that stuff. Making him do it would be sending him to his death. And then," he added, looking straight at Iseutz, "we'd all be in trouble. Well, wouldn't we?"

"I don't get all that," Giraut broke in. "They fight with sharps, right? So, obviously, from time to time people must get killed. You fight with real swords, it's got to happen. But we're being told don't kill anyone, don't get killed, or else there'll be a war. It doesn't make sense."

Addo shook his head. "I don't think logic's got much to do

with it," he said. "Besides, I get the impression that they fight with sharps here and don't get killed or cut up."

Giraut raised an eyebrow. "What makes you think that?"

"Well, the specimens we fought with last night, for one thing. They weren't all that badly scarred up, and they were grown-ups; our age, maybe a bit older. If they fought to the death here, we'd be facing a bunch of adolescents, because nobody would live long enough to start shaving."

"Maybe they start later," Iseutz suggested.

"I don't think so," Addo replied. "You saw, they were a pretty reasonable standard."

"They were rubbish," Iseutz said. "That's why we won."

"They were good enough that they must've started young," Addo said. "I don't know about you two, but I've been fencing since I was six years old."

"Seven," Iseutz conceded.

"Six," Giraut said. "But maybe they train with foils till they're sixteen or something, I don't know. Still, the point about scars is a good one. You can't mess about with sharp swords for very long without getting carved up."

"Not unless you're very good at it, or you've been trained since childhood. Or both, quite likely." Addo leaned forward a little. "Also, the books I was looking at last night, there's nothing in them about foils. And there's much more emphasis on wards and measure than what we're used to. Thinking about it, I think we won, or at any rate you two won, because you fight a much more aggressive game than they're used to. It stands to reason. We do safe fencing, so we don't care so much about taking risks – you misjudge it and get it wrong and you lose a point, that's all. Because you're both very good, you've also got very sound defences, but you're still fencing like you're using foils. Their whole approach is far less aggressive."

"I noticed that," Giraut said. "They're all wait-for-him-to-come-to-me. I got the idea he wasn't expecting me to come at him so hard, or so early."

Iseutz looked thoughtful, then nodded her head sharply. "I think you could be right," she said, "and it's worth bearing in mind. Come out hard . . ."

"Which is what I do anyway," Giraut said. "I know defence is my weak spot, so I always try and crowd out the fight."

"Possibly why you were chosen," Addo said, and suddenly Giraut went still and quiet. "Though you do need to be careful."

"And he's proved he can handle himself against sharps," Iseutz said. "Well, once, at least."

Giraut was about to say something, then thought better of it. Addo gave him a very slight nod, as if to say, *It's all right.* "Anyhow," Addo went on, "to get back to the original question, I think they do fight sharps here without causing undue mayhem, and we're expected to do the same. It's like boxing," he went on. "You can kill someone with your bare hands quite easily, but boxers don't slaughter each other. They know how to defend themselves and they don't tend to try and kill the other man, just knock him down. It's going to be hard on us," he went on, "and I really wish someone had seen fit to tell us before we left home."

"Phrantzes knew," Iseutz said grimly. "I know he did."

Addo shrugged. "They'd never have got a team if they'd told us. But we're just going to have to make the best of it and do what we can. And the same goes," he said, looking at Iseutz, "for the messers. We need to learn as we go along, think carefully about what we're going to do, and, I'd suggest, get some fairly intensive practice in before the next fixture. That's just common sense, surely."

Iseutz looked at him, then burst out laughing. "I'm sorry," she said, "but you should see yourself. Just looking at you makes me want to salute."

Addo turned away, blushing furiously. "Sorry," he said, "I really didn't mean to . . ."

"It's perfectly all right," Iseutz said. "It's just as well *somebody's* decided to take charge. And I really don't give a damn who it is, so long as it's not me."

Suidas wasn't in his room, and nobody could remember having seen him since the reception. Terrified, Phrantzes hurried out into the courtyard, where Totila's men were washing down the chaise. Totila wasn't there.

"Who's in charge?" Phrantzes snapped.

"Sir." A very young man in full armour, with a scarf wound round his face until only the tip of his nose was visible, sprang to attention. "Second Lieutenant Tzazo, sir."

"Have you seen Suidas Deutzel?"

"Confirmed." Phrantzes guessed that was military for yes. "I saw him leaving the building early this morning."

Phrantzes winced. "You didn't happen to ask where he was going?"

"I was unable to do so, sir. He was climbing out of a window." Tzazo stopped and looked at him. "Are you feeling all right, sir?"

"It's all right," Phrantzes said, once he'd caught his breath. "Which window?"

Tzazo pointed. "He got up on to the roof and I lost sight of him," he went on. He hesitated, then added, "I did report it to Colonel Tzimisces."

Colonel Tzimisces. "You did?"

"Yes, sir. About an hour ago. He said he'd deal with it."

Phrantzes breathed out slowly until his lungs were empty. "Thank you," he said. "You've been most helpful."

"Sir."

No time to waste. First stop, the market, which he'd noticed on the way in. The only thing of any potential value he'd been able to steal was a fistful of silver spoons, which he'd pocketed during the reception. When he examined them by lamplight in his room, he saw they were marked with some sort of crest, which was a nuisance. Still, there had to be competent metalworkers in this town who could grind off a simple engraving and make good. Silver was disappointing – he doubted it'd be worth much in Permia, in the same way salt water isn't valuable in the middle of the sea. But what he wanted to buy would be cheap.

He sold the spoons quite easily to a fat man with white hair, who gave him one tiny gold coin and four cartwheel-sized coppers, the faces worn completely smooth. By their weight, they were Eastern Imperial, and had presumably been circulating since before Independence. No silver currency in Permia.

Finding someone who'd sell him a messer was no problem. Choosing which stall to give his custom to was impossible. Not just one or two stalls, or half a dozen. When he asked someone in the fish market, he was directed to a walled courtyard with tall iron gates. It was packed to bursting with messer-sellers. For about a second he lost his balance; long enough to stagger and put his hand on the wall to keep himself from falling. People were watching him; a bit early in the day, their faces said. One or two looked as though they'd recognised him, but he couldn't help that.

It was like being deafened by a great surge of noise, except that it wasn't his hearing that was being overwhelmed; some other sense, one he hadn't realised he'd got, or only dimly guessed. There were at least twenty stalls; just tables, with a big cloth thrown over them, and on the tables lay messers, twenty or thirty of them on each. He'd never realised it before, but there were different varieties, styles and types and sub-types; messers with and without fullers, double-fullered, some deeply curved, some almost straight. There were rounded or sharply clipped points, blades of even width or swelling slightly towards the point; no handguard at all or a simple cross, or the tang drawn out into a rat's-tail that bent back to form a knuckle-bow. The tables filled three sides of the courtyard; standing in the middle, Suidas felt like he was facing a jury. There was no question of choosing one. He wanted them all.

But that wasn't going to be possible right now, and he desperately needed a messer, because if he didn't get one soon, he was going to stop breathing. They'd be after him, he knew that, and he didn't have much time. He walked up to the furthest stall and fought to keep his hands by his sides.

There was a man sitting behind the table. He was looking at Suidas as if he was trying to make up his mind about something. Suidas put his coins on the table and said, "What'll that buy me?"

"What?"

His accent. Also, he'd slurred his words. "What'll that buy me?" he repeated slowly.

The man shrugged. "How many do you want?"

Stupid question. "One. Two," Suidas corrected.

"All right." The man thought for an interminable moment. "What about this one and this one?"

It was a bit like asking a man standing at the altar, facing his veiled bride for the first time, if she'd do or if he wanted to see some other selections. But Suidas looked. The first one was unfullered, slightly longer than usual, only by an inch or so. The curve was quite pronounced and the false edge was about a thumb's length, making for a useful point. There was a plain, rather chunky brass cross an index-finger long. You could get both hands on the grip, which ended in a stubby bird's-head hook for a pommel. The scales were plain white wood, with three rivets. Someone had tried to make it look a bit nicer by filing notches and grooves on the back, but had given up about halfway down; probably just as well, because he hadn't had a very good eye. There were firescale marks and a couple of slag inclusions on the blade, and grinding marks from where it had been sharpened on a farm grindstone. He lifted it about half an inch off the table, and let it go immediately, like it was red-hot.

"Aren't you one of the Scherians?" the man said.

"Me? No."

"You sound like a Scherian. I saw you at the fencing."

"Not me," Suidas said.

The other one's blade was almost straight, flaring from an inch width at the hilt to an inch and three-eighths at the base of the false edge. It had three thin fullers, three-quarter-length. No cross, just a plain stag's-horn grip, the crown of the antler forming a basic handstop. There was a small nick in the edge two fingers down from the point.

"That'll be fine," Suidas mumbled.

The man nodded. "I'll throw in a bit of rag to wrap them in," he said.

"Thanks."

"You sure you're not one of the fencers? You look really like one of them."

"If I was a Scherian, I'd probably know."

The man shrugged, and twisted a piece of cloth three times round the messers. Even covered, they couldn't possibly have been anything else. "So," he said, "where are you from?"

"Mesembrotia."

"Never heard of it."

"It's a very long way away."

"Right, then. There you go. Good luck when you get to Beaute."

He tucked the bundle under his arm and fled, heading back the way he'd come. He hadn't given much thought to how he was going to get back inside the building; climbing the facade with two swords clamped in his teeth didn't appeal much, but neither did walking up to the guards posted on the door. In the event, he didn't have to decide. He walked though the gates of the courtyard and found Tzimisces waiting for him.

"I thought I'd find you here," Tzimisces said.

He really wanted to run. "Sounds like you were looking for me."

Tzimisces shrugged. "You shouldn't have stolen the spoons," he said.

"What spoons?"

Tzimisces ignored him. "The man you sold them to took them straight to the Guild," he said. "He knew he'd get a good price, in return for a description of the seller. It's hard to imagine anything more embarrassing. In case you've forgotten, we're guests in this country. The idea is to improve diplomatic relations, not cause an incident." He paused, then sighed and pulled a more-in-sorrow face. "Next time you want spending money, come to me. Understood?"

Under the cloth, two messers. He drew strength from them. "Understood."

"I said you wanted the money so you could go out and find a girl," Tzimisces said. "They weren't exactly impressed, but I thought they'd probably be able to relate to that better than if I told them the truth. You need to get a grip on yourself."

Suidas took a long step back into middle measure. "Nobody's perfect." But Tzimisces only laughed. "You'd better get back inside," he said. "Phrantzes is looking for you. He thinks you've deserted."

After he'd seen Phrantzes, Suidas went in search of food. He found the remains of breakfast: a few rock-hard crusts of bread, and the untouched pickled cabbage. He opened the jar, scooped out a medium-sized dose and swallowed it without chewing.

"You're a brave man." He hadn't heard Addo approaching.

"I was hungry," he said, wiping his mouth. "Besides, it's not so bad if you don't chew. We ate a lot of it during the War. Well, it was that or rats, and when you've had a hard day, you haven't got the time or the energy to catch rats."

Addo had noticed the bundle on the table. He didn't say anything about it. "I was meaning to have a word with you," he said.

"Sure. How's the face, by the way?"

"Stiff," Addo replied. "But they reckon it's starting to heal. Look, about these messer things. Will you teach me?"

For a moment, all Suidas could do was stare. "Please?" Addo

said. "Only I haven't got a clue, and I really don't want to be caught out again like I was last night. I thought we could get hold of a couple of the things and grind off the edges so we can practise safely. You know about them, don't you?"

Suidas hesitated, then nodded. "A bit."

"That's a bit more than I do. I'm guessing it's something like single sword."

"No, it isn't."

Addo nodded. "Just as well you told me, then. Well? It'd be a great help."

"Sure." Suidas realised he was rubbing his hands together so fiercely he was hurting himself. "I take it that means . . ."

"Yes," Addo said. "Well, you're better at longsword than me, so it sort of makes sense, doesn't it?

He was rubbing his hands because the scar was itching. "I don't like messers," he said.

"I'd gathered that." Addo was trying hard not to stare. Suidas covered as much of the scar as he could with his left thumb. "So, what d'you think?"

"Why not?" Suidas smiled, a big, deliberate grin. "I'll tell Phrantzes to get us a couple of the bloody things. Shouldn't be a problem. This country's awash with them."

Addo wasn't looking at the bundle on the table either. Presumably he'd learned from his father how to make things invisible. Tact and tactics, a gentleman's education.

"Have we got to?" Iseutz said.

"Yes." Phrantzes looked very sad. "It's expected of us. We did win the tournament, after all: three bouts to one."

There was a grim silence. Then Addo said, "Well, it can't be worse than having a tooth pulled. When do we . . .?"

"In about an hour. There's a big crowd already."

No kidding. The square was solid with people; a cat could have crossed it diagonally walking on their shoulders. And every single one of them seemed to be holding a picture on a stick.

"Where's the coach?" Iseutz hissed, as they stood in the Guild doorway. "I can't see it."

"Me neither," Giraut replied. "But I'm guessing it's over there."

He nodded towards the thin double line of Blueskins, hedging a narrow road through the crowd. They were holding their spears horizontally and pushing.

Iseutz pulled a face. "If this is how they carry on when they like us, I'd hate to be unpopular."

Phrantzes pushed past them and took the lead. Lieutenant Totila brought up the rear. "Please," he said, "don't dawdle, and don't stop to wave. Now, on three."

He counted, and Phrantzes stepped out of the doorway, and a great noise hit them and blotted out the world. Giraut couldn't see anything except the backs of armoured, struggling soldiers. Halfway down the road, Iseutz stopped dead. She was shaking her head and shouting, but nobody could make out a word of it. Addo caught her hand and towed her, with Giraut gently shoving against the small of her back. Suidas was trying to peer over the soldiers' heads. He was counting.

"About even," he said, once the coach door had shut and they could just about hear again.

"What?"

"The pictures," he said. "We're all more or less equally represented. Maybe just slightly more of you," he added, grinning at Iseutz, who scowled at him.

The chaise was moving. How that was possible, Giraut couldn't guess, until they left the square and he glanced back through the window and saw a clump of Aram Chantat horsemen forming up to follow them. *So the Permians are scared of them too*, he thought, and made a mental note to tell his father.

"These people are lunatics," Iseutz said.

"Quite," Suidas replied. "They like you best."

She ignored him. "Can you imagine *anything* making people behave like that at home? It's unthinkable."

"They're an emotional people," Phrantzes said. "And fencing's very popular."

Iseutz scowled at him, then noticed something. "Where's the creep?" she said.

"Excuse me?"

"Sorry, the *political officer*. He's not here. Where is he?"

"He'll be rejoining us later," Phrantzes said. "I believe he's had to stay on in Joiauz for a meeting of some kind."

"Yes!" Iseutz yelled, and Addo noticed she had a nice smile when she was genuinely happy. "That's the best news I've heard since we left home."

Phrantzes tried to look disapproving, but made a hash of it. "In the meantime," he said, "Lieutenant Totila will be our liaison."

Suidas grinned at him. "What's a liaison?"

"I'm not entirely sure," Phrantzes admitted. "But I'm sure Totila knows. He seems a very competent young man."

"Oh, the Blueskins are deadly competent," Suidas said. "Trust me."

There was an awkward silence; then Addo said, "I don't know if anyone's interested, but it seems that I carelessly packed a load of books in my bag from that Guild place. Of course, we'll have to give them back," he added quickly, glancing at Phrantzes, "when we get to the next stop, but I don't suppose it'll hurt if we read them first."

Suidas laughed. "All fencing books, presumably."

"Afraid so. Still . . ."

"Yes please," Iseutz said. "Well, it's got to be better than looking at the scenery."

Giraut smiled. "It's a bit bleak, isn't it?"

"Makes the war seem even more stupid, if you ask me," Iseutz said. "I mean, why the hell would *anybody* want a country like this?"

After four hours on the old Imperial road – dead straight, perfectly level, cut through the flanks of mountains and raised on vast shale and rubble causeways; magnificent, awe-inspiring and very, very dull – Giraut suggested they play a game. There was a slight pause, then Iseutz yawned ostentatiously and said, "Go on, then"; at which point Phrantzes took out the book he'd borrowed from Addo and started to read. Suidas grinned and said, "Sure. What did you have in mind?"

"How about dogs and frogs?" Addo suggested.

"What?"

"We used to play it on long journeys when I was a kid," Addo said. "It's very simple. Suppose I'm the dog, I think of the title of a book or a play or something, and I say it in dog language, and you've got to guess what it is. So, for instance, *The Return of Dolichenus* would be woof *woof*-woof woof-woof-*woof*-woof. And then you're the frog, so in frog language it'd be—"

"Let's not play that," Iseutz said firmly.

"How about frame of reference?" Giraut said.

Pause. "Just remind me of the basics," Suidas said.

Giraut nodded. "Well, if I start, then of course it's up to me to choose, but let's say I choose quotations. I start off with a quote from early Mannerist poetry, for the sake of argument; so I say, oh, I don't know, 'No temple hath Persuasion save in words.' Then you've all got to follow with quotes from early Mannerist poetry. But where it gets good is, suppose I lead with 'Maxentius at the gates of Ap'Escatoy', meaning it to be Rescensionist heroic ballads, and *you* come back at me with 'The theft of the golden cockerel', you've changed the frame of reference, you see, because Maxentius and the golden cockerel are both frescoes by Sisinna of Peribleptus, so I've got to follow with another northern impressionist fresco, when I was expecting to go with another Rescensionist ballad, and if I can't do that, you win." He stopped. They were looking at him. "It doesn't have to be art and books, it can be Ivy Crown winners or rivers or whatever you like. It's a really good game once you get into it."

"How about lies and scandal?" Iseutz suggested. "Everybody knows that."

"I don't," Giraut said.

Suidas stretched his legs out a little, taking full advantage of Tzimisces' absence. "I know a good game," he said. "It's called sudden death. We used to play it in the army."

The others looked doubtful, but Addo said, "Go on."

"It's pretty straightforward," Suidas said. "You say something you'd never do, not under any circumstances. Then I think of a situation where you'd do it. Simple as that. Come on," he added, as the others went quiet, "it's a good laugh. And you don't need to know the names of any rivers anywhere."

"All right," Giraut said suddenly. "I'll go first, then. I would never, under any circumstances, eat my brother."

Iseutz scowled at him. "You haven't got a brother."

"Fine. My father, then. Only that's a bad example, because we don't exactly get on."

Suidas shook his head. "A hypothetical brother will do just fine," he said. "Right, how about this?" He settled himself comfortably in his seat, his hands folded across his chest. "You and your entire family are travelling in a coach through the mountains. You're miles away from anywhere, and stupidly you've come out without an emergency supply of food. Your coach has a smash, it's not going anywhere. The horses run off, no chance of finding them again. In the smash, your brother is fatally injured. With his dying breath, he begs you to look after your aged mother and your crippled sister who can't walk. What can you do? It's five days' walk to the nearest village. All the food you've got is four loaves of bread. So, you leave the bread for the women, and you set off to walk to the village for help. But you need food for yourself, or you'll die before you get there. It's not just your life – you couldn't give a damn about yourself – it's your mother and your sister who matter. You'd do anything to save them, wouldn't you? And your brother's dead already, and he's made of meat." He paused and smiled. "Well?"

There was a silence. Then Giraut said, "That's a bit far-fetched, isn't it?"

"It's possible," Suidas replied. "It could happen. Well? Do I win?"

Giraut shrugged. "I guess so," he said. "But that's a really outlandish scenario. I mean, things like that don't really happen."

Suidas laughed. "Oh, I don't know. I mean, look at us. We're in a coach, in the mountains, miles away from anywhere. We've already had trouble with the coach, so you can't say that's unrealistic. And things like that do happen, believe me."

"I'm not sure about this game," Iseutz said. "It's a bit grisly, isn't it?"

"I've got one," Addo said.

Suidas nodded to him. "Go on, then."

"I would never," Addo said, "under any circumstances, kill my father."

"Oh for crying out loud," Iseutz muttered, but Suidas ignored her. "That's easy," he said. "We all know who your father is. He's a great man, right? Used to being respected. I guess things like dignity and honour mean a lot to him. So," he went on, "he gets a really nasty disease. It's the sort of disease you catch from getting careless in a brothel." Addo caught his breath, but Suidas said, "Hypothetical, remember? All right. This disease leaves him crippled, he can hardly move. And everybody can tell exactly where he got it from, just by looking at him, so there's the shame as well as everything else. The pain is agonising, and it never goes away. He can't move, he can't talk, he just lies there and looks up at you, and you know that what he wants is for you to end it, put him out of his misery. You love your father, you're a good son. So, what do you do?"

"Fair enough." Addo was looking down at his hands. "If it came to that, then I guess . . . "

"Of course you would," Suidas said. "That's the whole point of the game. The point is, there's nothing, absolutely nothing that any of us wouldn't do, if we had to. If you say otherwise, you're just kidding yourself. You can talk all day about right and wrong and good and evil; all it means is you haven't yet come up

against the situation where you've got to do it, you haven't any
choice. I mean, it's all garbage anyhow. At least half the story's
always the reason why you do something. You can give me a
whole string of things that normally you'd say were the most
appalling crimes, and then I'll give you cases where they're not
only justified, they're absolutely the right thing to do. Well?"

"All right," Iseutz snapped. "How about this? I would never,
under any circumstances, betray my friends to the enemy."

Suidas laughed. "Chestnuts," he said. "How about this?
You're a rebel, in a rebel army. The government soldiers catch
you. They go to a village and they line up all the women and
children in front of a great big pit, and they say to you: give us
your friends' names, or we kill the villagers. There's about a
hundred of them. What do you do?"

Iseutz shook her head. "I keep quiet."

"What?" Suidas stared at her. "You'd let them kill a hundred
civilians."

"Yes," Iseutz said.

"But that's . . . "

"It's not me killing them," Iseutz said, "it's the soldiers. I'm
not responsible for their crimes. Besides, they'd probably kill
them anyhow, for kicks. But just because they're evil, it doesn't
mean I have to be evil too."

Suidas scowled at her. "Tell her she's wrong," he said. "Go on,
tell her."

"They agree with me," Iseutz said. "Obviously."

"I wouldn't go that far," Giraut muttered. "Still, she's got a
point. What other people do can't be your fault. Can it?"

"You should know."

Giraut breathed in sharply, but didn't move. Addo's eyes
opened wide. Iseutz said, "*What* did you say?" Phrantzes ostentatiously turned a page of his book.

"Well in my case," Giraut said mildly, "yes it can, obviously.
If you're talking about the Senator I killed, I mean. I provoked
him."

Suidas nodded. "So you should've held still and let him kill you."

"Arguably," Giraut said.

"But that would've been wrong. He was taking the law into his own hands. He should have called the Watch, not drawn on you."

"So you're saying a man who doesn't fight back is aiding and abetting his own murder," Addo said gently. "That's an interesting point of view."

Iseutz laughed. Giraut shook his head. "It was just a mess, that's all. My instincts took over. I guess his did as well. I don't think either of us made any rational decisions."

"We should've played lies and scandal," Iseutz said. "This is a stupid game."

"Well," Addo said, "we've all had a turn. Maybe you'd like to have a go."

Suidas shrugged. "If you like." He thought for a moment, then said, "You know, I can't. Sorry, but I don't think there's anything I wouldn't do. If I had to."

"You're not trying," Giraut growled at him.

"Well, all right then. I would never, under any circumstances, kill myself. Or neglect a chance, however slight, to save my own life in the event of it being threatened. There," he added, "how's that?"

Iseutz gave him a scornful look. "Fine," she said. "You're dying of a really loathsome disease—"

"In the war," Suidas said, "I caught mountain fever. It's a form of dysentery, with the most appalling stomach cramps, like you simply can't believe. It's almost always fatal. My unit was being hounded by the Aram Chantat; they had to leave me behind. I lay beside the road for three days. I had a knife. I thought about it. I thought about very little else for three days. I'm still here. Because once you're dead, well, that's it, everything's over. So I kept telling myself, I'll wait another hour, just till the sun passes over that rock, and then I'll do it. And then I put it off another half-hour, and then another twenty minutes. The middle of the third night, I realised it wasn't quite so bad as it had been." He clicked his tongue. "I didn't cure myself, I was just lucky. I didn't *win* or anything, but I didn't throw the match, either. I reckoned, the fever's doing a pretty good job of killing me, damned if it needs any help."

There was a pause; then Iseutz said, "Is that true?"

"Yes."

"You had mountain fever?"

"Yes."

"Good God." She looked away. "All right, then. The person you love most in the whole world is going to die, but you can save them if you die in their place. Well?"

Phrantzes closed his book with a snap. "I think that's quite enough of that," he said. "If you all insist on playing a game, we'll play Frostbite. That's my final decision," he added sharply. "Well?"

So they played Frostbite, for three hours. Addo and Iseutz were the callers, and they won, twenty-seven games to twenty-five.

"Rematch?" Suidas said.

"No chance," Iseutz replied. "My stomach hurts too much from laughing. Besides, you're just a sore loser."

Suidas looked very grave. "Always," he said.

Later, when the others were asleep, Addo asked Suidas, "Did you really have mountain fever?"

"Of course not. I'd be dead if I had."

"Ah."

Suidas moved a little in his seat. "But I watched someone die of it. He got left behind, like I said. I stayed with him. After three days I cut his throat. The Aram Chantat were everywhere, and he wasn't going to get better." He shrugged, a sort of boneless gesture. "Don't tell her that."

"Sure." Addo frowned. "In the War—"

"I'd rather not talk about it any more."

"Of course. Only, no offence, but it was you who brought it up."

"That was the game," Suidas said. "I wanted to win."

Addo laughed. "I quite understand," he said. "You like to leave an opening, to draw the other man in."

"That's the whole secret of fighting messer," Suidas replied. "I'll show you, when we've got five minutes."

There were no horses at the inn. Totila was furious. He kept his temper while he was with them, but they heard him yelling at the innkeeper, who emerged from the interview a short while later, shaking slightly and nursing a split lip.

"Not to worry," Totila assured them breezily. "There's a long downhill stretch into Docavotz, we can easily make up the time. It's a nuisance, that's all."

The inn was a square grey stone block on a perfectly flat strip between two steep, bare mountains, precisely bisected by the road. There was a taproom, crowded with carters carrying ore from the mines to the refinery at Erba Fresc. "Don't go in there," the innkeeper's wife told them, "they'll hug you to death." So they made do with the couriers' dining room, reserved for government messengers and other important people on official business. It was slightly smaller than Giraut's father's house, and rather more splendidly furnished: two enormous oak settles, four magnificent carved oak chairs, fine rugs and tapestries. It was luxurious, Giraut reckoned, but somehow homely at the same time.

"You know why, of course," Suidas said. "All this stuff in here is loot, from the War. That's why it looks so damn familiar. This lot's all out of some big house back in Scheria." He turned to Addo. "One of your off-relations, most likely."

"But that's dreadful," Iseutz said. "We need to tell someone. I mean, if it belongs to someone back home, it ought to be returned to them. It's stealing."

Suidas laughed. Phrantzes said, "It's best not to worry about that sort of thing. It can cause bad feeling."

"You bet it can," Suidas said cheerfully. "Besides, you won't find many houses back home where there isn't some little souvenir or other."

"But this is a government building," Iseutz protested. "That's not the same thing at all."

Suidas couldn't be bothered to argue, and then the innkeeper's wife brought in a tray. There was a loaf, a big pottery jar with a wooden stopper, a brick of shiny white cheese and a tall stack of honey cakes, which proved to be edible.

"Any news about the horses?" Phrantzes asked, but the innkeeper's wife smiled sadly, as though he'd just asked her about the true meaning of life, and went away.

Suidas asked Phrantzes for money. Phrantzes borrowed some from Totila, and Suidas bought two messers from a carter he waylaid at the taproom door. There was a grindstone in one of the outbuildings. The wonderful thin cutting edges went up in a snowstorm of white and yellow sparks, leaving blue stains on the steel where the heat had bled through.

"This'll have to do," Suidas said. Their salle was an empty hayloft, floored with thick planks, slightly warped, that flexed disconcertingly under their weight. Light came in through the open door, outside which was a ten-foot drop on to the cobbled yard.

"The man said they don't use it any more because the joists are shot," Suidas said. "I hate fighting in condemned buildings. It's one more thing to worry about."

Addo made a decision not to ask for the back story, and said, "We should be all right. The planks seem sound enough."

"I'll remind you of that when you suddenly disappear. Right, you stand with your feet a shoulders' width apart, the usual thing. No, a bit more side on. Like that, you've got it."

"You're sure this is right?"

"You're thinking" – Suidas sprang forward and swung at him; a broad diagonal slash from right to left. Addo darted back and left, just in time to avoid a cracked skull – "in conventional fencing terms," Suidas went on, edging sideways crabwise. "Messer isn't like that. It's more" – he plunged forward, slicing upwards, right to left. Addo did a standing jump backwards to get out of the way – "about spaces than lines," he went on. "Fencing's about lines, and circles. Messer" – he charged, foot and blade together, sweeping his sword in a horizontal semicircle – "messer's more about shapes in the air. The idea is to make the space around you into a zone where nothing mortal can survive."

He launched another attack. Addo retreated, and found he was up against the wall. The blade was coming down at him, slanting, left to right. He had no room to dodge left, and if he went right the blade would follow and catch up with him. He felt a shock in his wrists and elbows, and discovered that he'd blocked the blow with his own blade, holding the tip end in his left hand and the grip in his right. He had no memory of deciding to do any of that.

Suidas took a step back. "Now you're getting it," he said.

"But that's wrong," Addo said. "If I'd done that with a sharp sword, I'd have cut my left fingers to the bone."

"Yes," Suidas said. "Now then, again."

It took him a while, but gradually he began to understand. There was no defence. If you tried to block, you needed both hands; you'd mutilate yourself for life, and you could only do it once. So: no defence. Instead there was attacking and avoiding, ideally at the same time, so that in escaping your opponent's attack, you formed and forwarded your own. That, he realised was the difference, and the reason why he'd done so badly at Joiauz. You couldn't just endure. It was pure aggression.

"Welcome to the messer," Suidas said, as they halted to catch their breath. "You can't protect yourself. Your only way out is to kill the other man."

"That's horrible."

"Yes," Suidas said. "And after a bit, it becomes a way of life. On the other hand," he went on, straightening his back and retreating into long measure, "it does wonders for your reaction times and your ability to assess people. You won't last two minutes in this game without a complete understanding of human nature."

Without warning he struck out; but Addo wasn't there. He'd read the impending assault in a slight movement of Suidas' left hand and flung himself out to the right. If he'd misunderstood, he'd have placed himself directly under Suidas' cut.

"What do you mean," he asked, "a way of life?"

Suidas explained with a rising cut, back-handed, aimed at his chin. He avoided it, but only just. "Instinct, you see," Suidas said. "All instinct. I bet you young Giraut'd be good at it, if somebody bought him a backbone." He swung; Addo dodged. "It's basic human nature to cut," Suidas went on, circling again. Addo tried to match him. "Rapier, longsword, single sword, all your business plays are thrusts. You repress the instinct to cut, because the cut's actually far less efficient, it's the thrust that gets the job done. But the messer's no good for thrusting, except in a bind. It's like ten centuries of scientific fencing hadn't happened." He offered a broad, slow feint, more clearly signposted than a marketplace, which Addo very nearly fell for. "No wonder the Permians can't fence rapier," he said. "It's a totally different language." He took two steps back and lowered his sword. "All right," he said. "Now you try and hit me."

"Actually, I'd rather carry on—"

Suidas shook his head. "You're still thinking like a fencer," he said. "You want to practise your defence before you learn to attack. But there is no defence, that's the whole essence of it. If you can't grasp that, you've got no chance."

Suidas started to move. Addo opened his fingers, and the messer hit the floorboards with a thump. "I can do that," he said. "After all, it's just a sport. It's not real."

"Then you forfeit the match. You lose."

"There's worse things."

Suidas stared at him as though he was some kind of intelligence test. Then he grinned. "Yes, but we're here to win," he said cheerfully, "and I'm going to teach you how. And I can't do that if your fucking sword is on the fucking floor? Agreed?"

"Fair point," Addo conceded. "Let's start again from the beginning."

Tzimisces arrived at some point in the night. They found him finishing off his breakfast in the couriers' room: cold pheasant, smoked cheese, rye bread and a bowl of fruit, from a wicker basket he'd brought with him. They made a point of not asking him where he'd been, and he didn't volunteer any information.

"You'll be pleased to hear you'll have a capacity crowd at Beaute," he said. "In fact, the Guild's begging me to try and fit in at least one extra fixture, but I've told them no. We've got nothing to gain from additional exposure."

"Good," Iseutz said. "They won't be disappointed."

"The feedback from Joiauz is extremely positive," Tzimisces went on. "You were a great success." He smiled. "All of you."

Addo looked up. "That's a comfort," Suidas said. "I never really thought of the Permians as good losers."

"However," Tzimisces went on, "it wouldn't do at all for us to get complacent. I hope you've all had an opportunity for some good solid training."

"With respect, Colonel." Iseutz looked straight at him, but saw no reaction. "No we haven't. We've been cooped up in the coach for a day, and we're back on the road as soon as we've had something to eat. I can practically hear my cramped muscles screaming at me. Now I suggest you adjust our schedule so that we get at least one clear day somewhere we can stretch our legs and do some practice before we have to go out in front of several hundred Permians and fight for our lives with sharp weapons. And some decent food wouldn't hurt either."

Tzimisces beamed benevolently at her. "Far be it from me to

tell you when and how to train," he said. "After all, you're the champion fencer, not me. I'm just saying you really ought to get in as much preparation as you can. It'll pay dividends, I'm sure."

Later, as they were waiting for the coach to be brought round, Addo said to Suidas, "I think Tzimisces ought to be the one fencing messer. He's got that whole defend-by-attacking thing down to a fine art."

Suidas was looking thoughtful. "When she called him Colonel . . ."

"Yes, I noticed that. He didn't react."

"He didn't deny it." Suidas picked up his bag. It was rather bulkier and heavier than it had been the last time Addo had seen it. "You know, I'd be interested in finding out what he did in the War."

"Any particular reason?"

"I collect people's war stories," Suidas said, and stood up. The bag clanked slightly as he moved it.

They were singing the *Solemn Mass for the Dying* by Areopagiticus in the Great Chapel; he could just hear it through four stone walls and a marble floor. It was one of his favourite pieces of music. He sincerely hoped it wasn't for him.

A doctor showed up, eventually – not Brother Physician, or even a brother from another house, but a layman: the Carnufex house doctor, no less. He proved to be a huge man, about forty-five years old, with shoulders and a back like a bear and the biggest hands that Abbot Symbatus had ever seen. You'd trust him implicitly if it was a matter of supporting a falling building while you scrambled to safety, but maybe that wasn't the point in this instance.

"What seems to be the trouble?" he asked.

"I'm ill."

The doctor sighed. "Right, let's have a look at you." Ah, Symbatus thought: the gruff, no-nonsense type. He preferred them to the oily smilers, but it was all as broad as it was long.

"Well?" he asked, some time later.

The doctor shrugged. "I don't know," he said.

A refreshingly novel approach. "What's that supposed to mean?"

"It means I don't know," the doctor repeated. "I happen to be one of the three best doctors in Scheria, but if medical science is geography, then mankind as a species has a map with three towns marked on it and a lot of blank space with drawings of sea serpents. I *think* it's your heart, but there's about a dozen other things it could be, half of which are trivial and the rest almost certainly fatal. How old did you say you are?"

"Seventy-two."

The doctor nodded. "If you've got any money saved up, I'd spend it."

"I've taken a vow of poverty."

"That's all right, then." He shook his head. "I'm sorry to have to tell you, your time's running out. But I get the impression you knew that already."

"Oh yes," Symbatus said. "It's common knowledge. But I'd be glad of any general indications."

"Somewhere between two and nine months, depending on such factors as stress, exertion, diet. That said, you're the sort of dilapidated old ruin that sometimes goes on for ever, out of force of habit."

The abbot nodded. "There was a floorboard like that in the house I grew up in," he said. "When it finally gave way, the carpenter said it was a miracle it hadn't gone years ago. Thank you, Doctor, you've been most helpful."

"Don't thank me," the doctor said, putting on his coat. "It was your cousin the general who sent me."

"Ah. And how is he these days? I haven't seen him in ages."

"Obscenely fit," the doctor replied. "Worried about his son, of course, but otherwise fine."

"Which son?"

"Adulescentulus." The doctor frowned. "Hadn't you heard?"

The abbot sat up a little. "I know young Addo's in Permia," he said.

"So you haven't heard the latest developments."

"Apparently not," Symbatus said. "And ignorance is terribly bad for my health. What are you talking about?"

The doctor lowered his immensity on to a small, spindly chair. "You know he was sent out to fence longsword? Well, they've got him fencing messer. The general's beside himself."

The abbot sighed. "I'm afraid I don't know very much about swordfighting," he said.

The doctor explained. Annoyingly, the pain chose that moment to wake up and extend itself, which made it hard to concentrate. "Just a moment," the abbot said. "What you're saying is Addo's . . ." He had to stop. He tried not to pull a face.

The doctor was looking at him. "Are you all right?"

"A touch of cramp," the abbot said. The words seemed too big to get out of his mouth. "So there's a real danger . . ."

The doctor wasn't listening. "What's the matter? Where does it hurt?"

"It's just cramp," the abbot whispered. "I'll be fine. Tell me . . ."

But the doctor wasn't there. He'd turned his back and was mixing something. "Drink this. Now."

"But I'm not thirsty."

"Do as you're damn well told."

Anything to satisfy him, so he'd stop fussing and answer questions. "Now," Symbatus said. "*Why* is Addo fencing with these messer things? It seems entirely . . ."

He fell asleep. The doctor watched him closely for a while, then got up and went outside.

"He's had a heart attack," he told the prior. "I was able to give him something, and he ought to pull through, this time."

"This time?"

"It's not the first and it won't be the last. If he's to stand any chance at all, he's got to have complete rest, peace and quiet. No

visitors. I'll be staying with him, so I need to send a message to
General Carnufex, to let him know I won't be back for a while.
Also, I'll need some supplies from my dispensary, I'll write out a
list. And remember, nobody's to go in there without asking me
first. Is that understood?"

"Luzir Soleth," Tzimisces announced. "It's not on our schedule,
but I've had a word with Lieutenant Totila, and we're actually
ahead of time, so we can afford to take a break. He's sent ahead,
so with any luck you'll have a quiet place to yourselves where you
can get some practice."

No chance. A mile outside the town, they were met by a
squadron of Aram Chantat, escorting the town council and the
mayor.

"It'll be touch and go," the mayor said, "but with your men as
well as this lot" (a nod towards the Aram Chantat, who had dismounted and were lying on their backs in the weak sun), "we
ought to be fine as long as we time it right."

They were sitting on folding chairs in a meadow littered with
fat red poppies. The chairs had been brought by the councillors,
along with a table, a tablecloth, the municipal silver and a large
hamper of food. A tall young man poured wine from a silver jug,
acting as though he was in the presence of gods. "It's such a
privilege to get a chance to meet you like this," the mayor said for
the seventh time. Iseutz gave him a look of mild disgust.

"Not a problem," Tzimisces said cheerfully. "After all, that's
what we're here for, to promote friendship and understanding."

"Absolutely," said a small man, some kind of town clerk.
"And it's so kind of you to take time out of your busy schedule
to visit our community. It's the biggest thing that's happened
here ever."

"Hence the crowds," the mayor added with a rueful grin.
"The whole town's out on the streets already. As soon as they
heard you were coming . . ."

There followed a long council of war. The mayor drew a map,

and Totila and Tzimisces worked out a plan of campaign. They would wait here until just before nightfall, then ride round in a semicircle, entering Luzir Soleth from the south, the direction they'd be least expected to come from. "That'll give us the element of surprise," Totila said, "but as soon as word gets out, there'll be chaos, everybody trying to get from here to here."

The mayor nodded. "The flashpoint's likely to be here." He prodded the map. "The corn exchange. The only way through is Coppergate, which is pretty narrow. If your men can block it here, by the fire altar, they'll have no choice but to go the long way round, past the tannery and up Sheep Street. A detachment of the Aram Chantat here . . . "

Tzimisces shook his head. "We can't rule out the possibility that some of them at least will go outside the wall and try and come in by this gate here." He rested a fingertip on the map. "Reluctant as I am to divide our forces, I feel it would be wise to cover this area here with a skirmish line, two or three companies. We can't stop them, but we can slow them up, buy ourselves time to get the coach inside the walls."

Totila nodded enthusiastically. "Then, if we leave the coach and cut across this alley here on foot . . . "

"Risky," Tzimisces murmured.

"It should be all right," Totila said. "If we send the coach on, as if it was going up this street here . . . "

"Linen Yard," the mayor said.

"Yes, right. They'll see the coach and assume the fencers are still in it, so they'll follow while I lead the fencers through these alleys here, and come out here, practically opposite the Guildhall. If we're quick, we'll be safe inside before they realise what we're up to."

Tzimisces frowned. "There's a problem with that," he said. "Assuming you can get them inside and close the door, you'll still have several thousand hysterical people outside, and only a door and a lock and a bar to keep them out. Your men will still be up at the corn exchange, the Aram Chantat will be on the other side of town. Who's going to keep the crowd from storming the Guild house?"

The councillors looked at each other. "We are," the mayor said. "And the Watch, of course. It'll look less suspicious, the Watch forming up outside the Guild. They'll be expecting them to do that. So, when the lieutenant here brings the fencers up from the alleys, the Watch'll be there to get them inside and hold the doors until your Imperials can get back from Cornmarket."

Suidas could see that Addo was itching to join in. He put a hand on his arm.

"Leave them to it," he whispered. "Not your war."

Addo hesitated, then laughed. "Fair enough," he said. "But it's funny, isn't it? We're planning a military operation against people who really like us."

"It's just tactics," Suidas replied. "Isn't that what you told me your father always says? Everything is tactics."

Addo nodded. "An old friend of the family told me once how my father set about courting my mother. Straight out of the *Art of War*. Trouble was, her father had read it too. Uncle Loic said in the end it was one of my father's hardest-fought campaigns."

Suidas looked at him. "But he won."

"Oh yes. An inspired outflanking movement followed by a determined siege. There was another man involved, apparently. I gather he ended up getting posted to the northern front. I don't know if he made it or not." He laughed, a little nervously. "Hence the proverb, I suppose. All's fair in love and war."

"No," Suidas said. "Not really."

It worked, after a fashion. The mayor assured Tzimisces that the riot was nobody's fault. It was asking too much of Totila's men to hold off a crowd estimated at seven thousand without using the sharp ends of their weapons, and young Tzazo had made the right decision in falling back rather than draw blood. By the same token, they couldn't blame the Aram Chantat for charging the mob as they came surging up the Broadway. They probably hadn't appreciated what was going on, most of them didn't even speak the language; so, when faced with a huge body of apparently angry people coming straight at them, their reaction was perfectly understandable. Fortunately, there had been only a handful of deaths and mercifully few injuries – which in itself demonstrated that the Aram Chantat had acted out of self-preservation rather than malice. In any event, the fencers were now safe inside the Guild house, with both the Watch and Totila's men guarding the entrance, and the crowd, although it showed no sign of breaking up, was relatively calm. It would, though, make a tremendous difference if the fencers could just see their way to putting on a bit of a show. Not a formal match, naturally, that would be too much to ask, but something in the way of an exhibition bout; after all, Tzimisces had said, they could do with the practice.

"No," Iseutz said, when Phrantzes passed on the request. "Absolutely not."

"I'd rather not," Giraut said. "I'd like to help out, naturally, but . . ."

"How about a few bouts with foils?" Addo suggested. "That couldn't hurt, could it?"

Phrantzes' face fell. "I don't think that's what they want to see."

"They'll never know the difference," Suidas said. "Well, maybe a few of them, up at the front. But the vast majority'd be too far away to see if there's little buttons on the ends of the swords."

"What about the messers, though? And the longswords?"

"Same thing. More than five yards away, you can't tell if a sword's got a blunted edge or not. You can fill the front rows with the tame ones, the local bigwigs, they won't make trouble. And the rest of them won't be able to see. Tell 'em it's that or nothing. Well?"

"It sounds like a good idea to me," Giraut said.

"Better than real swords, anyway," Iseutz conceded. "Though I'm not wild about the idea of fencing without a jacket and a mask, even with foils, if I don't absolutely have to."

The mayor and the Guild officers agreed, reluctantly, though they refused point blank to countenance the use of purpose-made foils, which (they said) wouldn't fool anyone. Instead, the fight would be with proper weapons, the points and edges to be ground off as unobtrusively as possible. Iseutz complained bitterly, pointing out that a ground-off smallsword was only marginally safer than a fully sharp one, but Phrantzes smiled sadly and ignored her. ("It's a pity," Addo said later to Suidas. "A lot of what Iseutz says is bang on the nail, but because it's her saying it, people assume it's just moaning and don't listen. Of course, it'd help if she didn't shout all the time.") She looked round for Tzimisces, with a view to lodging an appeal, but he'd disappeared again.

"Has it occurred to any of you to wonder," Iseutz asked, while they were waiting for the swords to be blunted, "what happens to the money?"

Giraut looked up. "Money?"

Suidas smiled. "The gate receipts, you mean? I must admit, the thought had crossed my mind."

"Presumably the Guild keeps it," Addo said. "As payment for the use of the building."

"Then they're doing pretty bloody well out of it," Suidas replied sharply. "How many people were there at Joiauz? Nine hundred? A thousand? That's got to be a fair bit of money."

"More than that. I counted the rows of seats. You know about that stuff," Giraut said. "What's the usual arrangement, back home?"

"Mostly you get a flat fee," Suidas said. "Guaranteed even if nobody shows up. Occasionally people fight for a share of the take, but we don't favour that. We like to know what we're getting."

"It must be costing the government a lot of money to run this tour," Addo said, though it was obvious his heart wasn't in it. "Maybe they're using some of the takings to offset the expenses."

Suidas laughed. "Let's see," he said. "Board, lodgings, cavalry escort and coach provided by the Permians. None of you lot's getting anything. Tzimisces is a military officer, so he's being paid already. No, I don't see it myself."

"You're being paid," Iseutz pointed out; and if she noticed the sudden drop in temperature, she showed no sign. "Quite a lot."

"Sure, I admit it," Suidas said angrily. "Nothing else on earth would've induced me—"

"So maybe," Iseutz went on, "our share of the takings is going to pay your wages."

"We don't know if the Permians are giving our government anything," Addo put in quickly. "So I don't think there's any point in speculating."

"I'm going to ask Phrantzes," Iseutz said. "Because if money's changing hands and *he's* getting all of it, that's not fair. Well, is it?"

Suidas gave her a poisonous look. "Look at it this way," he said. "I'm the only one who *needs* paying. The rest of you they could get for free, for various reasons."

Giraut winced. Iseutz opened her mouth to say something, but maybe the right words hadn't been invented yet, and she felt that the language as it stood wouldn't do justice to the strength of her feelings. Addo said, "This isn't helping. Well, is it?"

"It's all right for you," Suidas replied. "You don't need the money, any of you. It's just something that's naturally there, like air every time you breathe. Some of us—"

"Are risking their lives so you can get a nice fat payout," Iseutz said. "And you aren't even doing what you were *hired* for. You're supposed to be the one fighting with those disgusting meat-cleaver things."

"Look," Addo said – it was the first time he'd raised his voice, and it shut the others up instantly. "We don't even know for a fact they're charging money at the door. Well, do we? So it's pointless making a stupid fuss about it. And like he said, we don't need the money. We should be grateful for that, instead of picking on each other."

Iseutz glared at him. "Don't you have *any* principles?"

There was a short, stunned silence; then Suidas laughed. "Sorry," he said, "but I think you're fighting a losing battle there. From what I've seen, young Master Carnufex here has principles the way a dog's got worms. They're just not quite the same as yours, that's all."

"Leave it," Addo snapped. "Please," he added gently. "If we've got to have a blazing row about this, let's wait till we're safely on our way home again. It'll keep till then, I'm quite sure."

Iseutz shrugged. Suidas grinned. "Remarkable thing," he said. "Here we've got the son of the Irrigator, and all he wants to do is make peace. That's hardly the Carnufex way, is it?"

Addo turned and looked at him for several seconds. Then he said, "On the contrary, it's all my family's ever tried to do. Of course," he added, as Suidas looked away, "we've always sought to achieve it by slaughtering the enemy to the last man, but it's the thought that counts."

There was no fencing match. Giraut and Iseutz, who were billed to go on first and second, were waiting in the small anteroom at the top of the Guild house main hall when Phrantzes burst in looking terrified. He explained that something dreadful had happened, the streets were full of rioters, the building had been evacuated and they were on no account to go outside.

"What the hell do you mean, something dreadful?" Iseutz said.

"I really don't know," Phrantzes said, "but it must be something serious. Totila gave me the news, and he looked scared out of his wits. And I don't suppose much has that effect on that young man."

Giraut said: "You said there's a riot. Is it about us?"

"Again, I really don't know. Totila was about to line his men up outside the building, to stop anybody getting in, so we ought to be relatively safe, just so long as we don't go wandering about." He looked round, as though he'd just noticed something. "Where are the others?"

"Addo said something about grabbing ten minutes' practice," Giraut said. "To get used to the sword he'd be fencing with. God only knows where Suidas is."

Phrantzes closed his eyes, then opened them again. "If they come in here," he said, "don't let them leave. Why the hell people can't just stay put, I really don't know."

Suidas came in a few minutes later. "There's a mob in the street," he said.

"We know," Iseutz said. "And the match is off."

"Excellent," Suidas said. "Why?"

"Because of the mob," Giraut said. "Phrantzes was here. There's been some unspecified disaster, and we're not to leave this room."

"The hell with that," Suidas said. "I'm going to find out what's going on."

By the time he came back, Addo had drifted in, looking nervous and shaken. "I looked out the window," he explained, "and someone threw a slab of paving stone at my head. It's pretty lively down there, I can tell you. I thought they liked us."

"It's not us specifically," Suidas said. "I slipped out into the street by the back way, nobody's thought to put a guard there and the door's unbolted. Brilliant security. Anyhow, it seems that the local mine boss got himself murdered. Never heard of him, but I get the impression he was the next best thing to God in these parts. Hence the riot."

"Wonderful," Iseutz said. "Is anybody doing anything about it, do you suppose?"

Suidas shrugged. "I think the watch is out there smashing statues and burning houses with the rest of them," he said. "Totila's men are out front, nobody seems in a hurry to pick a fight with them, so we're all right. What I'm wondering is where those Aram Chantat have got to. If they decide to weigh in to the crowd, there's going to be a massacre."

Giraut shivered. "Is that likely?" Addo asked.

"No way of telling. They may decide it's a political matter, none of their business, or they may take the view that their duties include keeping the peace, in which case God help any living thing on the street. The danger is if they get carried away, or if anybody's stupid enough to fight back. If that happens, they could do anything. I'm not entirely sure they know the difference between Permians, Imperials and Scherians. We all look alike to them."

Giraut shifted uncomfortably. "When you say burning houses . . ."

"I saw an orange glow in the sky not far from here, and I don't suppose it was the sunset," Suidas said. "I can't see why a nation of fencing fanatics would want to burn down the Fencers' Guild, but fire has a tricky way of spreading. We really ought to think about moving closer to the back door, just in case."

Which they did, laying claim to a document store just down the passage from the doorway. When Phrantzes finally found them, he was not amused. "I've been looking everywhere," he said. "I told you to stay in the waiting room."

"We thought it might be wise to plan an escape route," Addo said. "What's going on? Have you found out?"

Phrantzes nodded and sat down on a packing case. "A senator by the name of Ashok has been assassinated," he said. "Tzimisces told me just now. He was a very important man, apparently, a senior member of the cabinet, and very popular locally. As soon as the news got out, people just went mad. They've had to send in the Aram Chantat to restore order."

Nobody spoke. After a moment, the door opened and Tzimisces came in. "We're going to have to leave the building," he said briskly. "It'll be all right, Totila's sent a dozen good men to look after us, and the back streets are relatively quiet."

Phrantzes' eyes grew very round. "Are you sure that's a . . .?"

"Better than staying here," Tzimisces said. "Things aren't going too well. Basically, the mayor's lost control of the town. The Aram Chantat are killing people in Fountain Square, and the crowds falling back from that area are so angry they don't really care what they smash up or set fire to. Also," he added quietly, "the crowd seem to be blaming the peace faction for killing Ashok. No idea if there's any truth in it, but that's what they've got into their heads, in which case mob logic makes us a subsection of the enemy. Totila says if we stay in town he can't guarantee our safety. Coming from an Imperial, that's quite an admission. So, we're leaving. Don't think about trying to collect your stuff," he added, glancing sideways at Suidas. "They'll try and find us some transport once we get outside the walls."

The alley was quiet. Tzimisces held up a lantern, and Giraut saw Tzazo and five Imperials lined up waiting for them. Tzazo had a cut lip and blood on his right hand, and the right shoulder-piece of one of the soldiers' armour had been torn loose and was hanging over his stomach. All of them looked terrified.

"Where's Totila?" Tzimisces asked.

"He's not coming," Tzazo replied. "I'm sorry, that's all I know. I think I'm in command now.

Tzimisces frowned; then Giraut watched as he dismissed the news from his mind. "Which way are you taking us?"

Tzazo rattled off a list of street names. Tzimisces seemed to approve; he nodded, and the six Imperials moved to form a square, with the fencers inside. "Hang on," Suidas said. "We're unarmed. If it's as bad as that . . ."

Tzimisces shook his head. "We're on foreign soil," he said. "We don't fight. That's what the soldiers are for. If one of you were to kill a Permian, even in self-defence, it'd be a disaster."

"Oh, right," Iseutz snapped. "And what'd it be if a Permian kills one of us?"

"Deeply regrettable," Tzimisces said. "Now then, I suggest we make a move, while the street's still clear."

It was hard walking inside the square in the dark. Twice Giraut trod on the heel of the man in front of him, who made no sound. Their boots sounded horribly loud, and were the only noise to be heard. It crossed Giraut's mind for a moment that the whole thing was an enormous practical joke – there was no riot, no crowd, no burning buildings, and at some point Tzazo and Tzimisces would double up with laughter and explain that they'd been had. But then he remembered that Suidas and Addo had seen the mob, and that Tzazo's face was cut. They won't hurt us, he told himself, we're not even from here, it can't be anything to do with us. He wanted to ask how much further they had to go, but didn't dare make a sound.

Addo nudged Suidas' arm. "I don't suppose you've got a couple of messers under your coat."

"No." Suidas was looking straight ahead. "Just the one."

"Oh. Actually, I was joking."

"Really." Suidas lowered his voice. "The only thing between us and a violent mob and the Aram Chantat is half a dozen Blueskins. I fail to see the humour."

"You heard what Tzimisces said ..."

"Screw him."

They turned right, then left, then left again. As they crossed a courtyard between two large buildings, they saw three dead bodies lying on the cobbles: two men and a woman. One of the men had lost an arm, though it was probably the head wound that killed him. Nobody said anything.

Some time after that – Giraut had no idea how long – Tzimisces said, "I thought you said you were taking us down Queen's Alley."

"This is Queen's Alley," Tzazo replied.

"No it isn't. This is Narrowgate. Queen's Alley is over there, to the left."

A pause; then: "Are you sure?"

"It's all right," Tzimisces said, in a tight, sharp voice. "We can cut across round the back of the tannery. It'll bring us out on Queen's Alley just past the orphanage."

"Are you sure about that? I thought—"

"How well do you know this town, Lieutenant?"

"Actually, I've never been here before. But I saw a map ... "

"Take the next left," Tzimisces said firmly.

The back gate of the tannery had been smashed down, and Giraut saw a few coins on the pavement gleaming in the lantern-light. He assumed Tzazo had noticed, and kept quiet.

They turned into a broader street, and the escort quickened the pace. For some reason, the extra width made Giraut feel more secure, though he figured it shouldn't – a wider street was more likely to be a main thoroughfare, therefore more liable to be used by rioters, or the Aram Chantat moving to deploy. He tried very hard not to think about it, but his stomach was tightening and his knees felt weak, as though he had a bad cold. He glanced back and saw Addo's face, or half of it at least, lit up by the lantern. He looked about twelve years old.

"And left at the top, into Moorway," Tzimisces said. He sounded happier, almost excited. "If I remember right, the livery yard's on the corner of Moorway and Cooper's Alley."

Tzazo didn't reply, and Giraut guessed he had no idea where he was. Then Tzimisces said, "Shit, this is Cotton Street, where did we—" and stopped short. A body of men, two dozen at least, were standing in the road looking at them.

Tzazo stopped immediately, and Iseutz barged into him, making him stagger. "Back up," Tzimisces said urgently, but he replied, "Better not." The men didn't move.

"I'm the ranking officer," Tzimisces said. "Back up, now." But Tzazo nodded sideways over his shoulder. Giraut turned his head to look. More of them, coming up behind them.

Tzazo took a deep breath. "I'll handle this," he said; then he added, "Please." Tzimisces dropped back without saying anything.

The men in front – there were women too, Giraut realised –

still hadn't moved. They were looking at the soldiers as though they'd never seen anything like them in all their lives. It's like a mechanism, Giraut realised; if we stay perfectly still, they won't move either. But a movement from us will set them in motion, like a cam tripping a sear and releasing a spring. It'd be a terrible mistake, the worst possible, to assume we're dealing with people here. There's nothing there to be reasoned with. It's mechanics, and chess. And we can't stay here for ever.

Or perhaps they could. Time seemed to have slowed down, and the fear — it hadn't gone away, no chance of that, but it had mutated into a fierce, painful concentration. Giraut could have sworn his sight and hearing had improved; he could see details of their faces and clothes, hear the barking of a dog in the far distance. He heard a woman in the group facing them laugh, and immediately he thought, *It's all right, they're going to let us pass*. Then he saw a man stoop down and pick something up. Maybe it was something he'd dropped. But he straightened up and took a step forward, then swung his right arm behind his back and brought it over his shoulder in a wide arc. Giraut saw something looping towards them through the air. Whatever it was, it fell well short; there was a chunky sound, as of a mason's hammer hitting stone. Several people in the crowd cheered, as if some sort of victory had been achieved. He heard Tzazo say, "Steady," in a deeply unhappy voice; and then it was almost as if he was inside Tzazo's mind, as if the young lieutenant was thinking with Giraut's brain rather than his own. *They're unarmed*, the thought ran, *they're civilians, just a rabble. They won't stand firm against a charge by armed soldiers. They'll run, and everything'll be fine.*

Giraut could follow the reasoning, but he knew it was wrong. He wanted to shout *No, stop*, but his mouth wasn't working. He felt the decision crystallise in Tzazo's mind.

"On three," Tzazo said. "Keep together, all of you. One . . ."

The thrower had stooped for another something-to-throw.

"Two, *three*." Giraut did manage to make a sound, but before it could become a word, he felt a terrific shove in the small of his back and discovered he was running, just to keep from being trodden on.

The thrower held his fire. Behind him, the crowd was moving strangely; those in front trying to back away, those behind pressing forward for a better view. The thrower swung his arm. Giraut watched; a speck became a shape, which became (of all the stupid things) a pickled walnut jar, just like the ones they had at home. Well, of course (it grew as it looped), they all come from the Western Empire, that's where all walnuts come from. It seemed to hang in the air as its velocity decayed. It began to drop. Giraut turned his head away. He heard a crack, and something whizzed past his face, making it sting.

He looked up. The side of Tzazo's helmet was smeared with red dust and shiny liquid; vinegar, he realised, from the jar. Tzazo didn't seem to have noticed. The crowd was trying to squash itself flat: front row scrabbling to get away, middle jammed up against the back, who were still trying to get forward. *No, stop,* Giraut thought; it was like being on a runaway cart, heading straight for a wall. You idiot, don't you realise, we're going to *crash*?

Then his chin hit the back of Tzazo's helmet, and something impossibly heavy and hard slammed into his back. He felt his ribs flex, as all his breath was squeezed out, like water out of a sponge. He tried to breathe in, but his lungs were too empty. Some kind of liquid splashed into his face, straight into his open eyes. He couldn't see. The obstruction in front gave way, and he lurched forward. Something hit him in the face. It hurt so much he couldn't think.

Here we go again, Suidas thought.

Just before impact, he turned as sideways as he could get, taking the force on his shoulders. That had been an early lesson (what to do if you're in the second rank), and because it was purely instinctive, it gave him time to think. Space was going to be the problem; all squashed up together, you can't do a damn thing. The only answer was to make space, by any means necessary.

Purely by chance, the impact shoved his right hand down and across his waist. His fingers bumped against the hilt of the messer, snuggled under his belt. There wasn't a conscious moment of decision, when he resolved to draw. It was as though someone had grabbed his hand and closed it round the hilt, and then his arm took over.

He didn't look down, because he didn't want to take his eye off the action. Directly before him was the turned back of some Permian, in a blue coat; the same Permian, presumably, who was standing on his foot. He didn't need to look in order to press the point of the messer against the blue coat, and push firmly. He heard a scream, which he assumed was the consequence of his action; then the blue coat gave way. He tugged sideways to free the messer, and as it came loose the momentum lifted his arm into a good position for striking. He was looking at the side of a man's head; a bald summit with grey slopes. He hit it good and hard.

Giraut was face to face with an old man. He was yelling something. Then a blade split open his head, and he died.

There was a sort of convulsion in the crowd – something was happening, but Giraut couldn't see what it was – and it flexed inwards, like a chest breathing in. No longer supported, the dead body came loose and flopped forward, landing on Giraut's shoulder. He blinked (his eyes were still messed up with the hot, sticky stuff) and tried to wriggle the dead thing off him, as if it was a spider. Then someone must've kicked his shin. He lost his footing and fell forward, banging his head hard against a head, which screamed. He grabbed with his left arm, caught hold of something that squirmed and flexed, but not enough to dislodge him. He was standing on something uneven and soft, and that was moving too. *The floor's made of people*, he thought, and the idea was utterly ridiculous.

Phrantzes was completely out of it for a second or two. When he opened his eyes, he saw a fist coming straight at him. Amazingly, he managed to get his head out of the way. The puncher barged up against him, overbalanced and went forward, but there wasn't enough room for him to fall.

He saw Iseutz screaming, putting her hand in front of her face. A Permian was swinging a messer – not at her, particularly, just generally, like a man cutting back brambles; but she was in the way. Then Addo stepped neatly in front of her, filling the space the Permian needed for a decent swing. His hand, rather than the blade, hit Addo on the shoulder; he got a grip on the Permian's arm, he was wrestling for the messer, and the Permian was trying to shake him off. A woman howled somewhere. Beside him, a Blueskin was trying to get his sword out of its sheath, but there wasn't room.

A hand appeared from nowhere and dragged obscenely across his face. He closed his mouth around a fingertip and bit as hard as he could.

When Suidas realised what the problem was, he could've laughed out loud. The reason why the crowd hadn't broken and run when Tzazo made his charge was that they had nowhere to go. They were backed up against a wall. Tzazo was trying to compress a solid.

He only found out because he'd cut a hole in the crowd. *For crying out loud*, he thought, staring at the wall. Then a woman tried to grab hold of his face, and he had to deal with her.

Now what? he thought.

It didn't help that it was too dark to see more than a few feet ahead, and then only general shapes rather than specifics. The path he'd cleared with such effort was closing up, leaving him stranded, away from the others. He heard a woman screaming, and it sounded like Iseutz's voice. He felt the familiar-from-the-old-days brief, sharp internal pain that registered the loss of a member of the company, followed by the surge of concentration as his mind automatically suppressed the fact. I've got to get out of this, he thought. Forward and back are out, which leaves sideways.

Suddenly he felt very, very tired. He had no idea how far the crowd extended, to left or right, so he made a conscious decision: to go right, because he was right-handed and it'd be easier to swing. As he lifted the messer he could feel its hilt pressing on the start of a blister. Some people wore gloves, for that very reason, but he didn't like to. You didn't have so much control in gloves.

A man with a beard turned his face towards him and shouted something he couldn't catch; he seemed angry rather than scared, as though something was Suidas' fault. That was obviously absurd. The hell with it, he thought; the sooner you start, the sooner you'll finish. He picked his target, and swung.

Suidas Deutzel hadn't wanted to go to war. He was fifteen, and his uncle had given him to understand that if he worked hard and learned the business, he could in due course expect to inherit the yard, the horses and the wagons. It was a solid, comfortable future, and he was looking forward to it.

Because of his previous experience, they'd put him in the transport corps. Fair enough. Since the military had also requisitioned the horses, the wagons and the drivers, there was a sort of logic to it. His uncle was furious, of course, but consoled himself with the thought that young Suidas would probably be all right. After all, he wasn't likely to come to much harm carting barrels of flour to supply depots well behind the lines.

But General Carnufex, in one of the most brilliant coups of the War, cut off and utterly destroyed the Aram Chantat brigade that had been harassing the supply lines. The Permians sent away for a replacement, which eventually arrived, from wherever it was the Aram Chantat came from. They were a different sect from a different tribe, and they didn't interpret their orders in quite the same way. Instead of targeting the strategically significant supply routes that brought food and equipment to Carnufex's Fifth Army, they went off on long, drifting raids in the Debatable Land and even into Scherian territory. These adventures didn't achieve much of military value, and the losses and disruption they caused were within acceptable perameters. The general had more important things to think about, and delegated the job of dealing with them to divisional level. Nobody at Division was sure whose responsibility it should be; it didn't quite fit in with mobile defence in depth, quick response didn't want to know, and highway maintenance objected angrily that they were engineers, not knights in shining armour. Eventually, the commission floated gently down as far as the desk of a junior colonel on the transport staff, who lacked the authority to do anything about it.

At the end of the wall was an arch. He stumbled through it into a long, narrow rectangular courtyard, where he collided with a set of steps. He howled and fell forward, landing on his forearms. He knew by the pain that he'd skinned his knees and elbows; his first injury of the evening.

He dragged himself to his feet, but the effort used up the last of his strength. He scrabbled in the dark till he found the messer, then sat down heavily on the bottom step. I shouldn't have to do this any more, he thought; I served my time, finished my tour and came home. But something must've gone wrong, because here I am again: in Permia, on my own, with a messer. It's like I've never been away.

He ought to get up, start running, but he couldn't. The skinned knees were a valid excuse. Stay here, catch your breath – he knew he was doing all the wrong things, disobeying a direct order from his brain, which could only lead to disaster; but what the hell. A lifetime spent trying to do the sensible thing in order to stay alive, and look where it'd got him.

Someone was coming. He grabbed for the messer, couldn't find it, panicked until his fingers closed round the hilt, like a young man too much in love reaching for his girl's hand to make sure she was still there. Back to business, he thought. He kept perfectly still.

"Come *on*," said a voice in the dark. "Please."

Suidas grinned like a cat, waited so as to time it exactly right, then said, "Watch out for the step."

He heard a sharp intake of breath, then a yelp. By then, Addo was close enough for Suidas to see his face. "Suidas?"

"Yes."

"Thank God."

Addo stood up straight. He had something in each hand: a messer in his right, Iseutz's wrist in his left. He'd been towing her, like a grain barge. "What about . . .?"

Suidas shook his head; the customary office for the dead. "What happened to you?"

"I'm not sure, really," Addo said, in a vague sort of voice; but the blade of the messer drooping forgotten from his hand gleamed wet in the moonlight. "What do we do now?"

"Excellent question." He leaned forward a little. "Iseutz? Are you all right?"

Addo answered for her. "She's a bit shaken, but not too bad. We saw a bit of a gap, and made for it." He drew in a deep breath, then let it go. "We really ought to get away from here," he said.

"Fine. Where did you have in mind?"

"Well, back to the . . ."

Suidas shook his head. "The Guild house was under siege when we left," he said, "so we'd be mad to go back there, even if we knew the way. We can't go to the authorities, because I don't think there are any, not any more. There's supposedly a coach waiting for us somewhere, but I haven't got the faintest idea where. I'm covered in blood, and I think you are too, so we're not exactly inconspicuous. Until further notice, we'd be wise to regard anybody we meet as a dangerous enemy." He paused, then added: "Well, then. In our shoes, what would Daddy do?"

"Get out of the town as quickly as possible, I guess," Addo replied, in a too-tired-to-fight voice. "What do you think?"

"No idea. I'm lost."

Addo was quiet for a moment; then he said, "Well, this yard points north."

"Does it?"

"I think so. I only got a quick look at the map, but I've got one of those see-it-once-and-remember memories. I *think* we're pretty close to the northern edge, so if we just keep going, we should be fine. We'll know soon enough, because there's a canal. If we cross that in the next half-mile or so, we're on course."

"I'm impressed," Suidas said. "All right, you can be the officer. Ready?"

He stood up. Addo saw the messer in his hand, then seemed to remember his own. "We ought to get rid of these, don't you think?" he said. "We'd be better off being victims."

"No way in hell," Suidas replied pleasantly, threading the messer through his belt and closing his coat round it. "And if I'm keeping mine, you might as well keep yours. Right, let's get going."

They followed the yard, passed through another arch and came out into a wide street. There was nobody to be seen. "The hell with it," Suidas muttered. "Which way?"

"Right," Addo replied. "I can't remember the name offhand, but I think this leads straight out of town. If I'm right, there should be a bridge quite soon."

They walked for a while in total silence, with Iseutz trailing behind like a tired dog on a lead. "You saw a map," Suidas said.

"In the Guild house. It was just lying about. I glanced at it, on general principles. I always like to know where I am."

"Heredity," Suidas said. "For which, right now, I'm profoundly grateful. This looks like that bridge of yours."

"Splendid," Addo said. "I think we may actually be going the right way."

A little later, Addo said: "I lost sight of Giraut and the others when we—"

"Forget it," Suidas said. "Not your fault."

They walked on in silence for a while further; then Addo stopped dead.

"What?" Suidas said.

"Look."

All Suidas could see in the moonlight was a row of barrels. "*What?*"

Addo took a few steps, and stopped again. "Barrels," he said excitedly.

"I can see that. What's the matter with you?"

"*Barrels.* Which means coopers. Cooper's Alley."

"I have no idea what you're talking about."

"The livery yard," Addo said, "is on the corner of Moorway and Cooper's Alley. I heard Tzimisces say so to the officer."

"That doesn't mean anything," Suidas snapped, but Addo was looking round wildly. "The street we've been walking down," he said. "That's got to be Moorway. I remember now, Moorway leads from the Circus up to the Northgate." He laughed, like a small boy. "We've come round three sides of a square," he said. "We were almost there when we . . ."

"Are you sure?"

"Look."

There was a small yellow square of light: a window. Addo grabbed Iseutz's hand and dragged her toward it; Suidas followed. They found a pair of tall doors beside the lighted window, by whose stray glow they saw wisps of straw on the paving stones, and an unmistakable pile of horseshit.

"Livery yard," Addo said.

"You're kidding," Suidas murmured. He shouldered past Addo, clenched his fist tight and banged on the door. There was a horrible interval of stillness and silence; then they heard footsteps, and the door opened. "There you are," said a voice. It was Tzimisces.

"You shouldn't have wandered off like that," Tzimisces said.

The coach was bigger than the chaise, heavier and more ornate, with red leather seats and a coat of arms painted on the door. Inside, it smelt of mould. Two horses were already between the shafts; they were waiting for the groom to lead out the front pair.

"After you left," Tzimisces was saying, "the Aram Chantat showed up. Things got a bit nasty at that point." He shrugged, a sort of these-things-happen gesture. "I got Phrantzes and Giraut out of the way, and we came straight here."

"What about Lieutenant . . .?" Iseutz stopped. She'd forgotten his name.

"Tzazo," Tzimisces said. "I don't think he made it. The Aram Chantat didn't charge straight away, you see; they held back and let off a couple of volleys of arrows, to loosen things up. It was dark, needless to say, so they had no idea what they were shooting at. That was when we left. We heard the charge go home, of course. Fortuitous," he added (and Giraut wondered where he'd got that particular word from, at that particular moment). "With all the mess they'll have made, nobody's going to notice that some of the bodies had slash wounds that didn't come from overhead." He gave Suidas a reproachful look. When it failed to have any effect, he turned it on Addo, who looked down at his feet. "We'll say no more about it," he went on. "But please, in future—"

"Hang on," Suidas interrupted. "Are you expecting more of that sort of stuff? Because if you are . . ."

"As far as I can tell, this was an isolated incident," Tzimisces said, "resulting from an extreme act and exceptional local circumstances. However, if anything like this happens again, I trust there'll be no repetition. Do I make myself clear?"

Suidas gave him a closed-door look. Addo mumbled something, presumably an apology. Iseutz said, "If Addo hadn't pulled me out of there—"

"You'd have been rescued by the Aram Chantat, like the rest of us. And now the matter's closed, as far as I'm concerned. I suggest we all reflect on it at our leisure, and try and learn the obvious lessons."

"Excuse me," Giraut interrupted. "What about our stuff?"

There was a moment's silence; then Suidas barked out a short laugh. Tzimisces ignored him.

"Naturally, if your belongings survived the attack on the Guild house and if there's an opportunity to have someone retrieve them, I'll do so. For now, though, we must assume that they're lost. I wouldn't worry about it. I'm sure our hosts will be happy to replace them."

"What happened to the soldiers?" Iseutz asked. "The rest of Tzazo's men."

"I don't know," Tzimisces replied briskly. "Well, it looks as if the coach is ready for us. No escort, I'm afraid, but that might be no bad thing. Having soldiers with us at this point would only attract attention."

The driver was an old, bald man in a huge coat. He had a boy of about fourteen with him on the box, most likely his grandson. The boy was eating an apple.

"Where are we going?" Suidas asked, as he shut the door and the coach moved off.

"North out of town," Tzimisces replied, "then we'll work our way east through the lanes until we pick up the main east road to Beaute. There's a post station about five miles along, where we can send ahead for an escort."

Giraut wondered what had become of Lieutenant Totila, but there was no point in asking. It occurred to him that Lieutenant Tzazo, and possibly Totila as well, and an unspec- ified number of their Blueskin escort, had died to protect him. It was an extraordinary thought. In his more romantic moments, when he was younger, he'd occasionally thought how grand it would be to lay down one's life for one's friend. He'd imagined it, once or twice, having contrived various scenarios to fit the dramatic requirements. In these little narratives, there had always been plenty of time – for deliberate choices, for speeches, farewells, dying words. The idea that you could find yourself in a situation, suddenly closing in around you before you'd had a chance to appreciate what was happening, where you'd be called upon to give your life for a complete stranger, struck him as quite bizarre. He wondered: at what point had Tzazo, or Totila, or any of them realised that this mess was one they weren't getting out of; had they seen a chance to run and nobly forsworn it, or had death simply swirled round them like floodwater, following the unseen bursting of a distant dam, and swept them away without giving them any chance to make a choice? Of course it was different if you were a soldier. Presumably you were trained, or at the very least you'd thought it through beforehand and decided that it (whatever *it* was) justified the risk. *To protect and serve the innocent and the weak*; something like that, at any rate, and once you'd made the decision and signed the piece of paper and been issued your uniform, your consent to whatever happened to you after that could be taken for granted. It was peacetime, after all. Nobody had to be a soldier if they didn't want to. Even so. He couldn't help imagining Lieutenant Tzazo making his final report before the Court of the Invincible Sun – *I died so that Giraut Bryennius might live* – and all around him the assembled cherubim and the glorious hosts of heaven staring at him as though he was not quite right in the head.

"Why've we stopped?" Suidas said.

It was a silly question, and Tzimisces didn't answer. He stood up, leaned across Addo (who somehow managed to shrink to about half his normal size without moving) and pulled down the window. A moment later, he sat down again.

"I don't know," he said.

"Well, don't you think you ought to find out?" Iseutz said.

Tzimisces sighed, stood up again, edged his way past Addo's

feet and climbed out of the coach. Nobody spoke until he came back, a long time later.

"The driver says this is as far as he's prepared to go," Tzimisces said. "He wants to leave us here and go back to town. I told him that wasn't acceptable."

"And?"

"He's just sitting there," Tzimisces said.

"I'll talk to him," Suidas said.

"That wouldn't be a good idea," Tzimisces replied.

"We could offer him money," Addo suggested.

"We haven't got any," Phrantzes muttered. "Have we?"

"Unfortunately, no," Tzimisces said. "I think our only option is to sit tight and wait. Sooner or later there should be a patrol – we're on the main road, at last – and I'll get the commander to commandeer the coach. We shouldn't have any trouble after that."

"What if he decides to drive us back to . . . ?" Giraut realised he'd forgotten the name of the town. "Where we just came from. Well, he lives there, so—"

"The hell with that," Suidas said abruptly. "I'll talk to him."

"Sit down," Tzimisces snapped, and after a moment Suidas subsided, like a pot taken off the boil. "May I remind you," Tzimisces went on, "we're in a friendly country in peacetime. Solving transport disputes at swordpoint isn't acceptable behaviour."

"We can't just sit here," Iseutz protested.

"On the contrary," Tzimisces snapped, "there's absolutely nothing else we can do, unless you feel like getting out and walking to Beaute. I wouldn't recommend it, though. This road is patrolled by the Aram Chantat. I have official papers, which they will respect. I'm afraid I don't have any spare copies to lend to individual members of the party." He paused – Giraut could practically hear him counting to ten under his breath. "Why don't we all settle down and sit quietly until the patrol gets here? Then it'll all be sorted out, you have my word."

"Fine," Suidas growled. "And if he does what Giraut just said, turns the coach round and heads back into town?"

"Then you have my full permission to climb up on to the box and cut his throat," Tzimisces replied pleasantly. "But he won't. I've told him that if he does, he won't get paid."

"But we can't pay him anyway," Iseutz nearly shrieked. "We haven't got—"

"Please," Tzimisces said wearily, "keep your voice down. He doesn't know that. And as soon as the patrol finds us, the coach will be requisitioned by the government and any issues of payment will cease to be relevant. I freely confess," he added, as Iseutz made a despairing gesture with her arms that nearly put a hole through the coach door, "the situation is far from ideal. But it is under control, and before too long we will be on our way. Until then, we must stay calm and patient. That's all there is to it."

There was a long silence. Then Addo said, "Colonel, as soon as we get somewhere where there's light to see by, I'd like to challenge you to a game of chess. I think you'd be a fascinating opponent."

Iseutz giggled. Tzimisces said, "I'm afraid you'd win quite easily. I'm not very good at chess."

"Really?" Suidas clicked his tongue. "I had you down for a master tactician."

"Indeed. And the golden rule is, don't fight battles you can't win. I'd only agree to play if I could be sure of ambushing my opponent's pieces on their way to the board and slaughtering them like sheep."

Intense terror followed by equally intense inactivity sent Giraut to sleep. He woke up to the sound of voices outside the coach.

"Sh," Suidas hissed at him. "It's them. The Aram Chantat."

Giraut listened hard. He could hear voices, though no words; Tzimisces sounding cheerful, occasionally laughing, and a high, musical voice, talking quickly. It sounded like old friends meeting after a long separation.

"It's not the patrol," Suidas said softly. "They're from the town, looking for us."

Giraut suddenly felt cold. He could tell from the sound of Tzimisces' voice and his knowledge of the man that he was putting on a high-quality performance, pulling out all the stops. Whether he was dissuading the Aram Chantat from arresting them or cajoling them into escorting them to Beaute, he had no idea. All he knew was, for that particular moment and that single purpose, he valued Tzimisces more than anyone else alive.

After a very long time, he heard Tzimisces and the voice both laughing together; then the door opened and Tzimisces climbed back in. He closed the door behind him and sat down, pulling his coat tight around him.

"Well?"

"It's all right," Tzimisces said, and his voice had changed; he sounded tired, possibly even shaken.

"What did they . . .?"

"Several things. For instance, they wondered if we could shed any light on an incident where six Imperials and about three dozen Permian civilians were killed, not far from our coachyard." He paused for breath. "I said I didn't know anything about it. Anyway, they're requisitioning the coach and they're coming with us, part of the way at least. They've sent ahead to meet the patrol." At that moment, the coach began to move forward. "Looks like they've just used their special blend of charm on our driver," he added. "I warned him, but he wouldn't listen."

They met the patrol just before dawn. Giraut was woken up by yelling. The coach lurched and stooped as if it had hit a wall, throwing him into Addo's lap. Nobody said anything.

After a while the shouting stopped, and all they could hear was horses going away at a gallop. Then someone banged on the door. Without a word, Tzimisces got up and went out. He was gone for quite some time.

There had been, he explained when he got back, sounding

as close to the edge as they'd yet heard him, a bit of a misunderstanding. The patrol—

"Cosseilhatz," Suidas said.

Tzimisces nodded firmly. "Exactly. Tribes," he went on. "Actually, that's entirely the wrong concept, but let's not get sidetracked. There's at least a dozen of them. The Chantat are just one, but we call all their different nations Aram Chantat, mostly because it's the only one we can pronounce. Anyway, the guards from the town are Aram Chantat, the patrol are Aram Cosseilhatz. They don't get on. And both of them being employed by the Permians isn't anything like a good enough reason for them not to fight it out to the death, if they're feeling that way inclined." He breathed out long and slow. "Fortunately, the patrol outnumbers our escort three to one. Unfair odds," he explained, "so they couldn't start anything, they could only fight back if the Chantat attacked them. Which they came pretty close to doing," he added, with a slight shake in his voice, "but their captain said no, their first duty was to hand over the – well, us to the patrol, because those were their orders. Business before pleasure, you might say. Of course, if it'd been the other way round, it'd have been completely different. The Chantat aren't bound by the unfair-odds rule, only the Cosseilhatz. Wonderful people," he added with feeling, "but complicated."

The coach was moving again. Iseutz said, "Hand over the what?"

"Excuse me?"

"You hesitated. What were you going to say?"

Tzimisces shrugged. "Fine. Technically, we're now prisoners. Escorting third-party prisoners is a supervening duty," he continued loudly over the beginning of Iseutz's howl of fury, "which overrides the obligations of the tribal feud. If we were just honoured guests, they'd have had to attack the Cosseilhatz, and we'd now all be dead. It's all right," he went on. "I'll sort it out when we get to the post station."

"Marvellous," Suidas said quietly. "So, whose prisoners are we, exactly?"

"The Cosseilhatz," Tzimisces said. "The orders were, hand us over to the patrol. Which they did. The Cosseilhatz were therefore obliged to take us. They're not exactly happy about it, but they'll do as they're told."

Addo cleared his throat. "Which post station?" he said. "It can't be the one you told us about earlier. We passed that hours ago."

"Quite right," Tzimisces said. "It'll be the next one along. The Cosseilhatz burnt the other one to the ground, two days ago."

There was a long silence. Then Suidas said brightly: "You know, I'm glad the War's over. It makes getting from A to B so much less stressful."

The post house was a square white building with a flat roof, sitting beside the road in the middle of a mile-wide level plain between two cliffs. It had no grounds, yards or garden, which made it look as if it had been carelessly dropped there, like a crate fallen from a cart. From a distance it looked like a hut, but the closer they came, the bigger it grew. "It's got to be the size of the New Year Temple," Iseutz said. Giraut thought about it and said it was probably bigger.

"It does seem pretty large for a relay station," Addo said.

Tzimisces yawned. "It was once a cathedral," he said, "in the central square of a city." He sat up a little and pointed through the window. "See that line there, in the distance? That was a river, hundreds of years ago. This plain was the breadbasket of Permia. But the river changed course, the city was deserted, nobody even knows what its name used to be. That thing over there is all that's left. The Empire used it as a bonded warehouse. When the Permians took it over they tried to pull it down, but it's so massively built they gave up. There was a battle near here in the War."

"Semont," Addo said. "So this must be . . ."

"Quite right," Tzimisces said approvingly. "This is Semont de Danzer. Not one of your father's battles."

"We were defeated, weren't we?" Addo said.

"The name rings a bell," Suidas said. "But I was never with the Third Army."

The coach came to a halt. Suidas yawned and stretched; Tzimisces reached past him and opened the door. "Last I heard," he said as he stood up, "there was a squadron of Imperials stationed here. I might just be able to persuade them to take us to Beaute, instead of the Aram Chantat. Don't get your hopes up, mind, but I'll see what I can do."

The post-house door was at least twelve feet high and six feet wide, green bronze, decorated with embossed friezes of human-headed winged lions and bird-headed men. In the very middle, someone had stuck a piece of plank to it with tree gum. On the plank was written, USE OTHER DOOR. Tzimisces, flanked by two oddly nervous Aram Chantat, walked up to it and gave it a gentle shove with his fingertips. It opened, smooth and totally silent. "Wait here," he said, and went in.

"Did you notice," Addo said quietly, "it's a different driver."

Giraut looked back. On the box he saw an old man in a coat two sizes too big for him. But he wasn't the same old man who'd picked them up from the livery yard, and there was no fourteen-year-old grandson on the bench beside him.

"All right," Suidas said, after a moment's silence. "The other driver refused to go on, so they replaced him."

"When?" Addo said. "I don't suppose the Aram Chantat patrols take spare coachmen around with them, just in case."

"We did stop twice for water," Phrantzes said mildly. "Perhaps they changed drivers then."

"In the middle of nowhere," Iseutz pointed out.

Phrantzes sighed. "What are you suggesting?"

"Actually, I wasn't suggesting anything," Addo said. "I just thought I'd mention it, in case it mattered."

The Aram Chantat, Giraut was uncomfortably aware, were grouped between them and the coach. They were talking to each other quietly in high, soft voices. "I get the idea they aren't too keen on going inside the building," Suidas said.

"I'll be so glad to see the back of them," Iseutz whispered.

"*You'll* be glad. Hello, he's back," Suidas said, as the door opened and Tzimisces came out. "Well?"

"There's an Imperial garrison here," Tzimisces said wearily. "It's manned by Imperials because the Aram Chantat won't stay here. Bad luck or something. I think the artwork's not to their liking. Anyway, that means the Imperials can't leave them in charge here to come with us. However," he went on, drawing a breath, "neither will they take us to Beaute, because this is the limit of their beat. The Imperial CO says he'll send a rider to the next house along; he'll borrow five men from there and give us five of his own, which is all either of them can spare, and the combined unit will take us to Beaute. With any luck, forty-eight hours. Till then, we're stuck here. Sorry, but that's the best I can do."

Phrantzes pulled a sad face, but Giraut and Iseutz grinned. "A couple of days off," Iseutz said. "I don't mind that."

"We've got a match booked at Beaute," Phrantzes said. "If we're stranded here for two days, we aren't going to make it."

"That faint sound you can hear is my heart breaking," Iseutz said cheerfully. "Now, I don't suppose there's even the remotest chance of getting a bath in this godforsaken place."

There was every chance. The bathroom was square and marble-lined, with an impossibly high ceiling, on which was painted a fresco of a sea battle in the late Archaic style of the Middle Empire. There were nine baths, side by side, scooped out of single blocks of grey basalt. Water came through a splay of lead pipes from a massive porphyry cistern supported by four fluted marble columns, still showing faint traces of their

original gilding. It was stone cold and smelt very slightly of
rotten eggs.

The station commander was an exquisite young Imperial by the
name of Captain Baudila. He greeted them wearing what looked
disconcertingly like a monk's robe, except that the hood was
lined with tiger fur. He wore red boots, with parallel rows of
nine silver hooks in the form of eagles' heads running up the
fronts. He would have been extremely good-looking if his nose
hadn't been cut off almost flush with his face.

("That means he was in some sort of political trouble back
home," Tzimisces explained. "Noblemen who get caught taking
part in plots and conspiracies have their noses cut off. It means
they're still fit for active service but they'll never be promoted or
eligible for high public office. The technical name for it is 'the
divine clemency of the Emperor'. Try not to stare," he added
helpfully.)

Dinner was in the post room, a vaulted chamber taller than
the Victory Tower back home. Baudila sat at the top of a long
table – "during the day, we use it for sorting the mail" – with his
guests clustered round him at the top. Twenty or so Imperial soldiers ate quietly at the bottom end. They had roast lamb
garnished with rosemary and flat white bread, slightly stale.

"By the sound of it, you were lucky to get out in one piece,"
Baudila said with his mouth full. "Apparently the Aram Chantat
went a bit mad and carved up a bunch of the locals. They're not
happy. I haven't heard anything about trouble anywhere else,
but it'd be a minor miracle if it doesn't spread to some of the
other big mining towns. Nothing for you fellows to worry about,
of course. Your next stop's Beaute, isn't it? You'll be fine there.
Different sort of place altogether." He paused, then shot a shy
glance at Addo. "I believe I have the honour of dining with the
son of General Carnufex," he said.

Addo looked up and nodded glumly. "Adulescentulus
Carnufex," he said. "Pleased to meet you."

"I studied your father's campaigns at the military college," Baudila said. "And my elder brother fought against him in the Hook River campaign." He made it sound like they'd been at school together. "Absolutely remarkable tactical mind, my brother always said."

They noted the past tense, but nobody said anything. "He speaks very highly of your people," Addo said awkwardly. "He told me once he was only ever scared of two things in his entire life, and one of them was the Imperial heavy cavalry."

Baudila looked delighted. "And the other thing?"

"My mother," Addo replied. Baudila thought that was a great joke. He wanted to discuss some of the finer points of the Verjan Delta campaign, but Addo politely declined. "I'm the civilian of the family, I'm afraid," he said. "I'm deplorably ignorant when it comes to my father's battles. I'm sure you know a great deal more about them than I do."

Later, when Addo was shown up to his room (on the third floor; the torso of a gigantic statue rose up through the floorboards and disappeared into the ceiling, suggesting that when they'd divided the upper space into storeys, they'd been unwilling or unable to demolish it and had built round it instead), he found a book on his pillow: *Inguiomer's Commentaries on the Campaigns of Carnufex of Scheria, Vols I–IV*. He sighed, and put it carefully on the floor.

Breakfast in the guardroom, a small space with a low ceiling. The room was crowded with tables and chairs, and three of the walls were covered by racks of spears, their blades polished, their cornelwood shafts shining faintly with newly applied oil. On the fourth wall was a mural, in a totally different style to the frescoes and mosaics that they'd seen elsewhere. The colours were startlingly bright against a white background, the style was crude but vigorous, and the title (painted in foot-high letters across the top) was *The Glorious Victory of Shinnath 15/7 1435 AUC*. It was a battle, mostly. On the left, a huge army of red and blue men, sticks for arms and legs, bobbles for heads, marched towards a blue wavy line, presumably a river. The same wavy line was repeated in the middle, where the red and blue stick men were beating the hell out of a small group of green and orange stick men. On the right, the red-and-blues escorted a long column of green-and-oranges to a grey box, some kind of building, and cut off their heads. Beside the pyramid of heads on the far right, in tiny gold cursive script: *Eternal Victory to Glorious Permia and Death to the Scherians.*

"Good morning," Baudila said, beaming at them. "I hope you slept well."

"Very well, thank you," Phrantzes said, deliberately not looking at the painting. He was trying to position himself so as to block Suidas' view of the wall, but he was too small and the wall was too big. Iseutz was looking straight at the plate of sausages on the table in front of her.

"Sit down, please," Baudila said. "I'm afraid there's only wine or goat's milk to drink. You simply can't get fruit juice here, and the water's not worth the risk."

They sat down. Suidas was looking at the painting and frowning. Addo said, "Excuse me, but is that a Stiban Urosh?"

Baudila nodded cheerfully. "He was stationed here, during the War," he said. "Do you like it?"

"My father collects Urosh," Addo replied. "We've got a lot of them at home, so I sort of grew up with them."

"Really." Baudila was impressed. "I didn't think the Naive school was particularly well known outside Permia."

"Actually," Addo said, "I believe he's got the companion piece to this one. Shinnath, but from right to left. He'd love this."

Suidas laughed. Giraut asked, "Are they valuable? These paintings you're talking about."

"Back in the Empire, I believe they're seriously underappreciated," Baudila said. "But recently there's been an increasing level of interest in the Naives. I was lucky enough to acquire a

small Brenna myself not long ago. In, say, fifteen or twenty years'
time . . . "

"Our colour sergeant lost a leg at Shinnath," Suidas said.

"My father was a young cavalry subaltern," Addo said. "But
his side of the army wasn't in the heavy fighting. It was the left
who broke and ran."

Phrantzes cleared his throat. "I was wondering," he said. "Is
there any chance we could borrow a room here, to practise in?
Only, since we're going to be here for the next couple of days . . . "

Baudila beamed at him. "I was just going to talk to you about
that," he said. "My men and I are – well, enthusiastic amateurs
is the best we can say for ourselves, nowhere near good enough to
give you a fight, naturally. But if you felt like it, and if it'd be any
help with your training programme, we'd be delighted to offer
ourselves as sparring partners." He hesitated, then added quickly,
"Of course, if you'd rather not, we'd quite understand."

"No, that would be most helpful," Phrantzes said. "Most
helpful. Do you think we could possibly borrow some equipment? We seem to have lost ours."

Equipment wasn't a problem. Giraut finally managed to
narrow his choice down to a matched pair of foils, first-quality
Mezentine, belonging to Baudila's second-in-command. Suidas
couldn't choose between the longswords, so he closed his eyes
and picked one at random. There was only one smallsword foil,
but it was a beauty; Iseutz's face lit up when she saw it, and its
owner blushed and begged her to take it as a present. There
weren't any messers, but Addo already had one of his own.

Giraut fenced five bouts with Baudila. He was pretty good,
though his style was distinctly old-fashioned, and the stoccata
came as a complete and terrible surprise to him; he stood looking
down at the foil blade arched against his chest, as if wondering
how in hell's name it could possibly have got there. Giraut taught
him the move, together with the volte and the scanso dritto in
straight time. "There'll be no stopping you when you get home
to the Empire," he said.

"I won't be going home, I'm afraid," Baudila said quietly. "Made it a bit too hot for myself, I'm afraid. Still, never mind about that."

Suidas was showing off. He'd spent an hour practising disarms, which he was very good at already, and he found the painting was getting on his nerves. "The hell with this," he said, giving back the sword he'd just taken away from a bemused-looking Blueskin. "Let's try something else." He leaned his sword against the wall and smiled. "Right," he said. "I want you to kill me."

"Excuse me?"

Suidas frowned. "You heard," he said. "You're armed, I'm not. Try and cut my head off. Pretend it's still the War or something."

The Imperial looked at Baudila, who nodded; then he took a long step forward, dropped into a high back guard and froze. Suidas sighed.

"That's no bloody use," he said. "Imagine I'm a helpless old man and you're going to cut me in two. Come on."

The Imperial frowned and transitioned from high back to middle. "Oh for pity's sake," Suidas said, and kicked him on the shin. As the Imperial staggered forward, he took his sword and pushed him over. Then he reached out a hand and helped him up.

"You know, I don't remember you people being quite so damned diffident at Mons Cauta," he said. The Imperial looked at him. "Were you in the War, soldier? You look old enough."

The Imperial nodded slightly. Suidas grinned. "Me too," he said. "I was one of the poor bastards holding the top of the ridge when your commander threw half a brigade at us. Of course, we sent you home in slices, but it was interesting there, for a while. Were you in that one, by any chance?"

The Imperial shook his head without saying anything. Phrantzes cleared his throat, but nobody was interested in him.

"Just as well for you," Suidas said. "Well, don't just stand there like a slab of pudding. Kill me."

The Imperial lunged. It was a business move, quick and angled. Suidas avoided it by a thumb's width, disarmed him and threw him over his shoulder. "That's more like it," he said, and kicked the sword across the floor towards him. "And again."

The Imperial didn't move. He was looking at Baudila, who shrugged. Then he got to his feet, picked up the sword and lunged again. He was a quick learner. He left no room for side-stepping; but just when Giraut was convinced the thrust was about to go home, Suidas reached out with his hands wide and open, clapped them on either side of the blade, lifted it over his head, stepped under it and stamped down hard on the Imperial's instep. He collapsed, and Suidas stepped back, holding his sword.

"That's how you grab someone's blade without getting your hands all cut up," he announced to the world at large. "One of the best tricks going, if you can do it, makes you next best thing to immortal. Trouble is, unless you can get it exactly right the first time you try it, you'll spend the rest of your life trying to pick your nose with your thumb."

Baudila coughed gently. "Would you mind terribly not damaging my soldiers?" he said. "They may not be much, but they're all I've got."

"Perhaps you could show me that." Addo took four long strides and put himself between Suidas and the Imperial, who showed no signs of wanting to get up off the floor. "It looks like just the sort of move I could do with."

Suidas looked at him as though he didn't understand; then he shrugged and said, "Of course. What we need is a long, thin piece of wood. Captain?"

Baudila was only too happy to oblige. Addo wore heavy gloves the first three times, but couldn't get the hang of it; Suidas hit him three times in the solar plexus, knocking out all his breath, until Iseutz yelled at him and he grinned.

"Of course you can't do it in gloves," he said, "you can't get the traction. Now try it with your bare hands."

This time Addo caught the pretend sword and was able to maul it out of the way. He beamed with pleasure, and Suidas laughed at him. "Told you," he said. "Now, again."

The Imperials had gathered round to watch. Suidas didn't seem happy about that, and muttered something about not teaching his best move to the enemy, but Addo made him do it again. This time he got a long splinter in his palm of his hand.

"That's because you're still trying to grab," Suidas told him. "What you should be doing is squeezing. Try again."

Addo didn't make the same mistake again. After four perfect captures of the piece of wood, he said, "Can we try that with the sword?"

"If you like," Suidas replied. "Up to you. Don't blame me if I break your fingers."

Addo took a step back, and Giraut handed Suidas the blunt-edged longsword. Suidas took a low middle guard and closed the measure; then, instead of thrusting, he lifted the blade and chopped down at Addo's head. Addo caught the blade perfectly, lifted it and closed in to block Suidas' arms.

"Now you're getting it," Suidas said. "It's knowing you can do it that makes it possible."

"A bit like flying," Addo replied. "Can we try it with the messer, please?"

Suidas frowned. "I'm not going to grind the edge off my half-decent messer, thanks all the same," he said. "You never know when I might need it."

"That's all right," Addo said. "Leave it sharp."

Suidas looked at him, and it was like looking into a mirror. "The thing is," he said, "I've never tried this play with a messer myself. The blade shape's different, and the balance. I don't know if it can be done."

Addo smiled at him. "Like flying," he said. "I'm willing to give it a go, if you are."

Phrantzes started to say something, and Iseutz said, "Addo, don't be so stupid," but Addo wasn't listening. Suidas looked at him again and said, "I don't like the idea. We'll grind off the edge. There's no point taking stupid risks."

"I thought the risk was the whole point," Addo said mildly. "Otherwise it's not really training, it's just playing a game."

"We've got a big wheel grindstone in the armoury," Baudila said briskly. "I'll get my armourer to do it, it won't take a moment."

Addo shook his head. "There's no risk," he said, "really. If we don't do it properly, we might as well not bother."

There was a look of horror on Suidas' face. "Sorry," he said, "you'll have to get someone else, in that case. Messers aren't things you play around with."

"Neither are swords," Addo said gently. "Please, Suidas. And don't pull the stroke. The Permian I'll be fighting in Beaute won't be faking it."

Suidas looked as though he was about to make a run for it, but he pulled himself together and said, "Please yourself, then. I'll go and fetch the messer."

"Use mine." Addo opened his coat. There was a messer hilt sticking out from under his belt. He drew it and handed it to Suidas, who took it as though he was handling something disgusting. Then he looped his forefinger round the guard and took a step back. "Ready?"

"When you are."

Suidas swung. He gave it everything, turning his wrist a little to align the cutting edge just right, snapping with his shoulder, elbow and wrist in sequence, as if the messer was a whip. He attacked at a forty-five-degree angle, for maximum shear. Addo stood quite still, and at the very last moment, clapped his hands. He stopped the edge about three-eighths of an inch from his neck, twisted it sideways and took it crisply out of Suidas' hand, as if picking an apple.

"Thank you," Addo said. Suidas was staring at him. "That's going to be very useful indeed. You've probably saved my life, in fact."

Suidas took a step back, as though Addo was about to attack him. His eyes were glued to the messer. He was trembling.

"Can we try it again?" Addo asked; and for some reason, Giraut thought, *That was cruel, that was the cruellest thing I ever heard.* "Oh for God's sake," Iseutz wailed. "Will you please put that thing away, before someone does somebody an injury?"

Giraut realised he was waiting for Tzimisces to come forward and put a stop to it; but Tzimisces wasn't there, he'd vanished again. So he found himself stepping forward, gently pulling the messer out of Addo's hand. He heard himself say something like, "That was amazing, the way you just caught it in the air. You two are going to have to teach me how to do that, as soon as we can get hold of a blunt one to practise with."

Addo smiled vaguely. Suidas was still looking completely blank, like a dead man pulled out of a lake. Giraut realised he was holding the messer in his hand. It felt unnatural, and he was frighteningly conscious of it. He wanted to open his fingers and let it fall to the floor, but he was scared that it would gash his leg on the way down. Nobody else seemed to want it. He looked round, then handed it to Captain Baudila, who put it on a table.

Addo was fast asleep when Iseutz came and banged on his door.

"It's Suidas," she said. "You'd better come."

"What's going on?"

"Now," Iseutz said.

He climbed out of bed, and noticed that the sheath on his bedside table was empty. He thought for a moment, and could distinctly remember Baudila giving the messer back to him. "Just a moment," he said. "I can't find my boots. Oh, here they are."

Suidas was in the post room. He was standing in the middle of the floor, holding Addo's messer in a low middle guard. He'd been busy. A statue, life-size, presumably some pre-Imperial goddess or other, was lying on the floor with its head knocked off. A table had been cut to pieces, and there were deep gashes in several of the door frames.

"I think he's asleep," Iseutz whispered. "But his eyes are wide open."

Addo nodded, put his finger to his lips and walked forward, taking great care not to make any noise. Even so, Suidas appeared to have heard something; he spun round on his heels to face the direction Addo was coming from and transitioned from low middle to high back. Addo froze, watching him carefully, then started forward again. Suidas was looking just past him, as if watching someone standing shoulder to shoulder with him. Iseutz jammed her fist in her mouth.

Addo stopped, just short of long measure. "Captain Deutzel."

Suidas looked puzzled. Addo waited for a moment, then said, "Sergeant."

"Sir."

"What the hell do you think you're doing, Sergeant?"

Suidas looked at him – straight at him, but couldn't see him. Iseutz could tell by the look on his face that he was trying to figure out where the voice was coming from. "Sir?"

"Stand down, Sergeant. Now. That's an order."

Suidas didn't move. Addo frowned, then walked round him in a tight semicircle. Then, so fast that Iseutz couldn't follow the movement, he stepped in and punched Suidas on the side of the head. There was a clatter as the messer hit the floor, but Suidas was still standing. Addo punched him again, and this time he fell. He twitched once, then lay still.

"Iseutz." His voice was high and shaky. "Get a doctor."

"I don't know—"

"Get a doctor," he repeated. "Quickly."

The Blueskin doctor was binding Addo's knuckles. "No harm done, luckily," he was saying. "You could easily have broken something."

"I'm fine," Addo repeated. "Really."

"Of course you are," the doctor said wearily. "Right, that ought to do. Try not to use that hand for a day or so. You ought to take more care," he added. "We need you to be fit for the big match. I tried to get tickets, but I was too late."

Addo gave him a poisonous look, and he went away. "How is he?" he asked.

Phrantzes looked up and scowled at him. "Did you really have to hit him quite so hard?"

"He had to punch him twice," Iseutz said. "He wouldn't fall over."

"What the hell was all that about?" Giraut asked. "Was he asleep, or what?"

Phrantzes sighed. "Apparently it's not the first time," he said. "His – well, the woman he lives with, she told us he's done this sort of thing before. But she said he was over it, and there hadn't been an episode for six months."

"There was a man in my father's regiment," Addo said. "And by all accounts he was a model soldier, the bravest man in the corps, my father said. But sometimes he'd get up in the middle of the night, walk across the camp and start killing horses. He had no idea what he was doing. When he woke up and they told him, he couldn't believe it. I think he killed himself, in the end."

"Thank you so much," Iseutz snapped. "That's exactly what we needed to hear."

"I'm sorry, I didn't mean to suggest—"

Phrantzes coughed loudly. "The doctor believes it's an imbalance in his choleric humour. He's prescribed some medicine to put it right. He told me these cases are entirely treatable. It's all a question of diet, apparently. Too much salty food and not enough fruit."

When Suidas woke up, he stared at them as though he'd never seen them before. Then he asked, "What happened?"

Phrantzes opened his mouth but Addo got in first. "You were walking in your sleep," he said. "You had a blow to the head. The doctor says you'll be fine."

Suidas frowned. "Did I do anything?"

Addo smiled. "Nothing terrible," he said.

"Thank God for that," Suidas said. "Sontha told me once I threatened her with a sword, thought she was Aram Chantat. She nearly left me because of it." He breathed out and lay back on the pillows. "I'm glad it wasn't anything like that."

Addo grinned. "Nothing like that," he said. "Do you remember anything?"

"Not a lot. I was dreaming." Suidas scratched his head, then winced. "I was taking a bath, as a matter of fact, in that amazing bath house they've got here. And the dried-up river started flowing again, and water came shooting down on me from the cistern. I thought I was going to drown."

"The doctor says you've been eating too much salt."

Suidas laughed. "They always say that, the Blueskins. Too much salt or not enough greens. That and bowel movements, they're obsessed. Bloody good doctors, though."

"We'll let you get some rest," Phrantzes said. "There's still a day before our escort gets here, so stay in bed and try to sleep."

Suidas gave him a thin smile. "In the circumstances," he said, "are you sure that's a good idea?"

Tzimisces reappeared late in the afternoon. He'd picked up a slight cold since they'd seen him last, which probably explained why he didn't seem to hear Iseutz when she asked him where he'd been. Instead, he blew his nose in a huge green silk handkerchief.

"The bad news," he said, "is that the trouble is definitely spreading. There's been rioting in several large towns and at least three important mines, and that's just in this area. The good news is, the Aram Chantat have stayed loyal to the government and they've dealt with the riots in their own charming way. Which is fine by us," he added, with a sideways glance at Suidas. "It means our own little spot of trouble back in Luzir Soleth will just sort of merge seamlessly into the general carnage, and nobody'll give it a second thought."

Phrantzes had a vaguely hopeful look on his face. He said,

"With all this trouble going on, I can't believe the Permians will want to carry on with the tour."

"Really?" Tzimisces smiled at him. "What makes you say that?"

"I'd have thought the last thing they'd want would be large, volatile gatherings of people. A fencing match would be just the sort of flashpoint that could lead to a riot. They'll have to call the whole thing off, it's the only possible course of action."

"I don't think so," Tzimisces said, sounding like an indulgent parent dismissing his child's particularly far-fetched suggestion. "You've seen how crazy these people are about fencing. In fact, cancelling the matches would be the surest way of starting a riot anyone could think of. No, by the time we get to Beaute all this nonsense will have burnt itself out, and we can get on with the job we came here to do. You can be absolutely sure about that."

Their new escort commander was called Major Cuniva. He was about forty years old, bald – completely hairless, in fact, like a freshly scalded hide – and enormous, as though he belonged to a completely different species. He was the first Imperial they'd met who didn't seem to be permanently frozen to the bone; he wore a fur-lined coat and a scarf, but no hat or gloves. He was missing the top two joints from the index finger of his left hand.

"We shouldn't have too much difficulty making up time to Beaute," he said cheerfully, in a voice so deep that Giraut was sure he felt the floor shake under his feet. "We can leave the main road at Chauzida and cut through the mountains. There's a pass I know that'll bring us back on the road just outside Dosor." He paused, waiting to see if anyone dared contradict him, then went on, "You must be Adulescentulus Carnufex, the general's son. It's an honour to meet you."

Addo gave him a weak smile. "I take it you were in the War."

"Ten years," Cuniva replied. "I started as a young second lieutenant, and ended up as a captain attached to the general staff. Of course, I've studied all your father's campaigns. In fact," he added, with just a touch of diffidence, which suited him like a straw hat on a dragon, "I've written a short essay on the Belcors campaign. As it happens, I have a copy with me. I'd be extremely grateful if you could glance through it and give me your opinion."

There was a faint but unmistakable leaden weariness in Addo's voice as he said, "Of course, I'd be delighted." But Cuniva's face lit up with joy, suddenly and unexpectedly transformed into a thing of beauty.

"I have absolutely no idea if this is any good or not," Addo announced later, as the coach bounced along the main road. "I've never even heard of half the things he's talking about."

"Just say it's marvellous and wonderful," Suidas said. "He'll be your slave for life."

"Yes, but what if he asks me specific questions? He'll realise straight away that I don't know the first thing about the rotten Belcors campaign."

"Really?" Tzimisces was looking at him.

"Really and truly," Addo replied. "My father's never talked about it much."

"It was a great victory, wasn't it?" Giraut said.

Addo shrugged. "I guess so. But I don't think it was one of his favourites, if you see what I mean."

Giraut noticed that Phrantzes was looking out of the window; something he didn't usually do, because he said it made him travel sick. Tzimisces said, "I know a bit about that campaign. If you like, I'll skim through it and give you a few notes."

It sounded for all the world like the offer of a minor act of kindness, but Addo hesitated. "You really don't want to wade through all this," he said, pleasantly enough. "For one thing, it's vilely written."

"Ah." Tzimisces smiled. "Let me guess. Flowery periphrases, back-to-back literary allusions and quotations from thousand-year-old authors. A marked reluctance to use one word when twelve can be jammed in if you sit on the lid."

Addo smiled. "Something like that."

"All the hallmarks of the approved Imperial military literary style," Tzimisces said. "It's used for everything they write, from dispatches to supply requisitions. They teach it at the staff college. You can't get promotion unless you can churn it out by the yard."

"That's stupid," Iseutz said.

"Not at all," Tzimisces replied earnestly. "It's one of the subtle filters the Imperial military uses to keep riff-raff out of the higher echelons of the military hierarchy."

"That's stupid, too."

"You clearly don't know your Imperial history," Tzimisces said. "Several hundred years ago, they had nearly a century of on-and-off civil wars. Seventy-four emperors in ninety-one years, of whom precisely two died of natural causes. All because of talented, ambitious men rising through the ranks to command large provincial armies, which they then used to seize power. It was very nearly the end of the Empire." He paused to blow his nose. "But nowadays it doesn't matter a damn how talented and ambitious you are. If you can't balance a pair of antitheses while using the appropriate quote from Post-Realist poetry, you'll never make it above major. Which would probably account for our new friend out there. He's clearly an efficient and experienced officer, but he's got an Eastern accent you could cut with a knife. Which is good luck for us," he added cheerfully. "This is his big chance to impress someone and maybe get called back home, after seventeen years in this place. He'll be trying his hardest, you can bet on that."

"Wonderful," Suidas said sourly. "Assuming he's on our side."

Giraut was still watching Phrantzes. Ever since Tzimisces had asked to look at the stupid essay, he'd been staring out of the window, perfectly still, like an animal trying to escape the notice of a predator it knows it can't outrun. He reminded himself that he wasn't there to look after anybody but himself; even so, he hoped Addo or Iseutz would notice, and do something about it.

Maybe Addo had got the message after all. He lifted his book
level with his nose and started reading again. Tzimisces' kind
offer had clearly been refused. Not that Tzimisces seemed put
out in any way; he wiped his nose with the monster handkerchief, closed his eyes, snuggled his chin on his chest and
appeared to go to sleep. Addo carried on reading, but from time
to time he lifted his head and peeped over the top of the book, as
if it was a battlement, in Tzimisces' general direction.

When the news of the riots in Luzir Soleth reached Scheria, the
chairman of the Bank called an emergency cabinet meeting.

The situation, he told the Board, was bad. As far as he
could tell, the explosion of public anger following the assassination of Minister Ashok had been entirely spontaneous, and
was spread across the full spectrum of Permian society. By its
very nature, a spontaneous outburst lacked focus and direction; the people were very angry, but as yet they didn't really
know who they were angry with, let alone what it would take to
appease their wrath. That, he pointed out, was both good and
bad. Bad, because until they made their minds up, or had them
made up for them, it was impossible to formulate a coherent
reaction or to know which side to be on; good, because they
had a little bit of time in which to try and make sense of the
situation.

"Getting down to cases," he went on, "I'm not sure there's a
great deal we can do. It's not like the rioters in the streets are
going to be particularly interested in what we think about anything. In fact, I'd say the worst thing we could do is interfere
visibly at this stage. The latest reports say the army's stayed
loyal to the government, and obviously, as long as they've got the
military on their side, sooner or later they'll put down the riots
and things will get back to normal."

"Quite," someone interrupted. "But we've got to bear in
mind the nature of the Permian military. They're practically all
mercenaries."

"Indeed," the chairman said. "And at the moment, the only entity in Permia with the money to pay their wages is the government, so of course they're staying loyal. And if the disorder can be put down while it's still just a mob throwing stones, before it crystallises into an organised opposition, that'll be the end of the matter and we can go back to where we were. But if the mob finds leaders, and the leaders get money, you can more or less guarantee what'll come next. There'll be a brisk auction, and whoever wins gets Permia." He paused to drink a little water. "Really," he went on, "on one level it's pretty simple. If we want to get ahead of events and put together a set of useful contingency plans, we need to look at where the money is."

"Excuse me," said somebody else, "but wouldn't it help to know who killed this Minister Ashok, and why?"

The chairman shook his head. "Interesting to future historians, maybe. Right now, we need to know who's going to win, and I can see three possible outcomes. One, no coherent opposition arises, the government wins, we're back to where we started from. Two, there's an opposition, it outbids the government and takes over. Three, there's an opposition, but the government wins the auction and stays in power, the opposition goes on the defensive and digs in – strikes in the mines, that sort of thing – and there's a nasty stalemate until something changes and the balance of power shifts."

"Fine," someone said. "Which one do we want?"

The chairman sighed. "Good question," he said. "We aren't exactly wild about the current Permian government, but they could be a lot worse. There's reason to believe that if the mob favours anyone, it's the war faction. But if this government survives, it'll only be because of the military. The soldiers and the line officers are Blueskins and savages, but the senior command is still basically Permian military aristocracy; in other words, the war faction. Two sides of the same coin."

"So what we want is the stalemate," someone said.

"Not really," the chairman replied sadly. "That just puts off the crisis for a while, allowing it to build up a really good head of steam for when it does eventually explode."

There was a tense silence. Then somebody said, "Aren't we getting ahead of ourselves just a bit? We don't know if the trouble's spread, or whether it's confined to Luzir Soleth. It could turn out to be nothing but a minor local problem. If we over-react, surely that's the worst thing we could do."

"He's right," said someone else at the far end of the table. "We can't put together a policy until we know exactly what's going on over there. I mean, if the rioting spreads to some of the other mining towns, or the cities, even, that's definitely a problem for us. But we don't know that's what's going to happen. We've just got to hold our water and see how it turns out."

Afterwards, Turcuin Boioannes, director of investment policy, tracked the chairman down to the small cloister just off the southern quadrangle, where he was sitting on a stone bench, reading a document and eating bread and cheese. "What was all that about?" he asked.

The chairman gave him a sad smile. "You don't want to know," he said. "Believe me."

Boioannes sat down beside him. "Probably not," he said. "Look, I'm on your side. What's going on?"

The chairman sighed and put the papers down on the paved floor."What the hell," he said. "You'll find out soon enough, I'm sure. We've got a problem, and it's my fault."

Boioannes grinned at him. "A wise man once said, there's no problem that can't be solved by a kind word, a five-figure payment or three inches of sharp metal. What have you done?"

"I've lent forty million nomismata of the Bank's money to the Permian government," the chairman said. "And I neglected to tell anybody beforehand."

For a while, Boioannes was completely unaware of the passage of time. "We haven't got forty million nomismata."

"Not in actual money, no. Most of it's a line of credit secured on Bank stock. If we're called on it, someone, the Empire presumably, is going to end up owning the Bank."

Boioannes breathed in and out slowly. "What on earth possessed you to do such a thing?"

The chairman smiled at him. "Desperation," he replied. "Turcuin, the Bank's about to go under. I haven't told anybody because I couldn't bring myself to do it, but we're this close to the edge. We're massively overcommitted to long-term loans to small farmers, small workshops, practically everybody in the country's borrowed from us, and we've had to borrow the money from the big Imperial banks, secured on future tax revenues we know aren't going to happen because the country simply can't afford to pay them. We all know this, deep inside, but nobody's dared say it out loud. Meanwhile, I've got to pay the Stewards of the South Gate Temple a quarter of a million by the end of the month, and then I've got to find a hundred and ten thousand for the Caecilius brothers, and so it goes on. There's nothing like enough coming in from our debtors, and I've got to show the Imperials *something*. And then I had this wild, crazy thought. Why not make up a whole lot of pretend money, lend it to the Permians and pay off our creditors with the interest?"

Another long silence. Then Boioannes asked: "Why the Permians, for crying out loud?"

"They asked." The chairman's grin widened. "They're broke too. During the War they sold silver futures to pay their mercenaries. It doesn't matter how much silver they dig out of the ground in the next twenty years, because none of it's theirs, it already belongs to the Eastern Empire." He paused for a moment while what he'd just said sank in, and all the blood drained from Boioannes' face. "Meanwhile, they've got thousands of Blueskins and Aram Chantat right in the heart of their territory who need to be paid or else who knows what they'll do. They really need the money, trust me."

"But . . . " Boioannes shook his head, as if trying to clear it. "There's no chance in hell of them ever paying us back. The

Empire's not buying their silver any more. The Regia process—"

"Doesn't matter," the chairman said. "It's pretend money anyhow, most of it, so if we lose it . . . " He laughed. "The interest, they're paying that in Permian government bonds, which the Western Empire banks are quite happy to take from us, as interest payments on our debt. But if the Permian government falls . . . "

Boioannes closed his eyes. "Talking to you purely as a friend," he said, "if I were you, I'd go home and pack. As an officer of the Bank—"

"It could still be all right," the chairman said quietly, and a shaft of sunlight, passing through the stained glass of the rose window at the far end of the cloister, drenched him in red fire. "Have you got any idea how much silver, iron, copper, God knows what else, there is lying under the ground in the DMZ? If we can only get a treaty, then the Permians can go in there, formally claim the mineral rights, sell the futures, pay us the capital, the forty million; with that money, I can pay off the Western banks, and suddenly everything will be just fine. Miracle. Magic wand. *That's* what I was thinking of, Turcuin, and it's a stroke of genius, I know it is. We could have it all signed and sealed in a month, if only we could get that stupid bloody treaty." He sighed. "And I was so close," he went on, "thanks to my friend, ally and kindred spirit in the Permian cabinet, who's been pulling strings and twisting arms on this for the last six months."

Boioannes winced. "Minister Ashok."

"That man was a hero," the chairman said, "the best, he really understood what had to be done. The thought that anybody could be *stupid* enough to kill him . . . " For a moment he seemed to have difficulty finding words. "*Stupid*," he repeated. "It's like picking up a red-hot iron off the fire and poking it in your own eye. Of all the idiotic, suicidal things to do. I can't begin to imagine . . . " He paused, then said, "Well, of course I can. Ashok's main agenda was reconciling the old military aristocracy with the mine owners, with a view to getting the exiles who were thrown out at the end of the War pardoned and recalled. A lot of the people in power helped themselves to the exiles' land and property, which they'd have had to give back if the exiles were pardoned. I don't think you need to look further than that for a motive. Unfortunately, those are the people who helped us stitch up the peace, and who we're having to do business with right now."

Boioannes nodded. "The peace party, in other words."

"Precisely. It's a crying shame that the good guys had to be a bunch of thieves and embezzlers, but what can you do? Anyway, that's what I've been carrying around with me for the last three weeks." He turned his head slowly and looked at Boioannes. "What are you going to do, now I've told you?"

"Me?" Boioannes looked vaguely shocked by the question. "Forget this conversation, for a start."

The chairman didn't look convinced. "Not sure you'll be able to."

"I can try. Also, I can delay the general audit." The chairman's eyes opened wide, and Boioannes laughed. "You'd forgotten about that, hadn't you?"

"God help me, yes, I had. Look, can you do that? Because if not . . ."

"It'll be my head nailed up next to yours on a gateway somewhere," Boioannes said, with feeling. "I don't see that I've got a choice. And really, we need to tell a few other people about this. If we want to get the treaty expedited—"

The chairman moved so fast that Boioannes didn't have time to react. Before he could shrink away, the chairman's hand was on his collar, pulling it tight around his neck. "You tell them," he said in a rasping whisper. "Say you've found out, you're utterly appalled and once it's all over you're going to have to do something about it, but meanwhile you desperately need their co-operation if the Bank's to be saved. I can't do it, they'd be so angry they wouldn't hear me out. But Goidas and Maniaces, on the foreign affairs committee, they'll listen to you."

Boioannes nodded. "I was thinking of Rimbaut Mezezius. He'd be the man to push the treaty through."

"Would he . . .?"

"If he wants to marry my niece," Boioannes replied grimly. "Listen, leave it to me. I still can't believe you've done this appalling thing, but since you have, we'd better try and make the best of it. Meanwhile, you'll have to use your contacts in Permia." He paused, and looked worried. "If you've still got any, I mean."

The chairman nodded slowly. "Two," he said, "both in the cabinet. Neither of them's mad keen to get directly involved, but I guess the prospect of the Aram Chantat declaring that they're open to offers might just make them feel a degree more energetic. I'll put pressure on them to renew the treaty negotiations, if you can make sure that our side'll be on board when it happens. If we do this together, and if there's still a government in Permia we can do business with, we may possibly come out of this in one piece. Otherwise, we might as well send a polite note round to the Irrigator asking him if he feels like forming a government."

Boioannes went home and wrote seven letters. Five of them he gave to servants to deliver. The other two he handed to his sons. They weren't best pleased at being called away from their studies to carry letters across the city, but they knew their father well enough not to argue when he had that particular look on his face.

With that out of the way, he put on a light coat (the sun was coming out) and walked up the hill to the Longest Day monastery. The porter knew him by now, nodded and opened the door.

"How is he?" Boioannes asked.

"He's wonderful for his age," the porter replied guardedly. "You know the way."

Boioannes found his uncle in the walled garden, on his knees, hand-weeding round the onions. He sat up when he heard footsteps on the gravel path, and looked round.

"Oh," he said. "It's you."

"Afraid so," Boioannes replied. There was something about his uncle in his monastic robe that made him feel about twelve years old. "Have you got a minute? I need to ask you something."

The old man shrugged. "I'm just a simple brother of the Order, I've got all the time in the world," he said sourly. "You're the incredibly busy man of affairs. To what do I owe the honour?"

Boioannes sighed and slowly lowered himself to his knees, taking care to kneel between the rows and not crush any onions. He reached out, wrapped his fingers round a clump of soft light green weed, and pulled gently. "I've just had a very disturbing talk with the chairman," he said.

The old man clicked his tongue. "That boy's a fool," he said. "I should never have promoted him out of the copying room."

Boioannes laughed. "Well, you did," he said, "so I guess this is as much your fault as anybody else's. Really, I should make you come out of retirement and sort it out."

The old man held up both his hands. "Never," he said. "Forty years in the Bank was quite enough for me, thank you very much. You have no idea how much happier I am here."

"Getting up at three in the morning for early mass?"

"I have a dispensation from the abbot," the old man said gravely, "because of my knees. Now, what exactly has the idiot boy done this time?"

"He's lent forty million to the Permian government."

The old man kept quite still for five, possibly six seconds. Then he began to laugh.

"I take it back," he said eventually. "The child has a certain degree of imagination, not to mention courage."

"We haven't got—"

"Of course we haven't," the old man said. "Presumably he's put up Bank stock to cover it."

Boioannes nodded his head. "It's so the Permians can pay the Eastern Empire for the hire of the Blueskins and the Aram Chantat," he said. "But there's been dreadful rioting in Permia, and the government could fall. In which case . . ."

"Yes, I heard something about that," the old man said, with a deliberate vagueness that made Boioannes want to hit him. "So, let me see, the only asset the Permian regime has got left is the hope of the mineral deposits in the Debatable Land. Presumably the idea was to hurry through a treaty, get the Permians to sell the futures, pay back the loan and thereby turn forty million imaginary nomismata into forty million real ones. Yes, I like that. It's rather a nice idea."

Boioannes stared. Fifty-two years he'd known his uncle, and still the old monster could surprise him. "You *like* it?"

The old man shrugged. "It's probably what I'd have done if I was still at the Bank," he said. "After all, there's absolutely nothing else that could be done. There's nothing left. The War's taken it all. This way, we get assured peace and genuine solvency, both of which are otherwise hopelessly beyond our reach. Bless the child, I was right about him after all. I'm never wrong about people," he added. "It's my one talent."

"But Uncle . . ."

"What's the alternative?" the old man demanded sternly. "As things are now, the Bank will collapse within the year. The military barons will then stage a coup, repudiate our foreign debt, and get us in a war with the Western Empire and Permia simultaneously. We'll beat the Permians, the Westerners will beat us, we'll appeal to the East for help and be annexed to the Eastern Empire. That's what Carnufex and his people have wanted all along; he trusts the Easterners, they absolutely worship him, he can see himself as commander-in-chief of the Imperial army in ten years' time. And there's no question but that the Easterners will run this country far better than we ever could. They've got the resources, after all." He smiled, and teased out a nettle, gripping its stem hard between forefinger and thumb so it couldn't sting him. "I've been resigned to that for some time," he said. "In fact, I've been reading up extensively on fire worship. I should be reluctant to have to convert at my time of life, but it's always sensible to be prepared."

Boioannes blinked, as if he'd been staring into a bright light. "You might have told me," he said. "I'm supposed to be governing this country. How can I do that if people won't tell me anything?"

"If you can't be bothered to find things out for yourself," the old man said mildly, "then I have absolutely no sympathy. If I can figure it out kneeling in an onion patch . . ." He shrugged. "Well, there it is. And really, I don't see a problem, provided the treaty can be forced through."

"But these riots . . ."

"In five towns," the old man said, "in the north-west mining belt. And I believe the savages have the situation well in hand. Just so long as nothing else happens, I don't see that there's an insurmountable problem. After all, you've still got the Permian chancellor and the interior minister in your pockets."

Boioannes managed to catch his breath, just enough to ask the question he'd been wanting to ask for the best part of fifty years. "Uncle," he said, "how the hell do you know all this?"

The old man pulled a sad face. "Turcuin, you idiot," he said. "You're a good boy, but you never did master elementary arithmetic. We know more or less how many mercenaries there are in Permia."

"Do we?"

"Yes," the old man said firmly. "And we know how much they're paid. Forty million isn't enough."

Boioannes frowned. "It isn't?"

"Good heavens, no. It's about two-thirds, if that." He flicked out a dock root, noted with a scowl that he'd taken an onion with it, and carefully pressed it back into the loosened soil. "And who do you think lent the Permians the other twenty million?"

Before Boioannes had recovered sufficiently to think about

the implications of that, the old man nudged him in the ribs and slowly hauled himself to his feet. A young monk was standing on the path, looking more than a little scared.

"Well?" the old man said.

"Father Abbot would like to see you," the monk said. "In his study. If it's convenient."

"I think it'll have to be," the old man said. "You can find your own way out, can't you, Turcuin? My nephew," he explained to the young monk, who smiled nervously. "He's just leaving."

Boioannes walked slowly on the way home, as though he didn't really want to get there. It was late, and the Watch were clearing the streets so that the food carts from the country could come in and make their deliveries. In a couple of hours' time, Westgate and Coppermarket would be jammed with every type of wheeled vehicle imaginable, all part of the vast and horribly overengineered mechanism that brought food to a huge assemblage of people who had no land and no livestock to feed themselves from. Years ago, as a small boy during the War, he'd asked his father what would happen if, for some reason, the carts stopped coming. No need to worry, his father had told him, we have three public granaries, as well as a dozen private corn chandlers; there's enough food in the city to last a month, easily. Yes, he'd replied, but what if the carts stopped coming for a month? What'd happen then? Well, they won't, his father told him irritably, and that was the end of the conversation; mostly as a result of which, he'd reached the conclusion that the old government had to go and someone – the Bank, as it turned out – had to get control and start taking these things *seriously*.

Well, he thought. They'd had three years' supply of grain left in the city granary at Flos Verjan when the Irrigator opened the sluices, and a lot of good it did them. War had to be avoided, at all costs, no matter what, because war killed men and burnt cities, evaporated money, drained resources, ruined everything. The chairman understood about war, which was why he'd made the decision to take Scheria away from the military aristocracy – and, presumably, why he'd been prepared to lend forty million to the enemy, even though the Bank didn't have forty million, or four million, or four hundred thousand. When the enemy is swinging at your head, you raise your arm to block the cut, even though it means losing your right hand.

Even so . . .

His uncle, now; probably the most brilliant financier in Scherian history, who'd resigned from the Board and entered a monastery (he was also Scheria's most prominent atheist) because he didn't hold with the Bank interfering in politics. At the time, nobody had been able to make sense of it. Of course the Bank interfered in politics, every day at every level; it had the money, without which politics simply wouldn't work. But the old man had seen a line that nobody else could see and refused to cross it, and they'd all been trying very hard not to think about that ever since.

("All right," he remembered arguing, desperately trying to talk his uncle out of it, "what about the Temple interfering in politics? Isn't that just as bad?"

"Oddly enough," his uncle had replied, "I don't have a problem with that."

"But you don't even believe in the Invincible Sun."

A sad, you-ought-to-know-better look: "Oh come on, Turcuin. Since when has belief had anything to do with organised religion?")

Brother Perceptuus, who had been Dancred Boioannes when he was still in the world, sat beside the abbot's chair until he woke up.

"I'm sorry," the abbot said, once he'd taken a moment to recognise him. "Have I kept you waiting very long?"

Perceptuus smiled. "I was weeding onions," he said, "and talking to my idiot nephew. Only too glad to be interrupted."

The abbot nodded. "Disturbing reports from Permia," he said.

"Quite," Perceptuus said. "And that's not all." He hesitated. Abbot Symbatus looked terrible: white and thin, his skin stretched over his bones like a hide drying in the sun. On the other hand, he was the right person to tell, and nobody else would do. "The Bank has lent forty million nomismata to the Permian government."

For a moment he was afraid the abbot hadn't understood; that he was too weak, no longer capable of handling information of that order of magnitude. A complicated train of thought passed through his mind: a new abbot – at the worst possible time; six or seven likely candidates, all of them instantly assessed and found wanting, which meant he'd have to do the job himself, which was something he really didn't want; then how to get himself elected, all the compromises and threats and fuss that that would entail. So he was mightily relieved when the abbot smiled and said, "Now that's interesting. Tell me about it."

Which he did. Afterwards, the abbot was quiet for a while. Then he frowned and said, "You'll have to go there, you realise."

"Where?"

"Permia." The abbot closed his eyes, then opened them again. "I'm dreadfully sorry, I know it'll be a burden, but—"

"That's all right," Perceptuus said, a little too quickly. "Always wanted to see the place, as a matter of fact."

The abbot smiled. Lies, it was commonly believed, bounced off him like arrows off tempered armour. "It's a great shame," he said, "that you've never found the comfort of faith. I've been lucky. I really do believe in the Invincible Sun. It makes doing what has to be done so much easier."

Perceptuus shrugged. "I believe in the Order," he said.

"That's not quite the same thing. It's like believing in justice, or the universal brotherhood of Man. It imposes responsibilities, instead of taking them away. Never mind, you may still come to it in time. It's possible that this business may tip the balance, I don't know."

Perceptuus smiled. "You think so?"

"Oh, I have high hopes," the abbot replied gently. "After all, there's nothing more conducive to faith than a clear and evident miracle. Which is what we'll need," he added with a smile. "A miracle of unprecedented magnitude and scope, big enough to convince even a hardened sceptic such as yourself. I, on the other hand, am quietly confident, because I have faith." He closed his eyes and folded his hands on his chest; doing a quite creditable impression of a dead man, Perceptuus thought, or maybe he's just getting in some practice beforehand. "Come and see me tomorrow," he said, "before you go."

Before he retired to his cell for the night, Perceptuus went to the scriptorium, where he begged a scrap of waste parchment and the use of a pen and some ink from a brother who owed him a favour. He had to write small in order to fit it all in. Then he went to the gatehouse, where the porter's young nephew was guzzling an illegal meal of leftovers.

"Exactly who I wanted to see," he said cheerfully, as the boy tried to hide a huge mound of cold mashed swede behind his hand. "Do me a favour, and take this letter over to the Bank. Tell them it's important, for Director Boioannes from his uncle. Go on," he said, "the food'll still be here when you get back. I might even use my influence with the buttery and find you a couple of sausages."

Which he did; but the boy didn't eat them. Instead, he wrapped them carefully in his left sock and took them home for his mother.

You'll know it when you get there, he'd been told. Just watch out for a ruined tower on top of a hill shaped like an upturned bucket.

He'd been looking, and of course every hill in Permia looked like an upturned bucket if you stared at it long enough. So far, however, he hadn't seen one with a ruined tower on the top. But there had been mist, and driving rain, and of course they hadn't followed the road they'd been expected to go by, and there had been times he'd fallen asleep in spite of himself. Then there was the problem of how to stop the coach, get out and go away for an hour without drawing attention to himself. The more he thought about it, the more impossible it became; but he'd been told, it's vitally important, whatever you do, make sure you go to the ruined tower on the upturned-bucket hill and see if there's a message waiting. It's our only chance to communicate with you, maybe warn you about some unforeseen disaster or notify you of a radical change in the plan.

In the distance he could see a long line of hills. They all looked like upturned buckets, and they were too far away for him to be able to see if one of them had a ruined tower on it.

The appalling business in Luzir Soleth must have changed everything, it went without saying. But how long would it take for a message to get from Scheria to the upturned bucket? A first-rate trained courier riding flat out, non-stop, with frequent changes of horses – but no chance of that in Permian territory, unless there was some sort of reciprocal arrangement with the Permian post for vitally urgent diplomatic mail. No, forget that: you wouldn't dare use official channels for a decidedly unofficial communication. Come to that, for all he knew, the Permians had intercepted the message. If ever he found the upturned bucket, therefore, he might well find Blueskins waiting to arrest him, or at best a substituted message, subtly phrased to subvert the whole mission.

Stop the coach, please: call of nature. Sure. Mere modesty wouldn't explain why he then chose to walk three miles and climb a hill. So far, the best explanation he'd been able to concoct was *I must've got lost and gone round in circles, I've been walking for hours*; and that wasn't going to fool anybody if they stopped in the middle of a featureless plain with a prospect of faint blue hills in the far distance. Really, it was too much to expect. You'd have thought they'd have trained professionals for this sort of thing, rather than relying on unwilling amateurs.

That made him remember the smiling face of the man who'd

given him his final briefing. *We have every confidence in you. After all, what you lack in knowledge and experience, you more than make up for in motivation. I mean, you do want to see her again, don't you?*

And if there was no ruined tower, no message, no radical change of plan, he'd have no alternative but to do what he'd been sent to do. The enormity, the sheer unthinkable scale of it, appalled him. *I won't lie to you, it's a horrible, dangerous job. If you fail, you'll die. If you succeed, God only knows how you'll live with yourself afterwards.* The grinning face, across a plain bare-wood table, by the light of a badly trimmed lamp. *Really, I can't think of any inducement that'd make me do it, not even if they threatened to kill my children. But clearly, you're more amenable.*

(Not for the first time, he considered telling the others; throwing himself on their mercy, explaining to them exactly what the real purpose of the mission was, begging them to help him find a way out of it. They were basically good people, after all. Iseutz had a kind heart and a strong instinctive sense of justice. Addo Carnufex seemed to feel at least a sense of the guilt that came with the family name; he was prepared to stand up for the others, if he felt he had to. They'd help him, wouldn't they, especially once they realised what they were blundering in to, what was about to happen, with them right at the epicentre. Three or four times he'd opened his mouth to say something, and each time he'd frozen, and the moment had passed. He'd pictured the look on their faces, the stare, the unspoken *How could you possibly have agreed to such a thing?* And besides, he didn't really know them, any more than they knew him – which, clearly, they didn't. If they did, they'd have strangled him and hidden his body in a ditch.)

If I try not to think about it, it'll go away.

Far away, outside the coach, he could see hills. Without any conscious thought, he scanned them for shapes and obtrusions. They looked just like a row of upturned buckets. On the top of one of them, he saw something that could have been a ruined tower, but it turned out to be just a particularly large tree.

"Ten miles to Beaute," Tzimisces said cheerfully. "We'll be there in an hour."

So, inevitably, the left-side lead horse went lame. According to Captain Cuniva, it had contrived to pick up a stone in its back nearside hoof. It was all right. One of his men was riding to Beaute to collect a replacement horse, they'd be back on the road in three hours, no problem at all. Until then, they might as well stretch their legs and have a breath of fresh air.

Having walked up and down and taken in the view, Giraut sat down on a large rock. In every direction, as far as the eye could see, there was nothing but brambles, head high and hopelessly tangled. Someone obviously came along and cut them back from time to time, to stop them swamping the road. Otherwise, there'd be no hope of crossing the plain. It occurred to him to wonder how on earth it had got like this.

"Charcoal," Tzimsices explained, and Giraut wasn't in the least surprised that he knew the answer. He knew everything. "Seventy years ago, this was all a huge forest, from Beaute right up as far as the Bec de Corbin. Then they built the big smelting plant at Beaute, and of course they needed charcoal. That's why they built it there, because it was so handy for an inexhaustible supply of fuel." He lifted his head, shading his eyes with his hand against the noon sun. "Well, the supply got exhausted. Under that lot, there's millions of tree stumps, which they never bothered to root out. They killed them when they burnt off the brash and the loppings, and the ash made the ground rich, so the brambles took over. I guess in a hundred years or so the stumps will have rotted away, and it might be possible to clear all this garbage and plough it up. But I wouldn't fancy it. By now, the briar roots probably go down a mile, so you'd never be rid of them. You wouldn't have thought it was possible to kill land, but it looks like the Permians have managed it."

"So this is all because of the silver works."

Tzimisces shook his head. "Iron," he replied. "There was a major iron seam, though it's all worked out now. This was where all the iron came from for the armouries, for the War."

Giraut looked again, and saw a sea of brambles, an inundation, waves saw-edged with thorns. "It came in handy, though," Tzimisces was saying, "it saved Beaute from Addo's dad. He couldn't get across this lot, so he turned south and took out Flos Verjan instead. Which was a stroke of luck for *us*, because of course Flos Verjan won us the War. If he'd stuck to his original plan and taken Beaute, we'd probably still be fighting." Suddenly he threw his head back and laughed, as if he'd just figured out a long and complex problem that had proved in the end to be ridiculously simple. "Wonderful, isn't it, how things turn out the way they do, and all because of things you wouldn't have thought were possibly relevant. The Permians build the biggest armoury this side of the Eastern Empire, and it wins us the War, all thanks to a shitload of brambles. It's a bit like chess, I suppose, only you're playing against someone who thinks ninety moves ahead, so once he's moved one pawn one square, you might as well give up, because you're as good as screwed already. Maybe that's why I'm so bad at chess," he added, with a pleasant smile. "I don't have the patience. My wife's the chess player in our family. I've given up playing against her. Two moves in, I can see what she's up to, so I resign. It drives her wild."

It hadn't occurred to Giraut that Tzimisces could ever have done anything so human as acquire a wife. Suddenly he wanted to know about her. How old was she? Was she pretty? How the hell could she bear to live with someone like that, even if he was virtually never at home?

The rider came back with a new horse and the latest news from the city. There had been riots. Several public buildings, including the law courts and the barracks, had been burnt down. The Aram Chantat had restored order, eventually, after some fairly intense fighting, but the rioters had broken into the armoury and helped themselves to enough hardware to outfit two regiments. It remained to be seen whether they were proposing to use the stuff, or whether they'd taken it simply because it was relatively portable and worth money. There was, of course, no question of cancelling the fencing match. On the contrary, it was imperative that it took place as planned, or else there'd be more riots. "Basically," Cuniva said, "they're relying on you to calm the situation, take people's minds off politics for a while until the mob's had a chance to cool down."

Phrantzes, looking terrified, mumbled something about whether the authorities could guarantee their safety. Cuniva gave him an indulgent smile.

"You don't have to worry on that score," he said. "They've brought in my old regiment, and two others, as well as a large contingent of the Aram Senhor. There's at least a dozen members of the Council who'll be attending the match, and three government ministers. You'll be in the safest place in Permia."

An awkward silence; then Iseutz said, "Splendid. So now all we've got to worry about are the people with sharp weapons who're *allowed* to try and kill us. Thank you. You've really set my mind at rest."

Cuniva looked faintly shocked, which made Suidas laugh. "Anyway," Tzimisces said quickly, "the internal political situation is really none of our business. Thank you, Captain. How soon can we get under way?"

Cuniva frowned. "There's a slight problem," he said. "While we were waiting for the new horse, I had my men look over the carriage, just to make sure everything's in order, and apparently a bolt's sheared in the offside front spring bracket. Just as well we found out now," he added, "it could have been messy if it had given way while we were travelling at any speed. I'd hoped we'd have got it fixed by now, but apparently not. It won't be long, though."

Iseutz sighed heavily. Even Tzimisces allowed himself the

indulgence of a frown before saying, "Ah well, it can't be helped, and I'm sure your people are doing their best. And, as you say, just as well . . ."

"I was wondering." Cuniva turned his head through ten degrees, disengaging from Tzimisces and focusing on Addo. "I don't suppose you've had a chance to glance through my Belcors commentary."

Addo gave him a sheepish look. "I was meaning to talk to you about that," he said. "I really must apologise, I can't think how I can have been so stupid, but I seem to have lost it. I've been through all my pockets, down the back of the seat, everywhere, and I simply can't find it. I'm dreadfully sorry."

"That's perfectly all right," Cuniva said, "I've got several other copies. But did you . . .?"

"I read it, yes. Perfectly splendid, and beautifully written. I almost felt like I was there." He gave Cuniva a broad, open smile. "You know, I'd never really quite understood the dynamics of the campaign before – and that's with my father explaining it to me. Now, though, I've got a much clearer picture in my mind of how it all worked out. Yes, thank you. I thoroughly enjoyed it."

A fierce joy, inextricably mixed with apprehension, burnt in Cuniva's eyes. "Would it be all right if I quoted you on that," he asked, rather too quickly. "I mean, if you wouldn't mind. I'll quite understand if you don't . . ."

"Oh, by all means," Addo said. "You can say I'd recommend it to anyone who really wants to understand the Belcors campaign."

Later, Tzimisces told him: "You know what you've done. You've just given him his ticket back to the Empire. An endorsement from the son of the Irrigator."

"Yes," Addo said pleasantly. "I thought it might be an idea to get him on our side, if we can."

"You've done that all right. That man would lay down his life for you in an instant."

"Really?" Addo frowned. "Then he'd never get home, so surely that'd be missing the point entirely. But I rather think it might give him an added incentive to keep us alive. And it never hurts to make friends with the enemy."

Tzimisces grinned. "One of your father's?"

"Mine, actually. But I think it's still probably true." He yawned, and covered his mouth with the back of his hand. "I remember my father once told me about how he came across a priceless archive of six-hundred-year-old pornographic books in a fire-altar library, I think it was during the Conort River campaign. He immediately sent them to the Imperial commanding the Permian heavy cavalry, who he knew collected that sort of thing; apparently it was the guiding passion of his life. Three months later he had the Permians bottled up in the Mesatges Valley and was trying really hard to negotiate a surrender so he wouldn't have to go in there and flush them out. He got in touch secretly with the dirty-books man, and was able to work out a very advantageous deal using him as his inside contact." Addo smiled. "I think he neglected to mention it in his official commentary on the campaign, but I dare say it's true. He kept one of the books, you see, and I found it, when I was nine. He said: always remember the enemy is human too. It's something you can almost invariably exploit to your advantage."

Tzimisces looked straight at him. "I collect Cerian porcelain," he said mildly. "Particularly the late Expressionist period."

"I'll remember that," Addo said. "In case I come across any somewhere. I mean, you never know."

Tzimisces turned to walk away, then paused and looked back. "Did you tell your mother?" he asked. "About the book?"

"Good heavens, no," Addo replied. "My father, yes, but not my mother. I'm what passes in our family for a peacemaker. Is it expensive, by the way? Cerian pottery, I mean."

"Porcelain," Tzimisces said. "And yes, very."

"That's all right," Addo said cheerfully. "Our family's got plenty of money."

Giraut, who'd fallen asleep in the coach, was woken by the sound of singing. At first he assumed it must be angels, but when he opened his eyes and looked out of the window, he realised it was a large body of Aram Chantat, riding in close formation around the coach, escorting it into Beaute. He'd never heard anything as beautiful in all his life.

They had to wait for the city gates to be opened. Then they rode through deserted streets, broad and lined with huge, tall buildings made from grey stone. On every intersection of major roads they saw soldiers: Imperials, mostly, but a few Aram Chantat – on foot, they looked like small groups of children playing at soldiers, smiling and laughing and jostling each other. Occasionally they saw bodies lying on the sidewalk, twos and threes, dragged there and laid neatly, face up, side by side. Mostly they were young men, but Giraut particularly noticed an old woman with thin grey hair and a hole in her throat he could've stuck his hand into. As they passed under some sort of triumphal arch (but so old and weathered that the bas-relief figures carved into it were just vague shapes with soft, round, featureless faces and no hands or feet), he saw a red banner stretched across it, on which were the words WELCOME SCHERIAN FENCING TEAM.

They climbed a hill and came into a square that was actually a rectangle. The far end was dominated by an enormous building like a castle, with a gate in the middle that was bigger than the city gate they'd just come in by. In through that gate they drove, and found themselves in a vast cobbled courtyard in the middle of the castle. A small group of old men in green velvet robes were waiting for them. There was a table, and a group of musicians in green livery, and some children holding garlands. The coach stopped. "Fencers' Guild," Tzimisces explained, as he reached across to open the door. "Best behaviour."

They had to stand still while the old men made speeches. Giraut tried to listen, but the words were absurd in the context of what he'd just seen – peace and understanding between our two great nations, going forward together in a spirit of brotherhood and trust. Four of them said more or less the same thing. The fifth, gazing at a point in the air about eight inches over the top of Addo's head, talked about the need for reconciliation and the moral beauty of forgiving our enemies, even though they'd done the most abominable things imaginable. The children then presented them with the garlands – the leaves prickled against Giraut's neck and made him itch all over – and the musicians played something very long and slow, while the old men held perfectly still. Giraut never did find out what the table was for.

Predictably, Tzimisces somehow contrived to disappear at some point in the ceremony. Iseutz said later that she'd been watching him like a hawk all through the performance, but one moment he was there, the next he wasn't, and how anybody could've got across that huge yard in a fraction of a second without using some form of magic she couldn't begin to imagine. "And there's strict laws against witchcraft in Permia," she added, "I remember reading about them, and they're still in force. Maybe we could get him arrested and burnt at the stake."

A long, thin old man with a head like a skull showed them silently to their rooms, which were at the very top of one of the towers that flanked the gate. His room reminded Giraut of the cell he'd woken up in, after he'd killed the Senator, except that the window was smaller and higher up the wall, and the bed wasn't quite as comfortable. Leaning up against the wall, he found a long, narrow rosewood box, with silver catch and hinges. Inside it was the most beautiful rapier he'd ever seen: cup rather than swept hilt, with a fluted ivory grip and a ball pommel the size of a crab apple. It seemed to float in his hand, barely making contact with his skin, and the point appeared to pull him, like an excited dog on a lead. He looked all over it for a maker's mark but couldn't find one. He put it back in its box and prayed to the Invincible Sun that his opponent wouldn't have one like it.

That evening, there was a reception in one of the side rooms off the main hall. Iseutz, who'd never felt less like meeting new people in her life, set off in search of the food, which she eventually found, spread out on a table the size of a cornfield, in the corner furthest from the door. There she found Addo, looking sad and chewing his way through a mouthful of pickled cabbage.

"I can only conclude they like the stuff," he said. "There's no other possible explanation."

There were seven – *seven* – different varieties of pickled cabbage, served in beautiful silver bowls engraved with the arms of past masters of the Guild. There was also a stack of brittle-looking bread rolls, and a yard-across wheel of cheese, armoured in snow-white plaster. "It's all right," Addo said quietly, as Iseutz stood wordlessly staring. "I had a word with Captain Cuniva, and he's sending us up something from the guardhouse later. Apparently they're having lamb in a sort of mustard and pepper sauce."

Iseutz nodded gratefully. "Like the old fart said," she muttered. "Reconciliation and the moral beauty of forgiving our enemies. I'd forgive a *lot* for a plate of roast lamb."

"However," Addo said, "it'd be indescribably rude if we didn't eat something now." He took a plate and dumped pickled cabbage on it out of a silver-gilt ladle in the shape of a preening swan. "Pretend to chew it, then swallow it whole. That way, you barely taste it."

"What about the bread rolls?"

"I wouldn't," Addo said gravely. "I dropped one on the floor just now. It shattered. You could cut your tongue to ribbons on something like that."

She gave him a mournful look, took the plate, separated two strands of sand-coloured cabbage from the general mass, and put them in her mouth. Addo nodded approvingly. "According to

Phrantzes," he said, "the fight'll be in the main hall, tomorrow evening. Three thousand in the audience, and they'll leave the big casement window open so someone can describe the action to the crowd in the courtyard. As far as I can gather, they're expecting practically the whole city to show up."

"Fine," Iseutz said. "So far, I think I've seen about four people, apart from soldiers. Do you think anybody lives here?"

"Curfew." Tzimisces had appeared out of nowhere, a few inches from Iseutz's elbow. She jumped and nearly dropped her plate. "Nobody's allowed on the streets before dawn or after noon. They're lifting it tomorrow, so people can come and see the match. In the meantime, anybody caught out of doors faces having to explain themselves to the soldiers. It appears to be working," he went on, "there's been no trouble since they imposed it. They're hoping the worst is over now."

"So who are all these people?" Addo asked.

"Half of them are Fencers' Guild, so they live here. The rest have got passes – local worthies, town councillors, nobody particularly special. The really important people, government ministers, mine owners, that sort of thing, won't get here till tomorrow." He took a plate and piled it with pickled cabbage. "Have either of you seen Suidas Deutzel since we got here?"

"Yes." Iseutz frowned. "I think so. Actually, I'm not sure. I thought I saw him talking to some old man in a blue gown over by the door when I came in, but—"

"I haven't seen him," Addo interrupted. "Why, is there a problem?"

"With Deutzel? Yes, usually. Tell me," he went on, lowering his voice, "have either of you seen him take a drink since we came on this jaunt? You know, wine, spirits, anything like that."

Addo thought for a moment, then looked at Iseutz, who shook her head. "No, I don't think so."

"Nor me," Tzimisces said. "That's why I'm worried about him."

"Because he's *not* . . .?"

"Yes." Tzimisces put down his plate. "We had a long talk with his girl, once we'd recruited him. Very interesting woman, quite intelligent. Anyhow, she said he did two kinds of drinking. One was basically just to take the edge off things, and she'd more or less cured him of it. The other was when something really got to him, or brought back a certain sort of memory. When that came on, she always made sure there was a bottle in the house. Lesser of two evils, you might say. Really, I can't see how on earth she puts up with him." He moved away; they could see him aiming himself at the door, like an arrow. Then he turned back and said, "If you do see him, you'll let me know, won't you?"

Subtle had been Suidas' reaction when they showed him to his room, *really subtle*. He had no doubt whatsoever that Tzimisces had seen to it that his accommodation was ninety feet up in the air, accessible only by way of a winding single-track staircase, easily guarded by one sentry. It was just as well, he decided, that he relished a challenge, and was fairly buzzing with energy that needed to be got rid of.

He'd lost weight since he'd been with the fencing team, and that was fortunate, too. Three weeks ago he wouldn't have been able to squeeze through the narrow window without losing a significant amount of skin.

Once outside, hanging on to the slightest of crevices with his fingertips as he balanced on the knife-edge sill, he considered his options and decided to go up. If he remembered right, from the quick glance that had been all he'd had time for, there was a square turret at the top of the tower. It could quite easily be ornamental, with no way down except the way he'd just come, or it might be functional, with access to the battlement (which might or might not have a catwalk leading to the opposite tower). He'd just have to find out when he got there. To make things more interesting, it was raining.

Suidas Deutzel hated climbing. Unfortunately, he was quite

good at it, which meant it was a viable option when he needed to plan a course of action. He groped upwards, feeling for the grooves between the stone blocks. On old buildings like this, water gathered in the pointing and ate it away, just deep enough to hook a fingertip into. *My hands'll be useless tomorrow*, he thought. *Pity*.

When he was just over halfway to the top, he came to a place where there were no handholds. He reached up as far as he could stretch and drew his fingers down lightly over the stone, but he could make out nothing but smooth, unbroken granite. At the same time, he could feel his feet beginning to slide out of the crack he was resting them in. No wonder: he was supporting his entire weight on the welted seam of the toes of his boots, where the sole was sewn to the upper. At that moment, it occurred to him that he could die because of that. It hadn't crossed his mind before, but now he came to think of it, death was a perfectly plausible outcome. After all, there was no earthly reason why there should be convenient handholds on every wall in the world. There was no chance he'd be able to go down, with nothing to hold on to while he found his footings. Any moment now, his balance would fail, and that would be the end of it.

He was astonished at how calm he found he was. Fear of death had always energised him, making him move far more quickly than his body should have been capable of, accelerating his reactions and his thought process to a quite incredible level. This time, though, he only thought, *Oh*, and realised that he didn't really care all that much. He could feel his responsibilities, the love of others towards him, the unfulfilled possibilities; they were like a child's hand trying to pull him up, doing its best but simply not strong enough for the job. Above all, there was no blame. *I tried to climb a wall, but I couldn't, and there it is*.

Then his left index fingertip lodged in a groove, and the other fingers found it, and he clenched his hand – he could feel the damage to the overstrained tendons, but no pain – and a strength that was nothing to do with him hauled him up, so that he was able to lift his knee and paw at the wall for a foothold, which he found; and not long after that he was lying on his stomach on the top of the battlement, shifting his weight to topple him forward on to the wet stone slabs of the turret floor. He lay in a heap for a moment, wondering, *What was all that about?* but he couldn't make sense of it. He'd been closer to death than at any time since the War, and now he was safe, and he couldn't for the life of him figure out what had happened in between.

Not to worry; he was here now, the place he'd expended so much energy and suffered so much damage to achieve. For a brief, panic-stricken moment he couldn't remember why he'd wanted to get there; then he remembered. From the turret, maybe he could get on to the battlement, into the opposite turret, and down an unguarded staircase into the world.

Not quite that simple. The turret, as he'd feared, proved to be entirely ornamental; there was no trapdoor and no access to the battlement, just a leaded roof on a slight slope, surrounded by fatuous crenellations. He looked down at the stretch of battlement linking this turret with its neighbour; directly under it was the gate, and set above the gate, he suddenly remembered, was a clock. And the truth about clocks, he thought happily, is that they have to be wound; and since only fools and desperate men go in for unnecessary athletics, there was bound to be an easy way up to the clock, on the inner side of the wall. It was far too dark to see it from where he was, and maybe he was wrong, and the lay brothers of the Guild wound the stupid thing once a week using a very long ladder, but what the hell. If millions of people across the West could believe that the sun was a god, there was absolutely no reason why he shouldn't believe in the existence of a clock-winder's staircase. Faith, he told himself. Confident hope of a miracle.

There was no way he'd be able to climb down the side of the turret, but it wasn't that much of a drop. The trick would be landing on a relatively narrow wall that he couldn't actually see very clearly (and slippery, because of the rain). He grinned. A sane man would stay where he was, and as soon as the sun rose and people started moving about down below, would start yelling for help. Then men would come with ladders and get him down, by which time he'd have had a chance to think up some kind of story to account for how he'd got there. That's what a sane man would do, oh yes. He wouldn't scramble up on to the battlement, take his best guess and voluntarily jump . . .

For God's sake, Suidas, his few remaining friends had been known to say to him, *why do you insist on wearing those big clumping army boots? They make you look like a farmer.* Because, he'd never replied, my feet are used to them, when I'm wearing them I know exactly what I can and can't get away with; so, if at any point I'm called on to climb a sheer face or jump ten feet off a tower on to a narrow wall, say, I'll have the best possible chance. As it happened, he landed just right, his knees folding up to absorb the shock of landing, leaving him squatting on top of the wall like a cat on a fence. He was amazed, and wonderfully relieved.

And because he'd had faith, there was a platform sticking out of the wall directly behind the clock, with a roof, with guttering; he hopped off the wall, slid down the roof, grabbed the guttering and swung himself on to the platform, as if it was a form he'd practised a hundred times in the salle d'armes. And there was a narrow staircase, with a handrail. Faith, you see. For two pins he'd have bowed three times to the Invincible Sun, except that it was well after sunset.

He scampered down the stairs with his hands in his pockets. He felt absurdly cheerful, as if he'd been proved right about something that mattered. On the far side of the courtyard, he could see yellow squares of light; the reception, of course. He smiled. Right now, he thought, I could murder a stiff drink. But I don't do that any more, he quickly reassured himself. He brushed the dust and grime off his knees and sleeves, instinctively felt for the hilt of his messer and remembered, no, I left it behind, on purpose; then he walked across the yard and walked up the steps that led to the great hall.

There was a guard on the door. "It's all right," Suidas said, "I'm one of the fencers."

The guard looked at him. "Well, you would be. Fencers' Guild. Invitation."

"I haven't got one."

"Then you can't go in."

Suidas sighed. "They're expecting me. I'm one of the guests. The Scherian fencing team."

"Is that right." The guard seemed very interested in the backs of his hands, which were bloody and raw. He couldn't remember damaging them, but he'd had other preoccupations.

"Look," Suidas said. "Get Phrantzes, or Tzimisces. They'll vouch for me. I'll wait here, all right?"

"Who?"

"Fine. Why don't I talk to your superior officer?"

That, it turned out, could be arranged, but it took a certain amount of time, which Suidas spent locked in a charcoal cellar. Then, eventually, the door opened and Phrantzes stood in the doorway staring at him. "Where have you been? We've been so worried."

Suidas grinned. "I must've taken a wrong turning somewhere. I got lost. I've been wandering around this place for hours."

"What happened to your hands?"

"Slipped and fell over in the dark, would you believe. Look, can you please tell them who I am and get me out of here? It's filthy dirty, and I don't have a change of clothes."

Halfway across the yard, flanked by soldiers with halberds, Phrantzes said, "And you're sopping wet."

"It's raining."

"So what were you doing out of doors?"

"I told you, I got lost. This place is the size of a small town."

Phrantzes gave him a sad look. "Have you been drinking?" he asked.

Suidas laughed. "No, of course not. Smell my breath if you want."

"No, that's fine, I believe you." Phrantzes stopped dead. "Suidas, you haven't done anything stupid, have you?"

"More times than you could possibly imagine." Suidas grinned. "But not recently. At least, I don't think so. Why? What am I supposed to have done?"

"We've been looking for you. You didn't come down to the reception with the others."

"That's it? That's my crime against humanity?" Suidas started to walk towards the steps. "Pull yourself together, will you? A man can go for a walk if he likes, even in bloody Permia."

For as long as he could remember, Giraut had been trapped in a corner, talking to a tall, bald man and his spherical wife about gardening. He knew nothing at all about gardening and cared less, and he wasn't entirely sure who these people were; they'd told him, but his mind had shed practically everything they'd said to him, the way a sheep's fleece sheds rainwater. He had an idea they were something vaguely important, so he couldn't just say, "Excuse me," and walk away. He wished very much that he'd paid a little more attention when his cousin from the country had bored him half to death talking about roses; but he hadn't, and it was far too late now.

Then, like the Invincible Sun bursting through clouds, Tzimisces appeared and grabbed him by the elbow. "Giraut," he said, "there's someone I want you to meet. Minister, you'll excuse us, I'm sure."

As simple as that: the siege was relieved. "Who was that?" Giraut whispered, as Tzimisces towed him across the room.

"Didn't he say? That was Minister Balouche. You've been talking to the fourth most important man in Permia. Minister of Production. Why, what did he tell you?"

"A lot of stuff about ericaceous compost," Giraut replied. "I'm sorry, I wasn't taking notes or anything."

Tzimisces laughed. "Come over here and look pretty for the war minister's wife," he said. "She likes beautiful young men half her age, and you're the closest thing we've got. And I gather you're good at chatting up inappropriate women."

Giraut reckoned he deserved that. "I thought the government people weren't arriving till tomorrow."

"Change of plan. We got fed the official misinformation, same as everyone else. That's her, the woman over there who looks like a hawk." He gave Giraut a shove that nearly toppled him off his feet. "For Scheria," he said, and disappeared.

The woman turned on him and smiled, showing all her teeth. "Who are you?" she said.

Giraut told her. "I'm not really interested in fencing," she said. "Tell me, which one's the Carnufex boy? I'd quite like to meet *him*."

Giraut looked round, and caught sight of the back of Addo's head. "I'll introduce you," he said.

The short, elderly man Addo was talking to proved to be the woman's husband. Giraut made good his escape, quickly looked round to see if he was being pursued, then fell back in good order on the table with the food on it. There he found Iseutz, radiating a barrier of unfriendliness he could feel from five yards away. She relaxed it just long enough for him to approach.

"Have you seen Suidas?" she said.

"As a matter of fact, yes," he said. "He came in with Phrantzes, just a moment ago. Why?"

"They've been looking for him. I don't know why."

"Well, they found him." Giraut looked at the food and realised he wasn't hungry. "I noticed his hands," he said, "they were a real mess. Like he'd been fighting or something."

Iseutz's eyes opened wide. "Do you think he tried to make a run for it?"

Giraut shrugged. "No idea. I wouldn't have thought so. I mean, this place must be harder to get out of than a prison. If he wanted to run away, he's had plenty of better chances."

She took a bread roll off the plate, picked at it and put it back. "You know earlier, in the coach. That stupid book Addo was reading."

"The military commentary."

"Did you happen to notice how nervous Phrantzes was acting? Something was really bothering him."

Giraut wasn't sure what to say. "I thought I was just imagining it."

"So you saw it too."

"And I think, on balance, I was right. Probably he was just fed up from sitting still for so long."

"No." Her eyes were shining. "I saw it too. He was definitely worried about something."

Giraut let out a rather overdone sigh. "Do you spend your whole time watching the rest of us? I wouldn't have thought we were that interesting."

"You're useless," she snapped, so fiercely that he took a step backwards. "We've been dragged here and dumped in the middle of some stupid, horrible thing, and you're just letting it happen to you. I can't understand how anyone could think like that. For God's sake, Giraut, there's dead bodies lying about in the streets. Don't you take anything seriously?"

"All right, there's dead bodies," Giraut replied, before he could stop himself. "But that's their problem, not ours. We aren't responsible, and there's nothing we can do about it. It's not our country. And . . ."

He'd stopped just in time. Well, maybe not. She gave him a cold stare. "And what?"

Well, if he didn't say it, she'd say it for him. "And they're the enemy. If they want to slaughter each other, let them." He waited for a moment, but she didn't say anything. "So? You can't pretend the War never happened. And if they're killing each other, they're not killing us."

Iseutz turned away, and Giraut got the distinct feeling that he didn't exist. He felt profoundly tired, as though he'd been carrying a heavy weight all day and nobody seemed prepared to take it from him. "Look," he said to the back of Iseutz's head, "I don't hate the Permians. They're weird, and how they can eat what they cook I'll never know, but they're just people. But their politics is nothing to do with me. I don't want to be here and I don't want to get involved. I'd have thought you could understand that."

She turned round so fast she nearly crashed into him. "Giraut, you clown," she said, "don't you get it? Something is going on, and we're right in the middle of it. Tzimisces always disappearing. That man getting murdered. Everywhere we go, there's trouble. It's something to do with the War, and people wanting another one, and they're *using* us. A fencing tour, for crying out loud; we were supposed to be here making things *better*, and now there's dead people in the streets and soldiers everywhere, and I don't *understand* . . ."

He sighed. "You're imagining things," he said. "You're wound up and stressed out because of – well, just being here's enough, and then we discover we're fighting with real swords, which is downright barbaric, and then the riots and all this stuff. But I don't think there's anything dreadful and sinister going on in the shadows. It's just a mess, that's all."

"You're wrong," she said. "You know that. It's just a pity you're such a coward you won't admit it."

He knew he ought to feel angry, but there wasn't the faintest trace of anger or resentment in his mind; it was a luxury he knew he couldn't afford. "I'm sorry you think that," he said. "And I hope you're wrong." He might as well have been talking to the wall. He turned away, and wondered how long it would be before they'd be allowed to leave. He looked round for someone to talk to. Suidas was in the centre of a ring of Permians; he was grinning and laughing, and they seemed delighted with him – fencing fans, presumably, thrilled to meet the Scherian champion. Phrantzes had been pinned in a corner by Minister Urosh and his wife (maybe he knew about gardening), and he couldn't see Addo anywhere. While his attention was thus occupied, a short, square Permian with long grey hair in a ponytail materialised in front of him and accused him of being Giraut Bryennius.

"Yes, that's me," he said.

"You're fencing rapier."

"That's right."

The Permian nodded. "Why? Isn't Suidas Deutzel your national rapier champion?"

Oh for crying out loud. "Yes, that's right," Giraut said, "but we needed Suidas to fight messer, so—"

"But he's fighting longsword. Adulescentulus Carnufex is fighting messer."

"Well, they swapped. Anyhow, Suidas can't do longsword *and* rapier, so they got me instead."

Clearly his answers were unsatisfactory. "I've been following the Scherian League for some time," the Permian said, "and I don't know you. Why didn't they get Gace Erchomai-Bringas to fight rapier? He was the silver medallist in this year's Trophy."

"I guess he couldn't make it," Giraut said wearily. "But I was available, so . . ."

"Have you ever fenced professionally? Your name doesn't appear in the Scherian Guild lists."

"Not as such, no. I'm sorry, I don't think I caught your name."

"Tuchoman. Secretary of State for Culture and Religious Affairs." Oh, Giraut thought. "Why is Carnufex fencing messer if Deutzel was selected? I don't understand."

"Well." Giraut opened his mind in the hope of snagging a stray speck of inspiration. "Addo's never tried messer before, but in practice we found he was so good at it—"

"He didn't put up a very convincing performance at Joiauz."

"He was nervous. Anyway, he's been practising. You're in for a treat tomorrow, I can promise you that."

Minister Tuchoman looked dubious. "I hope so," he said.

"You'll find the people here are a very discerning audience. I notice you tend towards the Vesani school."

Do I? And what in hell is the Vesani school? "A bit, I guess. Mostly, though, I just make it up as I go along."

He'd said the wrong thing. "I can't accept that," the minister said. "I read the transcript of your bout at Joiauz. You combined elements from four distinct Classical schools of fencing. It's the main reason why I've come here to see you."

Transcripts? "You came all this way just to see me?"

"To see post-orthodox Vesani straight-time techniques in action, yes. I've read about them all my life, but never actually seen them." A severe look. "I do hope you won't disappoint me."

With that, the minister made a perfunctory excuse and stalked away, leaving Giraut mumbling *post-orthodox Vesani straight-time* under his breath, so he could look it up in Addo's book. He hoped very much that it translated as keeping out of the way and not getting killed, because that was what he proposed to do, and the hell with the expectations of his audience.

"You know, they aren't such bad people after all." Suidas came up from behind him. He was holding a glass: clear water. "I've just been talking to a man who organises commercial tournaments, down in the south somewhere. Guess how much he offered me for five bouts, rapier, with foils."

Giraut moved away a little. "No idea."

"Five thousand nomismata. A thousand a bout, for rapier. And, guess what, he's got no problem with foils, none whatsoever. Apparently it's only the Guild that insists on using sharps, and they only control about a third of the fencing in this country. The punters don't mind, it's just a bunch of lunatic purists. There's good money to be made here. And that's not counting exhibition matches, private coaching, political endorsements . . ."

"Political . . .?"

"Oh, it's big business here. They pay you a heap of money and you say how much you admire some politician. Five hundred nomismata, they reckon I could get, being Scherian champion and all. More, if I put on a good show in the last two matches of the tour. I must say, it throws quite a different light on it all. Eighteen months here and I'd be set up for life, I could retire, set up a fashionable salle, spend the rest of my life coaching the likes of – well, you, I suppose – and never have to fight anyone for real ever again. One of those men I was talking to, little shrivelled chap, he said that for five per cent he could set me up solid, and no sharps whatsoever." He stopped, and frowned. "God, I hope there isn't going to be another war. That'd screw everything up."

Giraut stared at him. "You're seriously thinking of staying in Permia?"

"You don't understand." Suidas' voice was suddenly hard and quiet. "Sorry, Giraut, but you simply haven't got a clue. Money's never been a problem for you, has it? Always been there, you never give it a thought. It's different if you haven't got any, believe me. Well, I'm sick to death of being poor. It's a drag and it drains you till you can't think about anything else, and if I can get rid of it just by doing eighteen months in this shithole – frankly, I don't have a choice."

"But I thought you were—" Giraut cut the words off, but Suidas understood all right.

"Getting paid for being on this tour, yes. Twenty-five thousand. That's a lot of money, but it's not enough. Sontha . . . " He stopped, and frowned, as though trying to remember something. "It's not enough," he said. "It's enough to last me five years, and then where'll I be? I need double that, for the salle, to be *safe*. Otherwise it'll just make things worse, in the long run. No, this is the place. God bless Permia, I say. Wonderful country, beautiful people, and let's just pray there isn't going to be a war." He took a deep breath, which came out as a kind of a laugh. "I never did hold with war," he said. "Bloody stupid way to deal with a problem, always makes things worse, and people . . . Anyway." He looked round, reached out and grabbed a decanter of wine off a nearby table. "I think this calls for a drink, don't you?"

"Suidas . . ."

"Oh, screw you." He hesitated, then put the decanter back. "I'll give it some serious thought, anyway," he said. "I mean, what's eighteen months? You get longer than that for stealing apples."

Finally, just when he'd given up hope, the reception came to an end. It thawed gradually, like a harsh winter, as the important people withdrew, leaving the lesser mortals to talk excitedly to each other about who they'd just met; at which point Giraut realised that for the purposes of diplomatic protocol he counted as an important person and was free to go. He headed for the door, where a pair of Imperials in gilded lamellar armour fell in beside him. The position they took up – dead level, about six inches behind his shoulders – brought back old memories.

"Am I under arrest?" he asked.

"Escort, sir. For your own safety."

It was mildly unnerving to be told you were being protected when you hadn't realised you were in danger, but he'd been in Permia long enough not to let that sort of thing prey on his mind. Feeling no more than mildly self-conscious, he allowed himself to be protected across the yard and up the narrow spiral staircase, where one guard went in front and the other brought up the rear – the true danger, he couldn't help feeling, was treading or being trodden on by his protectors and tumbling down the lethal staircase to his death. They opened his door for him and stood back to let him go in. After the door had closed, he listened hard. He didn't hear a key turn in a lock, but he didn't hear footsteps clattering away down the stairs, either.

(Well, he thought, here we are again: trapped at the top of a tower, with the watch only the thickness of a door away, and still stubbornly alive. He wondered whether his life chose to assume such obvious patterns as a way of making a point, or whether these were simply the shapes it was predisposed to adopt, the way a rope naturally falls in loops if you throw it.)

He couldn't be bothered to undress, so he lay on his back on the bed (which would've made a smith a good anvil), closed his eyes and demanded to be sent to sleep. Sleep, of course, resolutely refused to happen. Instead, his mind picked over a wide range of issues, like a crow on an old carcass. He considered the death of two statesmen (one Scherian, one Permian), the unanticipated abandonment of a strategic way station on the Great East Road, Tzimisces' ability to vanish into thin air, Addo's loss of a borrowed book and the backs of Suidas' hands. He drew a number of conclusions, but none of them made him feel better. Nevertheless, he resolved to try and make some sort of sense of them, and in doing so he fell asleep.

He was woken by yelling: an angry man with a loud voice shouting orders. He sat up, noticing that the lamp that had been burning when he came in had now gone out, and tried to make out words in the furious voices. Then his door opened. Light burst in like floodwater. Against it he could make out the silhouette of an Imperial helmet.

"What's going on?" he mumbled.

"Sorry, sir. Nothing to worry about. Just checking you're all right." A different guard. "I'm fine. What's all the noise?"

"Nothing to worry about," the guard repeated. "You get some rest, sir, big day tomorrow." The door closed, the light went out, and for a count of ten there was silence. Then someone else started shouting, from a slightly different direction, and he could hear running on the stairs.

The next door Lieutenant Teudel opened was that of Suidas Deutzel. He'd been told to keep his eye on that one, but found him sitting in a chair writing a letter, resting on a book balanced on his knee.

"What the hell's going on?" Deutzel asked.

"Routine check, sir," Teudel replied. "Just making sure you're all right."

Well, he wasn't paid to be convincing. He shut the door,

reminded the guards stationed outside it that no one was to enter or leave (as if they needed reminding) and passed down the corridor to the next door: Adulescentulus Carnufex, the Irrigator's son. Something, Teudel thought, to tell his grandchildren. But young Carnufex was fast asleep, so that was all right. Shivering slightly from the cold, Teudel withdrew and applied himself to the next door: the team manager, Phrantzes. He adjusted his parameters accordingly.

"There's been an incident," he replied to the obvious question. "With one of the guests. But everything's under control, nothing to worry about. Sorry to have disturbed you."

He closed the door before Phrantzes could ask another question, and moved on to the last door. Slightly awkward, as the occupant was female. Different protocols therefore applied. He knocked, and waited.

After a moment the door opened a crack, and a plain young woman scowled at him. "What the hell is . . .?"

"Just making sure you're all right, miss."

"Why wouldn't I be?"

"No cause for alarm. Good night, miss."

"Wait a minute." She had the gift of command. "What's all the yelling about?"

"Sorry, miss. Just a drill."

"Like hell. What's going on?"

"Thank you, miss. Sorry to have troubled you."

He applied his knee gently to the door, easing it shut. The two guards looked straight past him as he walked away. As soon as he was safely out of range, they'd be laughing. He cursed them with early promotion, so that they'd be the ones who had to deal politely with stroppy females with diplomatic status, and returned to the guard post. There he found Captain Lozo, the duty officer, looking weary and terrified, searching frantically for the ink bottle. Teudel took it from the desk drawer and gave it to him.

"Sir, what the hell's going on?" he asked.

"Bloody good question." Lozo fumbled with the ink-bottle stopper, forced it out with a violent twist, and spilled ink on the desk. "Some bloody fool of a government minister's got himself killed, apparently. We think. We don't know. Main thing is to close this place right down, make sure everybody stays put, and under no circumstances is anybody to leave the building until further notice. We think they're trying to keep it quiet until they can bring in enough Aram Chantat. Once the news does get out, of course . . ."

He didn't need to expand on that. "And is it true? Which minister?"

"Don't know, don't care," Lozo replied. "Right now, all I'm concerned with is getting a status report out to Division, and then they can send someone in to take charge and I'm off the hook." He frowned at the pool of ink on the desk, as if he couldn't begin to imagine how it could possibly have got there. "All the Scherians safely contained?"

"Yes, sir."

"That's something, I suppose. God knows what'd happen if one of them contrived to get killed, we'd have another war on our hands in no time flat." His frown deepened, and he turned and looked at Teudel as though he was a prophet on a holy mountain. "Do you suppose that's why they're here?" he said. "To get killed, to start another war."

"I . . . " It wasn't the sort of question lieutenants in the Imperial service were supposed to address themselves to. "I don't know, sir."

"It'd get the job done, though, wouldn't it?"

Once asked, however, it itched for an answer. "Do you think that's why the Permians asked them here?"

"Or why the Scherians sent them." Lozo sat absolutely still for a moment, as if a sudden movement on his part might scare away the revelation of perfect truth. Then he shrugged hugely. "None of our business, anyhow. If they want a war, I guess they might as well have one. Were you here for the last lot, Teudel?"

"No, sir."

Lozo nodded. "Too young. Well, you didn't miss much. It was a mess, basically. The Scherians are a bunch of primitives who just happen to be led by the most brilliant tactical mind in twelve centuries. Fighting them is therefore a pain in the arse. One minute you're slaughtering them like sheep, the next they're all around you and you're hiding in a ditch. And the Permians ..." He laughed. "I have this recurring nightmare where I come back from the dead and I'm looking at my gravestone, and on it there's my name and my rank and my unit, and under that in big curvy letters, *He Died For Permia*. Something like that'd really fuck up the afterlife, don't you think?" He sighed, and dipped his pen in the ink. "Dismissed, Lieutenant. Go away and guard somebody, there's a good fellow."

It was a direct order, but Teudel didn't feel like obeying it. Instead, he went back to the tower and prowled round for a while annoying the guards, until he was quite certain there was nothing he could usefully do there; then he retired to the gatehouse, on the assumption that it'd be a logical place for anyone to look if they wanted to find him. Another war: he didn't exactly relish the thought, but the fact had to be faced. In war, officers died, and their juniors were promoted to replace them. In peace, there was only old age, illness or disgrace, and he wasn't prepared to wait that long. But a really good public-order crisis; it was a possibility he hadn't considered in any detail. He couldn't help remembering the case histories of men, great and glorious men, who'd been started on their careers by incidents in times of civic turmoil; men who'd thought quickly and calmly on the spot and saved the day, and been rewarded. Most of them, though, hadn't had to operate in a confined space infested with the Aram Chantat. And careers could be ruined as well as accelerated in anomalous circumstances such as these ...

The night air made him shiver, and he remembered how cold it had been in young Carnufex's room. Hard to see how people's brains could work properly in the cold. His own thought processes slowed alarmingly once he'd reached the point where he could no longer feel his fingers. Fortunately, there was a good fire going in the gatehouse. He sat in front of it, and slowly came back to life. He listened hard, but there were no sounds of tumult and disorder from the other side of the gate. Probably just as well, he decided on balance. Plenty of time for that tomorrow, when there'd be light to see by.

He Died For Permia, though. He pictured the look on Lozo's face as he'd said it, and couldn't help laughing.

From her window, Iseutz could see a red glow. It could easily have been the sunrise, but it wasn't.

This is the safest place in the city, she told herself. It has to be, it's stuffed full of government ministers. That sounded entirely fine and reasonable, until it occurred to her that maybe it was the government and its ministers that the people who'd started the fires wanted to get at.

It was, of course, utterly intolerable that they should be stuck here in the middle of a revolution or whatever it was. Clearly whatever point the tour may have had was long since gone, superseded by events; in which case, the only rational course of action would be to get them safely away from centres of population (she didn't think they'd be rioting in the villages; too much work to do, and nothing to burn down except their own barns) and then back to Scheria, as quickly as possible. But no: here they were, in the biggest target in the city. The Guild house was an old building, with wood floors and oak-panelled walls; it'd burn for days. Wonderful.

She looked at the door. She knew there were guards posted there – for her protection, no doubt; two men who'd bravely die for her, seconds before she died herself: male logic. She considered the possibility of simply walking out and ignoring them; would they physically restrain her and put her back inside? On the balance of probabilities, yes, and she couldn't work up any enthusiasm for the idea of fighting them. One, maybe, with the element of surprise. Two, forget it. Besides, even if she got past them, where would she go? It was all very well imagining herself mingling with the crowd, slipping quietly away into the back streets, making her way to an unguarded gate; there was far too much Permia between her and the border, and what would she eat, and where would she sleep? The horrible fact was that her future was out of her control, until further notice. The thought sickened her, but she choked it down.

So: sit still, like a good little girl, and wait for someone to come and get you. She clenched her hands until she was afraid she'd break a finger. Why did people have to be so *stupid*?

She thought about Addo. Whatever else he was, he wasn't stupid. Contingency plans and fallback positions would be second nature to the Irrigator's son. She'd noticed a dozen times how he assimilated the layout of every confined space he entered – other doors, ways round furniture, the geometry of the placement of guards. If there was a way out of this trap, Addo Carnufex would find it, and he'd feel duty-bound to take her, them, with him if he possibly could. His door, she remembered, was the next but one to hers. Worth bearing in mind.

The window was stuck, but after a short, energetic fight that cost her the skin off two knuckles she managed to get it open. The cold air splashed on her face like water. She held still and closed her eyes, but she couldn't hear anything: too high up, or too far away. That was probably good. If the rioters were laying siege to the Guild house, she was sure she'd be able to hear them. She remembered the soldiers in the streets. The Imperials had been wearing armour. There were over a thousand small steel plates in an Imperial cuirass (who had she heard that from? She couldn't recall offhand), ingeniously and meticulously arranged to move with the body, leaving no gaps for a point to poke through. Apparently, though, that didn't make them invulnerable against a furious mob, just as the walls of Flos Verjan hadn't protected the city from the river water. That much pent-up anger would crush anything. In the end it came down to quantity, volume, mass, weight of numbers; and a man who was prepared to open the sluices. How on earth could anyone bring himself to do a thing like that – open the gates, start a war, let go a flood that once loosed was beyond anyone's control? She couldn't imagine, and she really didn't want to try. She sucked her skinned knuckles and tried not to think how much more a sword cut into the bone would hurt, or a messer to the head, or a deep thrust from a broad blade that prised the ribs apart. Well, at least the match tomorrow would be cancelled; but she hadn't been afraid of that, even though it was to be sharps. A properly regulated bout against a single opponent was at least under control, in its own rather bizarre terms. They'd dipped the sword blades in boiling water before the match at Joiauz, the way doctors boiled their instruments to avoid infection. She'd heard somewhere that most men cut up in a battle died later, slowly, from blood poisoning.

There was a knock at her door. She started, then despised herself for it – blood-crazed rioters would hardly knock, would they? – and turned the handle. It was Phrantzes, looking rather dazed.

"Well?" she said.

"It's riots," he said. "I've just had our friend Captain Cuniva to see me – he wasn't supposed to, but I think he likes us, after Addo said nice things about his book—"

"What did he *say*?"

"A government minister's been killed," Phrantzes replied. "Cuniva didn't know which one, or when, or where. He says they tried to keep it quiet, at least till morning, but apparently that didn't happen. There's huge mobs in the streets, they've called out the Aram Chantat, no reports so far who's getting the better of it. We're to stay here till they've restored order, Cuniva said. When that might be is anyone's guess. Meanwhile, just stay calm and—"

"If anyone else tells me to stay calm, I shall scream," Iseutz snapped. "They can't just lock us up like this. You go to them and tell them we're Scherian diplomats, we've got rights. I have no intention of sitting still and quiet in a locked room at the top of a tower. Cuniva's a captain, isn't he? He must outrank whoever's in charge of this staircase."

"He's waiting outside the door," Phrantzes said quietly. "If you like, I'll ask him in and you can talk to him. I wouldn't, though, if I were you. He's pretty strung up, and it wouldn't be sensible to annoy the only man in the building who seems to give a damn."

She could just about see the logic in that. "All right," she said, "I'll just sit here and wait to be murdered. What'll you be doing? I notice you're not locked up in your cell."

"I'm the liaison," Phrantzes said awkwardly. "Between us and the Imperials."

"Isn't that Tzimisces' job? Oh, don't tell me. He's gone again."

"He's with the Guild authorities." Their eyes met, and she thought: he can't stand the creep either. He's *afraid* of him. "They're doing everything they can for us, I promise you. It'll be all right."

Who was he talking to? Not her, she decided. And then it suddenly occurred to her: this was as good a time as any, and better than most. "Phrantzes," she said, "what've they got on you? Besides your wife, I mean. There's more, isn't there?"

He gave her a look of fury and terror, but it was too late now to disengage. "Well?"

She could almost feel him break. What little strength there was had left him completely. He dropped down into the chair, his hands hanging over the arms, his head lolling on one side. For a moment, she thought he'd had a stroke. "I may as well tell you," he said. "It won't make any difference, I don't suppose. And you won't tell him, it's not in your interests. Oh, the hell with it." He lifted his head, and she could see more misery than she'd have thought it possible for one man to carry. She wished she was somewhere else, a long way away.

"I was a transport officer in the War," he said. "I was attached to General Carnufex's staff, in the Belcors campaign."

Oh, she thought. "The one that Cuniva wrote that book about."

He nodded. "That's the one. I'm sure my name's in that book, in fact I'm certain of it. You see, I inadvertently won that battle, by making a stupid, careless mistake. The general sent a squadron of cavalry to attack a bridge. It was a feint, they weren't supposed to succeed, but they did. They chased off a detachment of Permians – not Imperials or Aram Chantat, I think they were mine workers, conscripts. I guess that's why they ran instead of holding their ground and driving our cavalry off. Anyhow, the general sent me a note telling me not to send a supply train down a certain road; it'd be too close to the fighting at the bridge, and enemy stragglers might bump into our carts and cause a problem. Well, I was under pressure, I had to get the supplies to the front line or there'd be a horrible mess, but there wasn't time to go the long way round. I figured, the attack's just a feint, there's no real danger of enemy soldiers streaming down that road to get away from the bridge. I sent the carts down the road anyway, and stuffed Carnufex's note in with a load of other papers. If ever I was called on it, I'd say I'd never seen it, and some fool of a clerk had filed it in with the other stuff." He paused, and swallowed a great gulp of air, as if he'd just come up out of deep water. "Well, there were soldiers on that road all right, the whole Permian unit, running like mad from our cavalry. They came round a bend in the road, and there were our carts. I don't think they were actually looking for a fight, but they were scared, and some fool on a cart shot an arrow, and that was all it took. They slaughtered the cart crew, trashed the carts and wandered off. My fault."

Iseutz looked at him. "You said you won . . ."

"Oh yes." Phrantzes grinned at her. "At the time, I thought it was the most amazing stroke of luck. You see, about an hour later, nine hundred Imperial heavy cavalry came charging up that road. They'd broken through our line and were swinging round to outflank the main infantry. If they'd made it through, we'd have been slaughtered, lost the battle; for all I know, maybe even the War. But the road was blocked with smashed-up carts, they couldn't get through. They dismounted and tried to get all the junk out of the way, but after a bit they realised they were too late, the moment had passed. By the time they'd cleared the road and executed their manoeuvre, they wouldn't be charging the rear of an unsuspecting infantry division, they'd be riding straight down the throats of the archers and the field artillery. So they gave up. They got back on their horses and left the battle-field – which was the only sensible thing to do, God knows. They even stopped to pick up the few wounded carters who'd survived the Permian attack. One of them—"

Iseutz's eyes were very wide. "Suidas Deutzel."

He grinned at her. "That's right. Nineteen years old, carter's mate. He'd got himself horribly carved up, he should've bled to death, but the Blueskins scooped him up and took him to one of their field hospitals, where a very skilful doctor sewed him back together again. Six weeks later, he was well enough to walk, so they let him go. They figured he'd never bother anyone again, not after what he'd gone through." Phrantzes closed his eyes for a moment. "They were wrong about that. Suidas joined the Fourteenth Land Auxiliary. You heard of them?"

Iseutz shook her head.

"Well, you damn well should have. They were a skirmisher unit, they weren't supposed to *do* anything, just go ahead of the proper soldiers and make a pest of themselves. But by some bizarre chance, every man in that unit was – well, I suppose it was the circumstances in which they came together. They were all survivors, you see, from other units that'd been wiped out. Most men in that position deserted, or were posted a long way from the fighting. The few that didn't got drafted into the Fourteenth Auxiliary. They were all men who just wanted a chance to kill the enemy, and they didn't give a damn about any-thing else. It was unbelievable. They'd charge whole Imperial regiments and go through them like they weren't there. They attacked wings of Aram Chantat – on foot, mind you, and the savages on horseback – and they just tore them to pieces. Fairly soon Carnufex realised what he'd got there and started using them for, basically, suicide missions; except they did the job, came back alive and nagged and yelled until they got sent out again. Suidas rose to be the junior captain of the Fourteenth, third in command. That's who you've been sharing a carriage with, by the way. They say he used to have a big leather bag on his belt, and it stank; it was full of the little fingers of Permians he'd killed, and he meant to clean off the skin and the meat and string the bones on a necklace, like the Aram Chantat do, but they went bad before he got around to it. I don't know if that's true, but I've heard it from several men who were in that unit with him."

He stopped, as if he'd completely run out of words. Iseutz studied him for a moment, then said, "Does he know?"

"That it was me who put him in the way of those Permians? No, of course not. If he knew, I'd be dead. But Carnufex knew, of course – he forgave me, because he won the battle, he thought it was a huge joke. Tzimisces knows, I'm sure of it. Presumably that's why I was chosen for this job. If I put a foot wrong, if I don't do exactly what they want, he'll turn me over to Suidas, and that . . . " He stopped. "So you can see why I was terrified when Cuniva gave Addo the book."

Iseutz nodded. "So you stole it."

"God, no. I tried, but you can't just creep up unawares on Addo Carnufex. No, for some reason he got rid of the book and told Cuniva he'd lost it." He shook his head. "I'm hoping and praying it was compassion, but he's Carnufex's son, I can't believe . . . " He lifted his head and smiled. "So now you know. They used my wife to get me here, cooped up in a coach with Suidas Deutzel, and now I'm here, they've got me so I daren't disobey them. And Suidas is slowly going to pieces, which they must've known would happen, and when he finally snaps there'll be hell to pay, and I'm guessing the reason I'm here is to carry the can, because I'm supposed to be in charge of the team. It'll be my fault. Which it is, of course. That's the truly horrible thing. I look at Suidas and I *know* it was me that put him through all that. He's my fault, there's no getting away from it. It's *justice*."

Above all, Iseutz realised, she was *embarrassed*. A respectable middle-aged man suddenly disintegrating into a wreck no more than a yard away from her was horribly unnerving, the sort of thing that shouldn't be allowed, grossly and intolerably intimate. She wanted to make some excuse and get rid of him, push him out into the corridor so he could self-destruct in dignified privacy and spare her the misery of watching him. But that didn't seem to be an option. She took a deep breath, choked down the disgust and contempt, lowered her voice and squeezed out a drop of compassion. "He's not going to find out," she said. "Tzimisces won't tell him. It'd ruin the mission. His job's to make sure it all goes well. It's just a bluff, to scare you."

Phrantzes laughed, a horrible grating noise. "I don't think so. I don't think this thing's about peace and reconciliation. I think we're here to start another war."

"That's silly," she said. "How could we . . .?"

"By getting killed," Phrantzes said. "Or else Suidas will go berserk and start slaughtering people. You know what he did during the riot, he was out of control. He got a messer in his hand and he started cutting people to pieces, just because they were there. For pity's sake, you stupid girl, can't you see it for yourself? It was a ridiculous idea from the very start, sending a sports team to Permia. It was never going to achieve anything. They must've known how bad the situation is here. And they deliberately sent a high-profile diplomatic mission right into the heart of Permian territory. They want a war."

Iseutz forced herself to smile. "So who's this *they*?"

"The military aristocracy," Phrantzes answered immediately. "Carnufex, that lot. They hate the Bank, but the people love it and hate them. But if there's a war, the Bank will have failed. It can't wage war, it wouldn't know how. They'd have to bring back the military. They know the Permians are weak, on the point of tearing themselves apart with a civil war, it's the perfect opportunity. Carnufex's people only lost power because they ran out of money, but if they can win a quick victory, annex the DMZ, do a deal with the disaffected mine owners, then there'll be plenty of money from the mineral deposits; they can sell the rights, restore their lost fortunes, they'll be back in power for the next thousand years. What I can't understand is why nobody else can see it, it's so painfully obvious." He turned to her and gave her a death's-head grin. "And if you want proof, ask yourself: why else would they have chosen *me*? I'm useless, I can't do this. They wanted me because they knew I'd screw up and I'm eminently expendable. Well? Can't you see I'm right?"

She looked at him, making herself stay calm and strong. It was like holding a door shut when someone was desperately pushing from the other side. "You're an idiot," she said. "You're overlooking something really important. And it's so obvious."

"Really? Please, enlighten me."

"Addo Carnufex," she said gently. "If we've been sent here to die, or even if there's a serious risk we might get killed, do you really think the Irrigator would've allowed his own precious son to be on the team? *Well?*" she added, imitating his tone of voice as cruelly as she could. "Do you? Really?"

She could see him struggling with the thought, as if he was trying to wrestle it to the ground. "I don't know," he said. "He's a ruthless man. And the loss of his own son – he'd be capable of it, for the sympathy."

"Bullshit," Iseutz said. "And you know it. Come on, Phrantzes, use your common sense. General Carnufex is a great strategist, and you know why? He doesn't waste resources. He doesn't throw away men's lives on half-chances and gestures, he conserves his forces, he does exactly what's needed, no more and no less. And a man like that, a *family* like that, sons are a valuable resource. You need them, for jobs where you can't trust anyone else. You need them for marriage alliances. You don't just throw

them away when you can get the job done by other means." She
paused. To let the argument seep through. "What you're saying
is ridiculous, it's melodrama. No, one thing's for sure. If Addo's
on this jaunt, it's because his father thought it'd be safe. And if
that's true, your whole theory comes crashing to the ground.
Doesn't it?"

"All right." He rounded on her: hurt, angry. "So why'd they
choose me? I've done nothing, all the time we've been here. I just
sit in a coach and get in the way. They don't need me.
Tzimisces—"

"Is a military intelligence officer posing as a diplomat," Iseutz
cut him off, "a spy, you know that. You're here as a figurehead,
that's all. Ex-fencing champion, and a capable administrator;
that's why they chose you, not because they're plotting to feed
you to the lions. The Suidas thing's just to keep you in line. And
probably because Tzimisces likes torturing people, when it
doesn't interfere with business. He's that sort of man, you can
tell just by looking at him."

He turned away, and suddenly she thought about the old children's story, where the stupid girl opens the box that God gave
her, and all the evils of the world fly out, except Hope, which
stays at the bottom; and she wondered what Hope was doing in
there in the first place, in with all the bad things. Then the
answer came to her, and she wondered how she could've been so
stupid. Hope was in there because it was evil too, probably the
worst of them all, so heavy with malice and pain that it couldn't
drag itself out of the opened box. "Think about it," she said.
"You've been scaring yourself to death for nothing, I promise
you."

"I'm sorry." He spoke the words as though they had jagged
edges, slashing his tongue as he said them. "I guess I haven't
been thinking clearly. Of course the general wouldn't let any
harm come to Addo. They say he's the only one of his sons he
really cares about. And if Addo's supposed to be safe, then I
guess we all are."

"And they had to choose Suidas," Iseutz said. "He's the Scherian champion, the only one of us the Permians are likely to have heard of. Obviously they'd send him. And they knew they could get him to join, because he's so desperate for money."

Phrantzes nodded gratefully. "Did you know he did an exhibition match at my wedding? It was meant to be a surprise, my business partner arranged it all. They thought I'd be pleased. If I'd known then who I'd got in my house, I'd have—"

"When did you realise? That it was him, I mean."

"When we were in the coach, before we reached the border. He asked me what I'd done in the War. And after that, having to sit next to him in that bloody coach, day after day . . ."

"There's absolutely no reason for him ever to find out," Iseutz said. "Trust me, it's not going to happen."

"Addo—"

"Addo got rid of the book because he's a decent human being." Had she really said that? Yes, apparently; in which case, presumably, she believed it was true. She was surprised, but on the whole not displeased. "What possible benefit would it be to him to do something that'd cause all manner of trouble and ruin at least two lives? It's lucky he was smart enough to see the danger and take the necessary action, but I don't see how he could've done anything else. It's what I'd have done."

He stood up, nodded to her and walked to the door. "I'm sorry," he repeated. "I shouldn't have burdened you with my problems. I was being stupid, and I lost my sense of perspective."

"Yes," she said. "But it's all right. Now why don't you go away and make that Captain Cuniva find out exactly what's going on, and when we can get out of here. If I have to stay in this revolting little room much longer, I'll go mad."

Cuniva eventually escaped from Phrantzes long enough to get down to the gatehouse, where they told him what they knew. There had been messengers: rioting right across the city, but the Aram Chantat had stayed loyal and done a good job. Heavy casualties, yes, omelettes and eggs. By morning it ought to be possible to withdraw the Aram Chantat and replace them with Imperials, maybe even possibly the Permian local militia, but the city prefect wasn't going to take any chances. If it looked like there was any danger of the riots breaking out again, he'd keep the Aram Chantat on the street, and never mind the body count. Meanwhile, they were doing everything they could to get the surviving ministers out of the Guild house, just as soon as they could be sure the surrounding streets were secure. The surviving ministers? Dear God, didn't you know?

"Here," Cuniva repeated. "In the Guild house, both of them. Their throats were cut while they were getting changed after the reception. Well, everybody thought they'd be safe in here. After all, the place was locked right down. Nobody came in or out without being checked."

It took a long time for it to sink in. "They were killed by someone . . ."

"Inside the building, yes." Cuniva was trying to stay patient. It was a mark of great respect, and entirely undeserved. Phrantzes stared at him, opened his mouth and closed it again. "Which means, as far as we know, whoever did it's still in the building, because nobody's left. We've been round checking off names. We had a complete list of who was on the premises before the gates were closed, and they're all still here. So the killer . . ."

"My God," Phrantzes said. "That's appalling. You've got to—"

"We've done everything we can," Cuniva said (and his calm voice was starting to get brittle; work-hardened, like an over-flexed spring). "We made sure everybody was confined to quarters, with guards on the doors. Lucky for you, your people are all in the north tower, it's airtight, nobody can get in or out without passing at least three guard positions. The government people are in the west tower, which is also pretty damn secure. At this stage we're guessing the killer infiltrated the Guild staff, probably the kitchens. They took on a bunch of outside workers to handle the catering for the reception. They were supposed to have checked them all thoroughly beforehand, but checks aren't foolproof, heaven knows. So, first thing we did, we rounded up all the servants in one of the drill halls, and we're interrogating them one by one, so really it's just a matter of time. And once we've identified the killer, with any luck we can find out who's behind all this, and actually do something about it." He paused for breath, then added, as casually as he could manage: "You wouldn't happen to know where your political officer's got to, Colonel Tzimisces? Only he sort of disappeared about two-thirds of the way through the reception, and nobody's seen him since. In actual fact, he's the only one we haven't been able to account for. Not that he's under suspicion or anything, but we ought to find out what's become of him."

"He's missing?" A wild hope spurted up in Phrantzes' head; maybe Tzimisces was dead, murdered by the assassin; lying on a floor somewhere, or his body folded and stuffed in a cupboard, along with the mops and brooms. "No, I'm sorry, I haven't seen him, not since the reception. He was definitely there for most of it, but after that, no, I can't . . ."

"We can cross him off the list of suspects," Cuniva went on, "because we have a fair idea when the murders happened, from the state the bodies were in, and we're pretty sure he'd still have been at the party; or at least, he'd still have been there when the ministers retired to their quarters and the guards closed off the corridors leading up there. So, unless he can walk through walls, he's in the clear." He shrugged. "For all I know, he's been summoned to a briefing at the Prefecture and nobody's bothered to tell me, so I shouldn't worry too much. I mean, it's not as if he's a likely target or anything."

I can think of someone who wants him dead, Phrantzes thought. But he's a coward, so we can forget about him. "Please let me know when you do find him," he said, doing his very best to sound concerned.

"Of course," Cuniva replied. "Meanwhile, I guess I'd better carry on reporting to you, if that's all right. We're going to release your people from their quarters and put them in one of the reception rooms. We can still keep a close eye on them, and they won't be quite so cramped and isolated. Perhaps you'd be kind enough to explain what's been going on, so they won't feel too hard done by."

The reception room Cuniva had in mind was the Porphyrotriclinium, and it proved to be almost unbearably beautiful. Forty fluted porphyry pillars tapered up from a red-veined marble floor; the lines of the fluting continued into the traceries of the vaulted ceiling, making them seem like the veins of leaves, with the pillars as the stems. The room was on the third floor at the end of the east wing, and there were stained-glass windows on three sides, flooding the room with coloured light that blended perfectly with the reds and pinks of the stone. The fourth wall was covered with mosaics of the Ascent by Fire, and the rippling water of a small fountain caught the red and gold light and made it dance like flames in the facets of the gilded tessara. In the centre of the room stood an empty pedestal of gilded alabaster; at noon, on a cloudless day, the sunlight shone through a particular window on to a mirror set into the wall at a precisely calculated angle, projecting a brilliant golden column on to the pedestal; the fire that burns but does not consume. The Guild, who'd taken over the building from the Fire priests during the Disestablishment crisis shortly before Independence, used the room as a closed file store, but it had been cleared out for the post-match reception, which would not now be taking place.

"That's one good thing, anyhow," Suidas said, when they heard the news that the match had been officially cancelled. "Who knows, maybe they'll see sense and let us go home now. It's obvious there aren't going to be any more matches, with the riots and everything."

"Not according to the Guild," Phrantzes reminded him. "The

fixture at Luzir Beal's still very much on. They made a point of confirming it."

"That's so stupid," Iseutz said. "We'll get there and they'll call it off, and we'll have had a long ride for nothing."

"They're confident the rioting won't spread to the capital," Phrantzes said. "It's the stronghold of the peace faction, after all. When the news of the murders reaches Beal, they'll be dancing in the streets, not throwing rocks."

Addo, who'd been gazing at the mosaics with a puzzled expression on his face, turned round. "Unless there's more trouble," he said. "Further developments, I mean. For example, if someone decided to kill a couple of the peace faction leaders, as a reprisal ... "

"Don't say that, for heaven's sake," Phrantzes wailed. "Look, nobody wants to go home more than I do, but at the moment, that's not on the cards. So we'll just have to make the best of it, and try and put on a good show at Beal. Frankly, I couldn't give a damn about the success of the mission. I think it's fairly obvious it's been overtaken by events and is now completely irrelevant. What matters is what they think of us at home, and if they decide we haven't been doing our very best, they won't be pleased." He paused and breathed out, as if he'd just tried to lift a load that was far too heavy for him. "Captain Cuniva's pretty confident that there's no immediate threat to our safety, and once we're out of here and on the road to Beal, we'll be leaving the danger area and heading into relatively civilised territory. Beal's not like the places we've been to, apparently, it's not a mining town. People say it's almost like being in the Empire."

Iseutz, who'd been looking at him for a while, said, "Where's Tzimisces?"

Phrantzes winced. "He's meeting with the city Prefect," he said. "He's been sort of unilaterally promoted to Scherian ambassador, according to Cuniva. I have no idea what it's all about, but it's possible we won't have him with us for the trip to the capital."

Iseutz beamed and Suidas let out a whoop of joy. "Now that really is good news," he said. "It almost makes up for having to go to bloody Beal." He paused and frowned. "He'll be joining us there, I suppose."

"Probably."

"Oh well, can't have everything, I guess. Even so." He jumped up from the window seat he'd been perched in and paced across the floor. "So when do we get out of this dump and back on the road? Any word on that?"

"Later today, possibly," Phrantzes replied, "it all depends on the security situation, naturally. Cuniva said he'd let me know as soon as he's got any news."

It was a dreary morning. Nobody wanted to play chess, there was nothing to read, and nobody felt like talking. Suidas found a knife from somewhere and carved his name on the base of the alabaster pedestal. Phrantzes registered a mild diplomatic protest, which nobody seemed to hear. When he'd finished, Addo looked over his shoulder. "You've spelt it wrong," he murmured. "Isn't there a u in Deutzel?"

Iseutz burst out laughing. Suidas threw the knife across the room and went and sat in a corner. Giraut, who hadn't been all that far away from where the knife landed, got up quickly and said, "Tell you what. Since we're stuck here with nothing to do, and it looks like we're going to have to fence at Luzir Beal, maybe we should get some practice in. Might help clear our heads, maybe."

Iseutz yawned. "Why not?" she said. "If we can get hold of some foils. That ought to be possible, in a Fencers' Guild."

"I'll see what I can do," Phrantzes said immediately. He scuttled away and came back soon afterwards with a bundle of assorted foils under his arm. The weight was more than he could manage and he dropped them, sending them skittering across the floor as though they were alive.

"Splendid," Iseutz said. "Giraut, you can spar with me. Damn, there's no smallswords, I'll have to use a rapier."

Suidas found a longsword foil, long and heavy with a huge button on the end. "Addo?"

"Sorry," Addo replied, "but I don't think I will, if it's all the same to you. I seem to have pulled a muscle in my back, and it'd probably be a good idea if I left it alone for a while."

"Fine." Suidas looked round the room. "Phrantzes," he said. "Come and spar with me."

Phrantzes stared at him. "I don't think . . . "

"Oh come on, it's just sparring. I need to sort out my foot-work."

"It's been fifteen years," Phrantzes said. "I really don't think I'd be much use to you."

"I'll take it easy, I promise. Come on, man, you used to be champion fencer. And I seem to remember someone saying something about you being our team coach."

Very slowly, Phrantzes crossed the room. He picked up a longsword foil without looking at it, and lifted it painfully into a middle guard. "I honestly don't think this is a terribly good idea," he said. "I was never much of a longswordsman, even when I was younger."

Suidas wrapped a handkerchief across the palm of his right hand and took a grip on the hilt of his foil. "Stop moaning," he said. "It'll come back to you, trust me. Right, I'd like you to attack me in high front."

He raised the foil in a low back guard and nodded. Phrantzes gave him a despairing look, transitioned into high front, and moved. It was so quick that Addo, who was watching intently, barely saw it: a fast eye-level thrust that proved to be a feint but which melted into a left traverse and a low downward cut to the right knee. Suidas just about managed to block – he had no chance at all to organise his feet – only to find that the cut was a feint too, as Phrantzes traversed again, giving himself just enough room for a rising cut to the chin. The best Suidas could do was take a long step back, dropping his guard completely; the tip of the foil went past, just grazing his skin, but his balance was gone. He staggered back, and Phrantzes rammed the foil into his stomach. He went down, landing painfully on his left elbow, and saw Phrantzes standing over him, hands drawn back for a final killing thrust to the eye socket . . .

Phrantzes felt like he'd suddenly woken up; the sort of terrified, embarrassed panic when you've fallen asleep in a committee meeting or a dinner party, and you know everybody's staring at you. He looked at the sword in his hands, and the man sprawled on the floor at his feet. He was aware that Addo had just shouted his name.

"I'm so sorry," he said, and then realised he was still wound up for a killing stroke and immediately let his arms wilt. "My dear fellow, are you all right?"

Suidas was staring at him. "What the hell do you think you're playing at?" he mumbled. "You could've broken a rib."

Phrantzes let go of the sword to offer a hand to help him up; the sword slipped free and clattered on the floor. Suidas wriggled away on his bottom and pulled himself to his feet.

"I'm so sorry," Phrantzes repeated. "I just . . . "

"No, that's all right," Suidas said, taking a step back. "My fault, I didn't read you. I tell you what, though. If that's you after fifteen years doing nothing, I'm glad I wasn't around when you were fencing for real."

"It was an accident," Phrantzes said. "You must've slipped or something, or you weren't ready. It's my fault."

"Stop apologising, for crying out loud," Iseutz said. "I was watching. You wiped the floor with him. Literally."

Suidas stooped and picked up his foil. "I think we should do that again," he said. "This time, I'll see if I can be in the same fight."

"No, absolutely not," Phrantzes said. "Are you sure you're all right? I did ask if they had any masks or jackets, but . . . "

"I'll spar with you," Addo said, stepping in front of Phrantzes and picking up the foil. "My back's not as bad as I thought it was. I'm sorry, I was being feeble."

"Ignore him, he's just being noble." There was a harsh core of determination in Iseutz's voice. Phrantzes swung round and stared at her, but she was looking past him. "This time, Suidas, try and stay awake. He's twice your age and nearly twice your weight, so you might just stand a chance."

He understood. Fight him, she was saying, and then you won't be afraid of him any more. There was a sort of obvious logic to it, the kind of thing you'd expect from her, someone who saw the world in straight lines and primary colours. But when Suidas came for him, it wouldn't be with a longsword. He'd have a messer in his hand, and two squadrons of Aram Chantat would hardly slow him down if they were stupid enough to get in the way.

And then a terrible thought broke open in his mind. He winced, but it was too late, it was there, already hatched and moving. "Well," he said, "if you think it'll help. But you'll have to promise to go easy on me. These days I get out of breath running up stairs."

Suidas laughed, and smiled. "Me too," he said, "but for God's sake don't tell Sontha that, she'll have me eating lettuce leaves and celery." He lifted his foil into a front middle guard. "Ready when you are."

And then Phrantzes found himself fencing again, and he didn't realise he was too blown to breathe until there was a natural break in the flow of the bout. He was moving well, turning his wrists and forearms quickly and neatly, seeing his path, reading his opponent. He'd lied when he'd said he was no good at longsword; he'd always preferred it to rapier (but his old school friend Bonones was better than him, and nobody could ever catch him in rapier play). He fought a tight inside circle, cramping Suidas' moves and constantly turning him, so he couldn't make a big attack without laying himself open to a counter in single time. He found himself thinking two or even three plays ahead, making the pace, dictating both the distance and the tempo. Suidas was treating him with enormous respect, watching his point, concentrating. On a sudden impulse, Phrantzes decided to close for a disarm and throw. He feigned a feint, caught Suidas in a bind, let him apply his superior strength, sideslipped, hooked his calf round the inside of Suidas' front knee, and dumped him on the floor as easily as if he'd just pulled a lever. As Suidas hit the floor he felt a burst of joy, ridiculously out of proportion, as though he'd just solved all his problems with one magnificent manoeuvre; then Suidas, rolling to one side, flailed out a foot, hooked both his knees, and toppled him like a felled tree. He landed flat on his back, the floor hit him like a hammer, and for a moment he couldn't breathe. When he dragged air into his lungs and opened his eyes, he saw Suidas standing over him, grinning and offering him a hand. The terrible thought, which had almost been washed away by the burst sluices of joy, swept back again. Suidas' hand closed round his, strong as a wrench, and his mind was made up. He had to do it. There was no other way.

"Tell you what," he heard Addo say somewhere behind him, "if my back's still playing up when we get to Beal . . ."

"That was a hell of a throw," Suidas said. "You'll have to tell me how you did that. I really didn't read it, not till I was on my arse on the deck. If you'd only remembered to move your feet, you'd have had me." He was still grinning, delighted, pleased for a man he suddenly regarded as a friend and equal. But that was, after all, the purpose of the exercise: to promote friendship and understanding among deadly enemies, until the time was right.

Giraut fenced with Iseutz. She had trouble with the weight and length of the rapier: "But that's fine," she assured him. "When I go back to smallsword, it'll feel light and quick." Even so, she scored seven points to his six. He wondered if he was really trying, and decided he probably was.

"Just as well I won't have to fight you for real," he said, in a pause between points. "You're good at this."

"I'm taller and lighter than you," she replied, "and muscle doesn't matter a damn. Also, you stand too open. It's because you're always looking for a volte. As long as I can keep on your inside, you can't reach me."

He hadn't considered that, but it was true. "Thanks," he said, "I'll bear that in mind. Again?"

They fenced three more points; Giraut won them all. "Told you," she said, after the third. "Now, your turn. What am I doing wrong?"

"I'm sorry, I haven't been watching," Giraut confessed. "Too busy keeping out of your way. As far as I can see, you're not doing anything wrong, exactly."

"Then why did you just win three in a row?"

"I'm better than you, I guess."

She scowled at him, and the next three points were very hard going. But he won them, just about. "I think I can see it now," he said. "You're trying too hard."

"Excuse me?"

"Trying to force the pace," Giraut explained. "You're attacking when you don't have to, even when my defence is strong. You should make me come to you a bit more."

She shook her head. "Not my way," she said. "I'm good at aggression but not so good at defending. So I attack."

Giraut nodded. "And you give good advice but you don't take it, and you can read your opponent but not yourself. Well, you did ask."

"I didn't want an honest answer, I wanted you to reassure me."

"You're doing fine," he said, and in the next point she hit him so hard in the solar plexus that he had to sit down and catch his breath.

Later, when both pairs had worn themselves out and they were sitting in exhausted, contented silence on the window seats,

Suidas said: "Do you suppose there's any food in this place? I'm starved, and we haven't had anything to eat all day."

"I got the impression the kitchen staff were all under arrest," Addo replied. "Isn't that what Cuniva told you, Phrantzes?"

"And being interrogated by the Imperials," Phrantzes confirmed. "In which case they'll be in no fit state to go back to work for a very long time. Also, you wouldn't want someone who's just been worked over by the Blueskins handling food. It wouldn't be hygienic."

"Marvellous," Suidas growled. "Some people have no consideration."

"I don't think the cooks got themselves tortured just to cheat you out of breakfast," Addo said mildly.

"I didn't mean them, I meant the guards," Suidas said. "Why couldn't they have let them at least bake the bread and then interrogated them? Wouldn't have made much difference in the long run, and we wouldn't be starving to death."

"Being in Permia's done wonders for your sense of moral perspective," Iseutz said. "But I agree. If they were going to lock up all the kitchen staff, they might at least have made alternative arrangements."

Suidas laughed. "I don't know," he said, "we're starting to sound like we're back in the army. I remember one time, we were ambushed, just outside Conort. My lot got clear, but the entire baggage train was slaughtered to a man. Didn't we ever curse them for getting themselves killed and losing all our stuff. The general consensus was, they were lucky the Aram Chantat got to them before we did." He turned and looked at Phrantzes. "You've told me and I've forgotten, were you in the War? I guess you must've been."

"Staff officer," Phrantzes said. "Well away from the front lines."

"Good for you," Suidas replied. "That was my idea. When I knew I was going to get called up anyway, I volunteered for the transport corps. I was actually six weeks under age, but the recruiting sergeant winked and let me through. I figured, if I wait till they come for me, God only knows where I'll end up. Didn't quite work out like that, but at least I tried."

"If there's another war . . ." Addo hadn't spoken for quite some time. "Would you join up again?"

Suidas shook his head. "Absolutely no way in hell," he said. "I'd drop everything and get myself over the Western border as fast as I possibly could. How about you? I guess you'd have no choice."

"I don't want to be a soldier," Addo said. "But I'm sure my father would keep me out of harm's way."

Iseutz looked at him. "Would he do that?"

"Oh yes." Addo smiled. "He knows I'd be a rotten soldier, and there's the family reputation to consider. I'd just let the side down. Giraut? What about you?"

Giraut thought for a moment. "Yes, probably," he said. "But for your reasons, Suidas. I'd join up early in the hope of getting put somewhere reasonable. Actually, I thought of applying for the engineers. I believe they make engineer officers do a lot of technical training. With any luck, by the time I passed all the aptitude tests, the war would be over." He stopped and looked away. "Why do you ask? Do you think it's likely? Another war, I mean."

"It's the sort of ridiculous thing that tends to happen," Addo replied quietly. "I mean, apart from a few people like my father, nobody wants it. It'll do a great deal of harm, almost certainly the end of Permia and quite possibly Scheria as well. A great many people will die, and a lot more will be left crippled for life; oh, and we can't afford it, so we'll all be dirt poor for generations to come. So yes, on balance, I think it's practically inevitable."

"They've cleared the streets you'll be driving along," Cuniva had assured them, "there won't be any trouble, I promise."

They drove out of the Guild house gates in a beautiful white and gold carriage, the ceremonial vehicle of the Master of the

Guild; the carriage they'd arrived in was a heap of ashes, but the Master assured them that they were welcome, and he wouldn't be going anywhere in a hurry, so they could keep it for as long as they needed it. The two coachmen wore Guild livery. On the box beside them, where the Master's pageboys usually sat, two Imperials in full armour perched unsteadily, clinging to the rails and swaying on corners. Cuniva was inside the coach, in Tzimisces' place. Their escort was a troop of fifteen Aram Chantat.

Giraut took a good long look at them before he got in the coach. They were young – he'd have guessed the eldest was no more than nineteen – beardless, with wavy fair hair down to their shoulders; short men even for Aram Chantat, wearing white full-sleeved linen shirts gathered at the wrist instead of armour and holding no weapons, though their bow cases and scabbards hung from their saddles. They were talking very fast, occasionally bursting into peals of laughter. Giraut guessed they were playing a favourite word game. As he climbed aboard the coach, he noticed a clump of dirty red-brown matting tucked between the point man's horse and saddle, just behind the crupper. Something dark and sticky caught the light as it trickled down the short hairs of the horse's coat. Scalps.

"It's all right," Cuniva said. He wasn't looking his usual elegant self. Instead of the gilded parade cuirass he'd worn for the reception, he had his business armour on. It looked old and comfortable, and the small steel plates were painted black, to keep his sweat from rusting them. "They're Rosinholet, they're fairly reasonable people once you get to know them. And they don't have any ongoing feuds with any of the other sects serving in Permia, so we'll be fine."

They took the main east–west thoroughfare, the Ropewalk, heading due east out of the city. It was a wide road, which was just as well; it was littered with smashed carts and carriages, trashed market stalls and traders' booths, apparently random objects dragged out of houses and shops and hacked or pounded into bits, and bodies, ever so many bodies: men, women, children, horses, even dogs. It looked bizarrely familiar, which made no sense, until Giraut remembered the last act of his recurring dream, the point at which the floodwaters receded and drained away, leaving the flotsam behind.

"They'll fail, of course," Cuniva was saying. He'd been talking for some time, but Giraut hadn't been paying attention. "They've got no leaders or resources, no weapons, no training, no plan of campaign. They're just a bunch of angry people who didn't realise what they were letting themselves in for. This sort of thing never succeeds so long as the army stays loyal to the government. Which, of course, we fully intend to do."

"As long as they keep up the payments," Iseutz muttered.

"Exactly." Cuniva had apparently found nothing to object to in that. "And they pay in advance, so our loyalty's guaranteed for at least the next three weeks, by which time all this nonsense will have burnt itself out. And besides, when the army's loyalty wavers, it nearly always comes from the junior officers – me and my peers, as it were – because they can't stomach killing their fellow citizens. No such difficulty here, obviously. This is actually quite an opportunity for the junior field grades. You can get yourself noticed in actions like this. So you see," he concluded with a warm smile, "you've got no cause for concern whatsoever."

"Over there," Cuniva said, pointing vaguely through the left-hand window, "are the Verjan mountains. You can just see them, look."

Addo obediently craned his neck. Nobody else moved.

"And over there," Cuniva went on, pointing in what appeared to be exactly the same direction, "behind the big ridge, is Lake Prescile. Of course, you can't see it from here. But that's where it is."

"Good heavens," Addo said mildly. He picked up his book (Pescennius' *Art of War*, lent to him by Baudila; still, better than nothing) and made a show of reading it.

"It's such a shame," Cuniva went on, "that we're behind schedule. Otherwise we could've taken a detour and had a look. I've been there myself, of course, many times. It's a really rather beautiful place now, in a way; completely deserted, of course, even the main turnpikes are starting to grass over. The only thing you can see is the spire of the Orphans' Hospital, sticking up out of the water bang in the middle like a great big pillar. Otherwise it's just a big smooth lake, with the mountains reflected in it."

He was quiet for a while after that, and Giraut was just starting to nod off when they passed a column of soldiers, Imperials, marching the other way. "The Seventeenth," Cuniva informed them. "Headed for Beaute, presumably. They were due to go home later this month, but I guess they must've been rehired for the duration. Like they say, it's an ill wind."

Giraut could see Suidas clenching his fists, though his face was perfectly calm. Iseutz yawned. Addo turned a page. Phrantzes was looking out of the window on the other side, towards a distant range of hills.

"Actually," Cuniva said, fixing Giraut with a piercing stare, "if it's all right, there's something I'd like to ask you fellows. It's – well, a bit embarrassing, but I think we know each other well enough by now."

He had Iseutz's full attention, and Addo had lowered his book. "Oh yes?" Suidas said.

"The thing is." Cuniva hesitated, then took a rush at it. "I've always wondered why you people call my lot Blueskins." Everyone froze. "Not that it bothers me, you understand, it's quite all right, but you see, our skins aren't blue, they're dark brown. It's as if we went around calling you lot Redskins, when you're a sort of apricot colour. It doesn't actually make any sense."

There was a brief silence. Then Addo cleared his throat. "Oddly enough," he said, in a high voice, "I wondered the same thing, so I asked my father. He said that when our people encountered your people for the first time, they reported back that you had skins the colour of blueberries, just before they ripen. But Blueberryskin's a bit of a mouthful, so it got shortened. That's what he told me, anyway. I don't know if it's true or not."

Cuniva looked blank for a moment, then smiled. "How perfectly delightful," he said. "It so happens that I'm very partial to blueberries. Thank you. I wouldn't have asked, except that it seemed so odd. Not insulting or anything, just inaccurate."

That cut off any further conversation like the executioner's axe. Giraut studied his shoes for a while. Addo went back to *Art of War* (where he read about direct frontal assaults on the enemy's weakest point, and managed not to smile). Suidas closed his eyes and pretended to be asleep, but his breathing was all wrong for that. Iseutz sat quite still, frowning. Phrantzes went back to gazing out of the window.

In the late afternoon the road began to climb, as they approached the foot of a massive escarpment. Cuniva told them (nobody had asked) that this was the Chauzida plateau. The main road went round it, but they'd be going over the top. "It'll save us the best part of a day," he promised them, "and that'll put us back on schedule."

Giraut stuck his head out of the window. As far as he could tell, they were driving straight at a sheer wall of vertical rock. "Are you sure?" he said.

"There's a pass," Cuniva said. "You can't see it from here, it's narrow and pretty well hidden. But it's there all right. I've been this way loads of times."

Addo closed his book. "Would that be a path through a steep-sided defile with a sharp turn in it about half a mile along?"

"Yes. You know this place?"

Addo shook his head. "Not personally. But my father got caught in this pass when he was a young lieutenant. The enemy – actually, I think it was your people, Captain – they let our lot get in about halfway, then cut the road at both ends with big boulders and shot us to pieces with bows and light artillery from the tops of the defile. My father was one of about a dozen who made it out alive, out of around three hundred."

Cuniva looked shocked. "I don't remember that in any of the campaign histories."

"You wouldn't have. My father wrote them." Addo grinned. "Not one of his most glorious moments. He was in command at the time. He told me that if there was any justice he'd have been court-martialled and strung up for making such a stupid mistake. He said, one look at the place and he should've known. It's as though the Invincible Sun had designed it specifically for ambushing idiots."

Cuniva's eyebrows were practically touching his hair. "You do surprise me," he said. "But this was early in his career, presumably, one of his first commands . . ."

"No, actually. He was thirty years old and should've known better, was what he told me. But his uncle was the area commander, so they covered it up."

Cuniva shook his head, as if he'd just seen God throwing up in a shop doorway. "Ah well," he said. "Just as well this is peacetime."

The chieftain looked confused. "You're a priest," he said.

Brother Perceptuus decided it would be too complicated to explain the difference between a monk and a priest. "That's right," he said.

"A holy man."

"Yes."

Perceptuus was trying hard not to stare. The chieftain was a short man, five foot nothing; tiny little hands, like a girl. His face was round and deeply lined, almost completely bald on top, his long, thin back hair woven into a snow-white ponytail; somewhere between sixty and ninety; pale blue eyes and skin the colour of milk. His upper middle front tooth was missing. He wore a white shirt, spotlessly clean, with a lace collar, and velvet

knee breeches, a style that had been fashionable in the Western
Empire about seventy years ago. His feet were bare. He was sitting in a heavy folding chair made out of horses' leg bones.

"Excuse me," the chieftain said (he spoke perfect Imperial
with an upper-class Eastern accent), "but I find that surprising.
This is hardly a spiritual matter."

Perceptuus smiled. "There are times when the line between
spiritual and temporal gets a little blurred, don't you find?"

The chieftain frowned. "No," he said. "Where I come from,
priests are concerned with moral and ethical issues. They don't
do politics. Or money. That's strictly the province of the laity."
He shrugged. "Ah well," he said, "it wouldn't do if we were all
the same. I'm terribly sorry, I'm forgetting my manners. Would
you care for something to drink? I'm afraid we're a bit rough and
ready at the moment, but I can offer you a passable dry Vesani
white."

It had been many years since Perceptuus had had an opportunity to drink imported wine. "Thank you," he said. "That
would be most kind."

The chieftain nodded, and someone in the far corner moved to
the tent flap and crawled out.

"It was very good of you to see me," Perceptuus said. "At
such short notice."

"My pleasure," the chieftain said. "Now, how may I help you?"

He had a ring on his left middle finger, a huge red stone.
Perceptuus was only an amateur, but he was sure it was genuine.
If so, it was worth about twenty thousand nomismata. Don't
stare, he told himself. "It's rather a delicate matter."

"I thought it might be. Is that why your government sent a
priest?"

"I'm not actually here on behalf of my government,"
Perceptuus said, "not as such. I represent the College of the
Ascension; basically, the Scherian arm of the Studium. Nothing I
say should be construed as coming from the Scherian authorities,
or the Bank."

"Oh." The chieftain looked mildly confused. "Well, I'll bear that in mind. What can we do for the Invincible Sun?"

Perceptuus shifted a little in his seat: a plain wooden stool with a single narrow upright bar for a back, but remarkably comfortable. "I understand that your current contract with the Permian government is about to expire."

"In six weeks, yes."

"We were wondering . . . " A man appeared at Perceptuus' elbow. He held a brass tray, on which stood a cup, containing wine. It was made from a man's skull, with the apertures filled in with silver and niello.

"My predecessor," the chieftain said. "I'm sorry, you were saying?"

Perceptuus lifted it gingerly off the tray and held it up, taking care not to spill any wine. "You know, I've heard about these," he said, "but I've never actually seen one. How do they do the silver infill without charring the bone, I wonder." He rotated it in his hands. "Beautiful filigree work," he said. "You must excuse me, I used to collect fine silver."

"Keep it," the chieftain said, "please. You were about to say what you wanted."

Perceptuus took a sip of the wine. It was delightful. "Would you consider coming to work for us?" he said. "Once your term with the Permians is over."

The chieftain frowned. "I thought you said you weren't the government."

"We aren't."

"I see. And what would the Invincible Sun want with a mercenary army?"

Perceptuus finished his wine and took a moment to savour the aftertaste; dry, and with a hint of apples. "To protect our interests," he said. "We have substantial holdings of land, much of it close to the border with the Demilitarised Zone. We also have long-standing claims within the Zone, although of course we haven't been able to pursue them because of the war. Now, however, with mounting unrest in Permia and the possibility that the current regime may fall and the country might slide into chaos, we have to consider the risk to our tenants." He ran the tip of his forefinger over the embossed acanthus- and scroll-work around the rim of the cup. Exquisite. "From bandits," he went on, "wandering gangs, demobilised army units. You know the sort of thing that happens when a regime collapses suddenly."

The chieftain nodded. "Won't your government deal with all that?" he said. "That's what they're for, surely."

"Of course," Perceptuus said, "in theory. But the Bank may well have other priorities, and other calls on its resources. We like to take care of the people who depend on us. And, fortunately, we can afford it."

"I admit, I was wondering about that," the chieftain said. "To put it crudely, we aren't cheap."

Perceptuus put the cup down on the ground. "Our Order's resources in Scheria are limited, naturally," he said. "But we've discussed the situation with our brothers in the Western Empire, and any agreement you and I may make will be guaranteed unconditionally by the Studium; which means, in effect, by the Empire. So really, money isn't an issue."

The chieftain smiled. "You must excuse me," he said. "I'm only a simple shepherd, so I don't pretend to any understanding of international politics. Even so, I feel sure that for the established church of the Western Empire to underwrite the activities of a schismatic branch in a country still officially classed as in rebellion against the Empire, there must be something quite complicated going on, which no doubt you really wouldn't want to discuss with strangers." He lifted his hands and fluttered his fingers slightly; presumably that meant something, but Perceptuus had no idea what it might be. "You in turn must appreciate that the Aram no Vei have always maintained a strict policy of neutrality towards both empires, just as we are officially neutral as regards Scheria and Permia. Our presence here is a purely commercial arrangement. It doesn't represent public policy in any way. I would be grossly exceeding my mandate if I did anything that might be construed as breaching that neutrality." He turned the ring on his finger until the stone was underneath, and closed his fist around it. "In the circumstances, I think I'll have to refer your proposal to my superiors. It shouldn't take long," he added. "We have a fairly efficient system of communications."

Quite, Perceptuus thought. And in Scheria, how many simple shepherds would use words like *construe* and *mandate*? "I quite understand," he said. "But assuming they decide that there are no far-reaching diplomatic implications, do you think it's likely that they would agree?"

"That's not for me to say," the chieftain replied, and Perceptuus knew that all the siege engines and battering rams in Scheria wouldn't make a dent in that smile. "But as soon as I hear from them, I'll let you know, obviously. Meanwhile ... "

Afterwards, in the tent they'd provided for him (he'd never spent the night in a tent before; the cushions were silk, but he knew he wouldn't be able to get to sleep lying on the ground), Perceptuus composed a very brief report for Abbot Symbatus. *You were quite right*, he wrote, *they've had another offer, but who from and how much for I simply don't know. I think he believed me about the Studium, but I wouldn't put it past him to check up. What do you want me to do? When can I come home?*

He read through what he'd written, then splashed a quarter of a pint of the delightful Vesani white wine into the skull cup (there was even a dear little tulipwood box to keep it in, with hinges in the shape of leaping stags) and drank two mouthfuls. The cup he'd have to hand over to the abbey bursar when he got back, but there wouldn't be any of the wine left, he was quite resolved on that.

You probably know more about the situation than I do, he wrote, *but my man here believes the government will survive the crisis, assuming the trouble doesn't spread to the capital. He says the majority of the Aram Chantat contracts expire at the same time as his, but*

*he can't see the unrest lasting anything like that long. I would say he's
in a good position to judge. I gather the Aram Chantat have blanket
discretion to use all necessary force. They insisted on that, apparently; otherwise they refused to get involved. I get the impression they
don't really hold with the notion of rules of engagement, which they
regard as a contradiction in terms.*

He'd forgotten how strong real wine was. It was making him
feel stupid. He was sure there was something else he needed to
add, but he couldn't think of anything relevant that Symbatus
wouldn't already know; assuming, of course, that the abbot was
still alive. He shivered, and stood up to throw more charcoal on
the brazier. If Symbatus was dead, would there be anybody back
home who knew the whole of what was going on? He was
inclined to doubt it; Symbatus was notorious for keeping things
to himself, even in relatively trivial matters. Where something as
big as this was concerned ... For one thing, who was there he
could safely confide in? He tried to think of anybody at all, himself included, and failed. But if Symbatus were to die partway
through, with the complex mechanism he'd set up and which
only he knew about still working towards its unknown ultimate
objective, the result could be disastrous.

Well, he'd better still be alive, then, or we're all screwed. He lay
down on the heaped-up cushions and felt his head swim; bad
idea, so he propped himself up against the tent pole. He knew he
wouldn't sleep, too much on his mind. For instance: who else was
negotiating for the services of the Aram no Vei, why, and how
much could they afford to pay? The Permian nobility, for example; with the Aram Chantat on their side they could overthrow
the government in a matter of days. They had no money, of
course, but did that matter? Once they'd got power back, they'd
have the entire treasury at their disposal, not to mention the mineral futures in the DMZ. But would the Aram Chantat want
payment in advance? He realised that he hadn't asked that, and it
was vitally important. Somebody else should be doing this job, he
told himself, preferably someone with at least half a brain.

He sealed the letter; then he stood up, went to the tent flap, lowered himself awkwardly to his knees (he was still stiff from weeding onions) and crawled out. A guard was looking down at him, with a tolerantly neutral expression on his face. Perceptuus levered himself upright and smiled at him.

"I need to . . ." He stopped; exactly how do you do *I need to shit* in sign language? But the guard gave him an understanding smile and pointed to the edge of the encampment. Intelligent fellows, the Aram Chantat, he thought. Not too intelligent, let's hope, or we're all in trouble.

He walked about twenty yards and squatted down in what he hoped was a convincing posture. He hadn't been waiting long when he heard a soft cough and a quiet voice saying, "If you're not just pretending, I can come back later."

"There you are," Perceptuus snapped back at him. "I've got a letter, for Abbot Symbatus. Urgent. Can you . . .?"

"Sure," the voice replied. "Leave it on the ground when you go. How are you getting on?"

"I can't tell you that." Melodrama; still, why not? "What's the situation like in Beaute, do you know?"

"Under control. The fencers have moved on. Everything's fine. You'd better get back, unless you intend to feign intense constipation for the rest of your visit."

"Thank you, Colonel." He hesitated. It was dark, and he didn't actually know the man. "It is Colonel, isn't it?"

"I can't tell you that. Get along with you, before they send out a search party."

Tzimisces waited half an hour before retrieving the letter and making his way slowly and steadily back to the road, where he'd left his horse hobbled by a stream. He rode through the night, and as soon as there was enough light to read by, he took the letter out of his pocket and looked at it. Sealed, of course, but there are things you can do; a thin wire, red-hot, drawn through the wax was his favourite, with a smear of bow-maker's fish glue to put it back afterwards. He couldn't be bothered, though; he'd been listening outside the tent during the meeting, and the old fool had got nowhere, just as he'd anticipated. He could picture the look of mild annoyance on Symbatus' face as he read the letter (assuming Symbatus was still alive, but let's not go there) There was, in fact, no reason why it shouldn't be passed on and delivered; it could do no harm and make no difference.

He met the courier at the forty-seventh milestone: a tall, handsome young Imperial in a fur-lined riding coat, his teeth chattering in the comparative cold. "Take this letter to C7," Tzimisces told him. "Extremely urgent. All necessary measures to keep it from falling into the wrong hands. Understood?"

The Imperial nodded. "One for you," he said, and handed over a tiny square of parchment, folded over and over again to make it as small as possible.

"Thanks," Tzimisces said.

The Imperial saluted and rode away. Tzimisces sighed as he watched him go. Suborning Imperials was ruinously expensive, at a time when money was tight; a Permian civilian would've done just as well and would've been delighted to be paid a tenth of what the Blueskin must be getting. Still, he could see the logic behind the standard operating procedure; with enemies, as with senators, always buy the best you can afford. He unfolded the letter he'd been given and frowned as he read it.

"I'm sorry, I don't understand," Cuniva said, for the fifth time.

Iseutz sighed. "Oh for pity's sake. Look, why don't we play something else?"

"No, please." Cuniva looked troubled. "I'd like to learn, really. Could you go through it again just once more, and I promise I'll pay attention."

They'd been driving through the defile for nearly an hour. "All right." Addo had come up with a new patient voice they hadn't heard before. It was slow and soft and gentle, and Giraut wondered if it meant he was on the point of losing his temper completely. "It really is very simple. I say, 'The minister's cat is an *affable* cat' – affable starts with A, all right? The person sitting next to me then says, 'Because he's not *angry*.' Angry also starts with A, but it's the opposite of affable. Well," he added, "sort of, anyway. Then the person sitting next to him – that'd be Iseutz in this instance – says something like, 'The minister's cat is a *blue* cat' – blue starts with B, you see – and then Phrantzes, who's next to Iseutz, he says, oh I don't know, 'Because he's not *brown*.' And then you say . . . "

"Excuse me," Cuniva said, deeply ashamed, "I still don't follow. Brown isn't the opposite of blue."

"Yes, but if you're brown you can't be blue, so it counts. Like, if you're angry you can't be affable. So now you say something like, maybe, 'The minister's cat is a *cheerful* cat' . . . "

"Because he's not *cross*." Cuniva beamed like the sunrise. "Is that all right?"

"*Yes*." Iseutz closed her eyes for a moment. "I do believe you've finally got there. Right, can we get on, please? Whose go was it?"

"Suidas," Giraut said. "On G."

Suidas yawned. "You know what, I think I'll just look out of the window for a bit."

"You dare," Iseutz snapped, and he shrugged. "Fine," he said. "All right, the minister's cat is a gratuitous cat." He smiled, and said, "Your turn, Captain."

Cuniva looked stunned. "Gratuitous."

"Yes, that's right," Suidas said. "The minister's cat is a gratu-itous cat. And?"

"Because he's not . . . " Cuniva twisted his face and bit his lip. "I'm sorry," he said, "I can't think of anything."

"Suidas, for pity's sake." Iseutz glowered at him. "It's his first time playing. Why did you have to pick such a hard one?"

"It's perfectly fair," Suidas replied, "within the rules of the game. Naturally, I play to win."

"All right, then, you think of one."

"It's not up to me," Suidas said smugly. "Sorry, Captain, you're out and that's ten points to me. So, it's me to start again, isn't it? The minister's cat—"

"Quiet," Addo said. "Listen."

They heard it much more clearly up on the box, where the two Imperials grabbed for their shields, which they'd stowed under the luggage in the rack. The driver turned his head to see where the yelling was coming from, saw, and stared in horror, then looked back at the road just in time to pull back on the reins as they swung into the tight corner. An arrow went past his head, making that soft swish-swish sound as it spun. The Imperials looked round for their Aram Chantat escort, and noticed for the first time that they'd disappeared.

"We've stopped," Iseutz said.

Suidas' eyes were very wide. "Everybody get out of the coach," he said, in a level, brittle voice.

"Don't be stupid, they're shooting arrows." Cuniva was leaning over Phrantzes, scrabbling for the blinds. "It's open ground, there's no cover."

Suidas leaned forward slightly, drew his left hand back a little way and punched Cuniva on the point of his jaw. His head snapped back, his eyes closed and he slid down into his seat. "If we stay in the coach, we'll be killed," Suidas said gently. "Come on."

He edged across a little, drew his knee back under his chin and kicked the door with the sole of his boot. The door flew open and Suidas dived, as though into deep water, on to the ground. "Come *on*," he yelled as he scrambled to his feet. Then he burst into a frantic, jinking run.

"But where's the escort?" Phrantzes asked, in a dazed voice.

"Dead, probably," Addo replied. He was crouching in the doorway, peering out. "We'd better go," he said. "Iseutz, you next." He jumped, landed on his feet and swung round to grab

Iseutz by the wrist and haul her out. An arrow sailed over his head and glanced off the roof of the coach. "Phrantzes," he shouted, and then he ran, dragging Iseutz behind him.

Cuniva was sitting up, staring at the open door, registering the empty seats. "Shit," he wailed, and launched himself through the door. He ran five yards then dropped to his knees. He was still alive.

Phrantzes stared at Giraut, who just shook his head. He hesitated, then opened the other door, dropped bonelessly out of it and crawled under the coach.

Giraut sat perfectly still. *I'm not going out there*, was all he could hear himself say. He watched as Addo came tearing back, grabbed Cuniva by the arm and neck, hauled him upright and threw him forward, forcing him to find his feet. They staggered out of sight. An arrow hit the side of the coach, making it shudder slightly. Giraut could see half an inch of sharp, triangular point sticking out of a split in the woodwork. In his mind, it had hit him in the knee, socket-deep in bone, unendurably painful. He stayed where he was, and a voice in his head said, *The others have gone, so they'll think the coach is empty. So I'll just sit here, for now.* He was shaking, and he felt sick and chilled all over. He could hear his mother's voice, when they'd first tried to teach him to swim: *Don't be such a baby.* But all he'd been able to think of was water covering his eyes, filling his ears and mouth, and nothing they could say or do would induce him to let go of the big stone in the riverbank. He'd thought, *I'm safe here*; and then his uncle had lifted his fingers, one by one, until he lost his grip, and he'd been in the water, kicking desperately against nothing, and the water splashed into his nose, and he'd choked . . .

He dropped to the floor and crawled as far as he could get under the seat.

Later, Suidas could remember scrambling up the side of the defile – he'd missed his footing several times and landed on his knees, rasping the skin to pulp on the sharp shale – but nothing after that until he came to, as if waking up, and found himself standing over a dead body. There was a messer in his hand (he couldn't say for sure where it had come from) and his face and hands were wet and sticky. He hoped the blood was someone else's.

Someone had killed four Aram Chantat, with a messer. Whoever it was, he'd been hitting too hard, generally a sign of fear or panic; he'd cut through one man's right leg and deep into his left, and the man he was standing over was all but decapitated. Suidas frowned.

He made an effort, cleared his mind and tried to get a grip on the situation. Archers had been shooting at them from up here, but the dead men didn't have bows or quivers. The coach had stopped, so presumably the road ahead had been blocked. He had no idea how many of the enemy there were, or where. He had no shield or armour, and he was standing upright on the sky-line.

He knelt down quickly and looked round. From where he was, he could see the roof of the coach, with a dead man lying across it; the horses were dead in the shafts. The far side of the ravine was a vertical wall – if he'd only left the coach by the other door, he'd have been in good cover, because there couldn't be any archers on that side. But of course he'd jumped out of the left-hand door because it was the closest to where he'd been sitting. Idiot.

This is wrong, he thought. They've won, so what are they hiding for?

From his position, he couldn't see the coach well enough to shoot at it, not at the angle the arrows had been coming from. Therefore the archers must have been somewhere below him. He had no reason to suppose they'd still be there.

He turned his head and looked the other way, across the plateau. It was completely open, a flat tabletop of bare rock. If they were Aram Chantat, they'd have horses. A man on foot wouldn't stand a chance against horsemen on the flat. There was also the slight possibility that at least some of the others were still alive somewhere.

His skinned knees were starting to stiffen, and something he'd done recently had pulled a muscle in his back, but he had no choice. He glanced at the dead men, hoping for a shield, or something that might do for one, but they were infuriatingly unhelpful: shirts, trousers, bare feet, armed with sabres or single-hand axes, no bloody use to anybody. A thought struck him; he frowned, then shrugged, and reached out with his left hand for the head of the dead man lying beside him. It was still attached to the neck by a flap of skin, which he sliced through with his messer. He took a firm grip on the long hair and swung the head in a circle, until the hair was wrapped twice round his hand. It wasn't a shield, but it was something.

Going down the side of the defile made him wonder how the hell he'd ever got up it. The shale was practically a liquid, only taking his weight for a fraction of a second before falling away. He ended up running down, in a race with the shale to see who got to the bottom first. Just before he lost the race, he jumped.

He landed well, and found himself on the floor of the defile, about ten yards from the coach. He saw three men, Aram Chantat; they were kneeling beside the coach, prodding underneath it with their sabres, laughing. Suidas couldn't figure out what they were doing, but it didn't really matter. Miraculously, they hadn't heard him come crashing down the slope, so he had the element of surprise; that, a messer, and some poor fool's head for a shield. He sincerely hoped that that would do.

Instead of just running straight at them, he headed away ten yards or so, walking quietly until he reached the front, where the dead horses lay. That way, he could tackle them in column rather than in line; one at a time, rather than four at once. Of course he didn't know if there were more of them round the other side. He'd find out soon enough, if he lived that long.

The closest man saw him and jumped up, a single smooth transition from hands-and-knees to a modified low front guard.

Suidas took two long strides to close the measure and swung at his right arm with the head. He savoured the horrified look on the man's face as he flinched away, thereby opening the left side of his neck. Suidas took care not to hit too hard this time, so as not to exacerbate the pulled muscle in his back.

He thought, as he closed in on the second man: I like this messer, balance nicely forward, I wonder where I got it from. The third and fourth blurred into one; he smacked the left-hand man in the face with the head while draw-cutting the right-hand man's left hamstring. He killed left-hand on the ground; right-hand would keep. He peered round the side of the coach and saw two more. They were nearly too quick for him, but not quite.

He went back and dealt with the man he'd hamstrung, then stepped back and looked round. He was far too open and exposed, and there were no enemies to shield him if there were still archers out deep, but nothing bad happened. He counted: four up there, six here, ten. A typical Aram Chantat detached half-platoon was ten plus an officer. Damn.

"Suidas?" The coach was calling his name. He stared at it. "Suidas, is that you?"

"Phrantzes?"

"I'm under here."

It took a moment for that to make sense; then he laughed. "You clown," he said. "It's all right, you can come out now."

"No," Phrantzes said, "I can't."

At which point, Suidas figured out what the Aram Chantat had been doing on their knees in the dirt. "Are you all right?" he asked, which was a stupid question.

"You'll have to pull me out."

Suidas thought for a moment. "Stay there," he said. "I think there's one of the fuckers still loose."

"Suidas . . ."

"I'll be back for you as soon as I can. What about the others?"

"I don't know. I'm sorry."

"Stay there," Suidas said. "I'll be as quick as I can."

He took a few steps away from the coach, but he had no idea what to do next. The bastard couldn't have a bow, or he'd have shot by now. If he had the brains he was born with, he'd have taken his horse and . . .

Point. Horses. If I were the Aram Chantat, where would I have left my horses? Nowhere he could see; not behind, the way the coach had come, or they might have been seen. In front, therefore, round the bend.

The last man did have a bow after all, but he was either a lousy shot or too overwrought to aim straight. Suidas found him on the other side of the heap of stones they'd used to block the road. He proved to be a handful, smacking the messer out of Suidas' hand with a wild swipe and then lunging. Suidas was quite calm as he traversed right, warded off the thrust with the head and punched him at the point where the jaw met the neck. Then he retrieved the messer and finished the job while the man was still trying to get to his knees. Ten plus one. So that's all right.

Then he looked down, and saw the man lying at his feet. He'd fallen on his side, but his hips and legs were twisted round and faced upwards. The messer had cut through his neck to the bone; a good cut, strong enough but not too strong, it sort of made up for his earlier deficiencies in technique. There were fat spots of coagulating blood in the man's hair; odd, the things you notice. He had a nice-looking silver archer's ring on his right hand, but it wouldn't come off.

Suidas straightened his back and winced; his shoulder definitely wasn't right. He realised he still had the head tied to his left hand by its hair. The face was a bit the worse for wear after fending off several cuts and being used as a morningstar. He turned his wrist to unravel the hair, let it fall and booted it away.

Fencing practice, he thought. Well. He realised he felt completely calm, which was ridiculous, given the desperate situation he was in.

Phrantzes, he remembered, oh hell. He ran back to the coach, to find Phrantzes sitting with his back to it, and Giraut standing over him. A glance told him they were both more or less all right; enough to leave, at any rate.

"Giraut," he said, "the others. Any idea?"

Giraut shook his head. "I saw Addo run off with Iseutz, and then he came back to get Captain Cuniva after he got shot. But after that . . . "

Just a moment, Suidas thought. He did the mental geometry: sight lines. "Where were you?"

Giraut tried to look away, but couldn't seem to manage it. "In the coach."

Suidas frowned, then grinned. "Smart boy," he said. "Phrantzes, what about you? Did they get you?"

Phrantzes shook his head. "They were poking at me, but they couldn't quite reach. They were laughing. I kept expecting them to turn the coach over, but I suppose they didn't think of it."

"But you're all right."

"Cramp," Phrantzes said. "I couldn't move. Giraut had to—"

"*Cramp!*" Suidas exploded. "You bastard, I thought they'd cut your feet off or something."

"I'm sorry, I . . . "

"Forget it," Suidas said. "And get up, for God's sake, you look pathetic. We've got to look for Iseutz and the Carnufex boy, and that Blueskin. *Cramp*, for crying out loud."

Giraut looked at him. "What happened?" he said.

"What?"

"The enemy. What happened? Where did they go?"

Suidas noticed that the messer was still in his hand. He found it hard to let go of it, but he sheathed it (there was a sheath hanging from his belt; so that was where it had come from). "They're dead," he said. "At least, I think so. I found eleven, ten plus one; that's usual for a half-platoon."

"You killed eleven men?"

He sounded surprised; it made Suidas want to laugh. "Well,

obviously I did, or I wouldn't be here. You two, that way. I'll start
over there and work my way back."

Giraut found Addo; or rather, the other way about. Addo
jumped out at him from behind a rock, shoved him to the ground
and was about to drive his thumbs into Giraut's windpipe when
he suddenly froze, let go and said, "Sorry."

Iseutz emerged a moment later, looking white as paper but
unhurt. "Cuniva's dead, I'm afraid," Addo said. "What about
Suidas and Phrantzes?"

"They're fine," Giraut said, massaging his neck. "Suidas killed
the enemy. All of them."

Addo looked worried rather than surprised, but he said, "Well
then. What about the coachman, and the guards?"

Giraut hadn't even thought about them. "I don't know," he
said, just as he remembered seeing bodies that weren't Aram
Chantat. "I don't think so," he added. "And they killed the coach
horses."

"What?" Addo sounded very surprised by that. "All right,
where's Suidas? Is he all right?"

"Oh, he's fine," Giraut said. It had just dawned on him that they
were in the middle of nowhere, with no horses, food or water.
"Addo, what the hell is going on? I thought the Aram Chantat—"

"Obviously not," Addo said quietly.

Suidas thought he could hear a bubbling noise, like water sim-
mering. It was Iseutz, crying. He shot her a startled look and
moved away, as though it might be contagious. "We need to find
their horses," he said sharply, as if he'd found a fault in her that
linked cause with effect. "They didn't walk here, you can bet
your life."

Addo, who was staring at Iseutz, nodded. "My guess is they're
tied up round the corner somewhere. They'd be out of the way
there, less likely to be spooked by the noise."

"Yes, all right," Suidas snapped. "Why don't you run ahead
and see if you can find them?"

"I'll go," Giraut heard himself say, and he broke into a run. It occurred to him as he scrambled over the low wall of rocks that Suidas might have been wrong and there were more than eleven of them; a couple held in reserve, maybe, to watch the horses. Somehow, though, he felt he'd rather take his chances than stay with his friends. He stopped and looked round, and listened. Nothing. The road in front of him was straight, the sides of the defile sheer and vertical. You might just be able to hide six stone-coloured mice there, if you could teach them to sit perfectly still, but not eleven horses.

"They've got to be somewhere," Suidas growled, when he'd reported back. "And fairly close; the Aram Chantat despise walking."

"Maybe someone brought them here in a cart," Phrantzes said. It was the first time he'd spoken in a long while, and he might as well not have bothered. Suidas ran a little way up the shale slope, lost his footing and came tumbling down in a comical tangle of arms and legs, landing on his back with his feet in the air. Nobody laughed. He jumped up and kicked a stone, which went skittering down the road. "This is *stupid*," he said.

"They left someone to watch the horses," Addo said, "and he's taken them and gone off."

"There were *eleven* of them," Suidas roared. Giraut winced. Addo didn't move. "I'm guessing there were at least twelve," he said quietly. "I think we're going to have to walk."

Without a word, Iseutz sat down on the ground. Phrantzes said, "I think we ought to stay where we are. Sooner or later the Permians will realise we're overdue and send someone to find us."

"Oh for God's sake," Suidas shouted at him. "Who do you think sent those men? Who do the Aram Chantat work for? Well?"

Addo frowned. "Suidas . . . "

"And you can shut up, for a start. Where were you when the fight was on? You're pathetic, the lot of you."

"Yes," Addo said quietly, "but I can be pathetic and right at the same time, and yelling at us isn't helping. And you're right, we can't stay here, but I don't think there are any horses. We really ought to get going." He stooped and picked up a sabre. "Never used one of these, but I guess the principle's the same. Which way?"

"Straight on, surely," Giraut said. "After all, they think they've killed us, so they won't be expecting us."

"No, that's stupid," Suidas snapped. "We've got no idea where they may have come from." He paused to think, and nobody seemed prepared to risk making a suggestion. Iseutz wandered off and collected an armful of sabres. "But we might as well go straight on," Suidas said. "Really, it doesn't make a lot of difference. I don't think anywhere's safe in this country right now."

"Fine," Giraut said, in a high, loud voice. He suddenly felt very angry, though he wasn't sure why. "Let's go back, then. Scheria's that way, somewhere."

"What we need," Addo said, in that keeping-calm voice he'd used earlier, "is somewhere we can get food and water, if at all possible to steal or trade for some horses, and just maybe find out what's going on. Suidas, you're the only one of us who knows anything at all about this horrible country. Any suggestions?"

Suidas shrugged. "I never came this far. None of us did. All I know is, Luzir's straight on till we hit the main road again, then head east. How far I couldn't tell you. There's farms down on the plain, though," he added. "At least there were during the war. It's what passes for good farmland in Permia, about the only half-decent land they've got."

"Then we'll go that way," Addo said. "Problem solved."

They'd been walking for a couple of hours, in rather fragile silence, when Iseutz spotted a cloud of dust up ahead. They scrambled off the road into a shallow gully, wholly inadequate cover but all there was, and waited. After what seemed like a lifetime, it grew bigger and closer, and eventually turned out to be a large open-topped coach, drawn by four black horses. There were two men in it: a big, bald man and a young man in bright green livery, presumably the driver. Suidas pressed his finger to his lips, and they waited till the coach rolled past them. Then Suidas jumped up, vaulted into the back of it, stepped over, kicked the driver out, grabbed the reins and drew to a halt. The bald man sat frozen, his mouth open. Addo walked up to him and smiled.

"I'm dreadfully sorry," he said, "but we need your coach."

The driver was picking himself up off the ground. He got upright, then fell over again. He'd damaged his leg in the fall. The bald man didn't move or speak.

"We're duly accredited diplomats," Addo was saying, "so it goes without saying you'll be fully compensated for any expenses and inconvenience as soon as we get to Luzir Beal. Did you just come from there?"

The bald man was staring at the sabre in Addo's hand; also, Addo remembered, they were all fairly liberally spattered with dried blood, especially Suidas. "It's not as bad as it seems," he said brightly. "We had the bad luck to run into bandits. We fought them off, but not before they trashed our coach and killed our horses. And we really do have to get to Luzir as quickly as possible. I assure you, you're perfectly safe."

The bald man was still staring, but it was a different stare. "You're going to Luzir?"

"That's right. We've got a very important appointment there, which we absolutely can't miss."

"You're them, aren't you?" the bald man said. "The Scherians. The fencing squad."

For three heartbeats, dead silence. Addo opened his mouth, but no words came out. Suddenly, Suidas laughed – a terrible sound, like the roar of an angry predator. Iseutz went bright red, and mumbled, "Yes, that's us."

"My God," the bald man said. "I tried to get tickets to see you, but they're all sold out. My *God*."

"Tell you what." Suidas loomed over him like the biggest tree in the forest. "You take us to Luzir, and we'll get you the best fucking seat in the house."

"Really?"

"You have my word of honour," Suidas said solemnly, placing his right hand over his heart. "Our manager here'll see to it, won't you, Phrantzes?"

"I'm sure something can be arranged," Phrantzes said. "And of course we'll—"

"So that's a deal, then." Suidas sat down next to him. "You're happy, we're happy, everybody's completely bloody ecstatic. Well get in, for crying out loud," he roared at the others. "We don't want to keep this gentleman waiting, do we?"

Their host's name was Gosdaty Branko; he was a mining engineer, recently retired, lost his wife about eighteen months ago, living in one of the nicer suburbs of Luzir Beal, absolutely fanatical about fencing, been following it since he was a boy, never done much himself, of course, never had the skill or the stamina, but watching it, well, fencing was his life, always had been, although of course while he was working he hadn't had many opportunities, but the town he'd mostly been stationed at, Totas Partz, they wouldn't have heard of it, but it was roughly halfway between Joiauz and Beaute, so quite often they had warm-up fixtures there, it was a great opportunity to see the stars of the future before they became famous, so over the years he'd seen them all, Dushan, Stiban Meko, Porisa, now he'd actually seen Porisa twice, he'd been lucky, two weeks' leave and his wife away visiting her family, so he'd driven over to Beaute and seen him fight what's his name, they knew who he meant, Corta, which was a memory he'd treasure until the day he died, but if anyone had told him then that one day he'd be riding in a coach with the Scherian national team, well, he'd have laughed in their faces, and as for a front-row seat at the Luzir Guild house, well, things like that simply didn't happen to people like him, it was like sort of a

dream come true in a way, though who'd have thought, ten years
ago, that he'd have lived to see the day when a Scherian team
came to Permia, because of, they knew, the War and all that,
which he'd missed, of course, being in a reserved occupation, and
personally he bore the Scherian people no ill-will at all, all water
under the bridge as far as he was concerned, in fact he'd been following Scherian fencing on and off for years, always wanted to
see a Scherian fight, fascinating technique, but of course reading
about it just wasn't the same, and was it possible that the gentleman sitting next to him was none other than the great Scherian
champion Suidas Deutzel?

Addo, Giraut reckoned, was dying. On his left, the bald Permian
was slowly poisoning him with his incessant steam of drivel. To
his right, Iseutz was squashed so close on the narrow bench that
she was practically sitting in his lap, and embarrassment was
clearly driving nails into his soul. He likes her, Giraut suddenly
realised, rather a lot. He had to put his hand on his face and hold
his mouth still to keep himself from grinning.

Suidas, on the other hand, seemed happier than Giraut had
seen him before. He was sprawling in his seat, one of his legs
hooked over the side of the coach, his arms folded on his chest
like a neatly laid-out corpse. He was still covered in dried blood,
and smiling. Phrantzes was admiring the view, a strange thing to
do in such a miserable landscape. Every time the coach went
over a rock or a pothole, the driver groaned as the jolt jarred his
unset broken leg.

At least, Giraut told himself, there was now no question of
continuing with the tour. If Suidas' furious hints were right,
and he could see no reason why they shouldn't be, their hosts
had sent Aram Chantat to murder them on the road. Politics,
presumably; the war faction looking to provoke an incident,
although he had an idea that such an interpretation was hopelessly simplistic. It hardly mattered. The important thing to
bear in mind was that they were on their own, abandoned and

betrayed by their hosts, therefore relieved of their obligations towards them. If they could make it that far, they could go home.

In which case, Giraut couldn't help wondering, why were they heading for Luzir Beal? Obviously he couldn't ask, not with the Permian sitting there, but he was sure Addo and Suidas between them had a plan of some kind, and on balance he didn't mind not knowing what it was, since he was sure it'd scare him to death. He trusted Addo, or rather he could see no reason why he shouldn't; he clearly had more than a touch of his father's gifts of leadership and strategic ability, and somehow he seemed to have got Suidas under control, at least for the moment. Iseutz, he thought, was dangerously quiet. Either she'd collapsed or she was working up to an explosion, and neither possibility was likely to be helpful. Phrantzes obviously didn't count any more. Trust the Carnufex, he told himself, that's what Scherians do in a crisis. Even so, he was mystified. The logical thing to do would be to cut the bald man's throat and throw his body off the coach, then turn round and head for the border. But presumably that would come later. Patience was all that was needed, and everything would be fine.

So he was patient, and his patience was rewarded. Eventually, as the afternoon wore on into evening and the shadows grew long, the bald man talked himself to sleep; his head slumped forward into its ample nest of chins, and he started snoring gently. When Giraut was satisfied he was really asleep, he leaned forward, getting as close to Addo as he could.

"Addo," he said, "where are we going?"

"Luzir Beal," Addo replied.

A curious answer. He glanced sideways. Suidas was looking down, picking flakes of dried blood out of the hairs on the back of his left hand. "Why? Surely we don't want to go there."

"Oh, I think we do," Addo said crisply. "We'll be well behind schedule, of course, but that can't be helped. They'll just have to rearrange, that's all."

Giraut felt as though he'd just been kicked in the head. "Suidas?"

"Only place we can go," Suidas said, not looking up. "We won't last five minutes wandering around the countryside, not if they're trying to kill us. The only safe place for us is where there's loads and loads of witnesses. Think about it," he added. "They tried to ambush us in the middle of nowhere, right? And they wanted to be able to say it was bandits, or possibly rebels, I don't know. I'm not saying we'll be *safe* in Luzir Beal, but we stand a better chance there than anywhere else." He lifted his head and grinned. "Someone's going to be really, really pissed off when we show up," he said, "I'd love to see their faces when they find out."

"There's a chance we might be able to get in touch with our own people," Addo went on. "Tzimisces, for example. I can't believe he hasn't made some sort of arrangement for getting us out if things go badly. It pains me to say it, but he's probably our best bet. Anyway, Suidas is quite right. The last thing we want to do is make it easy for them by drifting round the wilderness in a small cart."

The bald man suddenly groaned, shuddered and opened his eyes. He blinked several times, then yawned. "Did I just nod off?" he asked.

"Did you? I didn't notice," Addo replied. "Sorry, I was miles away."

"That's all right," the bald man said generously. He looked away to his right – nothing but flat, rocky waste as far as the eye could see – and nodded happily. "We're almost at the edge of the Table," he said. "Be going downhill soon, and then it's just a short way to Luzir."

"How can you tell?" Giraut had to ask.

The bald man grinned. "Over there, see? On the skyline. See those hills?"

Admittedly, there was a pale grey smear that could have been hills. "What about them?"

"Third from the right, that's Scopoda. Soon as you see that, you know you're nearly there."

"I'm sorry," said Giraut. "I don't think my eyesight's as good as yours."

"Oh, you can't miss it. Plain as the nose on your face. Looks a bit like an upturned bucket."

Giraut shrugged. "You know this road well, then?"

"Oh yes, I was raised in these parts. Used to come this way with my dad, he was a haulier. Military work mostly, though he wasn't military, independent contractor. Made his pile hauling silver ore, then the War came, you know how it is."

Giraut fumbled in his mind for something to say. "It's very kind of you," he said, "giving us a lift like this. We must be taking you right out of your way."

The bald man did a big shrug. "Oh, it's my pleasure, really. The chance to meet the Scherian national team—"

"Where were you going, as a matter of fact?" Iseutz seemed to come back to life.

"Me? Oh, just a quick run out to Beaute. I've got cousins there, I like to see them now and again."

"That's very brave of you," Iseutz said, "with a civil war going on."

"Oh, I wouldn't call it that," the bald man said. "Just a bunch of layabouts and troublemakers with nothing better to do. The authorities'll have them sorted out in no time, you'll see. We're lucky we've got really good security forces. I know I'm biased, well naturally, but I think our police are the best in the world, no offence, I'm sure they're really good in your country too, but ours are pretty damn reliable if there's ever any trouble."

"You're not worried, then," Iseutz said. "About your cousins."

"Worried? No, not really. They're sensible people, they know to keep off the streets."

"Of course," Addo said. "Stay at home and don't go out, that's what a sensible person would do at a time like this."

For a fat man, he moved surprisingly quickly. Before Addo

could stop him, he'd opened the door and nearly made it off the coach. But Suidas grabbed him before he could jump, at which he produced a knife from nowhere at all and tried to stab Suidas' hand. Addo caught his wrist, then had to let go as the man tumbled backwards out of the coach. Suidas sprang forward and pressed the blade of his messer against the side of the driver's neck. "Stop the coach," he said. "Addo."

But Addo was already out and bending over the bald man's body. "His neck's broken," he said mournfully.

"Fuck," Suidas replied. "Never mind, we've still got the driver."

But the driver either didn't know or wasn't saying, even with Suidas at his most persuasive, until Iseutz made him stop. He gave up and told the driver to keep going.

Suidas sat down again. "Well, we've still got the coach, at any rate," he said.

"Who the hell was he?" Giraut demanded.

"Someone sent to pick us up," Suidas replied with a shrug. "Or to make sure we're dead. There's no money in this cart, or he could've been sent to pay off the Aram Chantat."

"Or bring them back," Iseutz said. "Since they didn't have any horses."

"Maybe." Suidas yawned. "I don't suppose it makes any difference in the long run. And we've got transport, so we're better off than we were."

They slept beside the cart, trying not to think about food. Finally, when the sky was roughly the middle blue of the Redeemer's robe in a temple fresco, they made a unilateral declaration of dawn. Suidas backed the horses into the shafts and they tried to wake up the driver, only to find he'd died in the night.

"That's stupid," Suidas said. "He had a broken leg, that's all."

"Presumably it was a bit worse than that," Addo said gravely. "Still, there's nothing we can do about it now. Suidas, you know about these things, you can drive one of these, can't you?"

"Sure." He grinned at them. "Like old times," he said. "This is a good coach, by the way. I suggest we keep it, if we can. Worth a bit of money back home, assuming we can get it there." He vaulted up on to the box and grabbed the reins. "Come on, then," he said, "if you're coming."

Phrantzes was still staring at the driver's body. Addo stopped and looked over his shoulder. "Internal bleeding, maybe," he said. "Not that I know anything about medicine."

"I think it was probably us," Phrantzes replied. "Wherever we go, people seem to die. Or hadn't you noticed?"

"My guess is, it's more likely to have been internal bleeding," Addo said briskly. "However, if you feel strongly about it, I suggest you consult a priest when we get home. I'm afraid religious stuff's never been my strong suit."

Suidas was annoyingly cheerful that morning, singing and chattering, not seeming to notice if nobody was listening. Giraut reckoned it was probably a bad sign, but dismissed it as being Addo's problem, since he'd apparently taken charge. He couldn't understand why anyone should want to do such a thing, though he was glad that it was Addo who'd done it; the thought of Suidas being responsible for his safety wasn't a comfortable one, Phrantzes was useless and Iseutz . . . You could see why the military aristocracy had run Scheria for so long, he thought. They might not be very good at it, but they're probably better than anybody else we've got. Particularly if there's got to be another war.

Something caught his eye: a pretty thing, a sparkle, a little gleam of yellow-gold light. He sat up, and Iseutz must've read his face, because she said, "Giraut, what's the matter?" He pointed. "Over there," he said.

"Wait up, Suidas," Addo said, but there was no need. Suidas had seen it too and stopped the coach. Just when Giraut had convinced himself he'd imagined the whole thing, Addo said, "Well, what d'you make of that?"

"I can't see—" Iseutz started, but Suidas cut her off.

"Imperials," he said, "got to be. Who else prances about in poncey gilded armour?"

"Agreed," Addo said. "In which case, why are they over there, instead of on the road?"

A sharp intake of breath from Phrantzes. "Who cares?" Suidas said. "The Imperials are on our side, aren't they?"

Addo looked at him. "That's rather a big assumption," he said.

"No it isn't," Suidas replied. "They're paid by the government, we're the honoured guests of the government, therefore they're obliged to protect us and get us safely to the capital. I say we go over and introduce ourselves."

"I'd agree," Addo said quietly, "if I knew why they're not using the road."

"I don't know, do I?" Suidas snapped. "Maybe it's a training exercise. They're nuts about training, the Blueskins, and it's peacetime. What else do soldiers find to do in peacetime? They train."

"I think it's a very bad idea," Iseutz said.

"Nobody asked you," Suidas snapped back, and Giraut saw Addo shiver a little. "Look, for all we know, there's Aram Chantat out looking for us. If they catch us on the road, on our own, we're dead. The Blueskins will be honour-bound to protect us, they believe in all that shit. It's the obvious thing to do."

"It would be," Addo replied calmly, "if they were marching along the road."

"I still can't see anything," Iseutz said. "Where are they?"

Suidas made a vulgar noise. Addo pointed. "See there, where there's a little dip in the ground? Follow that line, and you come to a—"

"Got you," Iseutz said. "Yes, you're right. There's a whole column of them."

"A hundred and twenty-five," Suidas recited, "one company, standard Imperial heavy infantry quick-response detachment. A hundred and twenty men, four sergeants and a lieutenant."

"Usually deployed to back up a cavalry squadron where

there's an emergency," Addo said. "And until we know what the emergency is . . . "

"Look." Phrantzes had shouldered past him, and was pointing at the skyline, where a cloud of dust was just faintly distinguishable.

"That'll be their cavalry," Suidas said. "Our ride to Luzir."

"Let's just sit still for a moment," Addo said.

"Yes, and let them get even further away. No, I don't think so. Look, we can't take the coach over the open ground, the axles won't handle it. We're going to have to walk. They move pretty quickly. We have to go now, don't you understand?"

"Not quite yet," Addo said.

"Screw you, then." Suidas jumped down and started walking at a furious quick march. Addo started to get up, but Phrantzes pulled him back. Addo shrugged off his hand, jumped down and ran after Suidas, who wasn't looking round. When he was close enough, Addo jumped. He landed on Suidas' back, shoved him down and got his elbow round his neck before he could reach for his messer.

"Let go; you're choking me."

Addo relaxed his grip; Suidas twisted round, kicked him in the chest, jumped to his feet and ran off.

"Oh for God's sake," Iseutz said, and hurried after them.

"The horses," Phrantzes said.

It didn't make sense for a moment; then Giraut glanced across and saw the reins lying loose on the box. He threw himself across and grabbed them. "What do I do?" he called back.

"I don't know."

This isn't happening, Giraut thought. He tightened his hands on the reins till they hurt, while keeping them as still as possible. "Be careful," Phrantzes shouted at him; in context, possibly the most useless piece of advice ever. In his mind he could picture, as clearly as if it was a memory, the horses suddenly bolting, dragging the reins out of his hands; the coach hitting a stone, overturning, himself being thrown through the air . . .

"It's all right, I've got them." Phrantzes was standing by the lead horses' heads, holding the rings at the corners of their mouths. Giraut looked up and realised he was shaking. He really didn't want Phrantzes to notice, not after the disgraceful way he'd behaved when the Aram Chantat attacked. "Can you see what's happening?" he asked.

"No."

Suidas was running towards the column waving his arms when the dust cloud turned into horsemen. That was more or less what he was expecting, so he didn't stop. He carried on running when the horsemen proved to be Aram Chantat (because this was Permia, and the Aram Chantat and the Blueskins were on the same side). When the horsemen's line split, peeled and swung round to envelop the column, he assumed it was just showing off, an exhibition of friendly antagonism, some kind of weird Aram Chantat thing that an expert like Tzimisces would've explained with a few words and a patronising grin.

Presumably the Blueskins thought the same. They had carefully planned, frequently rehearsed drills for coping with horse archers, but they carried on marching in column, even when the first arrows were in the air. By the time they realised they were being attacked, of course, it was too late. A third of them were dead on the ground.

They did their best. They formed squares, dropped to one knee, raised shields, hedged spears. The horsemen surged round them like a torrent of water in a flooded street, swirling and lapping against walls, searching for an open door or window. The tide drew out and swept back in again; not archers but lancers. It's no reproach to the building that it's not tall enough to hold off the water. The Imperials performed their drills flawlessly and kept perfect discipline almost to the bitter end.

Suidas realised he was standing upright in open ground, and dropped like a stone. Uppermost in his mind, shouting down the thoughts he ought to have been thinking, was: I'm privileged to be one of the few men still living who's seen the Aram Chantat fight the Blueskins. Always wondered who'd win. Now I know.

It made no sense. He was frozen and couldn't move because it made no sense whatsoever: the Aram Chantat against the Blueskins, like the arms against the legs. He watched as the horsemen slowed to a trot, then a walk, as they picked through the bodies on the ground for survivors and meticulously speared or shot them, then dismounted and made extra sure (attention to detail, a laudable trait), turning them over one at a time; no looting or robbing the dead, just a careful medical examination to make sure all life was extinguished. They took their time. Then, job done, they picked up their own handful of dead, collected their arrows and broken lances, mounted and rode away.

"Why?" Iseutz asked.

Nobody spoke for a long time. Then Suidas said, "Civil war. It's the only possible explanation."

"Not quite," Addo said. "My guess is, we're still two or three days away from that. I think what we just saw is preparations for a civil war, almost the same thing but not quite."

Suidas shrugged. "What makes you say that?"

"The careful way they gathered up all the evidence," Addo replied. "They even pulled out the arrows, did you notice? Like they didn't want anybody to be able to prove they did it."

"I don't understand," Iseutz said. "Why bother?"

Addo leaned forward, resting his chin on his hands. "I think the Imperials are still loyal to the government," he said. "I'm assuming the column was on its way to Beaute, to take charge of the city from the Aram Chantat now that the riots have been put down." He paused and grinned. "If they have been put down, that is; but that's another issue entirely. But whoever sent those Aram Chantat didn't want an Imperial garrison in Beaute, so they had them wiped out here in the middle of nowhere. It'll be at least a day before anyone finds the bodies, another day before the news gets back to the government in

Luzir; there's no physical evidence that Aram Chantat did this, so whoever's responsible can deny any involvement. They could even blame it on a third party – at a wild guess, Scheria. That's at least three days, maybe four, in which they can get all their other pieces in place and start the war in earnest. That's my interpretation, anyhow. I'm just guessing, obviously, but I think it covers most of what we know."

"You keep saying *they*," Iseutz interrupted. "Who's *they*?"

Addo smiled. "Good question," he said. "But, on the balance of probabilities, someone who wants a war with Scheria and who's got enough money to buy the Aram Chantat out of their existing contracts. I don't know enough about Permian politics to give you names, but you get the general idea." He sighed and straightened his back. "Not the government, not the mine owners, so who does that leave?"

"Does it matter?" Iseutz snapped, so violently that everyone looked at her. "To us, I mean? Oh come on, don't stare at me like that. Look, I couldn't give a damn right now about whether there's going to be a war, or who's playing what games, or any of it. I'm tired and I'm hungry and I stink like a pig, I've been wearing the same clothes since I can remember, my skin feels like it's crawling with ants, I hurt all over and I want to go *home*. That's all that matters, not stupid bloody politics. I'm so miserable I hardly feel scared any more, just completely bloody wretched. And I'm not a soldier, I'm a female civilian, so I really don't deserve to be put through all this. Look, we've got a coach and horses, we've got a driver, and we don't owe anybody anything. Can't we just go home? Please?"

Nobody spoke. Suidas was grinning, Phrantzes was gazing at his shoes, Giraut was waiting for someone else to say something, and Addo was looking at her with a fine blend of compassion, embarrassment and irritation on his face. She shrugged. "I guess not," she said. "In which case, screw the lot of you. You're all stupid."

Addo opened his mouth, and Giraut thought: he's about to try and explain, which is probably the worst thing he could do, bar laughing, like Suidas is doing. But evidently he thought better of it. He shook his head and said, "I'm sorry," and Giraut guessed it wasn't the first time he'd had to do something like that. Hadn't he had a girl back home, a girl he'd lost or who'd dumped him, shortly before he came away? He couldn't remember, and naturally he couldn't ask.

"You're sorry," Iseutz repeated. "Fine. That's an enormously huge lot of help, Addo. I thought you might be marginally less stupid than the others, but obviously I was wrong. Oh well."

Suidas smiled at her. "Have you finished?"

"For now."

"Good." He got rid of the smile and turned towards the others. "Now, as far as I can remember from the map, Luzir's no more than half a day's drive on the road from here, but obviously we can't do that. I say we dump the coach and walk. The coach can't go over the rough or outrun them anywhere, and it's easier to hide if you're on foot. Agreed?"

He was looking at Addo. Phrantzes said, "Agreed. I mean, it makes sense, I can see that." Suidas turned his head towards Giraut, who nodded and looked away. "Addo," Suidas said. "What do you think?"

"I'd rather not ditch the coach just yet," Addo replied slowly. "I don't like walking, and these boots are rubbing my heels."

"Addo . . ."

"We can't afford to waste time," Addo said sharply. "We've got to eat and drink, for one thing. Look at it, will you? Does that look to you like country you can live off? I don't think so. Also, we need to get to Luzir before the civil war starts in earnest. I'm not saying it'll be safe for us there, but it's got to be better than out in the open. You might be able to cope out there, Suidas, you're a soldier, you've done this stuff before. The rest of us simply aren't up to it. Besides," he added, softening his voice a little, "we're not a military unit or a government mission, we're just four men and a girl in a coach. We don't look anything like a target. Why would either side waste their time bothering us?"

"Because that's what happens," Suidas said. "I should know, I've done it. I've beaten up and killed civilians, just because I could. Force of habit, I guess," he added, as Iseutz stared at him. "Once you start killing Permians, it can get hard to stop. And there's always the chance their boots might fit you. Believe me, Addo, you really don't want to get caught on the road when there's people like me about."

"I said our chances would be better if we stuck with the coach," Addo said. "I didn't say they were good. We're not you, we can't march for six days on an empty stomach. And if we do meet soldiers on the road, there's every chance they'd be Imperials, and they don't do the bad stuff. Do they?"

Suidas shrugged. "Not if there's an officer watching, probably not. But you saw what happened to the Blueskins back there. Even if you meet some and they take you in, they can't protect you, not if the Aram Chantat are on the loose. See sense, for crying out loud. We both know the others'll do what you say, because you're the fucking Irrigator's kid. Stop pissing around and let's get going."

"Half a day," Addo said. "You said it yourself, we're just half a day from Luzir on this road. How long's it going to take to walk? Three days? Four?"

"Cavalry thinking," Suidas said, making it sound like the worst insult possible. "Get your head down and charge the massed archers. Well, you can if you like. I'll see you in Luzir, if you make it."

He halted the coach, threw the reins to Addo and jumped down. "Hold on," Addo said, "I can't drive this thing."

"Learn," Suidas called back over his shoulder. He was walking quickly, his legs stiff. "A clever boy like you shouldn't have any trouble."

"Addo," Iseutz wailed, but he sat perfectly still, watching Suidas' back, until he was just a dot against the grey rocks, moving slowly and steadily towards the horizon, a long, low range of hills, one of which looked rather like an upturned bucket. "Damn," Addo said. Then, quite expertly, he urged the horses into a trot.

"I simply don't understand you," Iseutz said, for the tenth time. "I can't believe you just let him walk off like that."

Addo had given up replying, which only seemed to make it worse. He fixed his eyes on the road ahead, which was climbing slowly up a broad, slow escarpment. On the other side of the ridge, he devoutly hoped, was Luzir Beal.

It was three hours since Suidas had walked away, and the road had been completely empty. Hardly surprising, since people don't generally tend to go about their usual business in the early stages of a civil war; they'd seen a few dust clouds in the distance, but none of them had been coming their way. The horses had behaved themselves, the road was straight and well maintained, the sun was shining. Welcome to beautiful Permia.

"We've got to go back," Iseutz said.

"Will you for God's sake please shut up?" It was the first time Phrantzes had said anything for a very long time, and the words seemed to break out of him against his will. "I'm sorry, but you know as well as I do we can't go back. It'd be madness."

"Actually, she's right." Addo's voice sounded curiously detached, as though he was a spectator offering a commentary. "I should've gone after him, and we ought to have turned back. Unfortunately, I've left it rather too long. I don't suppose we'd be able to find him now. It's my fault. I made the wrong decision. I take full responsibility."

"Addo ... " Whatever she'd been about to say, she thought better of it, or decided it was no longer necessary. She slumped back in her seat, just as the coach reached the top of the slope.

"Well," Addo said, "we're here."

Below them, laid out like a model in a sandbox, was a city. It was perfectly, unnaturally square, surrounded on all four sides by a bigger square of green, neatly subdivided into smaller squares bordered by straight brown roads. Tzimisces, if he'd been there, would have told them about Imperial grid-plan modular construction, and how Luzir was the best example of it outside the home provinces. To Giraut it looked unreal, like a painting, the backdrop for a play. Even the straight, regularly spaced lines of the irrigation canals were a bright, cheerful blue. If anything as untidy as people was permitted down there, they'd have to be small clay figures, beautifully painted – model citizens, he thought, and tried not to smile – carefully positioned to set off the architectural features, illustrating the size of the buildings. It occurred to him to wonder if Flos Verjan had looked like that, from the Irrigator's vantage point, just before he opened the sluices.

"That's Luzir?" Phrantzes said nervously. "You're sure?"

"Nowhere else it could be," Addo said. He sounded exhausted. "More by luck than judgement and two days late, but we made it."

"You made it." Iseutz was sitting up, looking at the city. "You got us here, and all I've done is whine at you. I'm sorry."

"Don't be," Addo said. "You were right and I was wrong. I shouldn't have lost my nerve." He shook his head. "Well," he said, "I suppose we'd better go and let them know we're here. I hope they'll be pleased to see us."

They were. Not at first: three bloodstained, wild-looking men and a snake-haired girl in a rich man's coach rolling into town covered in dust from the direction of the troubles drew brief, hostile stares from the country people in the perfectly square fields, and they had an awkward moment when they reached the city gate and the Blueskin guards quite obviously didn't believe them; fortunately, they sent for the duty officer, who'd been issued with a description of the missing Scherian touring party. It was, of course, wildly inaccurate – they'd got Addo's height and eye colour wrong, Phrantzes wasn't mentioned at all and Iseutz was supposed to be a man. But the Permian in charge of gate tolls was a fencing fan, who'd recently been dividing his time between rereading accounts of the match at Joiauz and bewailing the cancellation of the Luzir fixture. He vouched for them personally, swept Giraut up in his arms and kissed him on both cheeks (he was nearest) and took them off to his lodgings on the top floor of the gatehouse. For a while, Giraut was convinced he was going to keep them for his very own; but his sense of civic duty must have prevailed, because he sent a runner to the Guild house to let the Master know the Scherians had arrived. Then he ran a sort of controlled experiment to see how many honey cakes, almond biscuits and cream-cheese-with-chives-in-little-choux-pastry-horns he could stuff down their throats before the official welcoming committee arrived.

They came in a closed coach, the windows blacked out with shutters, and footmen lined up to make a human wall to keep the honoured guests from being seen. "You've no idea," the Master's assistant told them, as the coach started to roll through the broad streets. "When we got word you'd been trapped in Beaute and weren't coming, we nearly had a riot on our hands. Eighteen thousand tickets we've sold. They had me in up at the Prefecture. They were deciding which roads to close off, if things got nasty."

It was strange and rather unnerving to see streets filled with people again. Giraut couldn't resist pulling back a corner of the shutter, but the Master's assistant asked him not to. "As soon as word gets around you've finally shown up, it's going to be chaos out there," he said. "I had to promise the Prefect faithfully that we'd get you safely under cover before we broke the news."

Addo cleared his throat. "While we're on the subject of public order," he said.

The Master's assistant made a wide, airy gesture. "Oh, nothing like that here, I can promise you that. We're all good Optimates in Luzir. No, you're as safe as houses here. Well, so long as nobody sees you or finds out who you are, of course, otherwise you'd be hugged to death in five seconds flat."

"Optimates?" Iseutz said.

The Master's assistant hesitated and looked uncomfortable; it's because she's a girl, Giraut realised, presumably he's not supposed to talk to strange women. "The Optimate party," he said. "Politics. There's Optimates and the KKA. We're Optimates, where you've just come from is bedrock KKA country. That's why they've had all that trouble." He made it sound like a rather nasty disease, deliberately contracted. "But you don't want to bother with all that. Fencing's much bigger than politics in Luzir." He grinned. "That's why fencers are banned from standing in municipal elections, otherwise they'd be running the city. Almost certainly make a better job of it than the bunch of deadheads we've got on the Board of Guardians right now, but that's not saying much. Don't repeat that," he added. "As a Guild officer I've got to be completely impartial, of course."

To make conversation, Giraut asked, "What does KKA stand for?"

"*Kaloi kai agathoi*," the Master's assistant replied, "that's old Eastern Imperial for 'the beautiful and the good'. Which is what Optimate means in old Western Imperial. Don't ask," he added, "it's complicated. But basically, we hate them and they hate us. Only thing that ever kept this country together was the War. And fencing, of course, except that tends to split down party lines too. Luckily, we've got all the money, what there is of it. Right, we're here." The coach was slowing down. "Now, I'll take you straight to the Calidarium. Constant hot water, day and night. I imagine you'd all like a nice hot bath," he said, as Iseutz made a faint moaning noise.

There was a letter on top of the pile of fresh clean clothes waiting for Phrantzes in his room. He recognised the handwriting. He crossed the room in three long strides, snatched it up and froze. His hands were shaking so much he could hardly open it.

Sphagia to her Jilem, greetings.
    They've let me go. I can hardly believe it. They told me I was

going to have to spend the rest of my life in that place. But this morning the prioress came just after dawn prayers and told me, and now I'm back home, in our house.

I'm fine. Well, I think I've lost a stone and they cut off my hair – I'm so sorry, but I couldn't do anything. It'll grow back, I promise. I've done nothing but eat since I got home, I'd forgotten what real food tastes like. A horrible little man came round from the government – he said who he was but I didn't take it in – and he brought me thirty nomismata, in a little linen bag. He didn't say what it was for, just Sign here, so I did. Anyway, the point is, I'm fine, I'm safe and I'm all right for money. So please don't worry about me.

They told me you were fine too and everything's going really well. Are you, and is it? If you can possibly send a letter, please write soon. I miss you.

He tried to sit down, missed the bed and landed on the floor. He didn't move. It was like waking up out of a bad dream. He tried to think about Suidas, the man he'd made up his mind to kill, in cold blood. Now the idea seemed absurd; and besides, Suidas had gone, Tzimisces had gone, the problem had dissolved in light and gone away, like those insuperable worries that gnaw at you in the early hours of the morning and seem so ridiculous when you remember them in daylight. He was in Luzir Beal, a civilised city, calm, under control and safe. In a day or so they'd have the fencing match, after which they'd go home. Sphagia was safe, he'd done his job and therefore earned his free pardon, and even if there was another war he was too old to be made to fight. Against his expectations, against all the odds he'd made it and come through.

He was too weak to stand up but it didn't matter. He was perfectly happy kneeling on the floor for a while.

Later, he tried to tell them what he'd seen: the Aram Chantat slaughtering the Blueskins, the man whose coach they'd taken, all of it. They listened, but he got the impression they didn't believe him but were too polite to say so.

"Anyway," he concluded, "Suidas Deutzel felt he stood a better chance if he left us and made his own way here. He'd made his mind up, we couldn't talk him out of it. So he left us and we came on."

They looked at him. "If you could show us the place on a map," said an old man with a neat white beard, "we can send a search party."

"I'll try," Phrantzes said. "But I can't promise anything. It's pretty flat and featureless, so really, your guess is as good as mine."

"Did he have food and water with him?" someone asked.

"I'm afraid not. We didn't have any either, so there was nothing for him to take."

They looked worried; he wanted to laugh, and tell them: it's all right, we don't *want* Suidas found, we want him to be dead out there somewhere, and no more harm to anyone. Later he tried to feel ashamed for thinking like that, but he couldn't. They showed him a map and he did try and make an honest guess. He could afford to, since the map meant nothing to him. "About here, I suppose," he told them. "Somewhere around here, anyway."

"How fast did the coach go, after you left him?"

"Hard to say," Phrantzes replied, perfectly honestly. "Addo – Aduluscentulus Carnufex – he was driving, you could ask him. Some of the time the horses were going quite fast, sometimes the road was too rough and they were walking slowly. Someone who knows the road might be able to help you, but of course we'd never been there before."

They quite understood and thanked him for his help, and he went to join the others in the Master's day room. At the junction of two corridors, directly under a dazzling gold mosaic of a magnificent and entirely anonymous god, he met two of the men he'd been talking to earlier.

"There you are," one of them said. "Good news. We've rescheduled the match for tomorrow night."

Good news? Well, on balance, yes. The sooner it was all over and done with, the sooner they could all go home. All of them who survived the match, at any rate. "Splendid," Phrantzes was therefore able to say. "That's very good."

"And we've shifted the venue to the Procopian arena," the other one said. "It seats ten thousand, so we'll be able to squeeze in two thousand more than if we held it here. It's a very good arena," he added, with a hint of pre-emptive attack in his voice. "Very fine acoustic, and it was almost completely rebuilt just last year, after the fire, so there'll be no problems at all."

If Phrantzes had been a horse, his ears would've gone back. But he smiled and nodded and mumbled, "Excellent, splendid," and took a step forward. But they hadn't finished with him yet.

"So all we need," the first man said, "is your revised team." Phrantzes looked blank. "I'm sorry?"

"If Suidas Deutzel isn't available," the other one said, "obviously you'll want to rearrange your team. I imagine one of your fencers will have to do longsword as well as his own discipline."

Oh, Phrantzes thought. "Naturally," he said. "I'll discuss that with the team and get back to you as soon as I can."

"That would be splendid, thank you." Both of them beamed at him. "We'll need to know fairly soon, of course, because of making the announcement. There's a brief ceremony, nothing too arduous, but I expect there'll be a big crowd. Shall we say tomorrow, at noon?"

As he'd anticipated, the news didn't go down too well.

"You can rule me out," Giraut said. "I wouldn't fight longsword with foils, let alone sharps. No, I'm sorry."

Phrantzes hadn't been looking at him. He waited.

"No," Addo said, after a long pause. "No, I'm very sorry, but I don't think I can. Or if you really want me to fight longsword, someone else will have to do messer." Phrantzes saw Giraut flinch out of the corner of his eye, and didn't bother to turn his head. "And I think messer's what they'll be coming to see, so I'd better do that. You'll just have to tell them we won't be doing longsword, that's all."

This time, Phrantzes found himself in front of the entire Guild committee. They stared at him in silence for a long time.

"I'm afraid that's not acceptable," someone said at last. "I'm sorry, and I do understand how difficult it must be for you, though I do wonder why you came on this tour with no substitutes at all. Still, that's not for me to comment on. But we must insist. Someone will have to fence longsword. I'm sure that once you've explained the position to your people, you'll be able to sort something out."

Pleading, Phrantzes guessed, wasn't likely to get him anywhere; might as well beg the rain not to fall. "I'll ask them," he said, "but I really can't promise anything."

"We have every confidence in you," they said, which didn't help at all.

So he went back again, and there was a very long silence, with everybody looking away. Then Iseutz said, "But surely it's obvious. You'll have to do it."

For a moment, Phrantzes couldn't think who she was talking to. Then it hit him like a hammer.

"That's not a bad idea," Addo said, turning round and facing him. "Yes, that's perfect, it'd solve everything."

Phrantzes opened his mouth, but he couldn't seem to get his voice to work. Iseutz was beaming at him. "We know you can do it," she was saying, "we saw you fight Suidas, and if you can beat him, you can definitely handle some Permian."

"For God's sake." The words came out high and squeaky. "I'm an old man, I'm out of training, I haven't fought in competition for twenty years. I'll be killed."

Addo frowned. "I think you're selling yourself short there," he said. "Like Iseutz said, you showed you can handle yourself pretty well. And you didn't just fend Suidas off, you beat him."

Yes, but that's because I wanted to kill him . . . He couldn't say that. "It's different in public," was the best he could come up with, and it wasn't really good enough. "What if they put me up against some young thug half my age and twice my height? I wouldn't stand a chance."

Giraut shook his head. "Longsword is all footwork," he said. "You were moving pretty well against Suidas."

"A big young thug is just the sort of opponent you want," Addo said. "Muscle-bound and stupid. Work up your traverses a bit if you're worried. And it's definitely an advantage being the shorter man with longsword, you can close the distance and fight inside. Well, you don't need me to tell you that." He gave Phrantzes a reassuring smile. "As far as I can tell, the Permians are about thirty years behind the times as far as plays go, so you won't have to worry about dealing with anything you haven't met before. And stamina's not an issue either, not like rapier. Keep it short and close, you'll be fine."

In desperation, Phrantzes tried to outflank. "Maybe if I fought rapier, and Giraut—"

"No." Addo was completely firm, immovable. "He's just said he's not a longswordsman. But you are, you've proved it. The only other option is you fight messer and I'll do longsword. But I think that'd be a rather bad idea."

"And anyway," Iseutz added, "it may not come to that. Suidas could still show up. They've got lots of men out looking for him. Maybe they'll find him, and then all your troubles will be over."

So he went to the committee and told them he'd be the longswordman. They gave him a startled look and told him that would be just fine. "In fact," one of them said, with a strained expression on his face, "that'll do very well. After all, we've promised them a Scherian national champion."

"They always like it when someone comes out of retirement for one last match," someone else added. "It gives the proceeedings that extra edge, don't you find?"

They were taken to the Guild armoury to choose their weapons. It was in the basement, down five flights of narrow, winding stone stairs, worn slippery smooth and indifferently lit by horn lanterns in wall niches. At the foot of the stairs was a bronze door, which took two sets of keys to unlock and two men to pull open. Beyond the door was a vast natural cavern, lit by two shafts of light falling through glazed windows in the far-distant roof. The walls crawled with translucent limestone crusts, but "We don't seem to have a problem with damp," their guide assured them, "so long as we keep stuff well away from the walls."

It was a museum, an art gallery and a temple, and a prison, and a grave. The free-standing racks were in the middle of the cavern, directly under the light, which was dazzling against the surrounding darkness. The light was good enough for reading the smallest, most worn inscriptions – makers' names, presentations to honour victories and retirements, incantations to gods and Good Luck, bold on the spines of blades or nestling in thickets of acanthus-and-scroll engraving on ricassos or in the troughs of fullers. The longswords were stored upright, their quillons supported by pegs, so that they hung without the points touching anything, to guard against flex and set. The rapiers and smallswords rested horizontally, supported on five hooks. The messers – five messers to every longsword or rapier – sat by the dozen in buckets of black oil, like flowers in water. "Suidas would've loved this," Iseutz hissed to Addo, who grinned.

"Help yourselves," their guide said.

Addo pulled a messer at random from the nearest bucket and looked round for something to wipe the blade with. Giraut went slowly along the row of rapiers, lifting them, gauging the weight, resting them on the side of the knuckle of his left index finger to determine the centre of balance, holding them upright and smacking the blade with the flat of his hand to find the sweet spot for blocking. Phrantzes stood gawping for a long time, then took down a slim, long-handled Type Eighteen longsword, fumbled it and dropped it on the floor, jumped out of the way like a startled lamb, stooped, picked it up quickly and said, "This'll do fine," without examining it any further. Iseutz

stared for a long time without touching, and finally chose a
silver-hilted colichemarde, old-fashioned and a little heavy but
very strong in the forte for binds and parries. "Are there any
foils?" she asked. "You know, for practising."

Clearly she'd said something embarrassing, but their guide
was too well mannered to explain. "I believe we've got some," he
said, "in the salle in the east court. It's where the juniors train,"
he couldn't help adding. "I think the under-thirteens use them."

It was a long way to the east court. The salle smelt of sweat,
wet wool and boiled cabbage, and the polished wooden floor was
painted with lines and circles, neatly annotated with numbers
and letters, to help instructors explain to novices where they
should be putting their feet. The foils turned out to be wooden,
ancient, battered, haphazardly mended with bandage, rawhide
and glue. But they'd been good quality once upon a time; the
weights and balances were just right, and Addo said, "That's
fine, thank you," in a brisk, crisp voice. "Can we use this room
for practising?"

Their guide looked mildly horrified. "Well, yes, if you like.
But we've set aside the Long Hall for you. It's where we usually
hold training sessions before major competitions."

"This will do us just fine," Iseutz said firmly. "Could you
possibly get them to send us in some food? And if you could
rustle up a few masks and gloves, that'd be wonderful."

The guide clearly didn't trust himself to reply to such an infa-
mous suggestion; he scuttled away, leaving them in undisputed
possession of their new territory. Once he'd gone, a feeling of
unaccountable calm settled over them, as though they'd really
won a significant victory. Iseutz walked across the floor and carefully put her feet on 4 and 6. "This is actually a rather intelligent
way of teaching footwork," she announced, looking down the
dotted lines painted on the floor. "I wish I'd had something like
this when I was learning."

"We've got something a bit like it at home," Addo said, his
mind clearly elsewhere. "Smaller, though." He was picking at a

lump of encrusted grease on the blade of his messer. "Top of the north tower at the country house. It's a good room for a salle, because it's circular and it catches the light."

Phrantzes picked up a longsword foil, closed his eyes and took up a high back guard. Addo cleared his throat, though Phrantzes didn't seem to hear. "Ready whenever you are," Addo said. No reaction. He said it again.

"Excuse me?" Phrantzes opened his eyes and stared at him.

"Sparring," Addo said. "You and me. Help get you warmed up and into the swing of it, so to speak."

"I'll just do a few exercises, thanks," Phrantzes replied. He closed his eyes again, and flowed into a wide left traverse combined with a transition from front middle to high right. Addo had never seen it done better.

Giraut found a silhouette of a spread-eagled man stencilled on a wall. There were little white numbers to mark the preferred targets. He amused himself with it for a while, only thinking of a number once he'd committed to the lunge, transferring his weight to a foot hanging in mid air. He hit seven out of ten just right, and two more close enough for business. He knew that if he did another ten, he'd end up trying too hard and miss, so he looked round for Iseutz, who was playing a complex form of geometrical hopscotch with the numbers on the floor. "Fancy a few points?" he asked her. She thought about it for rather longer than he'd have thought the decision would take, then said, "All right. Actually, I need to practise passatas, if you don't mind getting killed for a bit."

Giraut shrugged. "Fine," he said. "Then can we do a few voltes?"

She frowned. "You're really good at the volte. You don't need to practise."

"Yes, but I like doing them."

Addo spent some time on the eight cuts, starting slow and speeding up, but practice was making him worse instead of better, so he stopped and watched the others for a while. Giraut was making an effort to help Iseutz, who was concentrating hard and improving with each reiteration. Phrantzes, as far as he could tell, was fighting a complex and difficult battle against an unseen opponent; not just a random set of moves, there was a narrative to it, and from time to time the invisible enemy came up with something Phrantzes struggled to deal with, though he was doing extremely well. His eyes were tight shut, and as often as not his feet were landing precisely on the numbers. Addo could see two weaknesses in his style; nothing fatal, but worth mentioning. He decided to do it later, when the invisible fight was over. Assuming, of course, that Phrantzes survived.

He heard a snapping sound and looked round. Giraut had closed Iseutz against the wall and gone for a big lunge. She'd demivolted (Giraut's best move) and prodded him gently in the ribs as he sailed past; he'd driven his foil into the wall with considerable force and snapped it. Iseutz laughed, which wasn't really the best thing to do. Giraut scowled horribly at her and walked away to join Addo.

"You were doing so well, too," Addo said.

"It's because she's a girl," Giraut said ruefully, "I couldn't resist trying to crowd her. Serves me right, I suppose."

"Yes," Addo said, and threw Giraut the wooden messer he'd been holding. Giraut caught it perfectly by the handle; so perfectly it startled him, and he looked down at it in his hand. "Would you mind?" Addo said.

"Sure," Giraut replied, and swung furiously at Addo's head. He just managed to avoid it, ducking his head instead of moving his feet. "Ready when you are," he said, and Giraut grinned at him. "I'll just attack, if that's all right," Giraut said. "I can dish it out, but I can't take it."

"That'll be just fine," Addo replied, and traversed well to get out of the way of a rising left-to-right that would've smashed his jaw into splinters. He had no trouble after that, and eventually Giraut had to stop to catch his breath.

"Horrible thing," he said, twirling the wooden messer over the back of his hand. "It makes you want to hit someone with it, really hard."

Addo nodded. "Talking of which," he said, "I hope he's all right."

"Oh, he'll be fine," Giraut said uneasily. "It's whoever he runs into on the way I feel sorry for."

"We should've gone back for him," Addo said firmly, then darted back and left to avoid a crushing downward cut to the head. "Steady on," he said reprovingly, then threw himself to the right as Giraut drove the messer straight at his face.

"Is it all right if I stop for a moment?" Giraut asked. "I'm out of breath."

Addo grinned at him. "*You're* out of breath," he said. "No, that's fine. You can—"

Giraut swung again, and Addo froze. He hadn't been expecting it, and for a fraction of a second he stared at the heavy wooden toy coming straight at him. Giraut tried to check the blow or pull it off course, but there simply wasn't time. He opened his mouth to scream—

And Addo had caught the blade, snapped it between his palms and jerked it sideways, plucking it out of Giraut's hand. Giraut stumbled forward and crashed into him; his jaw hit Addo's shoulder, and he felt his bottom teeth crush against his lower lip. He reeled backwards and tried to mumble an apology, but his mouth was full of blood. He wobbled, and Addo reached out and caught him, gently steadied him on his feet and then let go. He still had the wooden messer in his left hand.

"Sorry," Giraut said.

"No, that's fine," Addo said. "Are you all right? There's blood . . ."

"Just bit my lip, that's all," Giraut mumbled. "Listen, really, I didn't mean . . ."

"That's fine," Addo repeated firmly. "I know precisely how it feels. Even a wooden one, you just want to swing it and see what happens." He dropped the messer on the floor and pushed it away with his foot. "Apparently," he said, "most rural Permians carry one of the damn things with them wherever they go. It's a miracle there's anybody left alive in this appalling country."

Addo and Phrantzes fought a point. Phrantzes started off with a feint and a furious lunge and carried on attacking, like the sea crashing against a cliff, until one of his swirling from-the-roof shots just clipped the bottom of the lobe of Addo's left ear. Addo immediately called a hit, dropped his foil and took two long steps back. "You win," he panted, wiping sweat out of his eyes.

Phrantzes looked stunned. "Really?"

"No question." He dabbed two fingers to his ears, then held them out. "You see? Actual blood. Point and match."

Phrantzes put his back to the wall and slid down it on to the floor. "I can't keep that up," he said. "I just don't have the strength."

Addo sat next to him. "No, you're doing exactly the right thing. Keep on at him, in his face, like you were doing just then. If you've only got a limited amount of energy, it'd be crazy to waste it defending. Just make sure you keep tight inside, and carry on attacking till you get him."

"It's not going to work. I can't do it."

"You'll be fine," Addo said, gingerly rubbing his ear. It was bright red and swollen, and Giraut reckoned he could feel the heat radiating from it from the other side of the room. "Also, he won't be expecting it. Try and look really old and frail immediately before the start, and then go for the bastard. He won't stand a chance."

A brief ceremony, at noon, in the Procopian arena; nothing too arduous, they'd said. To get there, they were taken out through the kitchens and the stable yard just after first light and herded into a laundry cart, a rickety old thing with high wicker sides, into which bales of dirty washing were dropped from the upper windows. Cunning craftsmen had installed a false floor about halfway up the sides, creating a hidden compartment, with a low door for access, in which a small man could just about sit without bowing his head. Once they were in, the door was closed and bolted behind them, and the cart drove round the quadrangle; every time a bale of laundry hit the floor above their heads, the cart shook, until Iseutz said she'd never realised before what a thoroughly rotten time anvils must have. Addo, squashed up against the side, used the blade of his penknife to prise a small loophole in the wickerwork.

"The gate's opening," he told the others, "we're going through. I can't . . . Dear God."

"What?" Iseutz snapped.

"There's so many *people*."

If he'd been sitting on top of the gatehouse tower, instead of crouching in a cart at ground level, he'd have got a rather better impression of the scale of the crowd that had gathered outside the Guild house during the night. It filled the broad street on all four sides; the proverbial squirrel could've made a complete circuit of the building across the shoulders of the crowd without even having to jump. The main thoroughfares leading to Guildhouse Square were jammed for half a mile in both directions – everybody in the crush knew they hadn't got a hope of getting close enough to see the Guild house wall, let alone the fencers coming or going, but clearly they felt an overwhelming need to be there, as near as they could get, strong enough to justify the discomfort and the very real danger of being smothered, crushed or trampled to death. There were no guards or soldiers anywhere in sight, but that wasn't a problem. The crowd was too monstrously compacted together for anyone to raise a violent hand or throw a missile.

The laundry cart made its way through the crowd at the pace of water percolating through heavy cloth, until eventually it was able to turn off down a reasonably empty alley, the first stage in a horribly slow and tortuous progression through the rats' nest of

alleys, snickets, yards and entries that eventually brought them to
Victory Square, where the walls of the Procopian arena towered
over the surrounding rooftops like a singularly ugly hat. There
were crowds there too, seventy-five yards deep, so they had to go
back into the alley maze and tack and trim south by south-east
until they came to the boundary wall of the old Governor's mansion, a high-sided grey box the size of a modest arable farm.
There was a sally port in the wall just big enough for the cart to
squeeze through (they felt the wheel hubs foul the gateposts on
the way through) and then they were in an artificial canyon
between the outer and inner defensive walls, rolling quickly across
immaculately mown lawns. After about a quarter of a mile they
turned right into a long tunnel, and finally came out into the light
on the floor of the arena itself. A worried-looking man in a pale
green robe opened the door for them. "About time," he muttered,
as he bundled them out into the painfully bright sun. "We were
beginning to wonder where the hell you'd got to."

They'd been in the coach for four hours, which left just under
an hour before the start of the brief, not-too-arduous ceremony.
"We need to get you safely under cover before we open the
gates," somebody explained. "If they catch sight of you before
we've got the barriers up, it'll be a bloodbath."

Across fifteen acres of sand to a vast pillared gateway, to the
left of which was a tiny hidden door, leading to a corkscrew
wooden stair that brought them out on a plank-floored platform
high up on the wall. Beyond that was a narrow catwalk with a
rope handrail, which led to a door in the side of a square tower
built against the wall. They found themselves on a landing at the
top of a long, broad flight of marble steps, at the foot of which an
open door leaked light. There were three folding chairs and a
table on the landing. "Take a seat," their guide told them as he
walked away, "and for crying out loud stay put and don't even
think of wandering off. If you do, we can't guarantee your
safety."

Giraut, Phrantzes and Iseutz took the chairs. Addo perched

uncomfortably on the edge of the table, whose legs bent visibly under his weight. From outside came a noise, vague but deafening, somewhere between a furious argument in the Senate and the muted growl of the sea. They sat in silence for what seemed like a very long time, hardly daring to move. From time to time a trumpet sounded, and there were a number of inexplicable loud bangs and crashes, as if a wall had collapsed or someone was using a battering ram on a bronze door. Giraut leaned across and whispered to Phrantzes (he didn't quite dare speak out loud, in case the mob heard him and stormed the tower): "What exactly have we got to do in this ceremony?"

"No idea," Phrantzes replied. "I did ask, but they didn't answer."

Iseutz made an exasperated noise and muttered something about standing up in front of ten thousand people looking like a windmill; she had a point, Giraut was prepared to concede, because the clothes she'd been issued with didn't exactly flatter her. The most charitable explanation was that they still hadn't figured out she wasn't a man, but it was hard to think of any justification, however fanciful, for the cut of the sleeves. If she were to stand on a high place on a windy day and spread her arms, there'd be no knowing where she was likely to end up. But his own outfit wasn't much better, so his sympathy was muted. Phrantzes, in spite of his clothes, still looked exactly the same as always, and Addo – well, until you got to know him quite well, you had difficulty noticing he was there at all.

Trumpets blared directly overhead, and the crowd roared. Addo mouthed *Sounds like something's happening*, and a man appeared in the doorway they'd come in through, beckoning furiously and scowling. "All right," Phrantzes yelled, "we're ready." The man looked horrified and put his finger to his lips, then scampered down the broad staircase without looking back.

"Well," Giraut shouted in Addo's ear, "do we follow him or what?"

Addo shrugged, then set off down the stairs. The man had

reached the bottom; he looked back at them and thrashed his arms above his head, as though fighting off a swarm of three-inch bees. *I guess so*, Addo mimed, and he led the way, the other three trailing wretchedly behind him. A moment later, they stumbled through the doorway, and the sunlight hit them like a hammer.

"That was *it*?" Iseutz demanded furiously, as they were thrust back into the laundry cart. "That was *all*? Two minutes . . ."

Addo ducked and compressed himself into the seat next to her. "Plenty enough for me, thank you. I'm just glad it's over."

Giraut's ears were still ringing. "Did you see the size of the place?" he said. "It's vast. How is anybody going to see anything when we fence there tomorrow?"

"Two minutes." Iseutz was white with rage. "All that misery, just to walk out, shake hands with an old man and walk back in again. These people are—"

"Enthusiastic," Addo said, with a smile. "Oh come on, it wasn't that bad. We didn't have to make speeches or anything."

"Just as well Suidas wasn't here," Iseutz said. "He'd have—"

She stopped short, and nobody spoke until they'd been moving for several minutes. Then Giraut said, "Addo, what can you see?"

"Nothing," Addo replied. "Someone's been in here and filled in the hole I made. Now that's attention to detail. My father would definitely approve."

"Make another one," Iseutz commanded, but he shook his head. "Twice would be rude," he said, "especially since they've made it clear it's not allowed."

Another long silence. After a minute or so at walking pace, they'd slowed to a crawl. "Do you think he's all right?" Giraut said. "Really?"

"If anybody could make it, Suidas could," Addo said firmly.

"They'd have found him by now," Iseutz said, "if he was still alive."

"Not at all," Giraut said angrily. "There's miles and miles of open country, he could be anywhere."

"Even I could've walked to Beal from there by now," Iseutz snapped back. "Face it, Giraut, we won't be seeing him again. And it's his own bloody stupid fault."

Addo shook his head. "I should've—"

"His own fault," Iseutz repeated grimly. "If you'd tried to stop him, he'd probably have attacked you. It was obvious he was that close to losing it completely."

"Maybe he's gone home," Giraut said.

Addo frowned, and Iseutz looked at him. "That's a thought," Addo said. "Maybe he has, at that. Which would explain why they haven't found him, if he doesn't want to be found."

Phrantzes started to say something, then put his hand over his mouth. His eyes were wide open.

"He said we should come here, though," Iseutz said.

"Changed his mind," Giraut said eagerly. "Knowing Suidas, he figured that on his own he'd be able to make it through. Yes, I bet you that's what's happened. After all, if he's dead, surely they'd have found the body."

"It's possible," Addo said thoughtfully. "I don't know. Would he just up and go home like that?"

"If he's had enough, yes," Giraut said.

"Maybe. And yet only a few days ago he was saying how he'd had all these offers and how he was seriously thinking of settling in Permia and fencing professionally. Remember him telling us about all the money he could make here?"

Iseutz gave him a scornful look. "Maybe the civil war changed his mind," she said.

"Not much sign of it hereabouts," Addo said. "Mind you, he hasn't seen any of this. Otherwise, I'm fairly sure he'd want to fight tomorrow and then sign up for the most lucrative deal he could make. And good luck to him," he added, "the poor devil's desperate for money, and he could make a fortune doing exhibition bouts for those lunatics out there." He shrugged. "I really don't know. I hope he's all right, naturally, and if anyone could walk home from here to Scheria, it'd be him."

He was stiff from sitting still, something that had never come naturally to him. He was cold, though he'd learned to ignore that sort of thing. He'd stopped noticing hunger some time ago. Worst of all, he was bored. He tapped his fingernails on the blade of the messer; a dull pattering, like rain on a roof.

"Suidas Deutzel?"

The voice startled him; because it was unexpected, and because it was familiar. He held his breath, for no obvious reason.

"Suidas?" the voice repeated.

Well, he thought, and slowly stood up. It was, of course, too dark to see: no moon, no stars, no light even for his exceptionally keen night vision. "Over here," he said.

A pause; then: "You know, that's not particularly helpful. Where's here?"

Now he could see him; a slightly darker blur. "Directly in front of you." He waited for a moment until he heard a solid, chunky noise and a barely perceptible intake of breath. "Watch out," he then said, "there's a bank."

"Yes thank you, I gathered that," the voice said, rather ungraciously. "The hell with it, this'll do. You can hear me all right?"

"Loud and clear," Suidas replied. "Look, what the hell . . .?"

"You found it all right, then."

"Yes, eventually," Suidas said. "No thanks to the instructions. *A hill like an overturned bucket, you'll know it when you see it.* I ask you."

"Well, you found it."

"They could've told me it was right up close to Beal," Suidas growled. "It'd have saved me days of staring at the skyline. Which is littered, I might add, with hills like overturned bloody buckets."

"Ah well," the voice said, "that's because we didn't know

ourselves, not till the last minute. We could only go on what we were told."

"*You* could've told me."

"I didn't know either," Tzimisces said reasonably. "Not till I was briefed. I've been as much in the dark as you were."

Suidas breathed out heavily through his nose. "You might've mentioned you were my contact," he said. "We've been sitting in the same damn coach for as long as I can remember."

"It wasn't going to be me, originally," Tzimisces replied. "I'm a last-minute replacement. From which you can probably gather," he added, "things are a bit screwed up. The man who was supposed to be meeting you got held up in Beaute, because of the riots. It's mostly luck they were able to get a message through to me in time, or else we'd both be in Beal right now with absolutely no idea what we're supposed to be doing."

Suidas took a moment to dismiss the irritation from his mind. "All right," he said. "So what exactly am I here for?"

There was a long silence. Then Tzimisces said, "You didn't have any trouble getting away?"

Suidas laughed. "Define *trouble*," he said. "I don't know if you know, but a double company of Blueskins got cut to bits by Aram Chantat about four miles from here, day before last."

"Oh, I know about that. Go on."

"Well," Suidas said, "we happened to see it. The others got in a panic about what to do. I made it look like I'd had enough; we were in a coach on the road, and I said we should dump the coach and walk to Beal. They weren't having any, naturally, so I flounced off on my own."

"Fortuitous," Tzimisces said after a moment. "Good excuse."

"Well, I guess it was a bit more convincing than hold-on-I-need-to-take-a-leak. Anyway, the hell with that. What's going on, and what've I got to do?"

"Right." Tzimisces' voice dropped a little, though he was still perfectly audible. "You're up to speed on the background situation, I take it?"

"I thought I was," Suidas replied. "Now I'm not so sure."

"There have been certain developments," Tzimisces said carefully, "most of which I won't bore you with, because they're not really relevant. As far as you're concerned, though, it's basically the same as it was when we left Scheria. We have reason to believe that one of our party—"

"The fencers?"

"Yes. One of the party is out to make trouble. Your job's to stop him. Or her," he added. "We don't know which one, sorry."

"Don't you?" Suidas sounded surprised. "You ought to, you know. Your lot picked the team."

"Yes, we did," Tzimisces replied. "And we thought we'd been really clever. But obviously not. We got a tip from an impeccable source. One of the fencers has a completely different agenda, which, if not prevented, will lead to disastrous consequences. That's all we know, basically. I know it's not much—"

"You could say that," Suidas snapped. "So, what are you telling me? One of us is working for – who, for crying out loud?"

"That's a very good question," Tzimisces said calmly. "That's the problem, so many interested parties have got reasons for wanting trouble right now, our side and theirs. I'm guessing that trouble in this context means another war, but even that's just supposition on my part."

"But if you got this tip before we left home . . . "

"Quite. Narrows it down a little bit. Unlikely to be the leaders of the current insurgency, since as far as we know there wasn't an insurgency when we left Scheria; all that only started with the killing in Beaute."

Suidas frowned. "Maybe that—"

"No, I don't think so. Oh, sorry, I left a bit out. Whatever the big deal is, it'll happen in Beal. That's not from the original source," Tzimisces added, "that's from somewhere else, but we think it's someone connected to the first source, if that makes any sense. In other words, whatever it is, it hasn't happened yet."

Suidas sighed. "Fine," he said. "Couldn't your lot have told me all this before we left home?"

"Ah." Tzimisces sounded a little apologetic. "We'd hoped to have further and better information by now, which is why we set up this meeting. But we haven't, or if we have it's stuck in Beaute, which is why I'm here being not very much help, instead of the man who was supposed to be briefing you. Sorry about that. Not the intelligence division's finest hour, I'm afraid."

Suidas expressed an opinion about the intelligence division. Tzimisces laughed. "I quite agree," he said, "and I'm the deputy chief. Still, nobody's perfect, and to be fair, it's not like we've got a lot to go on. About all we can say for sure is that the assassinations might've been planned before we left home but the riots were spontaneous and unforeseen; likewise the current situation."

Suidas thought about that for a moment. "All right," he said. "So why are the Aram Chantat carving up the Blueskins? What's all that about?"

"Suffice it to say," Tzimisces was choosing his words, "we think that some factions within the Aram Chantat – the Cosseilhatz, maybe, and quite possibly the Aram no Vei – are under entirely new management, so to speak; in anticipation of the expiry of their current contracts, they've found someone else to work for, and maybe they've started early."

"That's not very likely," Suidas replied. "They don't change sides till the contract runs out, it's a point of honour."

"Absolutely," Tzimisces said. "But so are all the various blood feuds between the sects. It's a shame we don't know more about this sort of thing, because obviously it's really rather important, but we *think* that where there's a conflict, the obligation to pursue feuds overrides the duty to perform contracts until they run out. We think," Tzimisces emphasised. "But if that's right, it's not hard to see how someone could manipulate the no Vei, for example, into having a go at the Chantat proper.

Which would, of course, include their allies – in this case, the Imperials."

"That doesn't work. The Blueskins'd be the no Vei's allies too."

Tzimisces sighed. "It's complicated," he said. "It's also the sort of infinitely fine point of interpretation that appeals to the legalistic nomad-horseman mentality. I've often said, if ever an outsider managed to get inside the heads of those bastards and figure out exactly how their minds work, he'd be one step away from ruling the world. My fear right now is that that might just possibly have happened. Who this evil genius might be, however, I admit I haven't a clue. Probably by the time we find out it'll be too late. Never mind, though, that's not your problem. What you need to concern yourself with is which of our happy little band of pilgrims is about to fuck up the peace, and how, and how it can be stopped."

There was a long silence; long enough for Tzimisces to say, "Suidas?" to make sure he was still there.

Eventually: "Has it occurred to you," Suidas said, "that your secret traitor might be me?"

"You were the first one I thought of."

"Thanks. And what made you change your mind?"

"I'm not entirely sure I have," Tzimisces replied. "All I can say is, if it does turn out to be you, your Sontha will find it hard to pursue her theatrical career with no eyes and no tongue. The same goes, by the way, if you fail to deal with the problem. Oh, and we'll kill you too, of course, but I don't suppose you're particularly bothered about that." Suidas heard a faint rustle, as of a man standing up, but he couldn't pinpoint it accurately enough to justify making a move; not with the bank in the way, in the pitch dark. "There's a horse tied to a gatepost about a quarter of a mile down this bank. In the saddlebag you'll find a bundle of maps and floor plans, and a list of the most likely targets, stuff like that. If you go now, you'll be in Beal by daybreak. The others are at the Guild house. Give them my love."

Suidas waited, but there were no further sounds, and nothing to be seen.

He found the horse. It took him a while. He went up the bank when he should have gone down, and when eventually he did find it, when he tried to untie it, it bit him.

They decided they wouldn't train on the day of the match, in case of pulled muscles or similar injuries. The coach, they'd been told, would call for them just before noon. They passed the rest of the morning playing Snare.

"It's a bit like chess," Giraut explained. "I mean, you play it with a chess set, but the moves are different and you can play doubles. In fact, it's better as doubles. We used to play it at school."

Phrantzes didn't want to join in, but Iseutz and Giraut badgered him until it was less effort to agree than to hold out. He sided with Giraut against Addo and Iseutz. They laid out Addo's miniature chess set on top of a long rectangular marble thing that stood in the middle of the Senior Common Room, which was where they'd been put till they were wanted. There were only three chairs small and light enough to move, so Addo knelt on the floor.

"The main difference," Giraut explained, "is white always loses. That's the rule."

"Oh," Addo said. "Which are we again?"

"White."

"Ah."

"Yes," Giraut said, "but it's easier being white. Easier to win, I mean."

"But I thought you said . . ."

"It's *how* you lose," Giraut told him. "It's pretty simple really. Every time you take one of our pieces, we can take one of yours, only we can choose which one. If we take one of yours – in the ordinary course of play, I mean, not because you've taken one of

ours – then we get an extra go. After ten goes each, if we haven't
won yet, we get back all of our pieces you've taken, and all our
pawns turn into rooks or bishops. If we still haven't won two
moves after that, you lose all your pieces except the king. Then,
if we still haven't beaten you two moves after that, you lose automatically but actually you've won the game."

There was a brief silence. "I don't understand," Iseutz said.

Giraut went through it again, practically word for word.
"Being white's fairly straightforward," he added. "Just try not to
take any of our pieces and play for time. It's quite easy once you
get the hang of it."

Addo was smiling. "That's a very strange game," he said.

"Not really," Giraut said. "If you're white, the key to winning
is not to score any victories. If you're black, it's more or less like
chess, except the pieces don't move the same."

They played a game. Iseutz started off looking extremely
dubious and saying, "That's silly" every time something happened, but towards the end she got caught up in it completely.
Addo proved to be a superb player, though he gave every sign of
not taking it seriously. Giraut was trying to win, but Phrantzes
kept making obvious mistakes. After fourteen moves each side,
the white king was still in play.

"Does that mean we've won?" Iseutz asked breathlessly.

"Yes," Giraut said. He wasn't happy. "Well done," he muttered. "You got the hang of it pretty quickly."

"I've played something like it before," Addo said. "Only the
pieces are different and you play on an oval board. I can't
remember what it was called."

"Let's have another game," Iseutz said. "Go on, Giraut. You
two can be white this time."

Playing black, Iseutz and Addo were utterly ruthless, and the
game lasted a total of nine moves. "Being black's easier," Addo
said, "but white's more fun. One more?"

Giraut didn't look keen, but before he could speak, Phrantzes
suddenly said, "Why not?" and started to set up the pieces.

"We'll be white again, if that's all right," he said briskly. "I think I'm beginning to see how it works."

White lost in eight moves. Giraut now looked bored; Phrantzes set the pieces up again. "One more," he said, and it wasn't a suggestion. "We'll be white," he said.

"But you've been white twice now," Iseutz objected. "It's our turn."

"We'll be black," Addo said firmly. Iseutz scowled at him but didn't say anything, and Addo made the first move. Phrantzes hopped a knight across his pawn wall. Iseutz brought out a bishop. Phrantzes put the knight back where it had come from.

"Just a minute," Giraut said. "It was my go."

"Sorry," Phrantzes snapped, with a total absence of sincerity. Addo moved the bishop and picked a pawn out of white's wall. Phrantzes moved the knight again, the same move as the first.

Ten moves each later, white was reduced to their king and a solitary pawn, which fell at the next move. There were no black pieces to restore, since white hadn't taken any. All the black pawns turned into rooks and bishops. "Checkmate," said Addo.

Phrantzes was scowling furiously at the board. "But that's not fair," he said. "White can't win. It's impossible."

"That's right," Iseutz said. "That's what Giraut told us before we started."

"Yes, but you two won the first game."

"Ah well." Addo smiled. "Beginner's luck."

For an instant, Giraut was sure Phrantzes was going to knock over the board. But the moment passed and he leaned back in his chair. "Right," he said. "I suppose it serves me right, trying to win against the Irrigator's son. I should've known better."

That made Iseutz quite angry. "It wasn't just him," she said. "I'm here too, remember."

Phrantzes didn't bother to reply, which made her angrier still. Giraut started to put the pieces away. "You didn't help." Phrantzes rounded on him. "You kept making stupid mistakes."

"Did I?" Giraut sounded tired. "Well, it's only a game."

"That's exactly what I'd expect you to say."

"Well, it is."

"Fine." Phrantzes stood up sharply and walked away. There was an awkward silence, then Addo said, "You know, this marble thing, it isn't a table. It's a tomb. Look, there's writing on it."

"Don't be ridiculous," Iseutz said. "Who'd put a tomb in the middle of a common room?"

"I don't think . . ." Addo stopped, and got up. "I wish we had some way of knowing what time it is," he said.

"It must be nearly noon," Giraut said. "I feel like I've been stuck in this room for days."

"One more game." Phrantzes had turned to face them. *I've never seen him like this before,* Giraut thought, *except maybe when he fought Suidas.* "Come on," he added loudly, with a broad, humourless grin, "it's not like we've got anything else to do."

Iseutz gave him a worried look. Addo was frowning. "If you insist," he said. "Though to be honest with you, I'd rather save up my remaining luck for this evening."

"Fine," Phrantzes said. "Then you won't mind if I beat you."

"I think we may be missing the point," Giraut said. "It's supposed to be *fun,* not a duel to the finish."

"It is fun," Phrantzes said grimly. "Let's have some more fun, just to pass the time."

"Oh, let's do as he says, for pity's sake," Iseutz said nervously. "Addo, set up the board."

"Fine," Addo said. "Tell you what, let's have different teams this time, Giraut, you and Iseutz against Phrantzes and me."

"That's not my idea of fun," Phrantzes said. "Same teams as before."

Phrantzes and Giraut were black. They played five moves each. Then Addo moved a knight and said, "Checkmate."

They all stared at the board. Then Iseutz laughed, a little awkwardly. Giraut was gazing at the white knight in total confusion. "That's crazy," he said. "White can't win."

"I think we just did," Addo said gently.

Phrantzes grabbed the black king, lifted it and looked down at the board. He was quite still for what seemed like a long time. Then he laid the king down carefully on its side, stood up and held his hand out to Addo. "Well done," he said. "Thanks for the game."

Addo hesitated, then shook his hand. "My pleasure," he said. "I promise you, it really was a fluke. Sheer luck."

Phrantzes nodded stiffly. "Four consecutive flukes," he said. "A more likely explanation would be that you're a very good player. As is only to be expected."

Gently, Addo pulled his hand free. "My father always says you can tell a really good chess player by the way he always loses so long as there's no money at stake. He'd like this game, though. I must teach it to him when we get home."

Phrantzes' face registered a sort of smiling frown, as though Addo had just made a rather good joke but in very bad taste. "Quite," he said. "And when this is all over and we're back in Scheria, you must all come over and have dinner with Sphagia and me. She'd love to meet you, I know."

Addo put the chess pieces back in their box and tucked it in his pocket. Iseutz yawned and stood up. "It's got to be nearly noon by now," she said. "I hope they're going to feed us beforehand."

"I don't think I could eat anything," Giraut said with feeling.

"Probably best if we don't," Addo said.

"Nonsense." Phrantzes crossed to a huge carved-oak chair by the door, sat down and put his feet up on a small table. "When I was fencing competitively, we always used to have a three-course lunch with a bottle of decent white wine beforehand, and it never did anyone any harm. Micel Zeuxis, who was the champion before me, used to insist on clear soup followed by saddle of lamb and a fruit pie. He was a magnificent fencer. Before your time, obviously."

"I know the name," Addo said politely. Nobody else seemed to have been listening.

"I beat him, of course," Phrantzes went on. "I noticed he had a slight tendency to get square on when he was crowded on the outside. I'll never forget the look on his face when I landed the winning touch. He lost heart after that and gave up completely, which is a shame. I'd have liked to fight him again, just to prove it wasn't a fluke."

Iseutz shot Addo a why's-he-doing-this glance, which he saw but didn't react to. Giraut got up, crossed the room and leant against the marble rectangle that wasn't a table, pretending to be interested in the inscription, though it was too badly worn to be legible. Phrantzes folded his hands in his lap and closed his eyes. Giraut could tell by his breathing that he wasn't asleep.

Eventually, a steward came to tell them it was time to go. Phrantzes, who by that time really had fallen asleep, woke up with a ferocious grunt and looked round, terrified, until he realised what was going on. Iseutz, meanwhile, was pleading with the steward for time to go back to her room and fix her hair. Eventually Addo had to grab her by the shoulder and say, "Come *on*," at which she sighed and fell in behind him. Giraut brought up the rear, feeling strangely cheerful; one more fight, said a voice inside his head, and then it'll all be over and we can go home. The voice sounded just like his mother, on various occasions in his youth when she'd lied to him.

"I didn't even know they liked fencing," they heard the Master whisper to the Minister of War. "I never heard of them taking an interest in it before."

"Well, apparently they do," the Minister replied. "And there's no need to whisper. They don't speak our language."

He was, of course, entirely wrong about that; but the three Aram delegates (Auzeil, Cosseilhatz and no Vei) had guarded the secret carefully, and they'd learned not to grin, and where to look when someone said something especially unfortunate. There were times when the imbalance of knowledge made the delegates feel as though they were cheating. They knew everything they needed to know about the Permians, who'd never even bothered to ask them their names, on the assumption they wouldn't be able to pronounce them.

"What exactly is it we're going to see?" asked the Auzeil, in Aram.

"Swordfighting," replied the no Vei.

"Ah." The Auzeil frowned. "Some kind of trial by combat?"

"I don't think so," the no Vei replied. "As far as I can gather, the fighters have no quarrel with each other. Quite often they've never even met before."

"Then why do they fight?" the Cosseilhatz asked.

"So the people can watch," the no Vei told him. "Apparently."

"That's absurd," said the Auzeil.

"It's barbaric," the Cosseilhatz amended.

"Yes." The no Vei settled himself comfortably in his seat and folded his hands in his lap. He was ninety-one years old, and sitting still for any length of time made his knees ache. "But it's their national obsession. Almost like a religion. It's all the common people ever talk about, so they tell me."

"I'm curious," said the Cosseilhatz. "Do they only fight foreigners, or do Permians actually fight Permians?"

"Oh, this is an exception," the no Vei said gravely, "a special occasion, the first foreign team to fight in Permia since before the War. Usually it's Permian against Permian. Hence the excitement."

The Cosseilhatz shook his head. "Presumably they don't use real weapons, though."

"They most certainly do," the no Vei said. "Real and sharp. I understand that's not the case in Scheria. But in Permia, most definitely."

"Then how do they keep from getting injured?"

"With great difficulty, I would imagine. Ah, here's the First Minister and his party. You've met him, haven't you, Sichem?"

"Briefly," the Auzeil replied. "At a reception."

"What did you make of him?"

"He's an idiot."

The no Vei turned his head and bowed politely to the First Minister, who nodded back. "Yes," the no Vei said. "But apart from that."

"Weak, indecisive and scared," the Auzeil said. "Just intelligent enough to know what has to be done, but far too frightened of his own people to do it. Most of all, I think, he's terrified that there might be another war. Talking of which . . ."

"Not now," the Cosseilhatz said pleasantly. "I have an idea that man over there, he's something in the Treasury, might know a little Aram. Probably not enough, but let's not take unnecessary risks. We'll continue this discussion after the fighting's over."

"Oh dear," the Auzeil said. "I do hope there won't be any blood. It makes me sick to my stomach, and we're supposed to be ferocious savages who eat small children."

"Do your best," the no Vei said firmly. "They'll think it's rather odd if you're ostentatiously looking the other way."

"Look." The Cosseilhatz sat up straight. "Something's happening." He shaded his eyes with his hand. "Is that the Carnufex boy, do you suppose?"

"I don't think so," the no Vei replied, raising his voice to make himself heard over the roar from the benches all around them. "The first match is rapier, I believe, between—"

"What's rapier?" the Auzeil interrupted.

"I gather it's a long, thin sword with blunt edges. You can stab with it, but you can't cut."

"How curious. I'm sorry, you were saying?"

"Hush," whispered the Cosseilhatz. "I think they're starting."

Giraut completed the salute – a little stiff, but adequate – and composed himself into a high first guard. He wouldn't be able to hold it for long, but he sincerely hoped he wouldn't have to. The idea was to draw the enemy into a lunge from just an inch or so over middle distance, then volte or demi-volte and win the match in one play.

Nothing happened. He looked past the hanging point of his rapier at the man standing opposite him. Terrified, Giraut diagnosed. Not good. He'd been counting on contemptuous aggression.

The game is, white always loses. He'd made up his mind to play white.

Quite some time ago, in fact: in the bell tower, when he'd been leaking blood by the pitcherful. The idea back then had been to cheat by dying before they could get to him. A bit like resigning as soon as you lose your first capital piece; white always loses, but at least you get out on your own terms, defeated but unbeaten – a subtle distinction, but none the worse for that, and subtleties are the most you can hope for, if you play white.

The fool was just standing there. Annoyed, Giraut took a step back to cover the transition from high first to middle fourth; not a guard he favoured, but more comfortable for waiting in. It also sent a message: *You had your chance and you missed it, so now you're going to have to work for it.* Somewhere in the vast distance, somebody coughed. Then it was dead quiet again.

The points are sharp, Giraut told himself. A man could die of impatience. Make him come to you, he's a nervous wreck and you aren't. Let him come. Let someone else do the decent thing, for once.

White always loses; he really wished someone had bothered to tell him that earlier, because unless you knew, how were you supposed to make sense of anything? White wins by losing. It's the rules.

He knew, or at least he thought he knew, why the way station had been deserted, why the bandits had been allowed to roam unmolested through Scherian territory, why they'd been there, so improvidently close to a military outpost, at precisely that time. He had a good idea, or at least a plausible theory, about why Tzimisces kept wandering off, and why the Aram Chantat had turned on their allies the Imperials. He'd had his suspicions all along, but the revelation about white had allowed him to make the connections he'd overlooked, probably wilfully, up till now. He wondered if the Permian knew he was playing black. He didn't look like he knew, but maybe he was simply aware that in the game, there's always the possibility of a rogue element, as Addo had proved when they played the last hand. The points, he reminded himself, are sharp. But I have the advantage. You can't kill a man who's already dead.

Not strictly true, of course; you can, if he gets careless, you can kill him very dead indeed, and we don't want that to happen if it can be avoided, now do we? But if it does, at least we can console ourselves with the thought that it really doesn't matter all that terribly much. Dead then, dead now or dead about half an hour after I get home; who really gives a damn, anyhow?

He took a left-leg step forward; the Permian retreated. He leaned forward just far enough to enable him to tap the front two inches of the Permian's blade with his own point. The crowd laughed. The Permian was shivering. How pathetic can you get.

It had, of course, all been a trap, a set-up; a snare, excuse the pun. He wondered how they'd forced or manipulated the girl into agreeing to do it. Presumably they hadn't told her that her father was going to die. Probably they'd made out that Giraut was the intended victim, or else the Senator was certain to kill him and thereby get himself in trouble. Like it mattered. He should've guessed, of course. Now he thought about it, the girl had been ludicrously easy to get into bed. At the time he'd put it down to his irresistible charm, so really he'd deserved everything he'd got.

The Permian lunged. It was an apology for an attack, so carefully closed and guarded that aggression was very much an afterthought. He got out of the way with a simple step back, not even bothering to move his sword arm, and the Permian immediately retreated to exactly where he'd been. The crowd laughed again. He could see the enemy blushing with shame. Any minute now, he'll burst into tears. This is stupid, Giraut thought. I'm white, I shouldn't have to put up with this shit.

Slowly he lowered his sword until the point was resting on the ground. The Permian just stood there and stared. The crowd were booing. They hated their own man. Even if he won now, they'd still despise him as a coward. Even if he won, he couldn't win.

Giraut tried not to laugh, but he couldn't help it. He stood, sword lowered, laughing; and the Permian came at him. It was a good lunge, just inside middle distance, tending to his outside to make a volte problematic; he could only retreat and parry in single time, keeping the point upright, making the hand movement as small as possible. He forfeited the fraction of a second in which he could have riposted, and the Permian lunged again, but this time a little too fully. Before he realised it, Giraut's back foot had moved, his body was twisting, he had no control over them. He did try and pull his sword out of the way, but he'd practised the volte too often for that. His arm knew what to do and was determined to do it, regardless of any contradictory orders from the brain. The Permian stepped into the point, which entered him just under the ribcage, his own impetus driving it in deeper than Giraut's arm could ever have managed. Stupid fool's killed himself, Giraut thought, and stepped smartly backwards to let him fall.

"Oh dear," the Auzeil whispered, his voice clear as a bell in the unnatural silence. "Was that supposed to happen?"

The no Vei shrugged. "Yes and no," he said.

And then they cheered; which was obscene, Giraut thought, as he tugged on the hilt of his rapier (but the dead body was twisted, the blade was flexed, it wouldn't come out clean; he let go of the hilt. Not his sword anyhow). They cheered him, they were in love with him – love doesn't care what you do, it's utterly amoral – and if he'd been able to, he'd have ordered his army of Aram Chantat to close the doors and not stop killing till they were all dead. To express his contempt he swept them a low bow, then walked across the sand to the door he'd come in through without looking back.

Phrantzes was sitting on the stairs when Giraut burst through the door. He jumped up. "Well?" he snapped.

"You're on," Giraut said and pushed past him.

A short, wire-haired Permian with a big nose dropped down into the seat next to the no Vei. He was out of breath and sweating. "Terribly sorry I'm late," he said, in passable Aram. "I'm your translator."

"Splendid," the no Vei said, as the other two looked at each other. "You can tell us what's going on. I'm afraid it's all a mystery to us."

"No problem," the Permian said. "As it happens, I follow fencing very closely, very closely indeed. Now then." He leaned forward and peered down. "That's Jilem Phrantzes, fighting longsword for Scheria. He's a former All-Scheria champion."

"Isn't he rather old, for a fencer?" the Cosseilhatz asked.

"Ah." The Permian grinned. "Fencers are like wine, they get better with age. I saw the great Mathin Dusan defending his title when he was seventy-one years old, against a boy young enough to be his grandson. Let me tell you, one of them left the arena feet first, and it wasn't Mathin. Amazing man. So I'm expecting great things of this Phrantzes."

"Excuse me," the Auzeil asked, "but don't you want the Permian to win?"

"What? Oh, yes, naturally. But let's say I'm not exactly holding my breath. There's our boy, by the way. Luga Dusan – that's Mathin's great-nephew. Got a bit of the old man about him, but I've always maintained he's weak off the back foot."

The Cosseilhatz frowned. "What does that mean, exactly?"

"Shh." The Permian was crouched forward. "They're about to salute."

*

Giraut carried on up the stairs, past Iseutz, who said, "How did it go?"; up to the landing at the top, through the door and out on to the catwalk. No sign of Addo, but he was on last. He looked down into the arena, where two tiny figures were moving about, like insects on the surface of running water. He had no idea what he was looking for, naturally.

The perspective sobered him a little, and he ordered himself to think. Set up – well, yes: to kill the Senator, who was about to push through anti-slavery laws and other awkward measures. To kill him in as sordid a manner as possible, so his assassin couldn't be a martyr to the opposition. Better still, don't punish the assassin at all. Instead, send him to Permia. Only he won't get there. None of them will.

Think. The fencers are ambushed and killed by bandits, on Scherian soil, before they even get close to the border. Why? Because if they die in Scheria, they can't die in Permia; if they don't die in Permia, they can't be martyrs and a reason for war …

Because they can't be allowed to get to Permia, because if they do—

He heard a clank, loud enough to carry all the way up to the catwalk; steel on steel, a block, and not a very stylish one. He didn't bother to look down.

He'd been set up: to kill the Senator, yes, and then to die himself, two birds, one stone. And why him? What's so special about Giraut Bryennius? Precisely because he's nothing special, of no value to anyone, particularly once he's been thoroughly disgraced. Therefore expendable. Therefore capable of being useful *twice*.

A pretty good fencer at junior level, never bothered with it seriously, but good enough to look convincing in Permia, and then to die on a sharp point in a Guild house somewhere along the road to Beal. He thought about it and shook his head. It wasn't quite enough.

Looking at it from the wrong angle. All right, then, the others. Suidas Deutzel, because he'd had such a bad war, because he could be relied on to crack up when surrounded by messers and Blueskins and Aram Chantat – cause an incident, make a scene, start a war. Addo Carnufex, because he's the son of the man who drowned Flos Verjan and all those women and children; and because there was no way his death would go unavenged. Iseutz, because they needed a girl, also expendable, because the Permians are so inhuman they kill young girls as well as grown men: no, that's weak. But he couldn't do any better, and it wasn't essential to establish every part of the chain, not right now. Phrantzes: there had to be something about him, but he didn't know what it was. Add Giraut Bryennius, the walking affront to common decency. No, he wasn't there yet, not quite.

Tzimisces. For a moment he considered the possibility that the whole thing was simply a device for getting Tzimisces into Permia and giving him an excuse to wander about the place, doing whatever it was he had to do, without drawing undue attention to him. *Colonel* Tzimisces, political officer; sent by the Bank, or the Temple or the rump of the military, to outbid the Permians for the services of the Aram Chantat. He disappears, Aram Chantat horsemen wipe out an Imperial column. No, it didn't feel right. Almost, but not quite.

A single intake of breath from the crowd, followed by a tremendous roar. Bad news for somebody, presumably. Not that it mattered. All that mattered, he now knew, was *how* you lost.

"Giraut?" He turned his head and saw Addo. "What are you doing up here?"

"Watching the fight," Giraut replied.

Addo nodded. "Me too. It's not looking too good, I'm afraid."

It hadn't occurred to Giraut that Phrantzes might lose. He peered down, but he couldn't even tell which of the insects was his colleague and which was the enemy. In just such a way, of course, the Irrigator would have looked down from the heights of the Verjan mountains, while judging the perfect moment to open the sluices. "He'll be all right," Giraut said.

"Let's hope so," Addo said. "God forgive me if anything happens to him. It was me who talked him into it, after all."

Phrantzes was very nearly there. He'd reached the point every traveller recognises, towards the end of a long journey, between the first distant sight of the familiar landmarks of home and actually getting there: comfort, of a sort, in the knowledge that his road is now obvious and undisputed; weariness and frustration because there's still some way to go.

He blocked, again; clumsy and hopeless, but just enough to keep the other man's cutting edge off his skin. His block invited a low thrust, which came, which he put aside, just about, which made inevitable a rising cut to the chin, which he caught, just about, on his crossguard. He had no strength left at all. He couldn't slow his monstrous hyperventilation; he was drowning in air, unable to get enough breath no matter how hard he tried. Very soon, either he'd black out and collapse or the other man would finally make good on him. His defence had degenerated into an instinctive scramble, with no form or design to it. There was no way he could win from here. He was a man who couldn't swim thrashing about in deep water; he was in a flooded room standing on tiptoe to keep the gradually rising water out of his nose and mouth. He was very nearly at the stage where he couldn't be bothered to defend any more, but he wasn't quite exhausted enough, and his opponent wasn't quite good enough, and his reflexes wouldn't let him knock over the king quite yet. He blocked again, realised he'd misjudged and left himself wide open; but the fool opposite didn't see the gap until it was too late and he'd closed it. Idiot, he wanted to shout, but he didn't have nearly enough breath, even though he was sucking in air by the barrelful.

Another cut: from-the-roof, lots and lots of strength behind it, all wasted because the angle was rubbish. He deflected it, but he couldn't possibly lift his sword enough to make the counter-thrust. Instead he left it vaguely hanging, and the clown smacked at it, and the vibration ran up the handle and made the tendons of his elbows sing. If he'd had enough strength left to pick a flower, he could've drawcut the moron's throat from there; instead, he blocked another wild swish, and another, and his fingers on the hilt were the fingers of a man dangling from a cliff, or an archer holding a too-strong bow at full draw. The enemy was hardly blown at all, but he'd given up trying to think, he was flailing like a beginner vainly trying to breach the guard of his instructor, who grins smugly as he flicks away each mighty buffet. *It's not like that, you clown, you've won.* But he couldn't see that, evidently.

Another cut: number four in the book, horizontal, left to right, crossed hands; weak, slow, not recommended; usually compared to a man cutting hay with a scythe. Phrantzes tried to lift his sword to block but it was simply too heavy. He took a step back, and somehow the idiot contrived to miss; the useless force of his blow made him stagger – he was being dragged along by his sword, like a man with an unruly dog on a bit of string – and he landed on the side of his foot, turned his ankle over, wobbled for a moment and fell sideways. Phrantzes tried to get his sword out of the way, but by now the hateful thing weighed at least a ton. All he could do was keep the point down, so that when the idiot lurched into it, he didn't actually skewer himself. Instead, he sort of sat down on the edge – the false edge, worse luck, not the true edge, which was blunt as a pole from two dozen feckless blocks. Phrantzes let go, but the damage had been done. The edge had sliced deep into the halfwit's buttock, and he was leaking blood like a broken dam.

(And that's why you have to be so careful when you're fencing, because accidents happen . . .)

The fool hovered for a moment, then fell over. He ended up still sitting on Phrantzes' sword, in the dirt, spouting blood from his lacerated arse. For a split second the world held its breath. Then the crowd began to cheer.

Phrantzes was too exhausted to move, or he'd have fallen over too. But toppling himself would've required strength, and he had none at all. Slowly, like hemlock starting at the toes and creeping up to the neck, he realised he'd won. Which was ridiculous.

The yelling of the crowd battered his head like waves against rocks, and he hated them. He was full to bursting with anger and hate, but there wasn't anything he could do until his chest stopped heaving. As it was, his breathing seemed to have no effect. No matter how much air he dragged down, he desperately needed more and he wasn't getting it. He tried to tip himself over, but he couldn't even do that; just stood there, until eventually, about bloody time too, the gasping rate slowed and he realised he was going to make it.

He looked at the fool, who hadn't moved. He was sitting in a pool of blood, looking for all the world like a beetroot-eater who's pissed himself. For a while, Phrantzes was at a loss to interpret the stupid look on his stupid face. Then he realised: that infuriating, half-witted stare was his way of begging for his life, which was the victor's to give back or take away, as he saw fit.

"Get up, you idiot," Phrantzes said, and started to walk away. He managed five steps.

When they carried him in through the door, Iseutz was sure he was dead. She felt a sharp pain in her stomach, her throat was blocked and for a moment her vision was blurred. Not what she'd been expecting.

They carried him up the stairs to the landing, and Iseutz saw his lips move, though his eyes were closed. There was no blood that she could see. His skin looked a sort of bluish-grey.

"Phrantzes?" she shouted. "Are you all right?"

A faint, exasperated groan showed what he thought of that question, so she grabbed hold of one of the porters carrying (she noticed for the first time) the door he was lying on. "What's the matter with him? Is he badly hurt?"

The porter stared at her: useless. Phrantzes opened his eyes.

His lips were moving again, but she couldn't make out the words. "What?" she yelled at him. He looked at her, and she could tell how much effort trying to speak was costing him. "*What?*"

Phrantzes spoke in a high, shattered voice. "You're on," he said.

"What? Oh." She'd forgotten all about that. "Look, are you . . .?" All right? No, obviously not. Likely to die, alone, in the next twenty minutes? She'd have to take a guess on that one. "Stay there and rest," she said. "I'll be back. Count on it."

He didn't look utterly transported by joy, but she guessed that was a hurt man's privilege. She looked around for the stupid sword, grabbed it, patted the back of her head to make sure her hair hadn't burst free of its pins, and galloped down the stairs two at a time.

"Good heavens," the Auzeil said. "It's a woman."

"Oh yes," the interpreter said, nodding vigorously. "There's been a ladies' class in Permian fencing for, what, seventy years now. Of course they only fence smallsword, but some of them are really quite good. And the Scherians . . ."

"The swords aren't sharp, are they?" The Cosseilhatz wasn't really asking a question; more like seeking reassurance. But the interpreter nodded again.

"Oh yes. It's proper fencing. In Scheria I understand they use foils, though I find that hard to believe."

The no Vei frowned. "Foils?"

The interpreter had to shout, because the Permian girl had just walked out. "Swords with buttons on the end, to make them safe. But we don't. That's just for kids, really."

She was about five foot six, slim, and beautiful. She was dressed from head to foot in red velvet, and her straight black hair was held back with an ivory comb. Her salute was the most graceful thing Iseutz had ever seen, and when she'd made it, she smiled.

Not a mocking leer or any sort of a grin; a polite, friendly smile, from force of habit. *I can't fight that*, Iseutz thought furiously.

She told herself: don't look at the fencer, look at the sword. So she did; and it was thin and strong, triangular section with fullers, lighter than her colichemarde but just as good for parrying. The point was a needle, a geometric paradox, tapering by mathematical progression to the disputed place where nought-point-nought-nought-one subdivided into zero – an impossibility, but real nevertheless. I can fight that, Iseutz decided. Got to, in fact, or it'll kill me.

It occurred to her, suddenly and without warning, that the Permian woman was probably a better fencer than she was, and that she could well die. It wasn't the first time in her life that she'd been aware that she was in danger, but on the other occasions she'd been too busy to dwell on it: the fight with the bandits, the fencing match at Joiauz, a couple of times during the riots at Beaute. But now here was Death, in red velvet, pretty as a picture, making a graceful salute and taking a middle guard in fourth; her assurance, her perfect balance, the steadiness of her extended right hand. This woman's going to kill me, Iseutz thought, and there's not really very much I can do about it.

She thought about dropping the sword and running, tried to do it, failed. Her fingers were frozen to the handle, as though she'd grabbed metal outdoors in midwinter. Something she couldn't understand wouldn't let her run or give up; that made her furiously angry, mad enough to want to fight, but there was no escaping the fact: the Permian girl was better at it, and was bound to win. She couldn't feel her feet. Paralysed.

The Permian took a step forward, closing to long measure. Iseutz felt her own back foot slide out, her front foot following. The Permian edged towards her; she retreated. There was nothing else at all in the whole world apart from the point of the Permian's sword. She stared at it, but she knew she wasn't really concentrating. Her mind was a blank. She'd forgotten everything she'd ever known about fencing. Her feet moved without her orders or consent.

The Permian lunged; Iseutz put it aside to the left, moving the hilt but keeping the point still. The Permian disengaged quickly and smoothly and lunged again; Iseutz had to parry high and force the point down, and when the Permian disengaged again and lunged hard, all she could do was bunny-hop backwards into long measure, which was no answer at all. She felt panic surging through her, drowning all her practised reflexes, her instinctive responses. She tried desperately hard to open her hand to let the sword fall, but her fingers were cramped shut. The Permian lunged, and she tried to demi-volte, but she couldn't remember how to do it; instead, she managed a clumsy right-and-back traverse that just about got her out of trouble, in time for another lunge to come in directly at eye level. She had no idea what to do about that, but her left hand flicked out at the last moment and backhanded the blade away. The Permian pulled back sharply, and Iseutz realised she'd just missed a perfect opportunity for a counterthrust in straight time.

The Permian, however, seemed impressed, enough to back away and find a new line. *Pull yourself together*, Iseutz commanded herself, *for crying out loud*. Brave words; but it didn't alter the fact that she was fighting a superior opponent, and had just used up a year's supply of luck.

Suddenly, she remembered Phrantzes, the way he'd gone for Suidas like a lunatic or a drunk – no skill to speak of, and Suidas was far and away the better fighter, but Phrantzes had won. Wouldn't work, of course; the Permian woman would turn her aggression against her, and besides, you couldn't win at smallsword that way. Ah yes – Iseutz suddenly grinned – but you're not *going* to win. So that's all right.

The Permian was circling, choosing her line, clearly a perfectionist, resolved to make the most of the fight of her life, show off her skill in front of ten thousand connoisseurs. Iseutz kicked away from the sand with her back foot and shot out her right arm, as if she was trying to throw her hand at the Permian's face. It was a stupid move, because it left her wide open; a volte or demi-volte would kill her, or a deflection and counterthrust in straight time. But her point was moving very fast straight at the Permian's left eye. She parried and made space immaculately, but that didn't matter. Iseutz lunged again, even harder, even wilder; she knew she was going to die, but really, so what? She felt a muscle in her forearm tear – you can't lunge like that without doing yourself a mischief, so nobody does, so nobody practises a defence against it. A strong, sweetly economical parry put her blade aside, leaving her in direct line for a killing riposte. She ignored it and thrust again. The Permian parried, not quite so well this time, trying to bring herself round to Iseutz's inside line. The hell with that. Iseutz lunged at full stretch, and the Permian woman's point hit her in the mouth.

When Giraut saw Phrantzes collapse, he stood quite still for a moment, as if he'd been walking in a city and suddenly realised he was lost. Then he ran back along the catwalk. He assumed Addo would follow.

The Permians who'd carried him out of the arena were putting him down on the floor when he reached the landing. He pushed one of them aside and knelt down. "Phrantzes," he said. "Are you all right?"

"No. Yes, I'm fine, I'm just exhausted. What's happening with Iseutz? How's she doing?"

Giraut had forgotten all about her. "I don't know. I'll go and look." He hesitated. "You'll be all right?"

"*Yes*. Go on, quickly."

She'll be fine, Giraut muttered under his breath as he scrambled down the stairs, she'll be fine. He could hear gasps and shouts from the crowd, but that could mean anything; he knew they were perfectly capable of cheering for a Scherian. He reached the foot of the stairs and pushed the doors open, just in time to see . . .

The Cosseilhatz, who was short-sighted, leaned forward. "What happened?" he asked.

The interpreter frowned. "I'm not sure."

Addo, climbing back on to the catwalk, heard the deep rumble of the crowd gasping and froze. He glanced down, but there wasn't time. *My fault*, he told himself, and ran.

At the door, he stopped. He was covered in dust, and his shirt was ripped at the shoulder, where he'd caught it in a window stay, of all the stupid things. No fit state to go out in front of ten thousand people; but the noises the crowd were making suggested he'd run out of time for making himself look presentable. He patted helplessly at his knees and thighs, and told himself that everybody would be much too far away to see.

He'd left his messer on the table, but Phrantzes was lying there. He couldn't see any blood. "Have you seen my messer anywhere?" he asked. Phrantzes stared at him. "It was here on the table, but . . . "

"On the floor," Phrantzes said. "What's going on?"

"Sorry, I haven't been watching." Addo was on his hands and knees, looking under the table. "Ah, got it, thank goodness for that." He stood up, the messer in his left hand. "Is Iseutz out there?"

Phrantzes gave him a look he almost certainly deserved, and nodded. "I think you may be on now," he said.

"Right." Addo nodded. It was a strangely false gesture. "How did you do, by the way?"

"I won."

"Excellent. Right." Addo put the messer between his knees and rubbed his hands together, working some of the dust into his wet-soft palms. Not too much. "Where's Giraut?"

"Down there, watching."

"Splendid. Well, wish me luck."

Phrantzes didn't say anything. Addo turned and walked briskly down the stairs, like a clerk who's slightly late for the start of his shift.

"I'm guessing," the interpreter said, "that the Scherian woman had her mouth closed. I don't think it was a particularly strong thrust, so presumably her lips and teeth took most of the force out of it. Usually, a stab in the mouth is game over. She must've been lucky."

"And the Permian?"

"Stuck through the upper left arm, just above the elbow. Well," the interpreter went on, "they're just standing there, so I suppose that means they've given up and it's a draw. Simultaneous strike. Surprisingly rare. Ought to happen far more often than it does, if you think about it."

Iseutz spat out the mouthful of gravel that had been her front teeth. Her mouth was full of blood, welling out of her lips like floodwater. Strangely enough, it didn't hurt – no, that wasn't quite right. It hurt, but the pain was happening to someone else, the other Iseutz. She realised her sword was still a third of the blade deep in the Permian's arm, but she wasn't quite sure of the protocol for pulling it out. Should she ask permission first? It was such an intimate act.

The Permian had gone milk-white and frozen. She'd dropped her sword – reflex, not deliberate; now she was standing dead still, pinned to the empty air. Academic anyway, Iseutz realised, I couldn't say anything even if I wanted to. It'd come out a sort of bloody-spitty mumble. As gently as she could, like taking away your hand when you've just laid the last card on the roof of a perfect card house, she pulled the sword out of the Permian's arm. She saw her wince, and felt terrible about it. As soon as the blade was free, the sword dropped from her hand, like a ripe apple from a tree.

She was quite wrong about the pain. It did apply to her, after all.

Two men were helping Iseutz, each of them holding an elbow, helping her to shuffle along, like a very old woman supported by her grandsons. The violent tremor of relief he felt when he saw her surprised Addo, shocked him somewhat, but he didn't have the time or the spare attention to do more than note it and recognise that there would be implications, if he lived that long. Still, he thought, she's alive, and standing, that's what matters.

He felt empty as he walked through the gate, still holding the messer in his left hand. As he emerged into the light, there was a sudden, extraordinary silence, as ten thousand Permians got their first look at the son of the Irrigator. Then a roar; a bursting of sound from overhead, like – he shrugged off the obvious, inevitable simile that his mind had found for him. Yes, like the sound the water must have made, thundering down the mountainsides. Fine. He didn't know if the sound was hostile or friendly; probably both, he decided. Anyhow, it wasn't important. Iseutz was alive, so at least something was probably going to be all right. They wouldn't murder an injured woman in cold blood, no matter what. Would they?

Define murder. He looked round, but he was alone in the arena; the ten thousand in the stands didn't count. Then the sound nearly crushed his head, as the people of Luzir Beal welcomed the arrival of the Permian champion.

It would've been a good idea, Addo realised, to have tried to find out something about the opposition beforehand. But there hadn't been time, nobody to ask, and it had slipped his mind. Now he saw him, the opponent, the enemy, the other man. Addo resisted the temptation to smile. If he'd been given the job of making a Permian messer champion out of clay, and he'd had the necessary skill, working from first principles but without drawings and sketches, this was what he'd have come up with.

He was about six feet, very broad across the shoulders, about thirty years old; in fact, he looked like Suidas Deutzel with a beard. He wore a green linen shirt with big puffy sleeves, blue breeches and white woollen stockings, fencing pumps with silver buckles. He had a friendly sort of a face, very hard to read. He would undoubtedly have been in the War. His messer was the double-fuller pattern, relatively short and broad in the blade. Without that thing in his right hand he'd probably be a sensible, reasonable sort of fellow. He stopped just outside long measure and bowed. Addo responded in kind. The arena was suddenly quiet, so quiet that Addo could hear a bird singing a very long way away.

Concentrate, he told himself, but he was finding it difficult to keep his mind on this, and not the other thing. Slowly the Permian straightened up out of the bow. When his back was straight, the fight would be on.

Fight messer like you'd play a chess game. His father's only observation on the subject, and from what he'd seen of messer-play, entirely wrong and inappropriate. Still, in the absence of any supervening instructions from a source of equivalent authority, those were presumably his orders. He wondered if his father had ever seen a messer, let alone picked one up; but he opened with a mildly aggressive gambit and took a long pace forward, into middle distance.

The Permian swung at him. Cut number four, left-to-right horizontal; weak with any other weapon, practically unanswerable with a big, sharp knife. He jumped back out of the way, landed on both heels, traversed a half-pace left. The missed cut had become the potential for either a middle thrust or a number seven cut, rising from the right, kneecap or shin. He traversed another half-step left, crowding into the Permian's attack, the way you would with a civilised weapon. He tried to make it look like a mistake, but the Permian wasn't that stupid; he traversed right and restored the balance.

The solution to the riddle dropped neatly into place, and Addo cursed himself for not spotting it earlier. A simple matter of emphasis. Fight messer like *you'd* play a chess game. Of course.

So he dropped into a low back guard; left knee and shoulder forward and exposed, sword-hand back behind his right leg, see-me-I'm-the-target. Maybe a little bit too subtle; the Permian swung again, his lead foot following the blade, turning so he was practically hiding behind the sword as he hauled his body into the attack. Really? In the fraction of a second available, there was only one way to find out. Addo pivoted on the ball of his right foot, a textbook broadsword volte, stabbing for the Permian's ribcage as he went.

Thought not: he'd misread the Permian's line, which carried him wide and just in front of the thrust. Still, his position was awful, practically with his back to Addo, who traversed right as the Permian spun round through two-seventy degrees, cutting number four at chin height. All Addo could do about that was a rather clumsy block right in front of his nose; still, it worked, though the force of the blow knocked his hand back on to his face, crushed his upper lip against his teeth enough to draw blood. He darted backwards for living space, which gave the Permian all the time and room he needed to do whatever he liked.

A man, luckily, of limited creativity; he went for a straight, tight middle-guard thrust, which a lifelong longswordsman like Addo had no trouble at all in batting away, like a cat with a ball of wool. He flicked out a half-hearted wrist cut at the Permian's neck, just to keep him away, and converted it into a high middle guard while he tried to collect his thoughts.

Not doing this right, Addo decided, wandering away from the plan. He tried the same again: low back guard, inviting the attack. The Permian just stood there and looked reproachfully at him.

The hell with it, Addo thought, I haven't got time for this, and I need to conserve my energy. He asked himself: what's the worst, stupidest thing I could do from here, and how would I recover? Only one answer to that. He pivoted on his front foot and swung into a number one cut, right to left, diagonally down on the Permian's neck.

It was like controlling a puppet; no, it was like herding geese – you want them to go right, you take a step left. Immediately the Permian traversed left, making room to stab Addo in the stomach. Before he'd even completed the bound-to-fail cut, Addo let go of his messer – luckily it fell safe, instead of hitting his leg on the way down – and was nicely in time to clap his hands around the Permian's blade about three inches away from his skin.

It took him two inches to stop it – it would've been touch and go without the double fullers, which gave him purchase, something to press into – but after that it was a piece of cake. The Permian, who clearly didn't know it was possible to do that, made no attempt at all to hold on to his sword, which Addo nipped out of his hand and sent flying away to his left. Then, with rather more force than was absolutely necessary (he regretted it later), he kicked the Permian in the balls and, as he doubled up and his head swung forward, punched him sweetly and precisely on the point of the chin. Checkmate in six moves.

"Is that it?" the no Vei asked querulously. "That's all?"

"Yes."

"But it's only been, what, a few minutes." The Cosseilhatz clicked his tongue. "Not long enough to fry a pan of sausages. We came all this way just to see that?"

The interpreter didn't answer. He had a sort of dazed look, such as a lifelong atheist might wear after being jostled by God in the street. "Well?" the Auzeil demanded. "How was it? Was it a good fight?"

The interpreter shook his head. "I don't know," he said. "I mean, the Carnufex boy definitely won, but I don't know *how*. It's almost as though he caught the blade in his bare hands."

The no Vei shrugged. "He did. I saw him."

"But that's *impossible*," the interpreter said furiously. "You can't do that, it simply can't be done. It'd cut through your fingers like slicing beans."

"Is there going to be a ceremony now?" the Auzeil asked. "Prizes and medals and so on?"

The interpreter didn't seem to have anything left to say. "Oh, I should imagine so, yes," the no Vei answered for him. "Undoubtedly. For the ones who can still walk, anyway."

"Only," the Auzeil said, "the Carnufex boy left in a terrible hurry. You'd have thought he'd at least have taken a bow."

Addo ran up the stairs, three steps at a time. At the top he barged into Giraut, spun him round, yelled, "Sorry" over his shoulder.

"Addo," Giraut shoued after him, "where are you—"

"Doctor," Addo called back from the catwalk. "For Iseutz."

Along the catwalk, through the far archway, down the spiral staircase, along a covered walkway; short, agonised pause while he struggled to pull the fleeting glimpse of the ground plan back into his mind. See-it-once-and-remember memory. At the junction, he turned left. He still had the messer in his right hand.

As he'd anticipated, there was nobody about; not in the corridor, not in the back lobby of the Governor's mansion – he'd been there before, when the Guild officials had smuggled them in for the induction ceremony, a hundred years ago, yesterday. Lobby: in the far north corner, look for a discreet doorway, leading to a narrow stone staircase going down. He found it, ran down it far too fast, got away with it; found himself in a long oak-panelled gallery hung with portraits, turn right. At the end of the gallery, two doors. Left-hand door leads into the tunnel. The door might well have been locked, but it wasn't. Into the tunnel. It was broad, straight and paved with blue and yellow tiles. He ran.

At the end of the tunnel, a door, exactly as shown on the plan. And, in front of it . . .

"Excuse me," the herald said, "but where's the rest of you?"

It took Phrantzes a moment to parse the enquiry. "I don't

know," he said. "Giraut Bryennius was here a moment ago. I think Addo Carnufex went to find a doctor for Iseutz ..." He realised he'd forgotten her second name. Didn't matter. "I have no idea where she is."

"With the doctor," the herald replied. Then he must have noticed that Phrantzes was lying down. "Are you all right?" he asked.

Phrantzes sighed. "I suppose I've got to be," he said, and swung his legs off the table. "Presumably we've got to go somewhere and bow or something."

"There's a short ceremony, yes," the herald replied. "As soon as the First Minister arrives."

Phrantzes frowned. "What, you mean he wasn't here for the fight?"

"Oh yes, he saw the fight," the herald replied. "Now he's in his chambers getting dressed. Ceremonial robes. For the ceremony."

"Ah." Phrantzes nodded. It sort of made a kind of sense. "How long do you think he'll be?"

The herald looked vaguely shocked. "That's not for me to say. But they need you to be standing by, so that as soon as he gets here—"

"Fine," Phrantzes said. "Tell you what. I'll stand by here, and you can go and round up the others. They can't have gone terribly far, I don't suppose."

"Suidas," Addo said.

He was sitting on the floor, his back to the door, a messer lying across his knees. There was a brown smear on the blade that might just as easily have been rust. He looked dirty, exhausted and ill. "There you are," he said.

"Suidas." Addo couldn't help staring. "What the hell are you doing here?"

"You first."

"Me?" Addo frowned. "Looking for a doctor. Iseutz ..."

"No doctors down here, sorry." Suidas grinned at him. "This tunnel doesn't go anywhere. No, I tell a lie. It leads to the back stairs to the old Audience Room. How do I know that?"

Addo shrugged. "Suidas, I really do need to—"

"Tzimisces told me. Well, he gave me a map. Cut him off there, he said – meaning right here, this door. Who? I asked him. I don't know, he said, but whoever it is, he'll be coming up the tunnel heading for this door." He paused. "You know, I always thought I was quite bright, but I'm not, evidently. I was pretty sure it'd be Giraut. After all, he's got form for killing statesmen."

"Suidas." As though using the name gave him a measure of control. "What the hell are you talking about?"

"You," Suidas replied. "Your job. Sorry, your *mission*, you're too posh to have a job. Through that door, up the stairs, kill the First Minister of Permia while he's getting dressed for the presentation. Like you killed the politicians in the other cities. To start a war, for Daddy."

Addo took a deep breath, and let it go slowly. Then another. "That's simply not true, Suidas," he said. "Look, I don't know what's been happening to you since you—"

"Exposure? Bang on the head? Yes, actually." Without looking down, Suidas placed his hand on the messer handle, didn't close his fingers. "And you're right, I'm about this far from losing it completely. But I know you're going to kill the Permian. No, scrub that. You're not going to kill the fucking Permian. I'm not going to let you. Kill you if I have to."

"Suidas." Addo was pleading. "I really do need to find a doctor. Iseutz was hit, badly. There isn't *time* . . ."

"So it's you." Suidas pulled a sad face. "I wish it'd been young Bryennius. He's chicken, I could've dealt with him with one hand tied behind my back. You . . ." He shrugged. "God, I'm tired," he said. "Ran most of the way here, and I really don't like to run. Look, why don't you just piss off back to the prizegiving and save us both a lot of unnecessary effort?"

Addo's face changed, very slightly. "Sorry," he said.

"Really? I don't think—"

"And please don't play for time," Addo went on briskly. "I haven't got very long, and I need to go through that door." He hesitated, as though he'd ordered his body to advance and it hadn't obeyed him. "Look, I know you've got some crazy idea in your head, but really, I need to find a doctor, for Iseutz. If I don't, she could die."

Suidas smiled at him and rose slowly to his feet. "I'll try not to kill you," he said. "If you die in Permia, there'll probably be a war anyway. Presumably that was the plan."

Addo's hand tightened on the hilt of his messer. "My father once told me—"

"Fuck your stupid fucking father," Suidas said. "And fuck you too."

Addo sighed, then swung, front foot and sword hand together. Suidas moved, fast and confident, but he'd misread the line completely, right up to the last possible moment, when he winced sideways. The messer hit him on the point of the shoulder, cutting away the seam of his coat and a circular patch of flesh the size of a five-nomismata coin. Before he could recover, Addo hit him in the face with the elbow of his sword hand, sending him sprawling against the wall. The back of his head hit the stonework with a thick, solid thump, and he whimpered.

"Sorry," Addo said. "I really am."

Suidas sprang at him. He'd dropped his messer, and he grabbed with both hands for Addo's sword arm. Addo traversed about six inches left, smashing Suidas in the face with his left forearm as he fell past him. Suidas hit the door and bounced off it; his fingers were scrabbling on the floor for the hilt of his messer. Addo put his heel on Suidas' hand and ground his fingers into the floor. "This is *stupid*," he said. "Please, no more. I don't want to—"

But Suidas had got the messer in his left hand, a reverse grip, the way an amateur holds a dagger. He swung up to drawcut

Addo's shin, and got a kick to the forehead instead. He fell backwards, and the messer clattered on the tiles. Addo kicked it away down the corridor. "That'll do," he said. "That's enough."

Blood was welling up from a cut just above Suidas' eye, pouring down his face, flooding his eye socket; just the sort of wound you'd expect, Addo couldn't help thinking, from the son of the man who drowned Flos Verjan. He reached with his left hand for the door handle and turned it. Locked.

"Key," Suidas said, and grinned.

"Give it to me," Addo commanded.

"Ask nicely."

Addo aimed a kick at his face, but this time Suidas managed to get out of the way. He got both hands round Addo's ankle, and pulled. For a moment, Addo kept his balance, but Suidas was very strong; he felt his knee buckle, and then he was on the floor, lying on his side, on top of the messer, and Suidas' fingers were fumbling aside the cloth of his collar. He tried to push him away with his left hand, but it was cramped tight to his body, he couldn't get the leverage. Suidas' fingers were touching his skin, grossly intimate, and his breath was in his face. He slammed his forehead against the cut on Suidas' face, to cause pain; Suidas yelled, but his fingers tightened. *I'm not going to get out of this*, Addo thought, and it made him go cold all over. He flailed wildly with his feet, and his heel ripped down Suidas' shin and on to his instep. Suidas howled and let go for a moment, just for the moment Addo needed to shift his weight, pull the messer out from under him. Suidas must've seen, or maybe he sensed that the messer was loose and free; he sprang back, somersaulting on to his heels and leaping up. Addo swung wildly at his feet, to keep him away. He could see Suidas staring at the messer – *I've got one, you haven't*, as simple as that. He was frozen.

"I'm going to stand up now," Addo said, slow and clear. "Stay away from the door, and give me the key."

Suidas nodded slowly, and reached into his coat pocket with his left hand. He brought out a knife. He was holding it with his fingers extended, the thumb trapping the handle against his palm, the approved hold for knife-throwing.

He might miss, Addo told himself. Especially if I move.

He moved. Suidas threw. Addo felt something bash against the side of his face, but he was still alive and capable of movement. He swung the messer: feint to the head, turn the wrist for a horizontal cut to the left shoulder. Suidas read that one just fine. He traversed right, aiming a punch at Addo's jaw that would've cracked it like a featherboard plank if it had only connected; but Addo wasn't there. Somehow he'd managed to get out of the way and materialise just behind Suidas' left shoulder, the messer levelled for an underarm thrust to the stomach.

He's going to try and trap the blade, Addo thought; but he can't because I messed up his right hand. He thrust anyway, not looking down, for fear of what he might see.

He felt the messer go a little way and then stop, and Suidas cried out. But the messer hadn't gone home. Instead, Suidas had closed his right hand around it; he was gripping furiously with half-severed fingers, his grip failing as its own force drove the razor-sharp edge through flesh, tendon and bone. Addo got his hip behind the base of his hand and pushed. He felt the messer slice meat and something harder. Suidas yelled, and the resistance failed, not because Suidas had let go, but because he no longer had anything to hold on with. But he'd won himself enough time and room to wriggle away from the thrust; it gashed his coat and drew a little blood, but that was all.

Addo pulled away. Suidas stood upright, his mangled hand still a little way out from his body; two fingers were hanging by strips of skin, like ripe apples on a branch. He was out of position, backed into the angle of the wall and the door. A simple from-the-roof or a feint-high-stab-low would finish him, there was nowhere for him to go and he had nothing left.

He looked at Addo. "Well?"

Addo sighed: sad, disappointed, drained. It was as though

he'd come back from the War and found his home burnt to the ground. "Too late now," he said.

"What?"

"Out of time." Addo shrugged. "Even if I kill you now, by the time I've found the key and unlocked the door, he'll be gone. It's too late. There's no *point*." A tiny flare of petulance; he turned slightly and threw the messer away behind him, as if somehow rebuking it. It skittered and clattered on the tiles, like it was laughing at him. "You stupid bloody fool," he complained, "what did you have to go and do that for? You've ruined everything."

Suidas grinned at him; then he swayed, would've fallen if Addo hadn't lunged forward and caught him. "You idiot," Addo scolded him, "look what you've done to your hand, it's a complete mess. There was no need for that. I could've killed you, for God's sake. I thought we were *friends*."

He let Suidas slump gently to the floor. He saw him use his left hand to fold his right hand into a fist; not to punch with, but to keep the dangling fingers safe. He's trying to press them back on, he told himself, but that's not going to work.

Suidas looked up at him, still grinning. "I was right, then."

"What?"

"You were going to kill the Permian. Well, weren't you?"

"Yes."

"To start a war."

"Yes."

Suidas nodded, and closed his eyes. "You're right," he said, "I shouldn't have bothered. Heroics, good idea at the time . . . " He winced, determined not to let the pain show. "I thought maybe I'd kill you, or you'd kill me. Anyhow, it'd be over, clean, finished. I hadn't really thought about something like this . . . " He lifted his right hand a few inches. "Years and years and years to regret a few minutes of bloody stupidity," he said. "Should've killed me, much kinder. Still."

Addo's face was empty, as though his soul had fallen out, leaving nothing at all. "Come on," he said, "we'll find a doctor."

"Yes, good idea. A Blueskin, they're the best." Suidas made an effort to get up, not a particularly strenuous one. "I'm sorry," he said.

"What?"

"You're really going to be in the shit when you get home. Still, there it is. You should've stood up to the bastard from the start, instead of letting him shove you around."

Addo laughed, a sort of horrible release. "You can't stand up to my father," he said. "It doesn't work like that. You'd just get washed away." Gently, and with all his strength, he lifted Suidas until he could stand on his own. "I'm sorry," he said. "I know it's meaningless and it doesn't count for anything, but I really am."

Suidas shrugged. "You're quite right," he said, "it doesn't, not worth shit. Still, it's too late to do anything about it, so what the hell. It's all right," he added, "I can stand just fine on my own now."

Addo let go; Suidas tottered for a moment, then began to slide sideways. Addo caught him again, pulled his left arm over his shoulder. "For what it's worth, I don't want a war either," he said. "But I couldn't . . ."

Suidas took a step forward. "Did he tell you, straight out to your face, *you're expendable*? Well?"

"Not in so many words," Addo replied. "But it was sort of obvious from context."

"And you were all right with that?"

"Not particularly," Addo replied. "But I don't think my opinion mattered terribly much."

Suidas nodded. "Well, your father and I agree on something. What you're worth."

They made it to the end of the tunnel, but there was obviously no way that Suidas was going to be able to manage the stairs. "Stay here," Addo said, "I'll get someone. I'll be as quick as I can."

Suidas sat down and settled his back against the wall. "You do what you like," he said.

Addo nodded and started up the stairs; then he paused. "Suidas . . ."

"Oh for crying out loud." Suidas looked at him. "No, I'm not going to tell anyone, because that'd defeat the object of the fucking exercise. Yes, I might deal with you later, it all depends on whether I can be bothered or not. Also, I've got to be practical. I can't work any more and your father has a great deal of money. Now piss off and find someone. I'm sick of the sight of you."

"*Well?*" said the no Vei.

The translator blinked and shook himself. "Well," he said, "as far as I can make out, there was an attempt on the life of the First Minister. But he's alive and safe . . ."

The First Minister had just addressed the crowd. The no Vei sighed.

"Well, obviously," the translator said. "And apparently the attempt was foiled by the Scherians. Two of them, anyhow: young Carnufex, and Suidas Deutzel."

"Deutzel," the no Vei replied. "The older man with the big sword."

"No, that was Jilem Phrantzes. Deutzel didn't fence here today. It sounds like he got wind of this assassination plot and took it on himself to go after the men responsible. He's been terribly badly injured but he's going to be all right, the doctors are with him now. Young Carnufex came to his aid in the nick of time, and together they fought off the assassins." The translator paused and wiped his forehead. "Unfortunately, the assassins got away, but the authorities know who they are and they won't get far, the situation is completely under control, there's no cause for alarm. Well, they always say that, don't they? But isn't that the most amazing thing? The Scherians saving Permia, I mean. Absolutely extraordinary."

The three Aram Chantat looked at each other. "Quite so," the no Vei said mildly. "And such a satisfying conclusion, don't you think?"

The translator had to think about that. "Oh, I'm sure there's more to it than they're telling us," he said sagely. "There always is. Still, I never thought I'd hear myself say it, but thank God for the Scherians. If it hadn't been for them, who knows what could've happened?"

Tzimisces appeared out of nowhere to give them the latest news. "The doctors have done what they could," he said. "Imperials, naturally, they're experts at this sort of thing. They aren't promising anything, but they think they may have saved one of the fingers. They had to amputate the middle one. Six hours they were operating. Anyway, he's in no danger. You'll be able to see him quite soon." He turned and looked at Iseutz. "How about you? How are you feeling? No, don't try and talk. It's really not that bad. Once the cut's healed and the swelling's gone down, they tell me there won't be much of a scar. You were quite lucky, you know. Another inch and you'd have been dead."

Iseutz looked at him and turned away. Probably just as well, Giraut thought, that she wasn't up to saying anything.

"As for you." Tzimisces was looking at Addo, who seemed distinctly uncomfortable. "What can I say?"

"Please," Addo replied, "don't go on about it. It was Suidas."

"Yes, but on his own, he'd have ... " Tzimisces shrugged. "What makes it so special, of course, is that it was General Carnufex's son risking his life for Permia. I think I can safely say that that's what's going to make all the difference." He smiled, warm as the sun. "They're going to put up a statue," he said, "in the middle of Catasia Square. I should say you're the most popular man in Permia right now."

"That's stupid," Addo said. "All I did was—"

"Doesn't matter," Tzimisces said firmly. "It's what they believe that counts. And what they believe is that the Irrigator's son beat off a dozen murderous assassins to protect the First Minister. Talk about your fairy-tale endings. It's perfect." He smiled. "I expect your father will be very pleased with you," he said. "I know I am."

"Visitors one at a time," the doctor said. "And keep it short, for pity's sake. The poor devil's just had four of us sticking needles in him for six hours, he's not at his best and brightest."

Nobody wanted to go in first. In the end, Giraut volunteered, to get it over with. As he pushed the door open, he tried to think of something to say. *How are you?* didn't strike him as helpful or appropriate, but it was that or nothing.

"Not so bad," was Suidas' reply. "Actually, it brings back a lot of memories, having a bunch of Blueskins sewing away at me like I'm a quilt or something." He was lying on a low, narrow bed, his head propped up on a green silk cushion, his bandaged right hand on his chest. They'd washed and shaved him, combed his hair, even trimmed the nails of his left hand, but his face was as white as paper. He didn't look a bit like Suidas. "I gather we did all right in the fencing."

"Not bad," Giraut replied. "Phrantzes won, and Addo, and me. Iseutz drew. It went pretty well, I guess. Only Tzimisces is upset with me, because ... "

Suidas nodded. "I heard about that," he said. "It happens, even in Scheria."

"Maybe it happens to me rather more than most people."

"There's that. You know, you wouldn't think from looking at you that you're a killer."

"I didn't mean to, it was ... "

Suidas gave him a little frown that meant *shut up*. "If I were you, I'd quit fencing," he said. "In fact, you'd do well to avoid weapons of all kinds from now on. Seems to me they have a habit of leading you astray." He laughed. "They can be your best friends, but sometimes they're bad company. They keep you alive, but ... "

Giraut looked away. "I hoped I'd die in the bell tower," he said, "after I killed the Senator."

"Didn't, though, did you? And while the rest of us are marked up pretty bad, you've made it through all this shit with hardly a scratch. Sounds to me like you're addicted to breathing," Suidas said gravely. "You keep telling yourself you'll quit, but you never quite manage. I suspect you'll live for ever."

Giraut turned back to look at him. "Don't say that."

Suidas laughed. "I've seen your type before," he said. "You'll be all right. Can't say the same for those around you, but you'll be just fine. It's all right," he said, leaning forward a little. "Nothing wrong with being alive. It's what you're for."

"They set me up." Giraut was shocked to hear himself say it. "The Senator's wife, whoever's behind all this. They wanted the Senator killed, and they set me up. I've been thinking about it a lot, and I'm sure that's what happened. Then they sent me here, to get me out of the way, to get me killed. They thought I'd get killed. After all, I'm not a professional fencer, just an amateur, why else would they pick me for a team? They knew they fence with sharps here, and they thought I'd die and that'd help start another war. I think they meant for all of us to get killed. To start a war."

Suidas beamed at him. "That's bullshit," he said. "And you know it."

Iseutz was next. She looked down at him on the bed and said, "I can't talk much, the doctor says, or I could split the stitches."

Suidas shrugged. "That's fine," he said. "Nice to be able to get a word in edgeways, though I guess I'd have preferred other circumstances. Feels like cheating." He looked at her for a while, then said, "You know young Addo's in love with you."

"Oh for—"

"Shh," Suidas said, "you'll split your lip. Well, you should think about it, really. I mean, you'd never want for anything."

"Suidas . . ."

"And there'll be a scar," he went on. "And it's not like you can grow a moustache to cover it. Besides, you'd be good for each other."

"I'm not going to listen to this." She'd gone bright red, apart from her knuckles, which were white. "You're being completely—"

"Listen." He said it in the calm, irresistible voice he used for the horses. It'd work once, but no more than that. "I can't say I've got much time for Addo Carnufex, and his father's the biggest threat to the human race since the Great Flood. But if you marry him, you might just get to have a life, instead of growing old doing needlework and telling the cook to serve the leftover pork for dinner. If he marries you, it'll be in direct contravention of his father's orders, real never-darken-my-door-again stuff, so you'll be spared the joy of being a member of the Carnufex household. You'll get Addo away from that arsehole, and he'll be so grateful he'll worship you for the rest of your life. And be honest with yourself. You're not likely to get a better offer, or any offers at all, and I don't see you wanting to be the spinster daughter at home when you're forty. Think about it," he said through a big yawn. "He's not so bad, I guess. Considering where he's from and what he's been through, he could've been a damn sight worse."

She frowned at him for a few moments, as if he was written in a simple code that could probably be deciphered if she could be bothered. Then her face relaxed. "Suidas," she said sweetly, "you're so full of shit they ought to spread you on the strawberry beds. And the day I take advice from you about— Oh *hell*," she added thickly, through the web of the fingers she was pressing to her mouth. "It's started bleeding. Now look what you've . . . "

Tzimisces said: "Well?"

"Well what?"

"Were you surprised? To find out it was the Carnufex boy." He pulled out a chair and sat down. "Oh, I brought you some apples, by the way." He reached in his coat pocket. Two apples, to justify the use of the plural. Suidas looked at them. "You choose one," Tzimisces said, "I'll eat the other. Then you'll know they're not poisoned."

"You know what you can do with your apples, Colonel. Assuming they'll both fit in there."

"Suit yourself." Tzimisces smiled at him. "Don't feel bad about not guessing who it was," he went on. "I didn't know for sure, or I'd have told you. Still, with hindsight . . . "

"Yes, I know." Suidas yawned again. "Advantages to the Irrigator of sending his son: nobody suspects what he's planning, because they can't believe he'd send his own son to his death. If he succeeds, there's a war. If he fails, there's still a war. And no chance of Addo telling anyone or getting cold feet, because the son of the Carnufex does as he's told. Disadvantage: his son dies. But so what? The family history's just one long catalogue of sons buried by their fathers in a good cause. They're proud of it, which I think is disgusting. But I'm guessing he never really liked the boy all that much."

Tzimisces waited for a moment. "So what happened?"

"He won." Suidas lay back and closed his eyes. "Proved himself the better man, you might say. But he ran out of time. Once he'd realised that, he gave up. Not a killer, you see. I could tell there was a precise moment when he knew it was too late, and he . . . " Suidas sighed. "Not a killer," he said. "Or he'd have finished me off to shut my mouth. Now, of course . . . "

Tzimisces shook his head. "Nobody would ever believe you, your word against his."

"I realise that." Suidas stretched, stifled a yawn with his bandaged hand. "I don't think he does. But I reckon that's beside the point. *He* knows, even if nobody else ever will."

Tzimisces grinned. "A financial settlement, then, presumably."

"Among other things." Suidas frowned. "After all, it's because of him that I'll never be able to practise my one and only skill, so why not? Compensation. The Carnufex aren't exactly short of money." He sighed. "You know, it'll be nice to have the excuse. I was getting sick to death of bloody swordfighting."

"Well," Tzimisces said. "I've got something for you, by way of a reward."

"Money?"

"No," Tzimisces replied. "Better than that. Something money can't buy, as they say."

"All the things I like cost money," Suidas replied. "But go on."

Tzimisces drew closer; the closeness, and the intensity of his expression, made Suidas wonder if he was about to kiss him. But Tzimisces lowered his voice and said, "The first time, in the War, when you were a carter with the supply train, and some fool sent you on a collision course with a Permian column. You haven't forgotten that, have you?"

Suidas frowned. "What about it?"

Tzimisces came nearer still, until his face was so close, Suidas could smell the rosewater he'd shaved with that morning. It reminded him of Sontha. "Haven't you ever wanted to know the name of the officer who gave that order? And wouldn't you like to meet him? In some quiet place, where no one really gives a damn? Well?"

Suidas felt cold. "I can't say the thought hasn't crossed my mind."

"Would you like me to tell you his name?"

When Tzimisces came out, he looked straight at Phrantzes. "You next," he said.

"Is he all right?" Phrantzes asked. "I wouldn't want to bother him if he needs to rest."

"That's fine," Tzimisces said. "He'd like to see you."

Phrantzes stood up. In his pocket was a folding knife, a special sort the Permians made that you couldn't get in Scheria. When you opened it, a little spring locked the blade, until you pulled on a ring to release it. You could cut, or stab, quite hard, and the knife wouldn't fold up and cut your fingers. He'd seen a clerk sharpening a pen with it, and the clerk was a fencing fan and had heard all about the big match. "I'll go on in, then," he said.

Suidas was sitting up in bed. "Phrantzes," he said. "I gather you had a pretty rough time."

Phrantzes nodded. "I'm too old," he said.

"You won, didn't you? That's what counts."

"Well, I'm still alive." He took a step closer, like a man in a crowd pushed up against a barrier. "How are you feeling?"

"Tired," Suidas replied. "I just had Tzimisces in here. He's hard work."

"You ought to get some sleep," Phrantzes said.

"I'd like to," Suidas said, "but I can't seem to get comfortable. I think the pillows are too soft."

Phrantzes laughed. "Well, if you've been used to sleeping rough for a while, I guess they probably are." He took a step forward, through the invisible barrier, into close measure. "Here, let me see what I can do with them." He advanced, beside the bed, level with Suidas' head. There were two pillows. He lifted one off. "Lie back," he said. "There, that's better. The doctor says ... "

"I know," Suidas said. "But I'm not holding my breath."

Gently, almost tenderly, Phrantzes put his left hand on Suidas' head and pushed it back on to the pillow. "How long did they say you were on the table? Six hours? That must've been hell."

"It wouldn't have been so bad if the doctor hadn't been a fencing nut. But he wanted to hear all about the fight at Joiauz, every detail. Well, there wasn't that much to tell, so I had to make stuff up." He yawned. "That Tzimisces," he said. "I'll be so glad to see the back of him."

"Close your eyes," Phrantzes said. "Get some rest."

Suidas did as he was told. As soon as his eyes were shut, Phrantzes lifted the pillow in his right hand, dropped it on Suidas' face and lunged forward, laying his chest and forearms on it, crushing it down into Suidas' nose and mouth. Suidas' back arched; he kicked away from the bed, lashed out with his left hand, caught Phrantzes' chin in his cupped palm and pushed him on to the floor. Then he scrambled off the bed. By that time, Phrantzes had found his feet and opened the folding knife.

Suidas kicked it out of his hand, and smacked Phrantzes in the mouth with his elbow. Phrantzes tottered, tripped over his own feet and sat down hard on the floor.

"Well?" Suidas said, catching his breath. "Finished, or do you want to try again?"

Frantically Phrantzes looked round for the knife. It was in Suidas' left hand. He was folding away the blade, holding the ring in his teeth. He closed it up and threw it to Phrantzes, who tried to catch it and failed. It bounced off the tiled floor and vanished under the bed.

"Forget it," Suidas said.

Phrantzes looked at him. "I . . ."

"I said," Suidas repeated firmly, "forget it." He breathed out, long and slow and even; then he climbed back into bed and pulled the covers over his legs with his left hand. "I figured as much," he said. "You're a pretty good fencer, but you can't fight worth spit. Definitely not up to killing anybody." He laughed. "Not that that's a bad thing," he said. "One thing my life's taught me, fighting's a fairly useless way to communicate." He paused for a moment. Phrantzes was perfectly still, frozen with shock. "Killing's even worse," he went on. "But you couldn't kill me, even if you wanted to. And I don't really think you do." He was holding his right wrist in his left hand, keeping it away from his chest. "Tzimisces told me," he said.

"He told you."

"That's right." Suidas flattened his shoulders against the bed. "I think it was meant to be a sort of reward, for being good. Long story, you really don't want to know. He told me it was you who put the supply column I was with in harm's way, in the War." He shifted his head slightly. "Did you know?" he asked. "Before you joined up for this trip?"

"He told you."

"Yes. Presumably, the threat was, if you don't do as you're told . . ."

"I did everything that was asked of me," Phrantzes said.

"Which wasn't much," he added bitterly. "For all the good I've done, I might as well not have come. They didn't *need* me."

Suidas laughed. "From what I gather, this whole trip's been a bit of a disappointment. Or it would've been, if it hadn't been for young Addo. Thanks to him, I really do believe there won't be a war."

"Both of you, surely."

"Oh, I didn't do much. Anyway," Suidas said briskly, "I told Tzimisces his reward wasn't worth having. Too long ago, and too much has happened since. You know, there's some deadly secrets that are a bit like fine red wine. You keep them for too long and they go off." He closed his eyes. "You can get out now," he said. "Next time you want to smother a man with a pillow, for crying out loud just get on with it. Your big murder attempt was better signposted than the Golden Step Temple."

Phrantzes got up. "I'm sorry," he said.

"Oh, everyone's sorry," Suidas replied irritably. "Sorry for getting you all cut up, nothing personal, won't happen again. Like I give a shit. Assuming Tzimisces hasn't screwed me over, I've now got twenty-five thousand in the bank in Scheria, more to come, that's really all that matters. I'm out of it now, safe. All my troubles are over. And that's in spite of me doing the right thing, so it's probably more than I deserve."

"Even so," Phrantzes said. "I really am sorry. If I'd known . . . "

"Go away," Suidas said. "Please."

And then it was Addo's turn. He sat down and was perfectly still and quiet for a long time, until Suidas couldn't stand it any longer. "Well?" he said.

"You said you'd deal with me later."

"So I did."

Addo looked up. "Is it later yet?"

Suidas laughed. Addo gave him a disapproving frown. "You're

enjoying this, aren't you?" he said. "Holding court. You look like the Emperor lying there."

"Quite," Suidas said. "Champion fencer. I'm the one they came to see." He laid his head on one side, peering up at Addo like a puzzled dog. "If it'd been me," he said, "and you'd been in my way, you'd be dead now. Over and done with. I'm surprised about that. After all, you killed two, sorry *three* government ministers in cold blood. I'd have thought you'd have had no trouble."

"They were Permians."

"Ah." Suidas nodded. "Yes, I can see where you're coming from. Back in the War, I did a lot of that. Soon as you can turn them from people into the enemy, it's not such a big deal." He shrugged. "The enemy," he said, "the opponent, the other man. Targets, like the silhouette painted on the wall, with all the vulnerable parts numbered. Different when it's someone you know."

Addo shook his head. "They needed killing," he said. "You didn't. Therefore, there was nothing to be gained." He closed his eyes, then opened them again. "I asked you, is it later yet?"

"Later has been and gone," Suidas replied. "Apart from the shitload of money that'll keep me idle and happy for the rest of my life, I've finished with you."

"I see," Addo replied. "What have you done?"

"You'll see. It's not justice," he added, "because there's no such thing, but it's expedient. Makes the world a safer place. And your dad'll be livid."

Addo waited, but Suidas didn't enlarge on that; so he said, "And there won't be another war."

"Not tomorrow, at any rate. Later, maybe, but I'll be out of it by then, so it won't be my fault."

Addo smiled. "My father once said—"

"Oh, spare me, please."

"My father," Addo repeated firmly, "once told me I was his fault. I imagine it was the worst thing he could think of to say. He was in that sort of a mood."

"Your father," Suidas said, "is a turd. All right, you're dismissed. That's army talk," he went on, when Addo didn't move, "for go away. Thought you'd have known that."

"I'm not a soldier," Addo said.

Suidas looked at him. "I know," he said. "Be grateful."

In the square, they were chanting *Carnufex, Carnufex*. It made the First Minister smile. He looked to be out of practice, which was understandable.

"In a moment, you and I must go out on the balcony together," he told Addo, who winced and asked if that was really necessary. "Oh, most definitely," the First Minister assured him. "Unless you want to provoke a riot. They want their new hero."

Tzimisces beamed. "Yes, you've got to, Addo," he said. "It'll be one of those moments that people remember. The First Minister of Permia and the Irrigator's son shaking hands on the Guild house balcony. Seven years ago, nobody would've believed it possible. Shows how far we've come in such a short time."

"But it wasn't me," Addo said desperately, "it was Suidas. He was the one—"

"Indeed," the Minister said, smiling firmly. "Unfortunately, Captain Deutzel isn't well enough just yet. And besides, you're the one who's captured their imagination. The symbolism, you see: perfect." He laid a small, plump hand on Addo's shoulder. "We both know that Captain Deutzel was there too, but I dare say that in ten years' time, he'll have faded out of the story almost completely. It'll be one of those test questions: who was the *other* Scherian who foiled the assassination of Minister Lajos? And people will be really pleased with themselves if they manage to recall his name. That's history for you," he added cheerfully. "I've always thought of history as growing up around the truth like ivy on a tree. Not that it matters. The important thing is the moment, you and me together. They'll point to it in years to come and say, that was when the War finally ended."

"I really don't think . . . "

"Oh go on, Addo," Iseutz said. "Don't be such a baby."

"My people are going home," the old man said. "We've been here too long. The money's good, but there's more to life than money, don't you think? Besides, we don't really use money where we come from. It just ends up sitting in big wooden boxes, and they're a nuisance to carry about. I never did quite understand why they feel the need to make coins out of gold. It's so *heavy*."

Perceptuus tried not to let his face register what he was thinking. "So our agreement . . . "

"I'm not sure we ever had one," the Aram Chantat said mildly. "More an agreement to make an agreement if we wanted to and if the circumstances were right. But we don't want to, after all. So really . . . "

"Well," Perceptuus said, "it doesn't look like there's going to be another war, so maybe it's for the best. Less risk to our estates near the border."

The old man smiled. "There never was any risk," he said. "But certainly, if what I've been hearing is true and there are going to be real, genuine negotiations about shared access to the Demilitarised Zone, then I honestly can't see who your tenants are likely to be in danger from. Certainly not bandits. There'll be far too much activity in the Zone for bandits to feel comfortable there. And think," he added, beaming, "of all that money you won't have to spend on hiring us. That's one of the joys of peace. It's so much cheaper."

Perceptuus nodded slightly. "Have you told the Permians you're leaving?"

"Of course." The old man looked affronted. "It'd be terribly rude not to. I think on balance they were relieved to hear we're going. We make them nervous. And after the incidents in Beaute and that other place, Luzir . . . "

"Luzir Soleth."

"Yes, thank you, Luzir Soleth. I get the impression we're not popular with the ordinary citizens, the common people, especially in the large towns outside the capital. The First Minister is very keen on being popular at the moment – well, you can understand why, it must be so difficult having to be liked if you want to keep order. Not a problem where I come from. We don't have governments, as such. We don't need them."

"Well." Perceptuus put down his empty cup. "Thank you for seeing me, and I'm glad things have worked out for you. For both of us, really."

"For which," the old man said gravely, "we have young Carnufex to thank, or so I gather. You know," he went on, lowering his voice just a little, "it'd be quite interesting to find out what really happened." Then he laughed and shook his head. "No it wouldn't," he said. "The official version is entirely satisfactory, and that happens so rarely, it'd be a shame to spoil it, don't you think?"

"It came as something of a surprise," Perceptuus said.

"Oh, I should think it did. They do say," the old man went on, "that it was General Carnufex himself who first discovered the conspiracy. He had reason to believe there are Permian spies at the highest levels of your government, so he took it on himself to deal with it. Otherwise, why did he send his own son on what was by any criteria a highly dangerous mission?"

"They're saying that, are they?"

"People do like to speculate," the old man said. "And I don't suppose the general would be inclined to deny it."

"No, I suppose not." Perceptuus was suddenly thoughtful. "It'd do his popularity back home no harm at all, if people believe he succeeded in averting a war that the government was pretty much powerless to stop. That would be . . . "

"Satisfactory," the old man said. "It'd resolve matters, which is really all that counts. Well, it's been a pleasure talking to you, but now you must excuse me. We have arrangements to make, as I'm sure you'll understand."

Perceptuus drove on to Luzir Beal, where a letter was waiting for him. Abbot Symbatus was dead. The General Synod had met in emergency session and were pleased to inform him that he had been chosen . . .

He swore, and crumpled the letter into a ball.

Since most Permians didn't have a clue what Monsacer was or why it mattered, the presence of its newly elected abbot at the official thanksgiving ceremony hardly registered with the vast crowd in and around the stadium. Nor did they seem particularly disappointed when they heard that Suidas Deutzel was still too weak to attend, although there were a few cheers when his name was read out, They'd come, of course, to see Addo Carnufex.

And see him they did. He walked out into the arena with the First Minister on his right and a smiling old man on his left, followed by the surviving members of the Cabinet, the Guild master, the other Scherian fencers, the Imperial ambassador and various Permian notables who'd pulled strings or paid money to be there.

The First Minister was wise enough to keep his address to the crowd short and to the point. The War, he said, was over. Seven years of peace had been crowned by an act of supreme courage and selflessness performed by the son of their former enemy; an enemy no longer, since it had been General Carnufex who had detected the conspiracy and taken steps to forestall it. Now, thanks to the new spirit of mutual trust and understanding that must inevitably follow, negotiations were already under way for the shared development of the Demilitarised Zone; basically, Scherian shepherds would graze their flocks above ground, Permian miners would exploit the vast mineral wealth below it. Since peace was now assured, he went on, the government had decided to dispense with the services of the Aram Chantat –

(At least three minutes during which he couldn't continue because of the shouting and cheering.)

– who would be replaced by units of the Imperial Army of the

East, to guarantee the safety of Permia, in conjunction with their Scherian allies, under the terms of a new defensive and offensive alliance. In short, he could now guarantee peace. With peace would come stability, with stability prosperity, for themselves, their children and their children's children; and none of this could have happened had it not been for one man, one extraordinary man, who would now say a few words . . .

Tzimisces nudged Addo in the small of the back, propelling him forward. He didn't lift his head; instead, he looked down at the scrap of paper in his hand. It was just the right note of self-effacing modesty; a shy hero, the very best sort. There was absolute silence as he cleared his throat and started to speak.

He'd come to Permia, he said, to fence. It gave him great pride and pleasure to think that he'd helped, in some small way, to preserve the peace that had been his father's life work. Really, he hadn't done anything special. Anyone else in his position would have done the same, and of course he hadn't acted alone. Suidas Deutzel deserved as much credit as he did, if not more. In a day or so he'd be going home to Scheria, but he would never forget Permia and its people for as long as he lived, and he thanked them from the bottom of his heart for their goodwill and kindness, which he'd done so little to deserve.

Suidas was waiting for him when he came back from the arena. He didn't look particularly ill or weak. He was smiling.

"Nice speech," he said. "Your father's life work. I really liked that."

Addo gazed wretchedly at him, and then Tzimisces and the rest of the party came in, and Suidas turned away, looking frail and helpless. Someone slapped Addo on the back, making him lurch forward a step.

There was a reception, at the Senate house. Not long after they arrived, Addo looked round for Suidas, but he didn't seem to be there. Nobody else appeared to have noticed his absence.

He wondered if he ought to mention it to Tzimisces, but he couldn't see him either.

"I don't suppose you remember me." It was the old man who'd been on his left during the ceremony, and he was absolutely right. "Well, you wouldn't," he went on. "The last time I saw you, I think you were five years old. You were made to come down after dinner and recite *The Last Survivor* for your father's guests."

"I remember that," Addo said. "But I'm sorry, I don't think I know ... "

"My name is Perceptuus," the old man said. "And apparently I'm the new Abbot of Monsacer. At least, that's what they've just told me. I hope it isn't true, but I'm afraid it probably is."

Addo smiled. "You don't sound terribly enthusiastic."

"I'm not," the old man said. "Being abbot will mean admin-istration, responsibility, decisions, paperwork. Politics. If I'd wanted all that sort of thing, I'd have stayed running the Bank."

"Ah," Addo said. "You used to ... "

Perceptuus smiled. "Oh yes," he said. "My name used to be Boioannes. I ran the Bank for a long time, until I managed to palm the job off on my nephew and retire, as I thought, to the peace and seclusion of a monastic cell. Fat chance of that now." He turned his head and smiled to acknowledge a slight bow from one of the Permian ministers. "Someone's going to have to tell me who all these people are," he said, "before I offend someone and start a war. Although," he added, lowering his voice a little, "seems like that's not quite as easy to do as we previously thought."

"Actually," Addo said, "now I think about it, I do remember you. You'd had a bit too much to drink and you caught hold of one of the housemaids, and the buttons of her dress came off. My father was rather annoyed, but he couldn't say anything to you about it, obviously, so he took it out on my brothers and me later. Yes, I'm sure it was you."

"What a splendid memory you must have," Perceptuus said.

"Faces rather than names," Addo replied. "Of course, you had rather more hair back then."

Perceptuus gave him a chilly smile. "Eighteen years," he said. "A lot's changed in that time. For one thing, the War's over. And the Bank's now running Scheria. And your father's enjoying his well-earned retirement."

Addo gave him a weary look. "You'll know when my father's retired. You'll be walking behind his coffin, carrying a wreath. Look," he went on, "I don't know what you think about me, but my father and I don't get along terribly well. I know I've disappointed him, to the point where it's probably too late to do anything about it. He'll be livid with me when I get home."

"Because there isn't going to be a war."

"Yes."

Perceptuus nodded. "He sent you here to start one."

"I don't remember saying that," Addo replied. "But it's not exactly a secret that he doesn't like the Bank and that he reckons the old army families should be running Scheria, like they always have done. A war would've put things back the way they were. We'd have beaten Permia, and once we'd got hold of the mines there'd be plenty of money to make up for what we all lost in the war, so there'd be no more need for the Bank. That's how he sees it, anyway. You know that perfectly well."

"Is that how you see it?"

Addo shook his head. "Not up to me," he said.

"He sent you here to get killed."

Addo breathed in deeply and out slowly. "My father and I don't get along terribly well," he repeated. "Duty's important to him, and me too. I've spent my life trying to find a way to make him not disappointed in me. It looks like that's not going to be possible now." He shrugged. "I suppose I'll have to live with it. My problem, not anybody else's."

"Indeed." Perceptuus looked down at his hands; they were

calloused and split from gardening. "I imagine he'll try and make
the most of the situation, in spite of things not going exactly how
he meant them to. That was always one of his great strengths as
a strategist."

"He'll win in the end," Addo said. "He always does."

"Not if you stop him." Perceptuus kept very still, the way a
stockman keeps still when he's trying to catch a skittish calf. "If
you were to tell people back home exactly what happened here,
how your father sent you to start a war, how he was quite prepared to see you die for it . . ."

"Oh, I couldn't do that," Addo said.

"Couldn't you?"

"Certainly not. He's my father, it'd break his heart. And I
don't suppose anyone would believe me if I did. Besides, that's
not the way to handle someone like my father. Believe me, I
know all about that."

Perceptuus tilted his head on one side. "You've got an alternative."

"Well." Addo looked away. "You see, I was brought up to
believe that family matters: the honour of the house, its traditions, the way we do things. I believe that my father's done
wonderful things for our country, and he deserves to go down in
history as a great and good man, whose motives were always
pure and unselfish, and whose judgement was above reproach.
Now I don't think he'd want to be remembered as the man
who led a military coup and set up a dictatorship against the
wishes of the people. It'd spoil everything. I'm guessing he
wouldn't want that, but maybe his judgement's a little clouded
by what he sees as his duty to the state. You see, he thinks the
Bank is a very bad thing, and maybe he's the only one who can
get rid of it and put things back how they should be. If that's
how he sees it, he'd willingly sacrifice his personal honour and
reputation. He's always realised that you can't do the right
thing without making sacrifices. It's the greatest lesson he ever
taught me."

424

K. J. PARKER

Perceptuus frowned. "I'm not sure where this is leading," he said.

"Good," Addo replied, and he smiled.

The Aram Chantat left that night, suddenly, in the rain. The deep ruts left by the wheels of their carts filled with rainwater, which quickly dissolved into mud, which bogged down the grain and produce wagons coming into the City just before first light, which caused a gridlock at the major bottlenecks at Cornmarket and the Westgate, which blocked traffic in and out of the capital as effectively as a besieging army. The Imperials, sent by the City authorities to sort out the mess, closed the City gates until nightfall.

"No big deal," Tzimisces told them. "It's just one more day and then we'll be on our way out of here. That's a promise." He smiled. "But since we're here, and since we've got nothing better to do, I've agreed to a couple of additional engagements just to round the tour off, capitalise on the goodwill, that sort of thing. Nothing arduous, you have my word."

The rain had set in hard; sideways rain brought in on a sharp east wind. Luzir Beal had been built by Imperial engineers who knew all about drainage. There were drainpipes on every building, emptying into open gutters in the streets leading to underground sewers, but the grilles had silted up and the gutters were overflowing; several main thoroughfares were ankle deep in water, and shops and stores in the market district were flooded out; might as well be in Flos Verjan, Addo overheard someone say. It was a joke and the speaker's companion laughed, but Addo remained stony-faced.

The first engagement was a reception for the Permian Mine Owners' Association. There was white wine, hard biscuits and jars of pickled cabbage; the mine owners didn't seem particularly interested in the fencers, but Tzimisces and the elderly priest who'd shown up just after the big match held court for quite some time. After that they had to go and watch an exhibition

bout put on by the Permian Guild; Addo had to present the
prizes. The standard was low and the Permian fencers were
trying too hard. A young man fencing rapier tried to emulate
Giraut's trademark volte and got stabbed in the groin, apparently
by accident, and a longswordsman lost a finger, trapped against
the guard of his own sword in a high left block. The smallsword
bout was won by the girl who'd fought Iseutz; she seemed to have
made a remarkable recovery, but as she took her bow, Giraut
could see blood on her clothes, where she'd split her stitches.
Addo got a standing ovation, and a trio of terrified-looking children presented him with a wreath of white flowers. Giraut
watched Tzimisces while Addo bent double so that the children
could get the wreath over his head: *He's punishing him*, he
thought, but couldn't figure out what for. Iseutz, he decided,
probably thought the same. She was scowling at the back of
Tzimisces' head, and when Addo eventually escaped and went
back to his seat, she shot a quick, nervous smile at him that
made him turn bright red.

Suidas was waiting for them when they got back to the Guild
house. He was sitting on a huge trunk, one of a dozen piled up in
the entrance lobby. "For us," he explained. "To replace all our kit
and stuff. I haven't looked inside, so God only knows what
they've issued us with." He grinned at Iseutz. "I hope for your
sake they've finally established that you're not a man," he said.
"Otherwise . . ."

"Funny man," Iseutz said. "Well, they definitely owe us
something. I've been wearing these rags so long, they can practically stand up on their own."

"Maybe," Suidas replied gravely, "but can they fence?"

Iseutz couldn't be bothered to reply to that. Giraut said:
"Does all this mean they're actually letting us go?"

"Looks like it," Suidas replied cheerfully. "Apparently they've
cleared up the jam at the gate, so the road's open again. So unless
you lot've got any more ceremonies you want to go to, we can be
on our way."

426   K. J. PARKER

"No," Iseutz said loudly. "No more ceremonies. Absolutely not."

Phrantzes looked at Tzimisces, who laughed. "I'd sort of promised we'd put in an appearance at the Finance Minister's meeting with the mine bosses, but . . ."

"No," Addo said firmly. "We've done enough. It's time we went home."

"Fair enough," Tzimisces said. "Leave them wanting more, as they say. Actually, there's talk of making this an annual event; and then there's the reciprocal tour, them coming to us. One way or another, we'll be seeing quite a bit more of the Permians than we're used to."

"I've seen enough Permians to last me," Suidas said, and nobody looked at him. "One way or another."

The rain started again as they walked to the coach, which was really a cart with an improvised roof, drawn by six massive horses. Inside were two plain wooden benches. "Inconspicuous," Tzimisces explained. "I don't suppose you really want to be mobbed by cheering crowds every step of the way to the DMZ."

"It looks like a hearse," Giraut said.

"Oddly enough, that's exactly what it was this time yesterday," Tzimisces said. "Inspired choice on the part of our hosts, because Permians always look the other way when a hearse goes by. Respectful. You draw these curtains here, and nobody'll know the difference."

Iseutz wasn't happy. "We're riding back to Scheria in the pitch dark, are we?"

"Well, you've seen all the scenery already. Don't worry," Tzimisces added cheerfully, "we can draw the curtains once we're away from the city. And we'll have a Blueskin escort to the border, so that's all right."

Suidas said, "What about the luggage? There isn't room for all that stuff they gave us."

"It'll follow on in another cart."

Suidas sighed. "That's the last we'll be seeing of it, then. Pity. Probably worth a lot of money."

"That reminds me." Tzimisces turned, and a footman in Guild livery appeared out of nowhere. He was holding a flat burr-walnut case about two and a half feet long, with silver hinges and catches. "Present for you," he said. "From me. So you won't want to stop at every town and village."

Suidas looked at him. "I'm guessing ..."

"Yes. Finest quality. Matched pair. Best maker in Permia. By appointment to the Guild. I asked the Master who was the best man to go to. Cost me a fortune, but what the hell, the Bank's paying."

"No thanks." Suidas gave him a look of pure loathing. "Already got one. Here, Addo, you can have the bloody things. No good to me."

"Thank you," Addo said gravely. He took the box and threw it into the coach. It clattered as it hit the floorboards. "I'm sure they'll come in handy for something."

When the Minister of the Interior had asked Addo at one of the receptions if there was anything he could do for him, Addo had said he'd be really glad of something to read on the way home. As soon as the coach was out of the city, therefore, and Tzimisces allowed them to draw the curtains, he fished in the pockets of his coat and produced a small heap of tiny books, all apparently identical, bound in cream-white vellum. "The complete works of Callianis," he said, handing books to the others. "In twelve volumes. I suggest we read them and pass them round. Should make the journey go a little faster."

"Wonderful," Suidas said. "Who the hell is Callianis?"

"I don't actually know," Addo replied. "But I sort of got the impression I was supposed to have heard of him, so I said thank you very much. Well," he added, "it's got to be better than looking at the countryside."

Iseutz opened her book at random, squinted at the tiny lettering, opened her eyes wide and shut the book. "It's . . ."

"Yes," Tzimisces said. "Illegal to own in Scheria, of course, but I gather it's an exhaustive exploration of the subject." He opened his book and flicked through the pages. "No pictures," he said sadly. "Well, not to worry. I'm given to understand that the descriptions are incredibly evocative, so no great loss. Let's see," he added, turning to the title page. "I've got C to F. God bless the Minister of the Interior. Clearly a man of exceptional taste and judgement."

Addo closed his book and put it on the seat beside him. "I've still got my chess set," he said.

Iseutz dropped her book on the floor and wiped her hands on her sleeves. "Typical," she said. "Sharp swords, dirty books and pickled cabbage. Why has everything on this trip got to be horrible?"

Suidas leaned forward and picked up the book she'd dropped. He opened it, narrowed his eyes, held it almost at arm's length. "It's poetry," he said.

"Classic pre-Partition Imperial trochaic hexameters," Tzimisces said. "We used it as a set book in our verse composition classes at the Academy. Fifty-five thousand lines and never a misplaced caesura."

Suidas closed the book and put it in his pocket. "I don't go much on poetry," he said.

"That I can believe," Tzimisces said. "How about you?" he said to Phrantzes, who was sitting opposite him, keeping very still. "Very much your sort of thing, I understand."

Phrantzes looked at him. "I'm afraid my eyesight's not up to such tiny lettering."

"Ah well." Tzimisces grinned. "Take it home. Maybe your wife could read it to you."

Phrantzes nodded; then he drew back his foot and rammed his heel into Tzimisces' groin. Tzimisces gasped and his head shot forward, making it easy for Phrantzes to drive his left fist into his face. There was a cracking noise, and Tzimisces lolled back in his seat, clutching his head in both hands. Blood dripped from his chin into his lap. Iseutz whooped with joy. Phrantzes settled back into his seat, opened the book Addo had given him and started to read.

Suidas set Tzimisces' broken nose for him; not a particularly neat job, but, as he explained, the jolting and lurching of the coach made any sort of finesse difficult. "That's the trouble with riding in a vehicle with no suspension to talk of," he said. "You get thrown about all over the place, and accidents happen. Like just now." He pressed his thumb gently on Tzimisces' nose. "Isn't that right?" Tzimisces groaned. "He agrees with me," Suidas said, and wiped blood off his fingers. "Well, look at us," he said. "We've all been in the wars, haven't we?"

"Except me," Giraut said quietly.

"I guess you were just born lucky," Suidas said.

Addo spoke to the escort commander, who was under the impression that they were going home by way of Autet, Savotz, Bel Semplan and several other large towns. Addo quickly put him straight on that point. They were, in fact, taking the shortest possible route, avoiding all centres of population larger than a middling-sized farmstead, and under no circumstances letting anyone know they were the unbelievably famous Scherian fencing team. The commander sent a rider back to clarify the position, in case the authorities were under the same misapprehension and put out search parties when they didn't show up. He also apologised about the supply situation. If they weren't going to be stopping in large towns, the fencers would have no option but to take pot luck with the escort – plain military rations, nothing fancy. Addo, who had fond memories of Imperial plain military spit-roast lamb with pearl barley and apricots, said that he and his colleagues were prepared to rough it.

Two days out from Luzir Beal, they crossed a wide, bare moor. The road was ruler-straight, with perfectly squared milestones every three and a quarter miles. They saw a few crows and, very occasionally, a lark bursting out of the heather as they passed; otherwise, nothing living. Eventually, as it was starting to get dark, they came to a grey granite blockhouse; they didn't see it until they were practically on top of it, because somehow it blended perfectly into the black stems of the recently burnt heather. The door was open, the building was completely empty. As usual, the Imperials conjured up blankets, pillows and a disturbingly sophisticated set of cooking utensils out of their minimalist saddlebags. "Roast lamb again, I'm afraid," the captain said sadly. Nobody complained.

In the morning they started early, since they could all see a thick mass of iron-grey cloud directly behind them, softening the horizon until it was hard to tell sky from ground. "If we crack on a bit, we might well outrun it," the captain said hopefully. "I'd rather not get caught out in the open by that lot." But the rain swept over them shortly afterwards, carried in on a violent wind that tore open the curtains of the coach. The escort closed in on both sides to act as a human windbreak, but there wasn't much they could do. After an hour, the whole party was wringing wet, wiping rainwater out of their eyes with the backs of sleeves sodden into felt. The fencers huddled forward in their seats, eyes closed, feeling each raindrop, while the Imperials fretted about the depth of the mud and the danger of the cart bogging down and getting stuck. Then, quite suddenly, the cart stopped.

"Now what?" Suidas shouted, without lifting his head. No reply, so he jumped up, vaulted out of the coach and squelched flat-footed in search of an explanation.

He didn't have to go far. The Imperials were sitting bolt upright and perfectly still, staring at the plain in front of them. It was covered in dead bodies.

They lay as though they'd been dropped from a great height, arms thrown wide or folded under torsos, legs splayed, necks twisted at unendurable angles. The rain had soaked them, turning their clothes to black mush, washing channels through caked blood, so that for a moment Suidas thought they must have been drowned, in a great flood that had since drained away. But the actual cause of death was perfectly obvious: arrows, mostly, but towards the centre of the mass, great butcher's cuts that had sliced flesh and smashed bone. Soaked with rain, they didn't look like anything at all. It was only the dead horses that identified them as Aram Chantat.

"What in God's name happened?" Suidas heard himself say. Nobody answered. He lifted his head. The heaps seemed to go on for ever, covering the ground like the stumps of a clear-felled forest. *What a mess*, he thought, *what a hell of a job it'll be clearing all this lot away*. Weeks rather than days, to dig pits sufficiently deep to bury them far enough down that the first rain wouldn't wash them out again. To get an idea of how many of them there were, he tried to imagine them standing up, an army of living men rather than dead; he knew roughly how much ground a thousand standing men covered. But he couldn't do it. Five figures, at any rate. Aram Chantat, all dead.

He noticed that Addo and Tzimisces were standing beside him, staring, doing exactly the same as he was, but he found their presence intolerable and walked a few steps forward. The Imperial captain dismounted and went to talk to Tzimisces. He heard Tzimisces say, "No idea, sorry. Not my lot, I'm almost certain of that. I mean, they were going home. Why would we bother?"

It would be so easy to drown in a sight like that; but you could keep your head above water by clinging to curiosity. He recognised the arrows, and he was pretty sure the Imperial captain had done the same; Tzimisces too, quite definitely. The Imperials painted their arrow shafts, colour-coding them according to spine: green for the light self-recurves carried by the skirmishers and light infantry, red for the longbows of the infantry archers, blue for the heavy composites of the horse archers. The shafts sticking up out of the bodies and the ground were mostly red, but there were thickets of blue here and there (like bluebells in May). Nobody else in the world painted their arrows. But the wounds of the men who'd been cut to death: oh, those were so familiar, and only one weapon he'd ever come across did that to a human body. Here they fight, had fought, with messers, God help them.

He heard Tzimisces ask the captain, in a voice of detached enquiry, if the Imperials sold or gave consumable stores to the Permian militia; arrows, for example. The captain said no, they didn't. There were strict rules about military supplies. Imperial issue was for the use of Imperial personnel only. Tzimisces thanked him mildly. There was a pause, and the captain said, "Well, we'd better be getting along."

Nobody spoke for the rest of the day. But that night, which they spent in another empty blockhouse identical in every respect to the first one they'd stayed in, Giraut intercepted Suidas on his way back from staring at the rain. He was wide-eyed and pale; well, of course. Never seen anything like that before.

"I don't know," Suidas said. "But they were killed by Blueskins and Permians, that's for sure." He frowned. "I think they must've been Rosinholet and no Vei; the entire contingent. Roughly five thousand each. The Auzida and the smaller clans wouldn't ride with the Rosinholet, too many feuds. And five thousand sounds about right for the number of men the Permians were hiring."

Giraut's expression didn't change. "Why?" he said.

"Don't know," Suidas repeated. "I can only assume they didn't like them very much."

"That's no reason . . ."

"There doesn't always have to be a reason," Suidas said quietly. "Well, you could say the Permians wanted to get even after the way the Aram Chantat laid into the civilians during the riots, and the Blueskins may have had orders not to let so many unemployed braves go home, in case they turned up on the borders of the Empire in a few months' time. It could be something like that. It's not hard to come up with pretexts and justifications."

"Will there be a war?" Giraut asked.

"Oh, I don't think so," Suidas replied wearily. "If I'm right and that's the Rosinholet and the no Vei out there, then there simply aren't enough of them left back home to make any trouble, and the other Aram nations wouldn't put themselves out to avenge their ancestral enemies. Too busy wiping out the survivors, in all likelihood. That's the beauty of it. Nobody will be particularly upset to see them dead. In fact, if I was the Eastern emperor, I'd make whoever did this a duke and marry him off to my daughter." He grinned like a dog. "I wouldn't be at all surprised if this wasn't planned a long time ago. It makes such good business sense, especially doing it in another country. I expect someone'll be along shortly to clean up the mess, and then there'll be no evidence. No evidence, no war. Ten thousand pains in the arse wiped off the face of the earth."

Giraut shivered. "You make it sound like you approve."

"Well." Suidas looked straight in front. "I never liked the Aram Chantat, no. But that's all water under the bridge now. This is nothing to do with me. I just want to go home."

Giraut shrugged and went back into the blockhouse. Suidas stayed where he was, watching rain drip through a crack in the guttering and collect in a pool at his feet. If he only waited long enough, the pool would become a flood, and wash everything away.

He saw two Imperials hurrying across the yard, hunching their shoulders to make themselves smaller targets for the rain. "Hey, Sergeant," he heard one of them say, "what do you call ten thousand dead Aram Chantat in a field?"

"I don't know. What?"

"A start."

They ended up reading the books; even Iseutz, though she only gave in after they lost half the pieces out of Addo's chess set. She read with a puzzled frown, and kept turning back the pages, using her thumbnail as a bookmark. When they'd all read all the volumes, they traded them with the Imperial captain for *A Description of the Principal Cities of Permia*, a ninety-year-old-guidebook he'd been given by his grandmother when he first heard where his next posting was going to be. It described Luzir Soleth as a small, unspoilt market town, and stated that the people were peaceful and friendly.

One day, quite suddenly, the coach stopped in the middle of nowhere. Iseutz, Phrantzes, Suidas and Addo were all asleep. Tzimisces was writing a letter. Giraut sat still and patient for a while, then craned his neck to look out. There was nothing to see. They were somewhere on the flat, high moor, with no landmarks anywhere.

Tzimisces stopped writing and frowned. Then he carefully put the stopper back in his ink bottle, stood up and slid gracefully out of the coach, still holding the letter and the pen. Giraut sat back in his seat and closed his eyes. The coach was always stopping, for one reason or another.

He opened them when Tzimisces prodded his shoulder. "This is the border," he said. "Thought you might like to know."

For a moment, Giraut couldn't understand. "What, you mean Scheria?"

"Not quite." Tzimisces smiled. "The Demilitarised Zone. We're changing escorts here. The government's sent a half-squadron of cavalry to take us across the Zone."

"Scherians?"

"Well of course Scherians."

Incredible. Over the past few weeks, he'd almost come to believe that he and his fellow fencers were the last Scherians left on earth. "Where are they? Are they here yet?"

"Should be along any minute."

They were Scherians all right: provincial reserve militia, shepherds on bag-of-bones ponies, with three-quarters of a full set of Imperial kit and four spears between the ten of them. They stared at the Imperials and gawped at the coach. When Addo stuck his head out of the window, two of them started muttering to each other, while a third picked at the coach's black varnish with his fingernail. The Imperials gazed steadily at them, observing every movement they made without actually taking official notice of their presence, while the captain solemnly handed over a folded-flat packet of parchment to one of them, who stuck it in his pocket without looking at it. The Imperials formed up and bowed in the general direction of the coach, then turned and rode away at a perfectly synchronised rising trot. The Scherian who'd taken the packet gave Tzimisces a sad look, then plodded to the head of his short, shapeless column. These were men, Giraut decided, who most definitely didn't want to be here. Better things to do, in a better place. He really couldn't blame them for that.

The Demilitarised Zone, however, had changed. There were people on the road: shepherds, mostly, driving small flocks of thin sheep, but a few Permians in thick coats with fascinating-looking heavy brass instruments on their shoulders, or in the process of being set up on massive stands. If a group of Scherians passed them, each party ignored the other completely, even when the sheep knocked over the tripods and trod on the instruments. Once or twice a Permian looked up at the coach as it went by, frowned and suddenly froze, a stunned look on his face, as the shadow of the unbelievably famous Scherian fencing team rolled over him. They'll tell their grandchildren, Giraut realised; the thought made him feel distinctly uncomfortable, as if a sorcerer had stolen his soul in the mistaken belief that it was worth something.

They crested a hill, and saw the road straight and apparently endless in front of them, an arbitrary line drawn across treeless moor by a giant with nothing better to do. But as they descended the slight incline, they could distinguish some sort of man-made structure, and activity, and people.

The Scherians were building a frontier station. It was hard to see why. As a security measure it was completely worthless: go a mile to the south and you could cross the border entirely undetected. As a link in a chain of defence-in-depth outposts, it was equally useless, since it was little more than a shed and an outhouse, capable of accommodating three sociable men and two horses. It didn't have a roof yet, but they'd put up an eighteen-foot wooden gate right across the road. The coach driver stopped and waited, but the men walking about among the bare rafters paid no attention; they were builders, not soldiers or customs officers. The driver climbed down to open the gate, but it was closed with a padlock and chain. Tzimisces got out and went inside the hut; there was nobody there. He found a desk with a book on it, but no pen or ink. He came out again and told the driver to back up and go around the gate, which he did. Welcome to Scheria.

A mile or so on from the frontier post, the road forked. The coach went left, their cavalry escort went right. "What are they doing?" Iseutz asked. "They can't just abandon us like that."

"We're in Scheria," Tzimisces replied. "We don't need an escort."

Addo frowned; then he said, "No, I suppose not. Still, it feels odd. We've been escorted and guarded so long, it feels weird without them. Like walking around with no clothes on."

Suidas was watching the horsemen ride away. When they'd vanished out of sight, he smiled and said, "Stop the coach."

"What?"

"I said stop the coach."

Tzimisces shrugged and banged with the flat of his hand on the partition. The coach slowed to a halt, and Suidas stood up.

"Well," he said, "it's been interesting. You all take care now." He climbed carefully over Phrantzes' legs and got out.

"Where do you think you're going?" Tzimisces asked.

"I think I'll make my own way home from here, thanks,"

Suidas said. "Been cooped up a bit too long, I guess. Also – well, no offence, but . . ." He didn't complete the sentence.

Iseutz looked at him. "You're going to *walk* home from here?"

"Stretch my legs," Suidas replied cheerfully. "And I know the way, and I'm in no hurry."

"That's not a good enough reason."

"And I do rather want to *get* home," Suidas said. "Be seeing you." And he walked quickly away.

Iseutz rounded on Tzimisces. "You're not just going to let him go like that, are you?"

"It's a free country," Tzimisces replied mildly. "Well," he added, "relatively, anyway."

Giraut frowned. "Maybe he thinks the bandits . . ."

"Or something like that," Addo said quietly. "Or maybe he's just sick to death of us."

"But that's *stupid*," Iseutz protested. "He's got no food, no water, no money . . ."

Tzimisces leaned forward and bashed the partition. "He'll be fine," he said, and the coach rolled forward. "Probably get home before we do, if he finds a horse to steal."

"Addo," Iseutz said, but Addo just shrugged. "Phrantzes," she said, though with rather less enthusiasm. "Tell him. We can't just abandon him in the middle of nowhere."

Phrantzes shook his head. "If you want to try and stop Suidas Deutzel doing what he wants to, be my guest. Just don't ask me to do it."

"He left these." Addo was holding up the rosewood case of messers.

"I expect he's got another one," Tzimisces said. "At least one."

"And he took the book," Giraut pointed out. "You know, *Principal Cities*."

"I've read it," Addo said. "He's welcome."

Later, when the others had fallen asleep, Iseutz prodded Addo's shoulder and said, "I know why Suidas left."

Addo opened his eyes and yawned. "All right. Why?"

"Well," she said, "it was just after the escort went off like that. I think he thought we're going to be attacked."

"Really," Addo replied. "Who by?"

"I don't know, do I?" Iseutz snapped. "People are always attacking us, they don't seem to need a reason. But I think Suidas reckoned the escort dumped us for a reason. So he got out while he could. I mean, just us in a coach in the middle of nowhere, we're a nice big, slow-moving target. We wouldn't stand a chance."

Addo frowned. "Iseutz," he said, "we're in *Scheria*."

"So? We were in Scheria the first time, when the so-called bandits attacked us."

"We were on our way out then," Addo said kindly. "This time we're on our way back. It's over, the job's done. There'd be no point."

"Fine," Iseutz said irritably. "So why did Suidas . . .?"

"I really don't know," Addo said. "But I don't think it's anything horribly sinister. Really," he added, "I don't. We're home. We don't matter to anyone any more."

Giraut woke up out of a bad dream and opened his eyes to find it was dark. "Why've we stopped?" he asked.

"We're here," Addo said.

"What?"

"*Here*," Addo repeated. "We're home."

That didn't make sense. "Where?"

Suddenly he noticed that Iseutz, Phrantzes and Tzimisces weren't there, and Addo was standing up. "Outside the Fencers' Guild, I think," Addo replied. "I assume so, anyway. It's where we started from."

"What's the time?"

"Not sure. After midnight, I think." He stepped back out of the coach, so that Giraut could barely see him. "You coming, or are you going to stay there?"

Giraut scrambled up and nearly fell out of the coach. His legs were cramped and weak from sitting. Almost immediately, the coach started to move. Giraut had to make a conscious effort to stop himself from running after it. "Where are the others?" he asked.

Addo was looking round. "Already gone," he said. "Tzimisces had a carriage waiting, and he gave Iseutz a lift to her father's house. Phrantzes just sort of vanished as soon as he set foot on the ground." He saw something, and waved his arm. "That's my father's chaise," he said. "They must've been looking out for us. Well, so long. Take care."

"Addo." Addo stopped, and Giraut realised he had nothing he could say. What he wanted to say was, I don't know where to go, I can't go home, my father's disowned me. I never gave it any thought, because I didn't think I'd be coming back.

"Yes?" Addo said.

"Sorry," Giraut mumbled. "I don't know, I thought there'd be – well, someone to meet us, or something."

Addo grinned. "A reception, you mean? Dress clothes and pickled cabbage?"

Giraut shook his head. "Sorry," he repeated. "I just ..."

"I know," Addo said. He hesitated, then went on, "I'd offer you a bed for the night at our place, but I don't think my father's going to be in the mood for guests. In fact, things may be a bit fraught at home, it'd be embarrassing for you." He paused for a moment, then put down the coat he was holding and dug in his pocket. "Sorry," he said, extending a palm with coins on it, "that's all I've got on me. Should be enough for one night, if you can find anywhere that's open."

Two gold nomismata. Four months' rent, in the students' quarter. I wonder if this is how Phrantzes' wife used to feel, he thought, when they paid her, afterwards. He opened his hand and took the coins. "Thanks," he said.

"No problem. Look after yourself," Addo said, and walked away across the square.

*

Eight weeks later, Iseutz was upstairs in the morning room when the maid told her she had a visitor. She put down her embroidery and went downstairs. Addo was sitting awkwardly in the hall, in a chair far too small for his legs. He stood up when he saw her.

"Hello," he said.

He looked different. He was, of course, dressed entirely in black. Even the silver buckles of his shoes had been allowed to tarnish, or else they'd been dipped in vinegar, to darken them. But his hair was short and neat, and his various scars were shiny red patches instead of scabs. He looked older.

"Hello," Iseutz replied. "What are you doing here?"

"I came to see you," Addo said.

"Oh. Well, we'd better go in the garden."

"Fine."

Just as well that her parents were away. A son of the Carnufex, in their house; they'd have died of sheer aspiration. And he looked rather more the son of the Carnufex than she was used to: clean, looked after, not bloody. But he was still recognisably Addo, and for some reason her hands wanted to shake, though of course she didn't let them.

"Well," she said, as she pointed him at the bench under the window. "What do *you* want?"

She hadn't meant it to come out quite like that, but he didn't seem to mind. He smiled. "Settling in all right?" he asked.

"Bored out of my head, actually," she replied. Then she took a breath and said, "I heard about your father."

"I assumed you would've done."

"I'm sorry."

Addo shrugged. "So am I," he replied. "Which is strange. Actually ... " He was looking past her, at the horrible little marble cherub fountain in the middle of the lawn. Offences against taste of that kind, she imagined, were probably not a part of his everyday experience. If there had been a sledge-hammer handy, she'd have smashed it there and then. "Actually," he went on, "that was why I wanted to see you."

A total non sequitur, but also the only possible reason. She found it hard to breathe; a bit like drowning. Now there, she thought, is irony. "How did it happen?" she heard herself ask.

Addo frowned. "Our steward told me," he said, "that he drowned in the carp pond." He paused, as if preparing for an important speech. "Father loved painting and sketching. He always took his paints and his sketchbook with him on campaign. He was good at it, too, particularly landscapes. Well, there's a marvellous view out over the valley from the top of the old column." He smiled, looking away from her. "It's a sort of folly thing. One of my ancestors with even worse delusions of grandeur than usual had it built after he got back from his grand tour of the Empire. There's a family legend that he even hired a little man from the village to sit on top of it, like the lunatic hermits used to do, though personally I don't believe it. Even our lot wouldn't do anything that stupid."

Iseutz opened her mouth, then closed it again.

"Anyhow," Addo continued, "the carp pond is directly under the column, and what they believe is that Father was up at the top, and a freak gust of wind caught him and blew him off. He landed in the pond, the shock of hitting the water stunned him, and he drowned. They found the painting he'd been doing floating on the water, but the easel was up on top of the column, so it's a fairly plausible hypothesis."

Something in the tone of his voice made her skin crawl, but she couldn't figure out what it was. "I'm sorry," she said. "It seems . . . "

"Yes?"

"It seems such a trivial way for him to die," she said. "A horrible, stupid accident. I mean, it could've happened to just anybody. Sorry," she added quickly, "that wasn't a helpful thing to say."

"That's all right," Addo said briskly. "And you're quite right. It's the appropriate death for a minor country squire. All wrong for the Irrigator. He should've died in battle, of course, at the very moment of victory. Sword in hand, in the arms of his loyal and heartbroken second-in-command, with all the senior staff gathered round in suitable attitudes of desolation. That's how it always is in the paintings, we've got stuff like that on half the ceilings in the house. Death with a degree of purpose, death that achieves something; otherwise it's just such a stupid bloody waste, don't you think?"

She wanted to reach out, take his hand, something like that. But she found she couldn't. It was the same sort of strong reluctance that would've stopped her taking hold of something she had reason to believe was burning hot. "These things happen," she heard herself say, and wished she hadn't.

"Actually." Addo stood up. He looked like he was about to run; like a calf suspecting it's about to be grabbed and roped. "Actually," he said, in a harder voice than she'd ever heard him use, "it wasn't like that at all. In fact, he died in the very best traditions of the family. Quite possibly the best thing he ever did. At least, I very much hope so." He turned and looked at her, and it was like looking at a dead man, a drowned man: white and eyes bleached, inhuman. "I killed him," he said.

It was as though he was talking to her in a different language, one she didn't understand. "Addo?"

"I killed him," he repeated. "There's a big pipe that drains the water out of the pond, with a tap. We like to change the water now and again, to keep the pond from getting green and stinking. Couple of the men go down with nets and pick up the fish while they're thrashing about in the mud, put them in great big barrels; then there's a sluice you can open that brings water down from the mill race, to fill the pond up again. The night before, I crept out and opened the tap, drained out all the water. In the morning, early, I went for a walk, found the pond empty and all the fish dead, went back to the house, told Father. He was livid, of course; figured out it must've been done deliberately, went up to take a look. While he was examining the tap, I hit him over the head with a stone, knocked him out. I dragged his body into the middle of the pond bed, then ran up and opened the sluice. He never woke up. The water just flowed round him, and over him, and that was that. I'd stolen his painting stuff; I threw in a half-finished picture and his brushes and palette, and I put the easel up on the top of the column, where I'd be able to discover it later and solve the mystery. When the pond was full, I closed up the sluice, then ran back to the house all shaking and distraught. Didn't need to pretend much, of course, which helped, because I'm not a very good actor."

"Addo." Her throat felt as though it had been crushed. "Why?"

He turned away again. "Sorry to be a pest," he said, "but have you by any chance got anything to drink around here? My throat's a bit sore. Thanks," he said, as she poured him some water. He took the glass but didn't actually drink. "You want to know why I killed him."

"Yes. Addo . . . "

"Because it was the right thing to do." He put the glass down carefully on a table. "For his sake as much as anything. You know he wanted to take over, make himself dictator."

"No, actually, I didn't."

Addo shrugged. "He thought," he said calmly, "that that was the only way to save Scheria – take charge, get rid of the Bank, start a war, beat the Permians, use their money to pay off the debts, and then it'd be back to how it was in the old days, which was his definition of the perfect society." He frowned, as if deciding on a fine and difficult point of trivia. "I don't think he *wanted* power necessarily," he went on, "he just arrived at the conclusion that he was the best person to have it, and once he'd decided that, everything else followed logically on. Anyway, he was hell-bent on there being another war, which he was certain we'd win. He could well have been right about that," he went on, "but he was wrong about the rest of it. He'd have been a really terrible dictator. Too good a soldier, you see. He'd have expected everybody to follow orders, immediately and without question.

When they didn't – well, it wouldn't have been pleasant. And the end result would've been that he'd have destroyed Scheria, made everybody's lives utterly wretched, and gone down in history not as the finest general of his generation and the best of the Carnufex – which is what he was, no doubt about it – but as just another military adventurer who seized power and then made a mess of trying to use it. He'd have thrown away everything he ever achieved, and he'd have ruined the country instead of saving it; and he cared about Scheria, really and truly he did. So I killed him." He closed his eyes, then opened them and grinned. "For his own good."

"Addo . . ."

"And to stop him from starting another stupid, horrible war." Addo rubbed his eyes with forefinger and thumb. "Well, that's probably another issue, and there's stuff about that I won't bore you with. But basically, that's why. I loved him, more than anybody else in the world. So, what else could I do?"

"You *killed*—" She stopped. "Addo . . . "

"What do you want me to say?" He's exhausted, she thought. He doesn't need another fight. "The way I see it, one of us was going to do a terrible thing. I decided it had better be me. After all, I'm the expendable one, he made that perfectly clear, and I agree with him." He paused and looked straight at her, as if down the blade of a rapier in high first. "What do you think I should do? If I confess, it'd be the ruin of our family. I don't know if they'd hang me or not. Probably not, if I explained why I did it, but that'd defeat the object of the exercise. It wouldn't being him back, that's for sure. It might make me feel better, to go to the gallows for what I've done. Rather noble, don't you think? Very Carnufex." He raised his voice a little, as though reciting. "I loved my father, but I loved Scheria more." He shook his head. "But then I'd be the hero, and that'd be all wrong. I'm the hero's son, the one who does what has to be done. It's a fine distinction, but quite essential."

She stared at him: Addo, who she'd shared a coach with,

played chess with, who'd taken her seriously, and now he'd done this. It was a monstrous thing.

(Almost as monstrous as what Giraut had done, but she'd forgiven him: because he'd been weak and scared, because it was practically an accident, which made the Senator's death empty and meaningless. There was no point trying to punish Addo. Nobody in the world could do that half as well as he was going to do it, for the rest of his life. And what he'd done was *right*, and his motives had been good; and she'd killed others simply to preserve her own life, which was of no value whatsoever . . .)

"It's all right," she said.

"Excuse me?" He almost sounded angry. "It's most definitely not all right. It was—"

"Addo, be quiet." His eyebrows shot up, and he looked at her. "It's all right," she said. "It was the most appalling thing to do, but you had to do it. To stop a war. And for his sake. If anyone else had done it, I'd approve, I'd say he was a good man who'd done the right thing. It's just a shame it had to be you, but of course it couldn't have been anyone else, could it? You did it for kindness. You're a kind man, it's the best thing about you. You don't want people to suffer."

He was quiet for a long time; then he said: "He'd have suffered, no doubt about it. As soon as he realised he'd made a terrible mistake, and there was no way back from it. He'd have torn himself apart. And there wasn't any other way. He wasn't the sort of man you could *talk* to." He jumped up, got as far away from her as he could without opening a door. "I'm so sorry," he said. "I shouldn't have made you listen to this. It was selfish, and I apologise."

That made her smile, and the smile pulled on her lip and made her squeal. Now look what you've made me do. "That's all right," she said. "Really."

"There's nobody else I could . . . " He shook his head. "Thanks," he said. "I won't bother you again."

"I doubt that." She heard it before she realised she'd said it.

He looked round at her, desperate and frightened. "What did you come here for, Addo? To confess your sins?"

"No."

"Sit down, for pity's sake, before you knock something over."

He grinned and sat down, folding his ridiculously long legs neatly out of the way. "What did you come for?" she asked.

"Well." He was looking down at his feet. She wanted to hit him. "If you must know, I was going to ask you if you felt like getting married. But that's—"

"That's fine," she said.

He looked at her. "What?"

"That's fine," she said firmly. "Not ideal, but yes, on balance, I think so."

He sat perfectly still for an infuriatingly long time, then nodded. "If you're sure."

"No, I suddenly changed my mind. Yes, I'm sure. Oh for crying out loud, Addo," she snapped, "look at me when I'm telling you I love you."

Given the circumstances, the wedding was a fairly low-key affair. It was held at the Carnufex house: seven hundred and twenty-six guests, not counting the tenants, the musicians and the entertainment, which was provided by the students and instructors of the Deutzel school. Suidas Deutzel didn't attend in person; he pleaded pressure of work and sent his chief instructor, Giraut Bryennius, to represent him and make sure the show went off well, which it did. After the fencing there was a general exodus into the rose garden, but Giraut stayed behind. So did Jilem Phrantzes, who'd been deliberately avoiding Giraut all day.

"Hello," Phrantzes said. "Haven't seen you since . . ."

"No," Giraut said. "How's everything? Your wife?"

"She's fine," Phrantzes replied. "Couldn't be here today, not with the baby due any day now. You?"

"Oh, not so bad." Giraut smiled. "Working for a living, but otherwise I can't complain."

Phrantzes nodded. "How is Suidas these days? I haven't seen him."

"Oh, he's fine," Giraut said. "Having a great time running the school and not having to fence. He told me the other day he always hated fencing. But it was the one thing he was good at, so he had to."

Phrantzes nodded gravely. "I gather he's marrying that actress of his."

"At last, yes." Giraut smiled. "He told me she agreed to marry him as soon as he could show her forty thousand nomismata in the Bank. The day he cleared forty thousand and seven nomismata and twelve quarters, he went out and booked the Temple. That's what he told me, anyhow. Don't know if it's true, but it sounds like it should be."

Phrantzes smiled, then deliberately folded away the smile and straightened his face. "Tzimisces is dead," he said.

Giraut was more shocked than he'd have expected. "How?"

"Killed himself," Phrantzes replied quietly. "Poison. He was about to be indicted for treason, so I gather." He clicked his tongue. "That man always did have the knack of not being there when things got nasty."

Giraut took a deep breath and let it go. "No great loss," he said.

"No, not really. He was a thoroughly unpleasant man, and he had my wife locked up in a convent. Even so." He shook his head. "Not a great loss, but a loss nevertheless."

Giraut laughed. "Next you'll be telling me you're nostalgic for Permia."

"I don't think I could ever be that," Phrantzes said. "I suppose it's a bit like the people you meet who tell you they miss being in the army. Well, at least it looks now like there isn't going to be another war." He put down his glass. "We ought to go outside," he said.

"I'm not feeling very sociable," Giraut replied. "Tell me, do you ever think about – well, you know. What we saw. What we did."

"Not if I can help it. My wife says she always knows when I'm thinking about all that. Luckily, she's learned how to make me stop."

"Really? How?"

Phrantzes grinned. "Sex, mostly. And keeping anything sharp safely under lock and key."

A side door opened, and Addo and Iseutz came through. They looked furtive, as though they weren't supposed to be there. "We're meant to be admiring the wedding presents," Addo explained. "But we saw you were here, so we escaped."

"We climbed out of a window," Iseutz said. "In our own house. That's ridiculous."

It occurred to Giraut that *our own house* suggested a singular lack of understanding of her new position in life. "Thanks," he said. "Actually, I was hoping for a quiet word with you. Got something for you." He put his hand in his pocket and produced a small silver box. "From Suidas."

Iseutz looked at him, then at Addo. "That's nice," she said. "How is he, by the way?"

"Oh, fine," Giraut said. He turned to Addo. "He told me to tell you. First, it's not a wedding present. Second, it's something that money couldn't buy."

Addo took the box and looked at it as though it was a gateway to a dangerous place. "Well," Iseutz said. "Go on, open it."

The lid slid back. Inside, packed in coarse grey salt, was a man's finger. Iseutz opened her mouth, caught Giraut's eye and took a step back. Addo closed the lid carefully and put the box in his pocket. "Thanks," he told Giraut. "Tell Suidas I'll take good care of it."

The groom's present to the bride was to have the old stylite tower repaired, with proper stairs and a handrail. As time went on, she used to go there more and more often. She said that from the top of the column, she could see clearly where she'd come from. Addo had the carp pond filled in and turned into a strawberry bed, though it was too high and exposed for such a delicate fruit. When Addo was killed, at the age of sixty-two, leading his men to victory against the invading armies of the Western Empire, she had the column demolished and the stone re-dressed and used to build his cenotaph, where the old pond used to be. Two years later, after six weeks of unseasonal heavy rain following a dry spell, the mill leat broke down the embankment and flooded the hollow completely, turning it into the lake that can be seen there to this day.

Acknowledgements

My heartfelt thanks are due to Chris and Josh, the fencing instructors at Cricket St Thomas, who taught me the basics of classical foil so I could write this book. It can't have been fun for them getting poked at with a bit of wire with a button on the end by an aggressive, overweight, middle-aged novice. I hope the result in some ways justifies their ordeal.

extras

www.orbitbooks.net

about the author

Having worked in the law, journalism and numismatics, **K. J. Parker** now writes and makes things out of wood and metal. Parker is married to a solicitor and lives in southern England. For more information visit www.kjparker.com

Find out more about K. J. Parker and other Orbit authors by registering for the free monthly newsletter at www.orbitbooks.net

if you enjoyed

SHARPS

look out for

THE HAMMER

also by

K. J. Parker

Seven Years Before

When Gignomai was seven years old, his brother Stheno gave him three chickens.

"They're not yours, of course," Stheno said, "you're just looking after them. Food and water twice a day, muck 'em out when the smell gets bad, make sure the fox doesn't get them.

No big deal. Father thinks it's time you learned about taking responsibility."

"Oh," Gignomai said. "How about the eggs?"

"They go to the kitchen," Stheno said.

For a week, Gignomai did exactly as he'd been told. As soon as he woke up, he ran out into the yard, being careful not to slam the door in case it disturbed Father in his study, and went to the grain barrel, where he measured out a double handful of wheat into the battered old pewter cup he'd found in the barn. He scattered the grain all round the foot of the mounting-block, filled the tin pail with water, counted the chickens to make sure they were all there and made a tour of inspection of the yard palings. One paling was rotten at the base, and Gignomai was worried that a fox could shove against it, break it and get in. He reported his concerns to Stheno, who said he'd see to it when he had a moment. Nothing was done. Two days later, something broke in during the night and killed the chickens.

"Not a fox," his brother Luso said, examining the soft earth next to the broken palings. Luso was a great hunter, and knew everything there was to know about predators. "Look at the size of its feet. If I didn't know better, I'd say it was a wolf, only we haven't seen one of them for years. Most likely it's a stray dog from town."

That made sense. Town was a strange, barbarous place where common people lived, barely human. It followed that their dogs would run wild and murder chickens. Luso undertook to patrol the woods with his gun (any excuse). Stheno told Gignomai not to worry about it; these things happened, it wasn't his fault (said in a way that made it clear that it was, really), and if you kept livestock, sooner or later you'd get dead stock, and there was nothing more to be said. That would have been fine, except that he then issued Gignomai with three more chickens.

"Try to take better care of them," he said. "The supply isn't exactly infinite, you know."

For three days, Gignomai tended the chickens as before. For

three nights, he sat in the bow window overlooking the grand double doors of the hall. He was too young to be allowed out after dark, and from the bow window you could just about see the far western corner of the yard. He managed to stay awake for the first two nights. On the third night he fell asleep, and the predator broke in and killed the chickens.

"Not your fault," Stheno said wearily. "For a start, you wouldn't have seen anything from there, and it was dark, so you wouldn't have seen anything anyway. And even if you'd seen something, it'd have taken too long. You'd have had to come and wake me up, and by the time I'd got out there, the damage would've been done."

It was the same large, unfamiliar paw print. Luso still maintained it was a dog.

"You didn't mend the broken paling," Gignomai said.

"I will," Stheno replied, "soon as I've got a minute."

Custody of the remaining dozen chickens was awarded to one of Luso's huntsmen. The paling didn't get fixed. Two nights later, the leftovers from two more hens and the cock were scattered round the yard.

"We'll have to get a cock from one of the farms," Luso said. The met'Oc didn't condescend to trade with their neighbours, but from time to time Luso and his huntsmen went out at night and took things. It wasn't stealing, Mother said, but she didn't explain why not. Stheno tied the paling to the rail with a bit of twine from his pocket. Gignomai knew why he hadn't mended it: he had the farm to run, and he did most of the work himself because the farm workers were weak and lazy and not to be trusted. Stheno was twenty-one and looked like Father's younger brother rather than his son.

The next night, Gignomai climbed out through the kitchen window. He'd noticed some time before that the catch didn't fasten; he'd made a note of this fact, which could well be strategically useful, but had decided not to squander the opportunity on a pointless excursion. He took with him a horn lantern he'd found in the trap-house, a knife from the kitchen and some string.

The predator came just before dawn. It wasn't a dog. It was huge and graceful and quiet, and it nosed aside the broken paling as though it wasn't there. It jumped the half-door of the chicken-house in a single fluid movement, and came out a short time later with a dead chicken in his jaws. Gignomai watched it carefully, and didn't move until it had gone.

He thought about it. The predator was a wolf. He'd seen pictures in the *Bestiary* in Father's library, and read the descriptions in Luso's *Art of the Chase*. Quite likely it was the last surviving wolf on the Tabletop, or maybe in the whole colony. The met'Oc had waged war on the wolves when they first came here. Luso had always wanted to kill a wolf, but he'd only ever seen one, a long way away. This wolf was probably old, which would explain why it had taken to burglary; they did that when they were too old and tired to pull down deer, and when they were alone with no pack to support them. There was no way a seven-year-old could fight a wolf, or even scare one away if it didn't want to go. He could tell Stheno or Luso, but they almost certainly wouldn't believe him.

Well, he decided. The job had to be done or it'd kill all the chickens, and nobody else was going to do it because they wouldn't believe he'd seen a wolf.

He thought hard all the next day. Then, just as it was beginning to get dark and the curfew came into force, he went as unobtrusively as he could to the chicken-house, chose the oldest and weakest hen and pulled her neck. With the knife he'd borrowed from the kitchen and neglected to return, he opened the guts and carefully laid a trail of drops of blood across the yard to the woodshed, where he put the corpse on top of the stacked brushwood. He scrounged some loose straw from the stables and laid it in the shed doorway, and found a stout, straight stick about three feet long, which he leaned up against the wall. It was the best way of doing it that he could think of. There'd be trouble, but he couldn't help that.

The wolf came earlier that night. Gignomai had been waiting long enough for his eyes to get accustomed to the dark, and besides, there was a helpful three-quarter moon and no cloud. He watched the wolf's nose shove past the paling and pick up the scent of blood. He kept perfectly still as it followed the trail, pausing many times to look up. It was suspicious, he knew, but it couldn't figure out what was wrong. Old and a bit stupid, but still a wolf. He made sure of his grip on the lantern, and waited.

Eventually, the wolf followed the blood all the way into the woodshed. Gignomai kept still until the very tip of its tail had disappeared inside; then he jumped up, took a deep breath, and crept on the sides of his feet, the way Luso had taught him, across the yard. He could smell the wolf as he groped for the stick he'd put ready earlier. As quickly as he could, he opened the front of the lantern and hurled it into the shed, hoping it'd land on the nice dry straw. He slammed the door and wedged the stick under the latch.

Nothing happened for a disturbingly long time. Then he heard a yelp – a spark or a cinder, he guessed, falling on the wolf's back – followed by a crash as it threw itself against the door. He'd anticipated that, and wished he'd been able to steal a strong plank and some nails, to secure the door properly. But the stick jammed against the latch worked just fine. He could see an orange glow under the door. The wolf howled.

He hadn't anticipated that. It was guaranteed to wake the house and bring Luso running out with his gun. Luso would open the door and either he'd be jumped by a maddened, terrified wolf, or the burning lintel would come down and crush him, and there'd be nothing Gignomai could do. He considered wedging the house door with another stick, but there wasn't time and he didn't know where to find the necessary materials. Then the thatch shifted – it seemed to slump, the way lead does just before it melts – and tongues of flame burst out of it, like crocuses in spring.

Stheno came running out. Gignomai heard him yelling, "Shit,

the woodshed's on fire!" and then he was ordering people Gignomai couldn't see to fetch buckets. One of the farm men rushed past where he was crouching, unaware he was there, nearly treading on him. Quickly Gignomai revised the recent past. As soon as it was safe to do so, he got up quietly and headed for the house door. Luso intercepted him and grabbed his shoulder.

"Get back to bed. Now!" he snapped.

Gignomai did exactly as he was told, and stayed there until the noise in the yard had died down. Then he made his way down to the hall. Stheno and Luso were there, and Father, looking extremely irritable. Stheno was telling Father that the woodshed had caught fire; they'd tried to put it out but the fire had taken too good a hold by the time they got there and there had been nothing they could do. Luckily, the fire hadn't spread, but it was still a disaster: half the winter's supply of seasoned timber had gone up in flames, along with twelve dozen good fence posts. Father gave him a look that told him that domestic trivia of this nature wasn't a good enough reason for disturbing the sleep of the head of the family, and went back to bed.

Next day, Stheno went through the ashes and found the twisted frame of a lantern. Some fool, he announced, had left a light burning in the woodshed, and a rat or something had knocked it over, and now they'd all be cold that winter. It would go hard, he implied, with the culprit if he ever found out who it was. But his enquiries among the farm hands produced a complete set of perfect alibis, and Stheno had too many other things to do to carry out a proper investigation.

The attacks on the chickens stopped, of course, but nobody noticed, having other things on their minds.

Gignomai wasn't proud of what he'd done. Clearly, he hadn't thought it through. On the other hand, he'd done what he had to, and the wolf, quite likely the last wolf on the Tabletop, was dead and wouldn't kill any more chickens. That was important. The violation of the family property wouldn't happen again, so there'd be no need for him to repeat his own mistake. Accordingly, he didn't feel particularly guilty about it, either. It was a job that had needed doing, and he'd done it.

A little while later, when he thought it was all over, his sister came to him and said, "You know the night of the fire."

"What about it?" Gignomai replied.

"I was in the kitchen," she said. "I went down to get a drink of water, and when you came in, I hid and watched you climb out of the window."

"Oh," Gignomai said. "Have you told anyone?"

She shook her head. "Why did you burn down the wood-shed?" she asked.

He explained. She looked at him. "That was really stupid," she said.

He shrugged. "I killed a wolf," he said. "How many kids my age can say that?"

She didn't bother to reply. "I ought to tell Father," she said.

"Go on, then."

"But I won't," she said, after an agonising moment. "He'd just get mad, and then there'd be shouting and bad temper and everybody in a mood. I hate all that, specially when it goes on and on for days."

"Fine," Gignomai said. "Up to you, of course."

"You might say thank you."

"Thank you."

"It was still a really stupid thing to do," she said, and left the room.

After she'd gone he thought about it for a long time and, yes, she was right. But he'd done it, and it couldn't be helped, and it had to be done. The only criticism he could find to make of himself was idleness and lack of foresight. What he should have done was stack brushwood in the old cider-house, which was practically falling down anyhow (Stheno was going to fix it up sometime, when he had a moment) and would've been no great loss to anybody.

Next time, he decided, I'll make sure I think things through.

The Year When

His first real command were pigs. There were fourteen of them, quarter-grown light brown weaners, and it was his job to guard them while they foraged in the beech wood and keep them from straying. He dreaded it more than anything else. The men from the farm – proper stockmen who knew what they were doing – drove them up there from the house in the morning and led them back at night, but for the whole of the day they were his responsibility, and he was painfully aware that he had no control over them whatsoever.

Fortuitously, they were naturally gregarious animals and stuck together, generally too preoccupied with snuffling in the leaf mould to wander off and cause him problems. But he had an excellent imagination. What if something startled them? He knew how easily they spooked and once that happened and they started dashing about (they were deceptively fast and horribly agile) he knew he wouldn't stand a chance. The whole litter would scatter and be lost among the trees, and that'd mean turning out the whole household to ring and comb the wood in a complex military operation that would waste a whole day, and it would be all his fault. The list of possible pig-startlers was endless: a careless roebuck wandering into the clearing and shying; a buzzard swooping down through the canopy; the crack of a dead tree falling without warning; Luso down in the long meadow, shooting his stupid gun. Or what if a wild boar decided to burst out of a briar tangle and challenge him for leadership of the herd?

The first half-dozen times he performed his wretched duty ("It's time your brother started pulling his weight on the farm," his father had pronounced. Why couldn't they have told him to muck out the goose-house instead?) he'd spent the whole day at a breathless, stitch-cramped trot, trying to head off any pig that drifted more than a yard from the edge of the clearing, an exercise in counterproductive futility. It didn't help that the beech wood was on a steep slope. Since he clearly couldn't carry on like that for any length of time, he resolved to think the thing through and find an answer. There had to be one.

In the long barn, he knew where to find a large oak bucket, which everybody else had apparently forgotten about (the farm was crammed with such things, perfectly good and useful but long since mislaid and replaced). He also knew where they kept the yellow raddle. He got up very early one morning, mixed a pint of raddle in a derelict saucepan and used it to paint the bucket, which he carried up to the clearing in the wood. Next morning, he stole half a sack (as much as he could carry – actually, slightly more) of rolled barley and took that up as well, hiding it safe and dry in the crack of a hollow tree.

The idea was simple and based on sound principles of animal husbandry he'd learned from watching the stockmen. Three times a day, he fed the pigs from the yellow bucket. He knew the pigs loved rolled barley above all things – the sight of fourteen of them scrambling over each other and scrabbling across each other's heads to get into the bucket was really quite disturbing – and he made sure that each feed was preceded by a distinct and visible ritual, because pigs understand that sort of thing. When he walked to the foot of the hollow tree, they all stopped rooting and snuffling and watched him, still and tense as pointing dogs. When the sack appeared, they started barking and squealing. As soon as he moved, holding the sack, there'd be a furious torrent of pigs round his ankles, and he'd have to kick them out of the way to get to the bucket to fill it.

A great success, whose only drawback was that it was strictly illegal – he'd requisitioned equipment and drawn restricted supplies without authority, a serious crime, the consequences of which didn't bear thinking about, but the risk of detection, given the way the farm was run, was acceptably low. He took great pains to hide the yellow bucket when not in use, and was almost excessively careful in planning his raids on the rolled-barley bin. It was, however, a significant part of his nature that he didn't believe in perfection. The system worked just fine, but that didn't mean it couldn't be improved.

The most beneficial improvement would be doing without the barley, but he knew that wouldn't work, or not for long. He could rely on the squealing of the main body of pigs to draw in any outlying stragglers in an instant, but wouldn't it be better if he could train them, by association, to come to a feeding call of his own? The stockmen did it with the cows. All they had to do was call out, and the herd came quick-shambling to them right across the forty-acre meadow. He tried various calls, but the pigs just looked at him as if he was mad. In desperation, he tried singing. It worked.

His mother had once told him he had a fine singing voice (but then, she'd told Luso that he was handsome and Pin that she was pretty). He wasn't quite sure what "fine" was supposed to mean in this context. If it meant loud, Mother's words were a statement of undeniable fact, not a compliment. He thought he sang rather well, but he was realistic about his own judgement. In any event, the pigs seemed to like it.

To begin with, he restricted himself to a few short simple halloos and volleys, the sort of thing Luso used to communicate with the hounds ever since he'd lost the hunting-horn in the river. They worked perfectly well. By the fifth note out of eight, all the pigs came running, even if the sack was still in the tree (though he knew he had to keep faith and fulfil the contract by feeding them or the whole procedure would fail). Nevertheless, he felt the need for improvement or, at least, further elaboration. He extended the halloos into verses from the usual ballads, and the pigs didn't seem to mind. But he didn't like ballads much, they were plain and crude, and the words seemed a bit ridiculous taken out of their narrative context. So he began to invent words and music of his own, using forms from his mother's music book. He made up serenades to call them, estampidas for while they were feeding (the only form boisterous enough to be heard over the sound of happy pigs) and aubades for the minute or so of forlorn sniffing and searching before the pigs managed to accept that all the barley was really gone. Gradually, as he elaborated and improved his compositions, the singing became an end in itself rather than a function of practical swineherding, and the terrifying chore blossomed into a pleasure.

For the afternoon feed of the day in question he'd worked up what he considered was his finest effort yet. He'd started with the basic structure of the aubade, by its very nature a self-limiting form – but he'd extended it with a six-bar lyrical coda that recapitulated the opening theme transposed into the major key with a far livelier time signature. He'd run though the coda many times during the day, sitting with his back to the fattest, oldest beech in the glade. A wolf tree, the men from the farm called it. It had been there before the rest of the wood grew up, and instead of pointing its branches directly at the sky, it spread them wide, like his mother making a despairing gesture, blocking the light from the surrounding area so that nothing could grow there, and thus forming the clearing which generations of pigs had extended by devastation into a glade. When the angle of the beams of light piercing the canopy told him it was time for the feed, he got up slowly, brushed himself free of leaf mould and twigs, and hauled the yellow bucket out from its secure storage in a holly clump. Three pigs looked up, their ears glowing translucent against the slanting light. He grinned at them, and lugged the bucket into the middle of the clearing. Then he walked slowly to the hollow tree and felt inside the crack for the barley sack. Two more pigs lifted their heads, still diligently chewing. He cleared his throat with a brisk cough and began to sing.

La doca votz ai auzida . . .

(Lyrics weren't his strong point. They had to be in the formal language of Home, or he might just as well sing ballads and, in theory, he was fluent in it as befitted a boy of noble birth albeit in exile. In practice, he could pick his way through a few of the simpler poems and homilies in the books, and say things like "My name is Gignomai, where is this place, what time is dinner?" As far as writing formal verse went, however, he hadn't got a hope, so he tended to borrow lines from real poems and bend them till they sort of fitted.)

De rosinholets savatges—

He stopped suddenly, the next phrase congealed in his throat. A string of horsemen had appeared through the curtain of leaves and were riding up the track towards him. In the lead was his brother Luso, followed by half a dozen of the farm men and one riderless horse.

His first impression was that they'd been out hawking, because he could see a bundle of brown-feathered birds, tied at the neck, slung across the pommel of Luso's saddle. But there was no hawk on Luso's wrist. Had Luso lost the hawk? If so, there'd be open war at dinner. The hawk had come on a ship from Home; it had cost a fortune. There had been the most appalling row when Luso turned up with it one day, but Father had forgiven Luso because a hawk was, after all, a highly suitable possession for a gentleman. If Luso had contrived to mislay the wretched thing . . .

Luso looked at him without smiling. "What was that awful noise?" he said.

There was no way he could explain. "Sorry," he said.

They hadn't been hawking. They were wearing their padded shirts, with horn scales sewn into the lining. Two of the men had wide, shiny dark red stains soaking through their shirts, Luso had a deep cut just under his left eye, and they all looked exhausted. The birds on Luso's saddle were chickens.

"Keep the noise down, will you?" Luso said. He was too tired to be sarcastic. For Luso to pass up an opportunity like this, something had to be wrong. The men rode by without saying anything. Their horses had fallen into a loose, weary trudge, too languid to spook the pigs. He didn't bother trying to hide the barley sack behind his legs; Luso didn't seem interested. Under the chicken feathers, he could see the holsters for the snapping-hen pistols. The ball pommel of one pistol was just visible. The other holster was empty.

When they'd gone, he performed the feeding ritual quickly and in silence. It worked just as well without music. When the swineherds showed up to drive the pigs back to the farm, they were quiet and looked rather scared. He didn't ask what the matter was.

Father was angry about the man getting killed, but he was absolutely furious about the loss of the pistol, so furious that he didn't mention it at all, which was a very bad sign. Gignomai heard the shouting before they were called in to dinner – that was all about the man's death, how it'd leave them short-handed at the worst possible time, how Luso had a sacred duty by virtue of his station in life not to expose his inferiors to unnecessary and frivolous dangers – not a word about the pistol, but it was plain as day from what was said and what wasn't that the real issue wasn't something that could be absolved through sheer volume of abuse. Dinner was, by contrast, an eerily silent affair, with everybody staring at their hands or their plates. When the main course was served, however, Father looked up and said, in a terrible voice, "What the hell is this supposed to be?"

A long silence; then Luso said, "It's chicken."

"Get it out of my sight," Father said, and the plates were whisked away. No great loss, Gignomai couldn't help thinking; it had been sparse and stringy and tough as strips of leather binding, and he was pretty sure he'd last seen it draped over the pistol-holsters, in which case the chickens had been laying hens, not table birds, and not fit for eating. There was rather more to it than that, of course. They'd eaten layers before, when they'd had to, and had pretended they were perfectly fine.